In Dark Water

Glasgow-born Lynne McEwan is a former newspaper photographer turned crime author. She's covered stories including the Fall of the Berlin Wall and the first Gulf War in addition to many high profile murder cases. She currently lives in Lincoln and is in the final year of an MA in Crime Fiction at the University of East Anglia.

Also by Lynne McEwan

Detective Shona Oliver

In Dark Water
Dead Man Deep
The Girls in the Glen

In Dark Water

LYNNE McEWAN

CANELOCRIME

First published in the United Kingdom in 2021 by

Canelo
Unit 9, 5th Floor
Cargo Works, 1–2 Hatfields
London SE1 9PG
United Kingdom

A CIP catalogue record for this book is available from the British Library.

Print ISBN 978 1 80032 432 9
Ebook ISBN 978 1 80032 431 2

Look for more great books at www.canelo.co

Printed and bound in Great Britain by Clays Ltd, Elcograf S.p.A.

3

For my father,

John Faulkner McEwan,

the first storyteller.

Prologue

I'm way past scared. Panic's roaring through my veins like the first fix. Some punters like to see that you're feart. They get off on it. Sick. Does my head in. But this evil bastard's not a punter. He's a psycho, screaming at me to tell him stuff I don't know. I keep saying, it isnae me you want, but he doesnae listen. It's dark, the car moving fast. Me in the back seat, his arm around my throat choking me, and the fucker's got this knife inching towards my eye. Blood and piss on the leather seat, I'm slipping down. I try to call out to the driver for help, to stop the car, but then the cold metal of the knife touches my cheek and I freeze.

He picked me up from the squat in Carlisle. Flash car, a fourbie with tinted windows. Nice clothes, expensive aftershave. I've seen him around. Shaved dark hair, face like a skull. Said he was an old pal of Buckie's, but Buck didn't seem too pleased to see him. You'll be compensated for your time, that's what he said. Like I was doing them both a favour. Like I had a choice. Like my time was worth something.

I thought, this'll be class, I can squeeze some cash out of him. He said he just wanted to talk to me. We'd have a wee drink. I could tell him what my friends were up to. Well, that's a joke. Someone like me has no friends. When I laughed he hit me hard in the face, couldn't see the funny side. I wanted to shout at the bastard. My only friend is the next fix.

He won't be the only man to send me to oblivion. My father was the first. He belted me cos I gave him the cracked plate instead of the only good one in our house. I was about seven years old at the time. I'd spent hours making mince and tatties for his birthday cos I knew it was his favourite. Then he said I could give him a different present. I didnae know what he meant. I had no money for anything, none of us ever did. He showed me though.

Sometimes, when I read stories in magazines about women who were abused by their fathers, I laugh. There was never any of that 'you're my special girl' stuff or 'it's our little secret', not for me. He never threatened me, muttering in his beery breath what would happen if I told. He didnae need to. Everyone knew. My mother, my sister, the teachers. They all knew. Kept their heads down, did nothing. When they let me out of hospital the second time, bandages on my wrists like twin bracelets, I went south. But it was too late. Change of scenery, but really it was just the same old scene. Old habits die hard, as the nun said to the junkie. At least my kid is a boy. He might stand a better chance. You get big enough, you can hit back.

From the rear seats of the car, I can just see the bent flowerheads of the motorway lights. Bright blobs swimming through my tears. Watching over me. Flicking past like seconds counting down to the end. Skirt rucked up and a hole in my new tights. Snot and blood bubbling out my nose like I'm a wee girl. Car's slowing down. The fucker still got hold of me, but I'm not daft. If I see a chance, I'll run. For a moment a blue square with a white cross fills the window and I know where I am. I'm northbound on the A74. I'm going home. I know the sign. I know what it says. Welcome to Scotland.

Chapter 1

The call for assistance came into Kirkness Lifeboat Station on the Solway Firth on Saturday morning. Shona Oliver's pager sounded just as she was placing the teapot down in the dining room.

'Shout!' she called to husband Rob. She dashed into the kitchen, gave him a quick kiss, grabbed her car keys and ran from the house. The two B&B guests stared open-mouthed after her.

'Lifeboat. She's on call,' Rob explained as he entered the room a moment later and set down full Scottish breakfasts before the astonished guests, a husband and wife walking duo from Edinburgh.

'Oh, that's grand,' said the woman, thrilled to have acquired a nugget of holiday colour. Just the ticket for the postcards she'd already purchased. 'You must be very proud.'

'Actually, it's a bit of a pain,' Rob replied, glancing at his watch. Seeing his guests' uncertain expressions, he rolled his eyes and offered his most charming smile. 'Means I'll be doing the washing up.' They laughed nervously, invited to enjoy a joke they didn't quite understand.

'Oh, that's grand,' the woman muttered again, picking up her knife and fork. No one knew if she meant Shona's dedication to public service or the black pudding on the plate before her.

Shona was second in, behind coxswain Tommy McCall and just before Callum Stewart, the village's twenty-one-year-old postman. Within nine minutes of the alarm sounding, the *Margaret Wilson* was flat out at 25 knots heading up the Solway Firth, the green arms of Scotland and England stretched out on either side of them, hazy in the early light. Later, it might turn into a fine day.

'The maintenance boat from Robin Rigg Wind Farm reported seeing someone in the water,' McCall shouted to Shona and Callum over the noise of the wind and the outboard motor. 'The coastguard thinks the casualty has been washed up on Midton Bank.' He pointed to the chart on the screen of the lifeboat's electronic navigation console. 'With the tide running down they can't get any closer in with the big boats.'

Callum knelt in the bows and looked ahead, searching for any sign of their target. McCall, on the helm, nudged Shona. When she turned to look at him he mouthed, *unconfirmed delta*. She knew what that meant. Unconfirmed death. It wasn't looking good for the casualty. Tommy touched just beneath his eye with two fingers then indicated Callum. She knew what that meant too, keep a watch on Callum.

McCall was right. It was often difficult for newer crew members to deal with the recovery of a dead body. She remembered some of the fatalities she'd encountered when she'd lived in London and first volunteered at Tower Lifeboat Station on the Thames. She'd known nothing about boats, joining the RNLI with a yacht-loving boyfriend. He'd gone. She stayed, finding common ground with fellow volunteers from all walks of life – salesmen, drivers, plumbers. With police training she was better prepared than most for the deaths but it was still heart-breaking. The drunks, the accidents, the 'deliberate attempts to enter the water', as they termed the suicides, both successful and unsuccessful. Sometimes, without a living human being to return to the lifeboat station or hand over to the ambulance services it was easy to experience a sense that, on some level, you'd failed.

Saving a life was what it was all about. The feeling you got from that made it all worthwhile; the cold, the danger, partners left in restaurants and at parties or just at home with the washing up. The flash of irritation on Rob's face this morning, when the pager sounded and she'd kissed him goodbye, came back to her. Well, he could handle it. It was the end of the summer season, only a couple of guests. It had been his idea to move back to his home patch of Dumfriesshire, after he resigned from the bank two years ago. The B&B was supposed to be his thing. Their daughter Rebecca had been thirteen at the time, but already getting into trouble at school. It seemed a good idea to move out of London, a fresh start for them all. And it had been. The beautiful setting, the community. She'd fallen in love with it from day one.

The *Margaret Wilson*, named after the Solway Martyr, a young woman drowned for her religious beliefs, slowed as they approached Midton Bank. The Admiralty chart on the nav console screen now showed large areas of blank space where no attempt had been made to record this shifting, fluid world, neither land nor sea. Tide-washed sands in the middle of the estuary shone metallic grey against the low sun. Morning mist hung over the Cumbrian shore, making it difficult to pick out detail or judge distances. The locals said the tides here travelled faster than a horse could gallop. And if the tide did not catch you, the sinking pools of quicksand, invisible to the eye, would. Navigation was by local knowledge and respect. Shona was glad Tommy McCall, one of the most experienced skippers on the Solway Firth, was in charge.

Shona turned to Callum, handed him the binoculars, and motioned him to swap places. 'Keep an eye on the far shore,' she said as the engine noise dropped. 'Someone might be foolish enough to attempt to walk or drive out to the casualty across the sands.'

The tall, powerfully built postman gave her a thumbs up.

'I'll do a first pass up the length of the sandbank,' McCall said. Shona knelt in the bow and shaded her eyes from the sun. It wasn't long before she spotted a pale shape lying on the sands. At first, she thought it might be one of the grey seals who came into the Solway to pup in the autumn, or perhaps a length of driftwood. She looked away, then back again to check. A swag of blonde hair drifted, mermaid-like, in the shallow water.

Shona stuck out her arm. 'Target sighted, fifty metres.' All she had to do now was keep pointing firmly at the target as Tommy manoeuvred the lifeboat closer.

The shallow draft of the D–class inshore lifeboat made it perfect for the Solway sandbanks. Callum leaned over the side of the inflatable craft, calling the depth as they edged closer, until McCall judged they were as near as they could get without risk of stranding themselves in the falling tide.

'I'll go in and make a first assessment,' Shona said. McCall nodded.

At 5ft 4in in her stocking soles, the sea came up past Shona's knees, but the sand was firm beneath her boots as she waded through the shallow water. The body, partially clothed and probably female judging by the hair, lay on its side. It was tangled up in ghost gear, discarded or lost fishing net and lines. Crabs and other sea creatures had been at work.

Shona walked back to the waiting lifeboat shaking her head. 'Confirm life extinct,' she said. 'The casualty's been in the water for some time. Significant loss of definition to the face and hands. Identification will be difficult.' She looked at Callum. 'You up for this, pal?' When he nodded, she continued, 'We'll use the yellow stretcher. We'll also need to preserve what evidence we can, just in case. Tommy, can you make a note of our exact position?'

McCall indicated GPS fix on the screen. 'Already done. It's a tricky one. We're bang on the border between Scotland and England. Never come across that before.'

'Call the coastguard, ask them where they'd like us to bring the casualty in.' Shona turned back to Callum. 'First fatality?'

'Yes, but don't worry. I'll be fine.' His pale blue eyes showed a calm determination.

'I know you will.'

They walked together up the steepening curve of the sandbank. Already the distance between the casualty and the receding sea had lengthened. They needed to work fast, before the risk of grounding the lifeboat became too great. There was no way Shona would leave the young woman to the mercy of the next tide.

'There's a chance the body will break up when we lift it onto the stretcher. It's entangled in fishing net so that will help us, but all remains must be retrieved, understand?'

'Aye. I understand.'

Shona placed the flat plastic stretcher beside the prone figure. 'We're going to lift and turn her so she's on her back on the stretcher.' She looked down at the slight, pale woman, wrapped in her blanket of seaweed and netting curled up on the sand. 'I'll lift under her shoulders and head, you take her legs. One hand above the knees and one below. The joints may be loose. Okay, when you're ready.'

Shona noted the remains of jeans. One hand was gone, but on the other wrist there appeared to be a metal bracelet embedded in the discoloured skin. The criss-cross web of the ghost gear bit deeply into the greenish, bloated flesh, reminding Shona of a grotesque version of fishnet tights.

As they lifted her, a seabed miasma of rot and decay rolled heavily into their noses, mouths and lungs like an oily wave, coating the tongue and throat. Callum gagged but did not let go until the body was on the stretcher. Then he walked to the edge of the sandbar and vomited. Leaning forward for a moment, hand on knee, he took big gulps of fresh air. He returned, pale but composed. 'Sorry about that.'

'It's fine,' Shona reassured him. 'Always happens first time. You're doing well. Here, help me cover her up.' They fixed the orange plastic sheet over the body and carried the stretcher carefully over the tide rutted sand, back to the waiting boat.

McCall helped them manoeuvre the stretcher over the side and onto the flat bottom of the lifeboat. 'The coastguard want us to put in on Cumbria shore at Silloth. Paramedics and police are already there.'

They made good time and colleagues at Silloth Lifeboat Station towed the *Margaret Wilson* on their tractor into the boat hall where police were waiting to shut the doors.

'It's a crime scene now,' Shona said to Callum. 'We'll all need to give statements.' She nodded her thanks to a crew member from Silloth who'd brought out a tray of tea.

'Will the police find out who she is?' Callum asked Shona. 'She looked just a young lassie. Her hair, it was just like Paula's.' Callum's girlfriend, the barmaid of the Royal Arms, did indeed have long, blonde hair. Shona hoped the similarity wouldn't linger in Callum's memory for too long.

'They'll do their best, Callum.'

'But how did she end up out there?' he persisted.

'Well, it could be an accident. She may have been the victim of a crime. Or she may have taken her own life. Cumbria Police will investigate it once they know who she is. You've done your part now. It's okay to let it go,' she assured him.

'Do you always let it go?' He was studying her expression keenly.

'I try to, Callum,' she said. 'I appreciate that can sound harsh, but if you didn't you would just sink under the weight of it. The grief's natural, but it can stop you doing your job properly, and that helps no one.'

He nodded, satisfied by the honesty of her reply. 'Aye, I see how that could happen.'

She meant what she said, but it wasn't the whole story. The grief could be set aside, recognised it for what it was, the sense of sorrow at the loss of a life. But the anger? The anger that someone had taken a life? That someone had lost their life through despair or another's carelessness? That was something she could never let go of.

An hour later, the boat hall doors of the station opened again.

'Come on,' Shona said, clapping Callum on the back. 'Once we've talked to the police we can get back home and hope the rest of the day is quiet.'

Further up the slipway, Tommy McCall was giving his statement to two uniformed officers. Shona watched as a lean young man with cropped fair hair, a scrappy beard and a dark suit under his grey anorak went up to him.

'DC Daniel Ridley, Cumbria Police.' He showed his warrant card. 'What can you tell me?'

'Shona will fill you in.'

'She the doctor?'

'No, she's one of your lot.' McCall grinned at him.

Shona shook out her dark curls, walked over and placed the helmet on the ground at her feet. She extended her hand. 'Hello, I'm DI Shona Oliver, Dumfries CID.'

'DC Dan Ridley... ma'am,' he replied, noting her firm grip. 'I'd have thought you'd get enough excitement in the day job.'

'I assure you, Detective Constable, this is the kind of excitement we can all do without,' she replied quietly. 'The body was deposited on the sandbank by the tide. There was no other material with her. No handbag or other personal items. The PM is your best shot at identifying her.'

'Sorry, yes of course. Sorry, ma'am.' He reddened. 'Is she ours or yours, do you think?'

'We were instructed by the coastguard to bring the casualty in here, so she's yours. For the moment.' She looked directly up at him. 'Is that a problem?'

'No, no problem. Hear you're a bit busy anyway. Big drug inquiry,' he continued. Then, seeing her cool expression, he faltered. 'You know... my DCI has been in touch with your DCI.'

'Yes, DCIs. They do that, don't they.' She began pulling on her gloves. 'Not my operation, Detective Constable, so I can't help you on that.'

'No, ma'am. Sorry, ma'am. I hope I didn't speak out of turn.'

Shona batted away the comment, then fixed him with a steady look in her warm brown eyes. 'It would be good to know who she was, how she came to be out in the Solway.' She nodded across to Callum, standing pale but composed by the lifeboat, the blond hair at his temples dark with sweat. 'It helps the younger crew close the circle.'

'Yes, ma'am. I'll let you know.' He folded his notebook. 'Can't be easy. The RNLI volunteers do an amazing job.'

Shona searched his face for any sign of sarcasm but found none. 'We didn't manage to save her this time, but we recovered her body, and that helps the family.'

'Of course, ma'am.'

Shona paused. 'Like I said, ID will be difficult, but I noticed some jewellery. If you can't place her in Cumbria be sure to get in touch with me at Dumfries CID. I'd like to help put a name to her.'

'Thank you, ma'am. I'd appreciate that.'

'Good.' Shona picked up the helmet. 'Thank you, DC Ridley. Best of luck with your investigation.' They shook again, Dan gave her his card. Shona re-joined her colleagues who were washing down the *Margaret Wilson* ready for the return journey across the Solway.

'Set him on the right course then, Shona?' Tommy McCall raised an eyebrow at her as they climbed into the lifeboat, now positioned in a launch trailer and being backed into the receding tide by the beach tractor. 'Streak of English piss. No idea what he's doing.'

'Thanks, Tommy. Nothing like a bit of casual racism to brighten up the day.'

'So, you gonna do me for a hate crime then? You know it doesn't count if they're English. Common sense. They're rubbish at everything.'

'I'm sure he doesn't need my help,' Shona replied, refusing to be teased.

'Perhaps you'd like to take the helm on the way back,' he persisted. 'It's where you're happiest, after all.'

She wagged a finger at the smirking skipper. 'Enough of your cheek. Give Callum a go, he's earned it today.'

A smile lit up the young postman's face. 'Can I?'

'Go on then, Cal. Let's see if you can handle the lifeboat with more control than that post van you fly around the village in.' McCall shuffled round to give the beaming young man his spot by the outboard motor.

As the lifeboat slipped back into the water, Shona wondered if perhaps Tommy McCall had a point. She hoped the youthful DC was up to the job, that she was leaving the unknown woman in good hands. Shona looked back at the awkward schoolboy figure of Dan Ridley, watching from the shore. He raised a tentative hand in farewell. After a moment, DI Shona Oliver waved back.

Chapter 2

Detective Chief Inspector Gavin Baird looked up from checking his emails. Somewhere out of sight the high-pitched hum of a hoover and a cleaner's dirty laugh at her companion's comment were cut off behind the slam of a door. This early in the day, the executive floor of the Divisional HQ in Kilmarnock was empty. The fact that it was Saturday morning would reduce, but not eliminate, its later occupation. This high up, weekends were a thing of the past.

On the wall to the left of his desk was pinned an interlocking grid of Ordnance Survey sheets showing the old police territorial area of Ayrshire which ran from the western fringes of Glasgow and down through the Clyde's holiday coast, looping a couple of islands in the process. To the right, a matching mosaic map of Dumfries and Galloway, a rolling rural range stretching all the way to the English border.

On his desk, the studio-shot photograph of his local councillor wife and shiny bright children jostled with the crystal shard of his Scottish Policing Excellence award. The merging of eight regional divisions into a single Police Scotland in 2013 had given him a tail wind that he'd ridden ever since. Now he had the entire south-west quarter of Scotland under his eye. True, it didn't have the gritty glamour of the Glasgow beat or the powerhouse polish of Edinburgh where Scotland's MPs, moneymen and mafiosi rubbed shoulders until it was difficult to tell them apart. But his rate of climb was swift; it wouldn't be long before he joined the movers and shakers in the capital.

However, this morning's objective was to get through his workload and back to his wife Nicola and the kids, picking up essential supplies on the way. It was a fine day. She'd organised an afternoon barbeque, a chance to press the flesh with her political friends, and not even the Scottish weather would dare to rain on her parade.

He scrolled through the weekly updates from his three detective inspectors, based in Ayr, Galloway and Dumfries. Each was a checklist of Targets, Strategies and Local Outcomes and it only took a moment to see that they all had their areas under control.

When he'd started, straight from school twenty-five years ago, you learned everything you needed to know from your fellow officers down the pub. Now it was all emails and conference calls, but he knew his team personally. He'd worked the robberies, a big heroin bust, a kidnapping and the requisite number of murders with many of them as he'd risen swiftly through the ranks. A few had attempted to cling to his coat tails, others affected a studied indifference to the widening gap in their status, but everyone treated him with the correct level of deference.

Baird lifted the stack of manila folders he'd been working through and dumped them on the side for filing. He was putting the finishing touches to Operation Fortress, a big-money, county lines drugs op. If he handled this right, it would propel his career into the stratosphere. The surveillance portion of the job had gone like clockwork.

He'd used a DI and a couple of sergeants out of Ayr, from his old unit, officers he could rely on, to run the foot soldiers. Now he just needed local teams to sweep up the distribution network and he was done.

It had started with a tip from a contact. Names, addresses, supply lines, it was pure gold. By rights it should have gone to a Major Investigation Team but his super, Malcolm Munroe, was near retirement and wanted to go out with a bang. Over the years Baird had learned how to make deals. That way everyone got what they wanted. It was no more than his due.

He was a grafter, something he'd inherited from his coal miner father along with his stocky build and receding dark hair. But the pit at Bilston Glen had closed in 1989, the town absorbed into the poisoned strip of post-industrial wasteland that formed Scotland's Central Belt. By joining the police he'd cut himself off from his hometown, still scarred by the miners' strike, more completely than his £500 suits and polished accent ever could. He'd already met Nicola, middle-class and moneyed. She was excited by his bit-of-rough background, for about five minutes. Only occasionally did she play the my-husband-the-man-of-the-people card, and then she held it by its edges as if the taint of past poverty and deprivation would rub off on her soft, manicured fingers.

He checked the time, pushing back from the desk and freeing his jacket from the back of the chair. Nicola would skin him if the right sort of gin was sold out when he got to Waitrose and although it was only twenty minutes back to their house in Newton Mearns he might hit weekend traffic on the M77.

He scrolled hastily down the list. At the bottom of the screen he spotted an email from DS Murdo O'Halloran, based down in Dumfries, and deleted it unread. He already knew the contents. Let's meet for a beer sometime. They'd worked a big robbery together five years back when O'Halloran's local knowledge had proved useful. But he was a Borders plod who couldn't seem to take the hint that they were no longer drinking partners. They'd called O'Halloran 'Donut Cop' behind his back, after his fondness for deep fried bakery goods and a style of policing based on an episode of *Kojak* Murdo probably saw a kid in the 1970s. He was a joke. But his DI, this Oliver woman, wasn't a joke. Originally from Glasgow, she'd come up from the City of London Police. Fuck knows what she was doing in this backwater. Her husband had some connection to the area. She must be burnt out and running for home. A big fish coming back to a small pond. He knew little about her except she got good results. He doubted she'd be any competition. Baird tapped his pen absently against the desk, then retrieved the email from the trash. Maybe a single beer with Donut Cop would be a wise investment. Any unknown fish swimming in your pond are worth keeping an eye on.

–

Shona Oliver turned her back on the view from her living room. A precious Saturday was almost over. It was getting dark and Rob still wasn't home. Their house, High Pines, was built on three levels and the floor-to-ceiling windows in every room were the main reason they'd bought it. The downside was that you could never escape the spectacular views of Kirkness haven, the Solway Riviera some called it, this mercurial estuary backed by the low wooded hills of Dumfriesshire. Now it felt like the dimming blue of the evening sky was mocking her sense of a gathering storm.

After they'd returned to the lifeboat station, she'd had a cup of tea with Tommy and Callum. They'd completed the debriefing paperwork and the service return document recording how everyone was mentally and physically, any damage to boat or crew or any procedure that might be improved. Shona encouraged Callum to call the confidential trauma management phone line if he needed to. She reminded him and Tommy that the recovery of the body was a criminal matter now and not to discuss it outside of the crew.

Shona had hoped that she and Rob could go for a run out to Knockie Point. The waistband of her jeans was definitely getting tighter. The recent avalanche of paperwork and DS O'Halloran's fetish for donuts were the problem. Just inhaling their scent was enough to start the pounds piling on.

The latest guests, the talkative woman from Edinburgh and her silent husband, had left after breakfast. Becca had stayed at her friend's house the previous night and wasn't due home until teatime. Perhaps after the run and a shower she and Rob could even spend the afternoon in bed together getting properly reacquainted. She'd burst through the back door of the house when she returned and called out his name. In the utility room, silence and a laundry basket overflowing with guests' crumpled bed linen had greeted her. In the kitchen sink, a greasy film had congealed over the breakfast plates. There was no sign of Rob. His mobile went straight to voicemail.

After setting the house straight she'd pulled on her running gear and worn out her rage and disappointment pounding the five miles of coastal path to Knockie Point and back. The sun and the fresh air had moderated her mood but there was still the sense of an opportunity lost.

As the last glow faded from above the western bank, Shona washed up her mug at the kitchen sink and decided she'd waited long enough. What a waste of a Saturday. She could have gone down to the Royal Arms, but her appearance in the singular would have been noted. In a small community like this it was all that was needed to start the rumour mill turning. She tried Rob's mobile again. No joy. Becca was already back in her room zonked out from a sleepless sleepover at Ellie's. As she climbed the staircase to their bedroom Shona tried to put her irritation to the back of her mind and concentrate on the preparations needed for the week ahead. There were guests arriving tomorrow, CID budget and multi-agency meetings on Monday and a quarterly staff performance review to complete. Shona also wanted to tackle Becca about subject choices and university open days before she went back to school. She'd need to be up early to get through everything.

The front door banged open and there was a burst of song. 'South of the border, down Cumbria waaay'. Rob and his brother Sandy, a florid-faced bear of a man, lurched into view at the foot of the stairs. When Rob saw Shona's expression, he shushed Sandy and attempted to climb the bottom steps in an exaggerated tip toe.

'Where have you been?' Shona asked in a level voice. Rob stopped dead in his tracks and kept his head down.

'We've had a well-earned day out at Carlisle races, officer,' said Sandy, stumbling forward with a broad grin and a mock salute. 'All very innocent, officer.'

'Don't do that, Sandy, it's not funny.' She glared at her brother-in-law. 'Have you been driving?'

'No, no,' he insisted, his smile faltering. 'We're sensible lads. We took a taxi.'

'From Carlisle?' Shona smiled and nodded. 'Good idea, well done.' Sandy looked mollified, but Rob had turned pale. 'All the way from Carlisle,' she continued. 'Very sensible, gents. Oh, but I bet that cost you. On top of the drinking, and a wee flutter on the gee-gees, can't have much change out of a couple of grand, that be about right?'

Rob was motioning Sandy to keep quiet, but his brother blundered on. 'Yeah, 'bout right. £150 for the taxi, but better than losing your licence, eh?' Sandy nodded sagely.

'Is that right?' Shona stiffened. She came down the stairs until she was eye-to-eye with her 6ft 3in brother-in-law. 'Well, Sandy, I hope you like singing in a high register, because it won't be your licence you'll be losing when Caroline hears about this. Will it?' Sandy's formid-able wife was in Edinburgh visiting her elderly mother. Sandy opened his mouth and closed it again, pale and silent. Eventually he said in a small voice, 'She doesn't need to know, does she?'

Shona ignored him and turned to Rob, who queasily clung to the bannister. She leaned down close to his face and said quietly. 'Gambling? Don't take me for a mug. I really don't like that.' She stood upright and fixed them both with a final glare. 'We'll talk again when you're sober. Good night, Sandy, you know the way out.'

The realisation that Rob was gambling again had come like a gut punch. She turned and ran up the stairs, so he wouldn't see her tears. She knew he missed the high stakes game of investment banking and that risk-taking was part of his personality, as much as it was an element of hers.

But where she'd learned to harness the impulse, to coolly weigh up the options and shorten the odds, for Rob it was the risk itself, the chance of losing or winning it all that possessed him. That Rob had tried to keep it a secret from her was worse. When he'd left the bank and they'd come to this beautiful place, this new life, they'd made a pact to have no more secrets. But then didn't she have a secret just as big, just as shameful, something that could destroy them as surely as drink or gambling or infidelity? And there was one thing she knew for sure. It was something she was never, ever going to share with him.

Chapter 3

The following Wednesday Shona took the call from Detective Constable Dan Ridley of Cumbria Police. He could find no trace of the unidentified woman recovered from the Solway Firth. Would Police Scotland help? Shona agreed, and the next morning, Ridley was leaning on the front desk at Cornwall Mount, the Divisional HQ in Dumfries.

DI Oliver watched him for a moment from behind the reception security glass. He was not as young as she'd first thought. Minus the anorak, the coltish, schoolboy look had gone. He stood with his suit jacket slung over his shoulder and there was a mature muscularity beneath his fitted white shirt. She judged him about thirty, the same decade as her, although at the opposite end of it. He was gripping an A4 zipped folder in his left hand. No wedding ring and, based on the poor job he was doing chatting up Janet, the civilian receptionist, it was likely to stay that way for a while. The desk clerk's body language radiated a sullen boredom as she tapped the keyboard and glanced repeatedly at the wall clock. Shona decided to cut them both a break and buzzed open the door.

'Thanks, Janet,' she called. 'DC Ridley, come through.' They shook hands and she could see him taking in her own altered appearance, the RNLI waterproofs and life-jacket exchanged for a dark blue trouser suit, low heels, cream blouse, her unruly dark curls straightened into the smooth bob she always wore for work. They swapped pleasantries about Dan's journey and the weather as they climbed to the first floor.

'I'm about to start morning conference. You can brief us at the end.' Shona ushered him into a meeting room.

'Dan, this is DS Murdo O'Halloran.' A stocky, fair man in his forties, with a firm grip and a battered rugby player's face, got up and shook Ridley's outstretched hand. 'And this is DC Kate Irving.' Shona indicated a tall, fine-boned woman in her twenties, wearing a crisp white blouse, her fair hair in a high pony tail. Kate Irving nodded to him coolly. 'And DC Ravi Sarwar...' Shona scanned the faces around the table. 'Where is Ravi?'

'Community Engagement Team,' replied DS O'Halloran. 'You signed off on him giving a Diversity and Inclusion briefing to the specials.'

'You're right, I did. And if they can survive Ravi for a morning, the mean streets of Dumfries should hold no further fears. But Murdo, don't let the CET get too attached to him. I want him back, pronto.' She turned to Ridley. 'Find yourself a seat.'

The sun had edged round, and the small room filled with Shona's team and a dozen support staff was heating up. Windows ran the length of one wall. Dan Ridley chose a spot in the shade beneath them and sat down.

'Morning, everyone,' Shona addressed the group. 'I've just had conformation that we will be supporting Operation Fortress. Our role will be only to assist in the arrests of low priority dealer and drug users. DCI Baird will be coming in to brief you in the next few days.' There was a murmur of excitement. 'In the meantime, this is DC

Dan Ridley from Cumbria Police, he's here for reasons that will shortly become apparent.'

Shona pulled her chair in towards the table and flicked open her folder. 'Now, Murdo, can you bring us all up to speed on the overnights?'

All eyes slid to DC Ridley, a stranger in the room.

'Go on,' Shona commanded. 'There's nothing operational that isn't fit for Ridley to hear. Same side, even if he is from England where they do have funny ways.' There was a ripple of laughter and the room relaxed, attention switched to DS O'Halloran. 'Murdo, off you go. What have we got?'

'Couple of assaults and minor drug offences, they've been processed and will go before the Sheriff this morning.' Murdo paused and ticked off a list before him. 'Now, the baby milk thefts.' A groan ran round the room which Shona silenced with a frown. 'Co-op in town was hit last night. It's the same story we've been hearing over the last few months. This time two guys came in, and while the shop assistant's back was turned they cleared the baby milk shelf and walked out. Six cans. Gone before uniform could get down there.'

'Just the baby milk?' asked DC Kate Irving. 'No booze or high-value items?'

'Well, that's the thing,' Murdo replied. 'Seems the baby milk *is* a high-value item. Some stores have started keeping it behind the counter. I spoke to the Co-op's area manager this morning. Since it's illegal for stores to promote discounted baby formula – it's a Trading Standard rule – even half price cans will find an online market. But the whole situation is made worse by a world-wide shortage, caused by contaminated milk in China a few years back. It's been catnip to thieves for a while. They sell it online, mostly abroad. Stores have been rationing the milk to two tins per customer for a while, but demand is still high.'

'So, it's just a bit of enterprising shoplifting?' Kate Irving said, arching her eyebrows. 'Something for Ravi. He could ask around his community.' Shona noted her DC's scorn.

'Not on this scale it's not,' Murdo replied.

'How many shops were hit?' Shona cut in.

'Eighteen, so far. Approximately two hundred and fifty items taken.'

'So how much are they selling it for online?'

'Manager reckons between ten pounds and thirty pounds a pop,' Murdo said. 'So that's potentially...'

'...Between two and a half and seven and a half grand.' Shona beat him to the maths. 'Bit more than shoplifting.'

Kate Irving looked down at her notebook, a blush spreading across her pale complexion, ignoring the smirks from her colleagues.

'The calls are still coming in from the smaller shops who've just heard about it and are checking their stock.' Murdo consulted his notebook again. 'Tesco, Morrisons, the Co-ops, all the wee convenience stores, Spar, Boots in Dumfries have all now reported thefts. Some have been slow to come forward, it's often not worth their while prosecuting, and with supplies short they said they didn't want to spark panic buying. Now the media have got wind of it. I've already had the press office on to me.'

'Okay.' Shona nodded. 'Could be the work of an organised crime group. If it is an OCG then a Major Investigation Team may already be on it, working countrywide.' Shona leaned forward and tapped the table, making eye contact in turn with everyone around it. 'But this is our patch, so I want every piece of evidence we hand to the MIT to be top notch. No opportunity missed. Understood?'

Nods and murmurs of 'Yes, ma'am' ran around the room.

'New CCTV from the stores is already on its way,' said O'Halloran. 'I've got uniform compiling a list of potential witnesses from among the shop assistants and doing statements.'

'Good. Thank you, Murdo.' Shona pointed her pen at her DC. 'Kate, speak to the officers who've been dealing with this. Get a team together and do an initial trawl of the new CCTV when it arrives. I want to know how many individuals we're looking for. Is this a single couple or multiple groups? I want descriptions, clothing.' Kate began typing notes into her tablet. 'And a timeline,' Shona continued. 'I want a timeline. If there's a vehicle, or vehicles, identified get onto Traffic for potential ANPR hits. Let's establish if they're local or just visiting. Also check if we've already recovered anything with possible forensic opportunities. DNA, fingerprints. Did the perpetrators touch anything? Drop anything? There will be contamination, but we have multiple crime scenes. If we can find forensic links between them, we could have our suspects.' She turned to DS O'Halloran. 'And tell the press office they'll have that statement by lunchtime. Keep me updated. I want any leads as soon as we have them.'

Murmured conversation and a sense of purpose filled the room. DC Kate Irving was already leaning back in her chair talking to a young man and a middle-aged woman, two of the civilian staff, standing behind her. Murdo was scrolling through his phone. Dan wondered if he'd been forgotten.

'Now,' said Shona firmly, regaining their attention. 'DC Ridley has come in to ask for our assistance with a suspicious death. DC Ridley, would you like to take us through it?' She shuffled her chair sideways and motioned for the others to make room for him. She could see he was nervous. It was tough presenting to officers you didn't know. She gave him an encouraging smile.

'Morning, everyone. I'm DC Dan Ridley from Cumbria CID.' He slid the post-mortem photographs from his folder and passed them round. 'Last Saturday, a young woman's body was recovered from the Solway Firth by Kirkness lifeboat.' He paused and looked at Shona, but she nodded for him to go on. 'She'd been in the water some time and the PM showed cause of death to be internal injuries. A torn liver and ruptured stomach consistent with either a high-speed road traffic accident, where the seat belt can cut into the victim on impact.' He motioned across his torso. 'Or a severe beating. Someone kicking, punching or stamping on the victim, causing the fatal injuries.'

'Which does the pathologist feel is more likely?' asked DS O'Halloran. 'Given where she was found I'd say a car crash doesn't fit.'

'The pathologist, Dr Wilson, won't commit to either.' Dan replied. 'Said it wasn't his job to speculate.'

'What about defensive injuries?' Kate asked.

Shona stepped in. 'One of her hands was missing and there was extensive soft tissue degeneration due to immersion in sea water. It would have been difficult to tell.' She turned to Dan. 'How long did Dr Wilson estimate she'd been in the water?'

'Three weeks. She'd given birth at some point, though not recently. The state of her lungs also meant Dr Wilson...' Dan fumbled for his notebook. 'He said he couldn't rule out if drowning was a factor in her death.'

'You mean she could have been alive when she went in to the Solway Firth? Dear God.' Murdo shook his head.

'We haven't been able to identify her,' Dan went on, 'although we're still waiting for DNA. She doesn't match the description of anyone reported missing in Cumbria. I searched the UK Missing Persons database, but I got dozens of matches for blonde, young women aged twenty to thirty reported missing nationally, even without including Ireland or Europe.'

'There was no identification material with her, no purse or phone,' Shona added. 'Was there anything in her pockets?' Ridley shook his head. Shona continued, 'She was wearing a bracelet. What about that?'

Dan shuffled through the prints until he found the images of a thick silver band set beside a black and white forensic photography scale. He passed them round. 'No luck with a manufacturer. It's not sterling silver, so no hallmark either. Could have been made by a local artist or crafter.'

Murdo held up one of the pictures showing a flattened section of the bangle. Stamped into it were two overlapping hearts surmounted by a crown. 'It's a Luckenbooth.' When the others looked blank, he continued. 'Comes from Edinburgh originally. It's an old design for a brooch. Used to be given as love tokens, or to ward off the evil eye. Didnae work for this lassie, did it?' He shook his head again. 'Turns up on all sorts of jewellery nowadays. I gave Joan a pair of earrings like this for our anniversary. Doesn't mean our victim's Scottish, but it's a connection, of sorts.'

'If you could circulate the bracelet, ask around. I'd be very grateful,' Dan said.

Shona gathered up the pictures in front of her. The woman's body looked even more abandoned and alone against the cold stainless steel of the mortuary table than it had done on the Solway's sands. The mermaid hair was scraped back from the battered remains of her face. Somewhere a child had lost a mother, and a mother had lost a daughter. The ripples would spread out, touching family, friends, workmates and acquaintances, rolling on forever unless some resolution could be found. It was their job to find it. Shona could sense her team watching her, waiting for a decision.

'We, the lifeboat, recovered her tangled up in some netting from the sandbank halfway between Scotland and England,' she began. 'It was on the coastguard's instruction that this woman went to Cumbria, but only because emergency services were already standing by at Silloth. We're in a unique position here in Dumfries and Galloway Division, sitting as we do on the boundaries of Scotland, England and Northern Ireland. With that position comes the responsibility to aid our colleagues wherever they are. Though we may be on different sides of a border, we're all on the same side when it comes to achieving justice for the victims of crime.' She tapped the photographs. 'This could just as easily been our case, so I want you to think of DC Ridley as a member of the team and give him all the help you can.' Shona handed the prints back to Dan. 'Send me an electronic file of all the pictures and the PM report and I'll see it's circulated, and we'll put your contact details on the comms list.'

She turned back to the room. 'Right. Everyone know what they're doing?' There were nods as people packed up and split into twos and threes to start their assigned tasks.

'Murdo, we'll have a sit-down later.' Shona lifted her bag and folder. 'I've got a budgets meeting. Can you show DC Ridley out?' She nodded to Dan. 'Thank you for coming over.' Then she was gone.

DC Ridley and DS O'Halloran made their way downstairs and stopped by the front desk.

'What's your guvnor in Carlisle like then?' asked Murdo.

'Likes the sound of his own voice, preferably as loud as possible,' Dan replied, holding up the A4 folder. 'Thinks this case should be filed under unexplained death and no arguments. Doesn't hold with "fancy policing". That's anything introduced this century. You lot are getting off lightly. How's your guv, then?'

Murdo grinned. 'Let me tell you about DI Oliver. When she came up from London, she spent a couple of weeks with different sections, getting a feel for the area, how it differed from the city. She even did a day or two with Traffic, out on the streets, not sitting in an office. When she was with the Families Support Team, some low-life who goes by the name of Gringo – a six feet three inches pile of shite – had put his missus in hospital. DI Oliver and a young special constable went to get a statement. Gringo arrives, shouting the odds, and walloped the male special, who tried to stop him getting at his missus, still laid out in a hospital bed. Do you know what the boss did?'

'Called for back-up? Talked him down?'

'No. She picked up the constable's baton and gave Gringo a hammering. Bastard was on his knees when security arrived. Threatened to complain about police brutality but dropped the idea quickety-quick when he realised he'd have to stand up in court and explain how Wee Shona had beat him up. He'd be a laughing stock. His pals would never let him forget it.'

Dan pursed his lips and nodded. 'Impressive. Does she do martial arts training?'

Murdo's eyes twinkled with amusement. 'No, pal. Under that soccer mom exterior, she's as hard as fuck. Grew up in the east end of Glasgow. So, remember, don't get on the wrong side of her. No one gets off lightly with Wee Shona. She'll take your head off your shoulders, possibly even literally.' DS O'Halloran smiled and clapped Dan on the back. 'But, no worries, eh? Nice well-behaved lad like you? You'll be fine, won't you?'

Dan nodded obediently. 'What happened to the guy? Gringo?'

'The lassie pressed charges, after seeing what the boss did.' Murdo dropped his voice. 'Probably shouldn't say this, but Wee Shona's actions did more good than a month of community policing. Domestic violence prosecutions have gone up. It's like the women feel the police just might be on their side.' He opened the front door for Dan and they shook hands again. 'One last thing. Don't ever tell her I called her Wee Shona.'

Chapter 4

The next morning, DCI Gavin Baird appeared on the Skype screen. 'Shona. Thanks for your case list. Are you up to speed on Op Fortress?'

'Yes, sir.' The document he'd sent was thinner than she'd expected; Baird was playing this close to his chest. She'd scanned through the brief, noting how different their styles of policing were. She'd have made more use of Dumfries officers with local knowledge for the raids.

But she was already on her guard. Six months ago, DCI Baird had poached Vincent Greig, her visual investigations specialist, and Chloe Burke, one of her best information analysts. Shona had read the latest Operation Fortress document with the level of caution she would deploy for any suspicious package, one which might detonate without warning, removing members of her team and leaving her to deal with the aftermath.

Shona's door opened a fraction and DS O'Halloran quietly slid a sheet of notes onto her desk before pulling the door closed again. A printout from the local news website, *DnG24*, was clipped to the top. The baby milk story had made the headlines.

'We'll need every officer available for the co-ordinated raids,' Baird continued. 'I mean to hit this county lines drug network hard across Ayrshire, Dumfries and

Galloway. I'll be briefing everyone myself early next week.'

'It's a big job – can we set up a meeting to discuss this in more detail, sir?'

'Everything you need is in the document.' He waved away her concern. 'This is an excellent opportunity to exceed our targets and impact several local outcomes – anti-social behaviour, health and wellbeing.'

What happened to saving lives, locking up the bad guys, thought Shona. It was in there somewhere. But he was right, a big anti-drugs operation like this would cut crime at every level, from dealers' turf wars to the petty thefts and burglaries that fuelled the addicts' need for cash. The poverty and hopelessness would still be there waiting to bloom, though, in all its grotesque form. Addicts would not vanish. Supply and demand, the business of crime, would exploit these people in other forms. The multi-agency meeting she'd just come from was already primed for the expected surge in workload that Operation Fortress would generate; everything from child protection to drug rehab cases would increase. She hoped the agencies would cope, but they were already at full stretch. There was no magic money tree, as DCI Baird often reminded her, or reserve division of social workers to deploy.

'This Jane Doe in the Solway Firth…' Baird broke into her thoughts.

'Female, early twenties. Potentially a Scottish link, via her jewellery. I'm circulating particulars and checking local missing persons for matches.'

'I wasn't looking for an update. You can forget this one. I need you on the baby milk thefts.'

'Why?'

'Because you're a senior detective, and a crime that has a massive impact on the public and business communities has been committed.'

'And a young woman has died...'

'Yes, and it's Cumbria's problem, let them deal with it. From what I can see there's no clear evidence it's murder. Unexplained, yes. We don't have the resources to progress a case with no ID and little chance of success.' Baird's attention was being drawn by someone else in his office. Shona knew she'd already eaten up her allocated slot in his day. His PA would be signalling a more important caller or some Divisional matter that he should be attending to.

'Look.' A flash of exasperation passed over Baird's face, but he smiled, composing himself. 'You're an excellent detective inspector, and these thefts have caused a major impact on the retail businesses of the area. Now the press have got it. It's trending on Mumsnet, for God's sake. There's gonna be flack if we don't shut this down quickly. You're right to highlight possible organised crime gang connections, but it's currently just your area affected. I need my best officer on it if it's not to spread.'

Shona recognised the casual attempt at flattery. They both saw it for what it was. He was ordering her to drop the body in the firth case but allowing her the fig leaf of self-esteem and himself the wiggle room to deny it, should there be any comeback. She wouldn't play that game.

'Are you telling me not to investigate this death, sir?'

'I'm saying we have other operational priorities, Shona. Oh, by the way,' he said, effectively ending any further discussion, 'are you still on for the Scottish Trade Against Crime reception next week? Kenny Hanlon will be announcing the new crime prevention initiatives his business group are co-funding.'

Shona hadn't realised that the STAC launch was so soon. A trek up to Glasgow to stand around smiling at business leaders who thought they were entitled to tell her how to do her job because they were paying for the drinks was the last thing she wanted. Baird, she knew, would be in his element.

There were several operational reasons why Police Scotland should suck up to Kenny Hanlon. Money was the chief concern, closely followed by positive press coverage. Hanlon was a celebrity businessman who had his own show on BBC Scotland, *The Enterpriser*, a kind of tartan *Dragon's Den* and *The Apprentice* rolled into one. The funding figures looked impressive and community groups would welcome it with open arms. Was this a serious attempt to cut crime or a vanity project for Kenny Hanlon? Shona had yet to decide. She resolved to treat the evening as a research trip, an opportunity to judge, and perhaps influence, how much in the way of extra resources could be channelled into her patch in the aftermath of Operation Fortress. 'Yes, of course. I'll be there.'

Baird cut the call. Shona scanned the main office through the glass panels of her room. Catching DC Kate Irving's eye, she motioned her to come in.

'Boss?' Kate stopped in the doorway, notebook in hand.

'How are we doing with CCTV on the baby milk job? Any updates?' Shona had run through the notes Murdo had left on the desk without learning anything new.

Kate slumped her tall frame against the door jamb. 'It's slow going. I've got Hannah and Ed on it, but there's multiple cameras from each store. It would be a lot easier if Op Fortress hadn't swiped Vinny the Visuals. One of the small shops sent us a CD. I spent most of yesterday afternoon trying to find a laptop with a disc player in it.'

'Have you cross-referenced the thefts with the timeline, given yourselves somewhere to start?' Shona asked.

'Well, we're trying. The store thefts began about two months ago, but there's dozens of statements, and some of the shops didn't notice the thefts until later.'

'You see, this is why a timeline is important on multiple incidents, otherwise you'll be running around like headless chickens. Page one stuff, Kate.' Shona pushed her chair back. 'Get a *provisional* timeline on the whiteboard, based on calls coming in. Get someone on statements adding to it, use the clerical assistants if you're stuck, one or two are quite quick at reading through pages of text. Then you, Hannah and Ed confirm dates and times based on CCTV. I want descriptions on the board in an hour. Suspects and any cars. We'll put a press release out in time for this evening's news. We'll get a lot of calls, mostly useless, but DCI Baird wants us to take this on.'

'We're not handing this over to a MIT?' asked Kate.

'No, it's ours. Opportunity to shine, Kate. Crack on.' Shona ushered her back through the door. Then she set the timer on her phone and when it pinged one hour later she looked at the satisfying list of paperwork accomplished and headed out into the main office.

'Listen up, folks.' Shona paused for a beat as heads turned from computer screens and calls were ended. When she had everyone's attention she continued. 'Update please, Kate.'

DC Irving jumped up from her chair. 'These are our suspects, ma'am.' She began fixing a series of around twenty screen grabs of mixed quality beneath the timeline on the whiteboard. Shona was reminded of the game she'd played with Becca when she was little, matching pairs. Cards laid out face down, then turned over for a moment before being replaced in their original position. Shona's eye for detail meant she'd quickly memorised the entire deck and their positions, but she always let Becca win. Becca was good at it too and rarely needed her help. Perhaps it was hereditary. The thought that she'd passed a useful trait on to her child gave a small moment of pride.

'They've been careful,' said Murdo, indicating the prints on the board. 'Baseball caps, hoodies, headscarves. Keeping their backs to the cameras.'

'Which suggests they could be local and know their targets,' said Kate, studying the display with serious grey eyes. 'Or that they're from outside the area but they're organised and did their homework. Either way, it's likely they checked out the shops before they hit them, so there may be footage from a previous visit.'

'But when?' Murdo pointed to the surveillance video frozen on Kate's laptop screen. 'Do you not think you've enough on your plate with that lot?'

Kate nodded glumly.

'Pairs,' Shona said. 'Ever play it as a child? It's a bit like Snap.' She began grouping together the photographs where the suspects showed similarities. 'Tall individual, probably male. The Co-op theft was reported as two males, but a previous witness said a couple, so the smaller suspect is probably female.' She held up another photograph. 'There's less of a height difference here and they've changed clothes. Heels? No, it's in the build too, but they could have bulked up with layers of clothing.' She stepped back for a moment before grabbing a marker pen and writing 'suspect A' on the board and gathering together all the prints of the tallest person.

'Kate?' Shona said, holding out the pen. Kate came forward, added 'suspect B', and placed all the pictures of the smaller individual in a group. The rest of the team made comments and pointed out details.

'We could really do with Vincent to look at this,' said Shona, inwardly cursing the temporary loss. 'He'd check the videos for possible links in how they walk, posture and mannerisms, but from these stills I'd say we are looking for minimum two, but more likely three or four individuals.'

She picked up two of the clearest images. One showed the couple from the back, but with a partial profile of the man just visible beneath his pulled down baseball cap. In the other image, the female figure was seen from the front, her head dipped beneath the hood of her grey sweatshirt. 'Is that a Nike logo?' Shona showed the image to the team. A few of them nodded uncertainly.

'Could be,' said Kate. 'I wondered if that was a strand of blonde hair?' She pointed to a faint pale smudge at the woman's collarbone.

'Perhaps,' agreed Shona.

'I thought that was the cord from her hoodie,' said Murdo.

'Okay, get these two out to the press,' ordered Shona, handing him the prints. 'If we can get a possible ID on even one of these individuals, it will be a start.'

'Press office want us to put up someone for interviews on this. TV and radio,' Murdo said, passing the images to one of the civilian staff. Kate looked up, hopeful. Shona was tempted to let her do it, just to teach her an important lesson.

'The press office should have more sense. Some smart-arse reporter will make a feeble joke, you know.' Shona threw up her hands in frustration. '"Is breast now best following a spate of baby formula thefts?" or "Are Dumfries Police feeling like right tits after baby milk heists?" Now that, see that?' She broke off and pointed at two smirking male support staff who quickly straightened their faces. 'That is exactly the reaction I'm talking about.'

Shona turned again to her DC. 'On camera you'll be forced to respond, Kate. Smile and play along, be a good sport and we'll look like we're not taking this seriously. Slap him down and you'll look po-faced and out of touch, that the police can't take a joke. It's a poisoned chalice. So, no interviews. A statement with an appeal for witnesses is the best fit until we have something positive to say. Understand?'

'Yes, ma'am,' Kate replied, looking suitably chastened.

'Right everyone, back to work. Murdo, a word.' Shona returned to her office, followed by her sergeant. The quiet hum of worker bees resumed as staff went back to their tasks.

'Murdo, get an appeal out for our unidentified woman in the Solway Firth and send out the picture of the bracelet with it.'

'Isn't that Cumbria's case? Division won't like that.'

'Well Division can lump it. I'll not ignore a young woman's death.'

'What did Baird say? Shouldn't you clear it with him first?'

'It's what I say that counts, DS O'Halloran. My manor, my rules,' replied Shona, drawing herself up and lifting her chin in defiance. Her first boss, a Cockney bruiser with thirty years' service, used to say that. He'd taught Shona all she needed to know about being responsible to the community you served. 'Call in favours with tame journalists if you have to, I want maximum coverage for this.'

'Okay, no problem. Will we be getting any more people? If we're working the baby milk thefts and a suspicious death and also supporting Op Fortress, we'll be pushed.'

It was true, Operation Fortress was bearing down on them like a truck with no brakes. It was a logistical nightmare. A dozen simultaneous early morning arrests involving uniform and CID teams, vans, sniffer dogs, the works. The culmination of months of surveillance, intelligence processing and planning. But it was Baird's operation, his officers were dealing with it. That made it Baird's problem, not hers. Her team would concentrate on the cases they had. 'No.' She shook her head. 'No more staff. It will just be us as usual. Keeping it in the family.'

'Does that mean there's a chance of overtime?'

'Do you want the Divisional response on that?'

'Does it begin, not a snowball's chance…'

'…in hell?' she finished. 'Yes, Murdo. That's the one.'

Chapter 5

Shona worked on until seven p.m. Then she told those team members who hadn't already left due to family responsibilities to go home. DC Kate Irving, facing the prospect of another Friday night in front of the TV with a ready meal, volunteered to stay for a while and sift the calls coming into the control centre after the evening news appeal. Shona reckoned the interesting tips might not come until Monday, when those with something to gain or lose by talking to the police had weighed up their options, and time had worked on both their consciences and their sense of self-preservation. For now, the majority would be fantasists or curtain-twitchers who already had suspicions about their neighbours and relished a chance to air them. But every tip needed checking and Kate could give them a head start by prioritising the initial intel.

The half-hour drive back from Dumfries HQ to Kirkness was Shona's buffer zone. A window of time in which to assess the business of the day and re-order her resources for the different challenges of home. She caught the end of *The Archers* on Radio 4, then switched to Classic FM as she left the A75. The road became narrower, winding down through the lanes until the first spirit-lifting glimpse of the bay. The tide had gone out, leaving a sheen of brightness on the mudbanks; a million tiny points of light sparkled in the evening sunshine. The first flames of autumn colour were tinting the far bank. Golden alders and larches, red rowans and the fiery glow of hawthorns licking upwards to the dark pines on the higher hills.

She parked the four-year-old Audi A3 next to Rob's brand new Mercedes V-Class MPV, bought to collect B&B guests from Dumfries rail station in comfort but used mostly to ferry Becca and her friends around.

Rob called out from the kitchen as she came through the back door. She took in the ordered laundry room and stacked guest supplies with an involuntary stab of guilt. Since Rob's outing with his brother Sandy to Carlisle races last weekend, he'd been a model of sobriety and contrition. Her worry that he'd been gambling again was beginning to feel like an overreaction. It was a day out with his brother, a letting off of steam built up by their first full season of demanding guests. It was the inevitable outcome of this period of adjustment, a single act he would not be repeating. He'd said all this in a profuse and credible apology at a lunch he'd made for just the two of them and followed by the attentive lovemaking only a relationship-threatening argument can inspire.

Rob had his back to her, washing up under the big window that faced out into the bay. He grinned over his shoulder as she wrapped her arms around him.

He turned and embraced her. 'Careful. Tommy dropped off some fish. I've been making a pie. I stink.' Rob's mother had once cooked at the nearby exclusive Palnackie House Hotel. He'd done a cookery course there soon after his redundancy and when he returned to London, he had a complete plan, spreadsheets, the lot. He still had occasional thoughts of opening a restaurant in an empty building at Tommy's boatyard. For the moment, he practised on the family. 'If you're hugging me now you must love me really.'

'Who says I love you? I could just be using you for sex, all the while planning to callously discard you.'

'Naw, you must love me. You followed me to this hell hole.' His expression clouded.

She looked at him seriously, examining his tanned, handsome face and blue-grey eyes for clues. 'You think this is a hell hole?' Beyond the window, the curve of the bay was a serene smile, the calm evening a gentle caress.

He pulled her close again, nuzzling her neck, then leaned back grinning at her. 'Course not, though *your* cooking could stand some improvement, lassie. That is a vision of hell. Lucky you've got me or we'd all starve.'

Shona glimpsed the pie in the eye-level oven, the golden potato crust browning nicely. Her stomach rumbled. Becca came into the kitchen wearing an acid yellow vintage top over leggings, her dark wavy hair loose around her shoulders. She had her mother's heart shaped face and colouring, but her father's height and cheekbones. She rolled her eyes at her parents. Shona detached an arm from Rob and pulled her daughter to her. At fifteen, Becca was already several inches taller than she was. She kissed her lightly on the cheek. For a second, Shona held them both in a fierce embrace, fixing the imprint of them in her consciousness, throwing a ring of protection around all that really mattered to her.

'Muuum,' Becca protested. Becca disdained, but never denied, these moments of affection. Perhaps her daughter loved her after all.

Rob detached himself. 'Right, food, ten minutes,' he said as he began laying the table in the kitchen. The jaunty theme-tune of *The Enterpriser* came from the small

TV suspended below the kitchen cabinets. 'Your pal's on again.' He indicated celebrity business guru Kenny Hanlon, all impossibly blond hair and loud suit, beaming like the risen sun from the screen. 'When are we meeting him?'

'Don't remind me. The STAC reception is next week.' She watched as the camera swooped wildly over the ecstatic studio audience. As the titles ended it came to rest on Hanlon, posed side-on, feet planted wide and arms folded. He turned, brandished a huge fistful of cash, and winked. The legend Your Business is My Business flashed up in neon behind him. 'God, this is trash.' Shona shook her head.

'Don't let the theatrical camp fool you. He's got a good commercial head on him.' Rob tasted the homemade ketchup he was stirring and nodded, satisfied. 'Mind you, he should have a rabies shot the way he goes after some of the contestants.'

'You a fan?' Shona raised her eyebrows.

'Oh, I wouldn't go that far.' Rob smiled diplomatically.

While Becca was upstairs finishing some homework, accompanied by the pounding rap of Stormzy, Shona quickly showered and changed into jeans and a sweater. Returning to the kitchen, she noted a bottle of chilled white wine, already half drunk, had appeared on the table, along with a glass of apple juice for Becca. When they were all settled with full plates in front of them Rob asked them both about their day. Becca responded with grunts and shrugs but her general mood suggested things hadn't gone too badly. 'I know better than to ask you for details,' he said to Shona. 'For *operational reasons*.' There was an edge of sarcasm in his words.

In the early years of their relationship they'd both agreed their jobs stopped at the front door of their home. She'd talk about cases only in the broadest terms. Rob's banking deals, when discussed at any length, quickly became an abstract string of numbers that Shona found a curiously impersonal way to spend your working day. But now Rob had no corporate life, no colleagues to confide in or grumble about the boss with. He was his own boss and could order his day in any way he pleased. She envied him the freedom. But it was a lonely sort of freedom, and perhaps a factor in his recent behaviour, the source of the restlessness and dissatisfaction she sensed below the surface of their life together.

'Actually, I need to ask your advice about something,' she began. He was surprised, but she could see his interest was piqued. 'Managing rivalry in your team.' She stopped short of detailing DCs Kate Irving and Ravi Sarwar's worst excesses. But Kate's constant sniping and Ravi's baiting of his colleague was having an impact. She didn't want to lose either; something needed to be done. She could give them a good talking to, but perhaps there was another way?

Rob barked a short, mirthless laugh and topped up his wine glass, draining the bottle. 'In banking you don't so much manage your team as keep them at bay with a pointy stick. It's like swimming with sharks, they'll gobble you up if you turn your back for a second. Want to keep them happy? Throw them a live victim and stand back while they try to tear each other apart.' He took a large gulp from his glass. Then, pinching the stem, he rotated it between finger and thumb, frowning at the swirling contents, lost in dark and unhappy remembrance.

'You must be so glad to be out of it.' Asking him had been a miscalculation. In a bid to change the subject, she said. 'So, what did you get up to today? Do anything special?'

'Don't do that,' he snapped at her.

'Do what?'

'Question me like a suspect. I know you think I swan around all day wasting my time, but I've been busy.'

'No point in lying to Mum. She'll always bust you,' Becca joked, but seeing the expression on her father's face, quickly slid from the table and deposited her empty plate into the kitchen sink. Mumbling something about more homework, she fled upstairs to her room and slammed the door. Shona glared at Rob.

'What?' he shot back, draining his glass. 'You think I'm gambling, but I'm not.'

Shona started to deny it, but he cut her off. 'It's all right for you,' he continued. 'If you're not at work you're down at your precious lifeboat. I spent an hour picking her up from school, then when we're nearly home I had to go back because she's left a course book there. Barely got a thank you. I spend half my time covering for you.'

'You're not covering for me,' she snapped. 'The school run is your job because you can fit it in around the guests. The B&B was your idea and I supported you when you left the bank.'

'I knew you'd throw that in my face.'

'I'm not.' She paused. She'd had a long day and couldn't face an argument. 'It's just when I run out the door, for the lifeboat or the job, I need to know you'll take up the slack at home. That's what we agreed.' She smiled and placed her hand on his arm, but he shook it off.

'But you never wanted to move here.'

'Not this again.' She stared at him, puzzled by this sudden squall in the middle of a perfect evening. They'd bought their salary-stretching Camden basement flat as honeymooners, for its tiny outdoor space. For Sundays spent reading papers in the garden. For gastro pub lunches and browsing second-hand furniture in Camden Market. When Becca arrived, Rob had just landed a big bonus, so they bought the flat upstairs and knocked through. Growing up, Shona would only have entered a house like that as the cleaner. Though this house, High Pines, was beautiful, it had been chosen for its B&B potential. For Shona, it would never be quite the home their Camden maisonette had been. She had her own reasons for leaving London, but the fact remained that this had been Rob's plan. 'I could see you were miserable in London. I wanted what was best for you and Becca. We're happy now, aren't we? It's working out? I love it here.' She felt her resentment at his petulant, ungrateful behaviour spring up like a cold draught. 'You can't blame me for making a go of it.'

He frowned at his empty wine glass. 'Becca hates her school, you know. I think she's being bullied.'

'She's not said anything to me.'

'Well now you're here, why don't you question her for a change?' He got up, unsteady, nudging the table as he did so. The empty wine bottle toppled over and spun like a rudderless ship across the polished pine surface. Shona put out a hand to catch it, but it skipped over the edge and smashed on the tiled floor. 'Rob, wait...' The jagged glass nicked her finger as she bent to pick it up. She swore as she gingerly walked to the cabinet with the first aid box, sucking the wound and unwrapping a plaster. In the hall, she heard Rob's footsteps and the front door slam.

Shona stared at the wreckage of the dinner table. How did that happen? Her husband's Jekyll and Hyde outbursts were always a sign of stress. She knew money was tight, the B&B business had narrow profit margins, but every time she asked him about it he said it was just the teething trouble of any new business and things were fine. Before Rob's mother died she'd recall her son as Wee Bobby, the golden child. Never cried, always a joy. But somewhere a switch had been flicked that couldn't be unflicked. Shona wished she could go back and fix whatever it was that would trigger these self-destructive bursts. Not change him as such, just adjust the levels, like those on his expensive Naim sound system that, until a few months ago, had squatted in the corner of their sitting room. Rob said he'd sold it because he preferred his iPhone since he rarely had a chance to sit down, but perhaps bookings were slipping. There was certainly something he wasn't telling her.

But mostly the outbursts just left her tired and wrung out. If Rob was right and Becca was being bullied, she wanted to know. She heard the front door again and from the kitchen window she saw her daughter slipping her red waterproof coat round her shoulders and heading down the path after her father. A fairy tale image rose up in her mind, but there were no wolves or woodcutters, no treacherous grandma's house for Becca to find refuge in. That was why they'd moved here. They wouldn't let Becca into the Royal Arms, Rob's most likely destination, so she would probably end up with Tommy at the lifeboat station. Shona would catch up with her there. Once she'd cleared up.

–

The lifeboat station was in the main street, converted from a pair of one-and-a-half storey white-washed Victorian fisherman's cottages. The boat hall took up half the ground floor and stretched all the way up to the rafters. On its high walls engraved boards detailing past rescues were flanked by photographs of the lifeboat and framed black and white cuttings from old newspapers. At the back was the closed-off crew changing space. The boat hall was overlooked on one side by a mezzanine level, its rail hung with airing immersion suits like the skinned pelts of marine creatures. This area, which sat above the ground floor shop and had a dormer window overlooking the firth, functioned as chart and radio room, a training space and as a lounge. With its kettle, fridge and biscuit tin it was a favourite spot for the crew to relax between shouts. This was where Shona found Tommy McCall, taking apart an ancient marine compass, the enamelled face and wooden case spread out on the crew room table. There was no sign of Becca.

'Any news on the lassie in the water? That Cumbria copper lived up to expectations?'

'Don't like the Cumbria police, do you? Anything to do with that ticking-off you got for speeding on the M6 last month? You were lucky not to get fined.' Shona pulled out a chair and sat down opposite.

'No, it's not. I don't hate the police.' Tommy indicated the teapot and Shona poured herself a cup, topping up Tommy's mug in the process. 'I don't mind you, do I?' he continued, 'though you're one of the lifeboat family now. Couldnae do without you. Callum's come on leaps and bounds since you joined us. I heard what you said to him. Doesn't get any easier, does it?'

Shona saw again the young woman's mermaid hair and ruined face. She sighed. 'Where do you think she went into the water? Pathologist reckons three weeks.'

'Well.' Tommy got up from the table and, cupping the mug of tea in his hands, crossed to the OS map of the Solway Firth pinned to wall. 'It's hard to say. If she was swept up the channel, then maybe as far away as Ireland or the Isle of Man. Remember thon fella reported missing in Douglas last year?'

Shona nodded. An elderly man, dementia, left his house on the Isle of Man to post a letter. His body washed up weeks later in the Solway.

'She could have fallen from a vessel or the Stranraer ferry,' said Tommy, his fingers skimming over sea and sands, the faded blue and the thin contour lines, as if divining hidden paths.

'Doubt it. No mis per report. No one's looking for her, Tommy.' Shona came to stand by his shoulder.

'So, we found her here.' He tapped the sandbank in the middle of the firth. 'The spring tides run high over the south side of Midtown Bank. She was in the water for about three weeks?'

Shona nodded.

'It's just a guess, mind,' he warned her. 'I'd say she went in the water either here, in the Wampool Estuary,' he pointed to an area of the north Cumbrian coast, 'or further up the River Esk. Or even the Sark.' He traced a blue line, fed by smaller rivers, that crossed the Scottish border at Gretna and meandered off into the lowland hills.

Shona sighed. 'This is not to go any further, Tommy, but it's looking like an unlawful death. A deposition site would probably need road access. But would a body really travel all the way downriver from Gretna and not be seen?'

'In three weeks? Aye, it could. The spring tides scour out that river a fair way upstream.'

'So, she could even have been thrown from a bridge?' It was Shona's turn to study the map, placing her finger over the River Usk where it was crossed by the M6 motorway. There were cameras everywhere on that stretch. It was an unlikely choice to dispose of a body, even in the dead of night.

'The lassie was wrapped up in green netting, wasn't she? What if she didn't pick it up in the firth?' He pointed to a bridge crossing the River Sark in the outskirts of Gretna. 'This wee industrial park here. It recycles fishing gear. Cockle bags, seine netting and the like. Plenty of kit lying about since the government got so concerned about low catch weights and banned some of the fishing. What if she was already wrapped up in it before she went in the water?'

'You mean to disguise the body?'

'Aye. Or to weight it down.'

'It's a possibility.' Shona nodded slowly. 'Worth checking out. Thanks, Tommy.'

Shona washed up the cups and hung them back on their hooks. 'Becca been to see you this evening?' she said as casually as she could, but Tommy looked at her shrewdly.

'No. Nor your Robert neither.' He slid the compass rose back into the case and spun the floating needle, checking its accuracy. 'They haven't gone far. They'll find their way back, don't you worry. You on call for us this weekend?' Shona nodded. Tommy continued, 'Go home, it'll all be fine.'

Shona smiled her goodbye to him.

Outside the lifeboat station the tide was on the turn, creeping in over mud and cockleshell beach, lapping up beside the Wee Pier, a granite runway built in the eighteenth century by the Kirkness fisherfolk. Shona sat down on the ancient stones, her legs dangling over the side, toes reaching down to the newmade waves. Her breath came slower, her shoulders relaxed. Tommy was right. Rob would sort himself out, one way or another, and Becca was a teenager and as changeable as the weather. There were bound to be storms. When she got home Rob and Becca would probably be sitting side by side on the sofa hooting at some awful comedy, everything else forgotten.

Shona pulled out her phone. After hesitating for a moment, she scrolled past Becca and Rob's numbers and made a call. It went straight to voicemail.

'Hello, Dan, it's DI Shona Oliver here. Can you meet me in Gretna first thing Monday morning, eight a.m.? I'll text you the address. I've got a lead you might be interested in.' She had time before her first meeting. No one at Cornwall Mount need know about her detour.

She dusted off her jeans and took a last look around the bay before heading back along the waterfront. The wind had dropped enough for a cloud of midges to gather round her. She swept her hand back and forward in front of her face.

Fifty metres from the Royal Arms she saw a flash of Becca's red jacket moving between the tables outside the front of the pub. A car had pulled up, music spilling from its open windows. Becca walked to the driver's side. A boy in the back leaned forward and handed her something. Shona saw her daughter's laugh turn to a frown, then she threw the folded paper back. A hand shot out, grabbing her arm.

As Becca struggled to free herself, Shona let out a shout. She broke into a run. The other rear-seat passenger turned, his mouth forming a perfect circle as he saw Shona sprinting along the seafront. The distance between them was rapidly diminishing – in three seconds she'd have them. Just as the car took off, Becca managed to jerk her arm free.

When Shona reached her daughter, she was rubbing her wrist and glaring after the vehicle already making the turn up the hill and out of the village.

'Are you all right?' Shona caught hold of her daughter. Becca was trembling, her long dark hair falling over her eyes, blinking back angry tears. She shook off her mother, walked to her table, picked up a glass of dark liquid and downed it in one.

'It's just Coke,' she said indignantly to a horrified Shona before flopping down on the bench. 'Want to check the glass?'

Shona took the glass from her outstretched hand. She fought the impulse to lift it to her nose and smell it. The table was littered with empty pint mugs and tumblers. Shona placed the glass amongst them and sat down next to Becca.

'Some people from school were here,' Becca said, wiping her nose on her sleeve. 'Paula, Callum's girlfriend, lets us buy soft drinks and use the free Wi-Fi.'

'It's good you're making friends,' Shona said calmly, but her heart was still hammering against her ribs. 'Who were those lads in the car?' When Becca didn't answer she continued, 'Dad said you we're being bullied.'

'Dad's a drama queen.'

Shona took a deep breath, letting it out slowly. 'Are they from your school? What did they say to you?'

'Just some crap joke. They're losers. It doesn't matter.' Becca slumped down in her seat as if pressed by a heavy weight.

'Becca, I hope you'd tell me if there was a problem.'

'There's no problem. It's just…' She sighed. 'It's hard to fit in sometimes. They've all got their friends. Had them since primary school and I'm just… different.'

The pain of being fifteen and not fitting in. Was that all it was? Becca kept up with few of her London friends, but she still wore the clothes she'd bought, second-hand, in Camden Market's vintage shops and played an eclectic mix of rap, Bowie, Fleetwood Mac and Queen. Her friend Ellie had introduced her to some Glasgow bands, but she still must have seemed like an exotic blow-in to the local kids. They probably mocked her London accent, while secretly coveting her city swagger. Becca was also pretty enough to turn heads and trigger jealous rivalries. But the talent for trouble that had got her expelled in London was rooted deep in her personality and perhaps Becca's refusal to conform to any set of norms was also causing problems with her new friends. And growing up was tough, no matter where you lived.

Shona tried hard not to let the things she'd seen and experienced as a police officer ebb into her family life, to resist her urgent desire to shield Becca from all that was difficult and frightening. But there had been times when she couldn't protect herself, so how could she expect to protect her daughter? It was impossible, she knew, but that just made her want it all the more. Shona saw that Becca was watching her, the crease of a frown between her eyebrows. 'Come on,' she said, in an effort to disguise her dark thoughts, 'let's get you home. I've a treat for you.'

'What?' said Becca suspiciously.

'How about some of my special hot chocolate?'

'Mum, I'm not a kid.' She fell into step behind her mother. After they'd gone a short distance she caught up, hooking her arm through Shona's. 'Okay, but only if there's mini marshmallows.'

'Deal,' said Shona, squeezing her arm and smiling. 'Sure you're okay?'

Becca nodded and smiled back. If only all problems, Shona thought, could be solved with a sugary drink.

Rob wasn't back when they got home. She put a pan of milk on the stove to warm and sent Becca upstairs to change into pyjamas. While she was gone Shona slipped her notebook from her bag and in neat, inked capitals wrote down the make, colour and registration number of the boys' car. She'd mention them to traffic and if she saw them again in the village, she'd be having a serious word.

Chapter 6

After a quiet weekend with no lifeboat shouts and easy-going B&B guests, Shona pulled the Audi into the layby on the outskirts of Gretna where she'd arranged to meet DC Dan Ridley. Rob had come home Friday night after closing time and, following a fulsome apology, had fallen into a deep sleep and woken to a hangover that had lasted most of the weekend. She hoped he'd suffered sufficiently to mend his ways, but she doubted it.

A burger van was moored on the layby's scrubby verge. Local workers, in drifts of threes and fours, tucked into their Monday morning breakfast rolls on the line of battered plastic garden furniture cast out in its wake. Dan, incongruous in his suit and tie, his hair gelled and light beard neatly trimmed, was drawing curious glances. He stood apart checking his phone in one hand and nursing a large polystyrene cup of tea in the other. Shona unlocked the nearside door.

'Hop in!' she called through the rolled-down window. He stood for a moment, uncertain how to accomplish this, before throwing his half-finished tea in a nearby bin and pocketing his phone. He opened the passenger door to the accompanying whistles and cat calls from the seated workmen telling him it must be his lucky day. Shona couldn't help smirking at his obvious discomfort.

'Morning, ma'am,' he said reaching for his safety belt, the car's acceleration already pressing him into the seat. They passed a squat sandstone inn advertising Sky Sports and offering Gretna Green wedding packages from £499. On the other side of the road was a small industrial estate, the grey metal blocks set against the silver of the Solway Firth behind them.

Ridley cleared his throat. 'I hear you came up from London, ma'am?'

Shona indicated and took a right turn into the estate. 'Yes, that's correct,' she confirmed. It wasn't a secret.

'I'd like to work down there one day. Must be exciting at the Met.'

'I wasn't at the Met. I worked with City of London Police.'

'Isn't that all financial crime and public order?'

'You mean serious and organised crime, international money laundering and counter-terrorism?' Shona pulled up next to a yard, its chain-link fencing running down to the River Sark. Seeing his deflated expression, she smiled. 'Don't worry, that's pretty much word for word what they said when they interviewed me for this job.'

When the DI's position in Dumfries had come up she was the dark horse candidate. Plenty of internals were queueing for the post. By then, Rob had left the Milton McConnell banking group, Becca was in trouble at school and the need to move was pressing. Shona had pulled out all the stops to get the position. Detective Superintendent Malcolm 'Mars Bar' Munroe was kirk elder in the Church of Scotland and a teetotaller not known for his progressive outlook, but he had seen something he liked in Shona and championed her appointment. His curious nickname, she was told, was due to his habit of celebrating a result on a big case by handing out chocolate bars instead of buying a round of drinks for his staff.

Shona motioned Dan to follow her as she got out of the car. 'Any idea why I've brought you here?' She watched him take in the bridge, the overgrown riverbank, the jumbled piles of fishing gear spilling from the large, white plastic containers in the yard.

'It's amazing how many secluded spots there are in a town,' he said, raising his eyebrows. 'You think this is where she went in the water?'

'I think it's worth checking out. The lifeboat helm, whose judgement I trust, reckons a body deposited this far upstream could stay in the Solway Firth for weeks.' She clicked the electronic lock on her car keys and zipped up her fleece jacket against the breeze.

'How does it work?' Dan asked. Shona frowned, not understanding. 'The lifeboat and the job, being on call?' he continued.

'Well, I'm in Cornwall Mount from Monday to Friday daytime. Murdo, Ravi and Kate are on a rota to cover call-outs on the weekend. Thankfully, we have one of the lowest crime rates in Scotland, so I'm rarely contacted at weekends. One of the few benefits of rank.' She smiled. 'When I'm in Kirkness I carry my RNLI pager and respond to shouts. We're well supported, and a fairly quiet station. It works. Why? Tempted to join? Did Silloth try to sign you up last week?'

'No chance. I get sea sick standing on a beach.'

'Well, Admiral Nelson was a famous sufferer and it didn't stop him. We may get you yet. Come on,' she indicated the industrial unit, 'let's go and see if anyone's home.'

The paint-peeled gates were propped open. A battered caravan sat in the far corner of the yard. Gulls wheeled above them but there were no other signs of life. Shona led the way between piles of fishing nets, their tumbled blue, green and orange flanks like the discarded skins of giant sea monsters. She thought again of the woman wrapped in their coils. Is this where she'd met her killer? It was certainly possible.

Dan crossed to the caravan, knocking and calling out a hello. A movement caught Shona's eye and she turned to see a balding, middle-aged man in filthy overalls, the thighs shiny with wiped-off oil, edging up behind Dan from the blind side of the caravan. He was holding an axe handle high in his right hand.

'Stop! Police! Drop your weapon!' Shona yelled, her right hand flying to her belt. As a London City officer, she'd regularly carried a firearm and the reflex was still strong. Finding only empty air she grabbed her warrant card and held it towards the man. 'Police! Drop it!' Alerted by Shona's shout, Dan darted back to where she stood and brandished his badge too.

'Police?' the man said suspiciously, his small, pale eyes darting between the officers. Strands of hair from his comb-over rose in the breeze like the crest of an angry bird.

'DI Shona Oliver, Dumfries Police.' She replaced the warrant card in her pocket and held up a pair of handcuffs. 'We're here for a chat. I'm not gonnae have to cuff you, am I?' Her voice was firm but calm as she sought to de-escalate the confrontation. It was a bluff. She wouldn't risk tackling him. 'Or shall I get a police dog down here?' The sight of big, sharp teeth usually did the trick, but she didn't think it would get that far. 'Last warning, put down the weapon.'

The man eyed the cuffs then held up his hands in submission. 'Okay, you are police. Well, it's about bloody time you lot showed up,' he boomed, not in the local Dumfries accent she'd expected but in flat Cumbrian vowels. He chucked the axe handle behind a battered wheelie bin. 'Sorry. Thought you were the bailiffs.'

'If you threaten Sheriff Officers with violence, I'll make sure you're very sorry,' Shona warned, tucking the cuffs back into her pocket. Dan stepped forward and searched the man for any other weapons. When he finished, she said, 'Now, why were you expecting a visit from the police?'

'Well, not expecting,' the man sneered. 'I live in hope, not expectation, where coppers are concerned. It were nearly a month ago I called your lot.'

'What was the call in connection with, Mr… er?' Dan said. Shona noted the increased interest in his voice. The time frame matched the period the girl spent in the water.

'Don't you know, lad?' he jeered. 'And it's Jones. Nathan Jones.'

'Let's start again, Mr Jones,' Shona said. 'This is DC Ridley from Cumbria CID, and we're here in connection with a missing person inquiry. We'd like to ask you some questions, out here or in there.' She nodded to the caravan.

Nathan Jones stepped between Shona and the door. 'Here's fine.' He adjusted the jeans below his overalls, which were fighting a border war of attrition with his overhanging stomach. 'Missing person?' He glanced suspiciously from Shona to Dan and back. 'That's got nowt to do with me.'

'Why did you call us a month ago?' Shona asked.

'Goings on. Next door.' Jones thumbed at the neighbouring building, a single storey metal box with no signage, set at right angles to his yard. 'Shouting at all hours. Squatters, immigrants.'

Shona and Dan exchanged a look. He got his notebook out and prepared to follow her lead.

'Do you live here? On site?' Shona guessed the terms of Nathan Jones's lease were for business use only, no overnight stays. The threat that she might report him sleeping here gave him an incentive to co-operate.

Jones shifted from foot to foot, searching the sky for an answer. 'My missus lives in Carlisle,' he said eventually, as if that explained his current domestic arrangements.

'So, you heard a disturbance next door?' Shona asked.

'It were late, midnight. I heard a car pull up. Shouting. A man shouting.' Jones screwed up his eyes in an effort to remember. 'Been comings and goings for a few weeks, always at night. Thought they might come round here and smash the place up.'

'Can you describe the people you saw?'

'Not faces, like. Don't know if it were the same folk every time or different.'

'What were they shouting, Mr Jones?'

'Dunno, just noise, like. Most likely they were drugged up, looking for trouble.'

'What makes you think drugs were involved?' Shona said, but Jones just shrugged. 'So who owns that unit?' she continued.

'No one, that's the bloody problem.' Seeing their blank faces, he spelled the word out, as if to a child, 'Car... mine. Them that went bankrupt? Used to be them that had it.'

'The Carmine Group? The building and infrastructure company?' Dan jotted a line into his notebook.

'Had it as a project office for that bypass that were never built.'

Shona scanned the surrounding buildings. Disposing of a body was all about ease. It would be easy enough here.

'Do you have CCTV?' Shona hadn't seen any cameras, but it was worth asking.

'Are you soft in the head?' He spread his arms. 'How would I afford owt like that?'

'You said squatters and immigrants. What did you mean by that?' She came closer, studying Jones's expression.

'Thought they were moving in there, set up a camp. It's what that lot do. Move in, take over.'

'Did you see the local TV news over the weekend, Mr Jones?'

'Dinna have a telly.'

'Did you ever see a woman?' Shona patted the air above her shoulder. 'A little shorter than me. We're looking for a girl. Young, blonde?'

'Aye, there were lassies. Slags and whores, up to all sorts, I'm sure.' He licked his lips and leered at Shona, who stared back impassively. He continued, 'Came in cars. I heard women's voices.'

'Makes? Registration numbers?' Dan asked.

'It were dark. But flash cars. BMWs and the like. There were always a gang of fellas. Big fellas.' Jones growled, as if his manhood was now in question.

'So, you can't say what these people looked like, what they were shouting or what cars they were driving?' Dan summed up.

'It's your job, to catch folk.' Jones bared a set of grey teeth and spat on the ground.

'But did you ever see a young woman with long blonde hair?' Shona persisted.

Jones eyed her, shaking his head, retreating behind his defences. She knew he was lying, but about what she couldn't say. Jones probably had plenty to hide from the authorities. They could at least check his story about calling into the control room. She told Dan to take Jones's contact details.

'We may need you to give a statement. Mind if I have a look around?' she asked when Dan had finished. She indicated the caravan.

Jones shifted uncomfortably. 'That's private.'

'I'm only interested in a missing person,' Shona persisted. 'Or I can get a warrant? Come back with the Sheriff Officers. Give the place a thorough going over.'

Jones hesitated, weighing up the cost of resisting. Eventually he shrugged. 'Have a deck about if you like. Makes no odds to me.'

Shona opened the door. A sour smell ebbed from the caravan's dirty interior, the floor covered with overflowing binbags of clothes and rubbish. A stack of porn magazines lay open by the unmade bed. She caught Jones's eye and he turned away, blushing. She stepped inside and made a quick search. There were no signs of violence or that a crime had been cleaned up. She'd be willing to bet there had been no cleaning up for a very long time.

'Thank you, Mr Jones. We'll be in touch.' She tapped Dan's arm and they turned and walked through the yard. Jones stepped into the caravan and slammed the door. Behind the dirty window, Shona could see Jones's shadow watching them.

They walked through the yard towards a gap in the fence where it bordered the river. Strips of plastic caught on the barbed ends fluttered like flags in the breeze.

'What do you think?' Shona said when they were out of sight of the caravan.

Dan shook his head. 'All charm, wasn't he? He didn't like it when you asked about the girl.'

'No, he didn't. Check out Mr Jones. Talk to the wife in Carlisle, will you? See what she says.'

'Okay. Do you believe his story about the disturbance next door? Do you think he could have killed the girl?'

'It's certainly possible,' Shona confirmed. 'He's a big fella. Not that fit, but strong enough. I think he was scared for his own skin when he called the disturbance in. Why draw the attention of the police if he killed her?'

'He doesn't strike me as that bright,' Dan said. 'A smokescreen? In case someone else reported seeing something.'

She furrowed her brow. 'He said immigrants. Do you think our blonde girl could be Polish? Eastern European? Russian, even? Paying off her traffickers through prostitution, and Jones was a client? We're at a crossroads here. The M6 motorway between England and Scotland.' Shona held out an arm indicating north. 'The A75 Euroroute to the ferry port at Stranraer, linking Ireland to the UK and Europe.' She spun round onto an east–west axis, as if orientating herself to magnetic pull of the earth might give her a direction to follow. 'If she was being trafficked, working here before being moved on, it might explain why no one's reported her missing.'

'I hope not,' said Dan glumly. 'No chance of identifying her if she was. And if Jones killed her, the traffickers would want payback. How come he's still breathing?'

Shona nodded, letting her arm fall. 'Immigrants, though? Why say that?'

'He's a Brexit voter. Bit ironic since he's a Cumbrian in Scotland, so technically he's an immigrant too.' Dan grinned, amused.

'So, how does an asylum seeker appear to someone like Nathan Jones?' Shona thought of the cafes and shops she frequented in London's East End where she would often be the only woman not wearing a headscarf. 'Dress or skin colour? It was dark. Language? But he claims he didn't hear what was said. The non-white population of Dumfries is about one per cent. Something made him think the people he saw were not local.'

'How does that help us?'

'Not sure,' Shona conceded. They came to the gap in the fencing and stepped through. The bank down to the water's edge was steep and littered with rubbish. The tide had left marks high on the muddy slope and Shona could see how a body deposited here could be sucked out into the firth by the combined force of the river and the retreating sea. The bank also gave access to the neighbouring unit. 'Let's check out next door.'

A faint fox-path ran through the grass to where the fencing had surrendered completely. The concrete posts uprooted, weeds grew up through the prone metal mesh of its remains.

The roller door at the front of the building had a newish padlock, but the fire exit at the back was propped shut with a length of wood. Pigeons fluttered across the broken skylights in the double height section of the warehouse, the oil stains on the floor suggesting it had once been used to store vehicles and machinery. At the back, a shuttered-off area provided an office. In the thick grey light, papers were strewn across the desk and floor and foam poked from the fabric on an office chair. A collapsed tower of cardboard boxes leaned in one corner.

Shona used her pen to turn over the pages of yellowed Carmine Group headed notepaper peppered with mouse droppings. On the floor beneath the desk something metallic caught her eye. There was a foil bubble pack of pills. She flipped it over, peering closely at the name embossed on the back. Xanax, a prescription-only tranquiliser. If they could find the pills' box, they might get the patient's name or a clue to the pharmacist who dispensed it. Shona turned to call Dan.

He was standing in the corner holding a length of damp cardboard by the edge and scrolling through his phone. The uplighting from the screen gave his face a ghostly, greenish tinge. Around his feet, a mound of foil strips like the one Shona was holding. 'Xanax. Valium.' He read from his phone screen. 'Quinox? I can't find that one, but I bet it's not a vitamin pill.' He looked up at her. 'Some of these other boxes are half full.'

'Quite the wee chemist shop,' said Shona, pulling out her own phone and tapping the screen. 'Hi Murdo, I need you down here. I'll text you an address. Get the troops and bring anyone you can find from forensics.'

Chapter 7

Murdo arrived at the industrial unit with DC Ravi Sarwar, who sported jeans and an olive-green, funnel-neck parka, both stylish and practical. He got out of the car and combed his dark, glossy hair into place with his fingers. Shona knew he had it cut regularly in one of Glasgow's trendy West End salons. He waved, flashing his mega-watt smile. A patrol car and a van containing three uniformed men and one disgruntled forensics officer pulled up behind them. Since the creation of Police Scotland there were no local Scenes of Crime staff in Dumfries. Most were now based in Glasgow, Edinburgh or the other major cities and requests needed to meet a twenty-eight-point attendance criteria. By chance, SOCO Peter Harrison, the slim man in his forties now balancing unsteadily on one foot as he climbed into a paper suit, had been in the Dumfries Cornwell Mount HQ for a meeting where he had been nabbed by Murdo.

Shona recognised one of the uniformed officers, a young but experienced constable based at Loreburn Street station. 'Matthews, I want a statement from Nathan Jones in the yard next door. He heard a disturbance a month ago and phoned it in. I've checked the call logs, Friday the third. A patrol had a quick drive-by a couple of hours later and reported it was all quiet. Butter Jones up, stress he's a valued witness. He was cagey with us, but he might let something slip if he thinks he's not in the firing line. Do that later.'

'Yes, ma'am.' The young officer nodded.

'But first,' Shona turned to the pair of nervous looking special constables in black fatigues and caps, 'what're your names?'

'I'm Lewis Johnstone,' said the taller one, his face a mass of orange freckles.

'Campbell Menzies, ma'am.' The second officer was older; his square build and ruddy complexion hinted at old farming stock.

'Have you both completed a forensics and evidence-gathering course?'

They shook their heads. Shona's lips pressed into a tight line.

'Okay, well, I want you to follow PC Matthews's lead. Gloves on. Search the riverbank. Our estimated time frame for the offence is four weeks ago. I'm looking for drugs paraphernalia, paperwork, any identifying documents. Also, clothing, especially women's clothing. Shoes, purse, handbag, mobile phone, anything like that. Hang on a moment.' She turned to the forensic scientist making his way over. 'Peter,' she called. 'I really appreciate you coming down.'

Peter Harrison looked like he was about to make a sarcastic comment about Murdo giving him no choice but thought better of it. 'What do we have here?'

'Haul of prescription pills, mostly tranquilisers.' She drew him aside. 'Peter, I've also got a woman's body recovered from the Solway Firth last week. I've no ID and no witnesses, but it's a suspicious death. It's also just possible that this is where she went in the water, so keep that in mind for me, would you?' She followed Peter's gaze to where it rested on Dan Ridley. 'That's a colleague from Cumbria CID, he's helping out.'

Peter sighed, pushing his glasses back up to the bridge of his nose with an index finger. 'Have I not got enough on my plate? Make sure I get elimination fingerprints from him.' He glanced at his watch. 'Look, I can do a quick assessment for you, photograph the scene and bag the drugs. Any signs of violence, any blood, I'll need reinforcements from Gartcosh and you'll need to put in a chit for that.'

'Thanks, Peter.' Shona smiled gratefully. 'We've taped off the riverbank too. I was thinking uniform could do a search while you're inside. Unless you want them for anything else?'

'Aye, off you go. It'll keep them out from under my feet anyway,' he grumbled, shouldering his cases and ducking under the blue and white barrier tape.

Shona turned back to the three uniformed officers. 'Any questions?'

'How far along do you want us to search?' Matthews asked, handing the specials long wooden poles like broom handles and heavy duty flashlights.

'To the Sark Bridge, on this side only.' Shona scanned the riverbank in the opposite direction. A row of high, spiked metal palings, running across the back of the factory next door, cut off access to the river upstream. 'Just to that fence. Anything suspicious, bag it and tag it.'

Shona turned her attention to the rest of her team. On the hardstanding beside the roller door at the front of the unit Murdo was introducing Dan to Ravi. She saw Ravi gesture to Dan's scrappy beard, then rub the flat of his hand against his own smooth face. Either they were bonding over male grooming or she'd just witnessed the start of an office romance.

SOCO Peter Harrison removed the entrance padlock with a set of bolt cutters, borrowed by Dan from a nearby garage. Together, they forced up the door, allowing some light into the building.

Shona fished blue forensic gloves from her jacket pocket and crossed back into the crime scene. 'Ravi.' She summoned him with a tilt of her head. 'How you doing? How was the community policing group?' She and Ravi were her team's only Glaswegians. Shona had grown up with Sunday afternoons of tea, samosas and Bollywood round her Punjabi friends' houses and the connection gave them a secret handshake of shared values. Their relationship was generally smoother than Shona's interactions with her other DC, the Edinburgh-raised geography graduate, Kate Irving.

'Good. I gave the specials a right going over.' He grinned. As a gay, vegetarian, Asian-Scottish police officer, Ravi was a one-man diversity dream-team, constantly in demand for training and community and school talks. But far from regarding these opportunities as a cushy number, he pushed hard for improvements and, Shona suspected, followed them up in his own time. 'The five campus support officers came in from the schools for a chat and I've put them in touch with some partner agencies.'

'That's good work, Ravi.' Shona nodded approvingly. 'But there's something here I want you to look at now.' She motioned him to follow her to the door of the unit. 'Familiarise yourself with the layout. One poten-tial witness next door, but that's it.' She indicated the office area at the far end of the warehouse. 'In there we found multiple prescription drugs. No address labels on the boxes. The building was apparently in use by Carmine until they folded. Firm that date up and find out who was in charge here.' She took her notebook from her pocket. 'Diazepam in various brands. Etizolam or street Valium. Methadone. Pregabalin, used to treat epilepsy and anxiety.' She held out the list for him to copy. 'Also, Xanax and a newbie, Quinox. Could be pharmaceutical or veterinary, agricultural, even marine in origin. Or a foreign brand name or a re-naming of an old drug or a variation or upgrading by adding something like caffeine.'

'It would have to be registered somewhere.'

'True, but not necessarily within the EU or the US. Find out what it is. Is it being sold locally? Is this a transit warehouse? Ask your community contacts.' She peeled the key to the Audi off her RNLI keyring and handed them to him. 'Take my car, I'll get a lift back with Murdo.'

'Okay, boss,' Ravi said, setting off in his long, loping stride towards the Audi, twirling the key in his fingers.

'Drive carefully,' she called after him, and he shot her a grin over his shoulder.

Shona spent fifteen minutes rescheduling her meetings and the rest of the morning supervising the evidence gathering and checking with Kate for updates on the baby milk operation. As predicted, the initial flood of calls had subsided into a steady trickle and Kate was keeping the civilian staff busy collating the information and scrolling through the remaining CCTV. Shona asked her if there had been any calls about the body in the Solway Firth, but, even after the media appeal on local TV and radio, no one had come forward to report a missing young woman. At lunchtime she sent one of the special constables back to the burger van for bacon rolls and tea for everyone. After talking to PC Matthews, she called Dan over.

'The riverbank search hasn't thrown up anything obviously connected to our unidentified woman,' she told him. 'It was always a long shot. There are a few items of clothing and discarded food packaging which we'll look at in relation to the drugs. Peter's found plenty of prints and what could be a few diluted blood spots, but we'll need to eliminate everyone who worked here when Carmine had the place. Could be a slow job. Thanks for your help. Your DI will be after my guts, keeping you here.' She watched Dan's face fall; he knew he was being dismissed.

'He'll think you're doing him a favour. I try to stay out of his way.'

Shona frowned. She knew the subtle, and not so subtle, ways in which officers were sometimes bullied by their colleagues.

'What's the problem?'

Dan shrugged, scrapping the soft ground with the toe of his shoe. 'I think it's important to gain the community's trust so they'll work with us. It's not a popular view with my DI. I know we're under pressure to get our solve-rates up but I think the right result is better than the quick result.'

Shona nodded. 'You did some good work here this morning. I'll be emailing your DI to tell him so and give him my thanks.' Dropping her voice, she took a step closer to him. 'Our girl. This isn't the end of the road, you know, whatever our bosses might think.' Her warm brown eyes looked earnestly up at him. 'If she's local, we'll find out who she is. And then we'll find out who did this to her. Understand?'

'Yes, ma'am.' He smiled, reassured.

'Good. Off you go. Keep me updated.' Shona was already moving away, zipping up her jacket. She waved PC Matthews over. 'Matthews, take Dan back to his car, it's on the main road. Then, when Peter is done, I want you to finish up here. Call Murdo if you have any problems.'

'Will do, ma'am.'

'Murdo, with me. Back to base.'

–

Ravi was waiting for her when she arrived, his parting grin still in place. He followed her into her office, carrying his laptop. 'You're gonna like this, boss.' Through the glass panel, Kate was shooting daggers at his back.

'My car still in one piece?' Shona said, hanging up her jacket and holding out her hand.

'Course,' he said, fishing in his jeans pocket for the key, and handing it over. 'Have a little faith in me.'

'Go on then,' said Shona, trying not to catch his infectious grin, 'amaze me, what have you got?' She indicated he should put the laptop on her desk.

'Think I've found your group of pharmaceuticals enthusiasts.'

'What? Already?' Shona couldn't hide her surprise.

'Aye. Nae bother. Magic touch, that's me,' he said, flexing his long brown fingers. 'Called one of the campus officers and checked with a pal at the Royal Infirmary. Both said they'd seen a big jump in the abuse of prescription drugs. Here's a heads up, boss. Expect a rise in addict deaths when the figures come in next month, cos A&E are getting more poly-addiction cases. Five deaths already. Mix heroin or booze with these tablets and it's lights out.

Suppresses the respiratory system. Some users are swallowing ten Diazepam at a time and topping up with a bottle of Buckfast. A one-way ticket to the undertakers, so it is.'

'Where are they getting them from? You said you'd found our group.'

Ravi adjusted the laptop and brought up a page.

'Our old friend Facebook,' Shona said, studying the screen. It seemed no drug operation nowadays was complete without a social media angle. 'Sweet Life? This is our supplier?'

Ravi nodded, suddenly serious. 'This is a closed group. The tabs are being bought online and sent out through the post. It's cheap, two pounds a tablet, and easy.'

Shona thought of Callum, her lifeboat colleague and postman. It was the perfect distribution network. No pusher at a fixed address the police could monitor, no dealers on the streets to attract attention, just the local postman on his regular route. On the screen someone calling himself @Diazaman had posted a picture of pills, the date scribbled on a piece of lined paper next to them and advertised as a tenner for the lot, payment via direct messaging, untraceable by the police.

'Even worse, you don't know what you're getting,' Ravi continued. 'Etizolam, that anti-epileptic you mentioned, it's being used to make fake Xanax pills. If you overdose, the doctors at the Royal have no idea what to treat you for.'

'Any chance we can trace this group?'

'Doubt it. Facebook might take it down for breaching their rules, but the dealers will just create a new group. In fact, they may have already moved on.' Ravi moved the curser down the page. 'They'll be on other social media like WhatsApp by now. The last posting on the site was a few weeks ago.'

'What about tracing any of the site users?'

'Possible, but they won't know who they bought from.'

'How do you know the Sweet Life group is local?'

'I don't know for sure, but this Quinox was mentioned by A&E. I checked with Divisional Intelligence and you were right, boss. It's a benzo brand name from the Far East, anti-anxiety, and seizures. Not widely available here.'

'Okay, write up what you've got and put in a request to Division for a drugs dog. Contact the Royal Mail sorting office and say we'd like to send it in to pick up any undelivered packages. Let's see where that gets us.' Shona's mobile rang; the screen flashed up DCI Gavin Baird's number. She picked it up, waving Ravi out the door while mouthing 'good work' and giving him a thumbs up.

'Shona, this prescription drugs find,' said Baird without preamble. 'I've decided it comes under the remit of Op Fortress. You'll need to send up everything you have. We'll be taking it from here.'

'We're just gathering initial findings now, sir.' Shona kept her voice even. 'There's a possible link to the body we recovered from the Solway Firth. I'd like to see any forensic results.'

'I thought that was Cumbria's problem. Even if you have an ID or a witness, get them to deal with it. I heard you put an appeal out over the weekend. Should have cleared that with me first.'

'Yes, sir. We dealt with it along with the baby milk press release as an efficient use of resources.'

'Fine,' said Baird flatly. 'But get everything you found today to me. I'll be down tomorrow to brief your team.

We're going for co-ordinated strikes right across the region within forty-eight hours.' He hung up.

Shona crossed to where Ravi shared a back-to-back desk with Kate. Both were busy, heads down, tapping away on their keyboards. They looked up as she leaned on Ravi's chair and called Murdo over.

'Orders from DCI Baird. Wrap up everything you've found on the Sweet Life group and the forensics from the Carmine unit. Get it up to Op Fortress by close of play today.'

'In the name of the wee man,' Murdo shook his head, 'do the officers on the ground not deserve a go at this? We've got the contacts; it's our patch folk are dying on. Ravi's played a blinder on this.' He looked at Shona for support, but she shook her head. Baird was out of order. This was no way to treat talented and dedicated officers, but she couldn't see how she could defy him over this.

'Sorry, guys. This is going up the line. Suck it up and move on.'

Ravi rolled his shoulders in a shrug, but an uncharacteristic frown gave away his true feelings. She couldn't blame him. Even Kate, who Shona had expected to crow over the decision, looked put-out. Op Fortress was turning into a ravenous beast, devouring resources and opportunities for her officers. Shona returned to her office and, between prioritising her paperwork, fantasised about exactly how she could put a certain senior police officer in a shallow grave and get away with it.

Chapter 8

Shona arrived at Cornwall Mount on Tuesday morning knowing she would need to tread the delicate line between rallying her troops and sharing their resentment at the loss of the Sweet Life investigation. The thing was to keep them busy.

'Kate,' she called, sweeping into her office and dumping her handbag on the desk, 'I want the baby milk update in ten minutes.' She scanned the outer room for her sergeant. Murdo was in the far corner, taking a call on his mobile. He raised a hand to acknowledge he'd be with her in a moment.

'Baird will be here this afternoon. Op Fortress,' Shona said when Murdo came into her office, handing over a white coffee in her Charles Rennie Macintosh mug. 'He'll be briefing the teams making the early morning arrests. Make sure we tie up any jobs we can and get everyone off early tonight. They'll need to be back here by four a.m. Has all the Sweet Life material gone?'

'It has. Can't say everyone's too pleased about that.'

'Well keep them at it today, Murdo. Let's see if we can bury some of that chippiness before Baird arrives. Results are what count. Get everyone into the conference room and let's get on.'

A bank of serious faces stared back at Shona. Some rested their chins on hands, one or two chewed the end of their pens. 'Right. Thoughts?' she said once Kate had outlined progress on the baby milk inquiry.

'The car,' said Ravi. 'Seems our best lead. We've got nothing else.'

Kate glared at him for stealing her thunder. 'It's a silver Ford Focus hatchback, SD55 RSF. Registered keeper is an address in Annan. One of our overnight callers mentioned seeing a man and a woman, he thought, loading bags into a silver Ford in a backstreet near Aldi. We've some CCTV and a couple of ANPR hits but not enough to place the vehicle at all the crime scenes. They seem to have been careful, not using the supermarket car parks, staying off the main roads.'

'Murdo, get out there and interview the owner, that's a priority.' Shona turned back to Kate. 'Go through the witness statements again, see how thorough the officers have been. I want a shortlist of the three witnesses who got the best look at our mystery shoppers and I want you to re-interview them personally. Take the CCTV images, see if we can get a better description, the pictures might jog their memories. Any little detail, cos at the minute there's, potentially, a gang of individuals walking around in broad daylight, helping themselves to property, and we have no idea who they are. We've got about twelve hours before the media, the public and Division start asking what we're playing at. Now, I want you all back here for an Op Fortress briefing at four p.m., so crack on everybody.'

By late afternoon Murdo had returned, solemn faced. Shona told him to take a seat while she finished an email. 'Okay, where are we with the car, Murdo?'

'Registered owner, a Peter Donnelly who was in his seventies, died last year. The son, also Peter, sold the car, cash in hand, through an ad in *Autotrader*. Seems the new owner never registered it, and Peter never completed the V5C documentation.' Murdo flipped a page in his notebook. 'The lack of ANPR hits since suggest it's been kept off road somewhere since it went bandit. There's plenty of wee farms and smallholdings in the area that will store a car on the quiet, for a fee. His description of the buyer was vague. Male in his thirties. Dark cropped hair. Scottish. Not a local accent, maybe Glasgow he thinks, but not sure.'

'How did the buyer contact him?'

'Phone. But he's since lost his mobile and didn't keep a note of the buyer's number. I've put a request in for phone records, but I'd bet my pension the caller used a burner. It's possible the car's been sold on again anyway.'

'Do you think Peter Donnelly could be involved?' Shona asked.

'Possibly. But he's no previous. He's single, unemployed. The house is a tip, garden overgrown. Struck me as vulnerable, a chaotic character.'

'Could he be a target for cuckooing?'

'Aye, maybe. Would be easy enough for someone to persuade him he was his new friend, then move in and use his place to package drugs or store stolen goods. But I think it's more likely a buyer gave him five hundred quid for his dad's old banger, and he was happy to take it, no questions asked.'

'Okay, Murdo, thank you.' Shona made a note on her pad. 'Get uniform to keep a look out.' Kate tapped on the door, Shona waved her in.

'I've re-interviewed our best witnesses and there's something of a consensus emerging for two of the suspects in the earlier thefts.'

'Go on,' Shona said, putting down her pen and giving her DC her full attention.

'A man of Middle Eastern or South Asian appearance, possibly Indian or Pakistani, was mentioned by all the witnesses, although no one heard him speak. About twenty-five years old, slim build, short hair and stubble beard. Non-descript dark clothing and baseball cap, as we can see from the CCTV.' She laid out the CCTV images on the desk. 'The woman, or women, that's more difficult. Two said she was dark and wearing a headscarf, one said blonde with a baseball cap and hoodie, but all said she was small, around five feet tall. So, it could be one woman in disguise. Crucially, they all said she was Scottish, and one heard her speak to the man and thinks it was a local accent.'

'Good work, Kate. Get mug shots of anyone with previous shoplifting or fraud convictions in the county who fits the description. See if our witnesses pick anyone out.' Shona's email alert sounded. She glanced at the clock. The time for the briefing was approaching without any heads up from the front desk that Baird had arrived. She hoped they hadn't started early without her team. 'Okay, Murdo, get everyone to finish off what they're doing. Kate, give the front desk a buzz, check where we are with the Op Fortress briefing.'

'Yes, ma'am.'

'Good, off you go.' Shona scanned the subject line and sender of the new email. It was from DCI Baird, probably some last-minute details. She clicked it open. Attached was a ream of documents, including a planning spreadsheet, that Shona hadn't seen before. She felt her jaw tighten. 'Murdo,' she called in a tone that made the whole office look up from their work.

'Boss? What's the matter?' he said seeing her expression.

'The briefing is delayed. Tell everyone to work on for a bit, then send someone out for chips.'

'Will DCI Baird be here by then?'

'DCI Baird isn't coming.'

'Who's doing the briefing then?'

'I am, and you're helping me.'

Murdo frowned for a moment, processing this change of plan. It looked like his promise of a pint with Baird had gone out the window. He'd been surprised when his old mate had agreed to the suggestion, so maybe he shouldn't be surprised it had fallen through. He shrugged. 'Okay. No worries. I'll let uniform know to come back at… what,' he checked his watch, 'six p.m.?'

Shona nodded grimly and hit the print button on her screen. The office printer began churning out page after page of close-typed instructions. When it stopped she divided the pile in half and crossed to where Murdo was back on the phone, telling his wife he'd be late and not to worry.

She glanced at the framed photograph on the filing cabinet next to her sergeant's desk. A group shot taken five years ago, when DCI Baird was a newly promoted detective inspector and rising fast, with Murdo beaming behind his shoulder. 'Donut Cop' was what Murdo'd been nicknamed behind his back; she suspected Baird had a hand in it. She could see how O'Halloran, looking for a role model and a leader, might idolise the man. On nights out O'Halloran would often appear in a black leather jacket identical to the one Baird wore in the photo. The man would take all this as his due and despise O'Halloran for it. Her DS was never going to climb the greasy pole, he'd be out of his depth in strategy meetings. But on this patch of Scotland nothing much happened that didn't twitch upon the thread of his intelligence network – the rugby club, the church, his wife Joan's Scottish Women's Institute group, the beat cops who remembered when he was in the squad car with them and respected him for time served. Murdo was much more than a cliche, and Baird should know better.

She left half the papers with Murdo and returned to her office to read her section. He joined her soon afterwards, and sitting side by side they went through all the pages one after the other.

'First thoughts?' Shona asked. Murdo fished out a page concerning transport.

Shona read a line of marked text. 'We need twelve vans.' She turned to him. 'How many are operational?'

'Ten, and last time I looked the magic carpet was still at the cleaners.'

She raised an eyebrow in enquiry. He brought out a printed sheet showing Dumfries and the surrounding area. 'Overnight road works on the main road.' He indicated on the map with his pen. 'Also, the quarry up at Jericho Bridge is moving a couple of excavators. It's an abnormal load. Their contractors are dealing with it, but this section of the A701 will become closed here,' he marked a pair of crosses, 'and here, between four and six a.m. We'll never make it if we're vans short.'

'Okay. What do you suggest?'

'Well, we need to hit them all at the same time or phones will start ringing and we risk losing some targets, so we send teams out this way.' He drew a dotted line through a maze of small country roads. 'They'll avoid trouble.'

'And we'll need two squad cars to pick up suspects,' Shona said. 'That's not ideal, I'd rather have them in the cage.'

Murdo scanned down the list of targets and circled two names. 'Couple of familiar faces. They're low level dealers, shouldn't give us much trouble. Put Guy Matthews, he's useful, and a special on one, and the two Kirsties, Jamieson and O'Carroll, on the other.'

'Are they up to it if things kick off? I don't want any mishaps with an operation this size.'

'Oh aye. They're handy lassies. Rock solid.'

They went through the rest of the briefing document until both were satisfied. O'Halloran stretched up and yawned. Shona was treated to a glimpse of his pale rounded stomach, like a whale surfacing for air, before it disappeared back beneath his untucked shirt. In the outer office, chip suppers were being distributed and Murdo went to claim his share.

The forty or so staff and officers in the briefing room accepted DI Shona Oliver's substitution for DCI Baird without a murmur. With Murdo's help she went through the schedule of suspects, locations and background checks and answered a couple of queries from the floor. An hour later, as the teams were filing out with their instruction, Shona was approached by PC Guy Matthews.

'Any problem, Matthews?' Since Murdo's vote of confidence, she'd ear-marked him as potential CID. Intelligent grafters were what she needed, and she hoped he wasn't going to ruin his chances by asking a basic question.

'No, ma'am. I just wanted to update you on Nathan Jones.'

Technically the Sweet Life investigation was no longer her case. But technically, Nathan Jones and his yard full of fishing gear wasn't really part of that case, beyond a vague witness statement. 'What can you tell me?' Shona asked.

'Not much, ma'am. He gave a very brief statement, wouldn't be drawn. He has a previous for drink driving and was interviewed about stolen outboard motors, but otherwise he's clear.'

'Nothing violent? No sexual offences?' Shona asked. Matthews shook his head. 'All right, thank you, Matthews.'

Shona gathered up her papers and followed the others out. It was frustrating. It had seemed a promising lead, but now it looked like she was no nearer to finding the identity of the girl from the firth, and her killer, than she had been when she'd folded her brutalised body into the plastic sheeting and brought her ashore.

—

On the journey home Shona would normally have felt the tightness in her shoulders ease with each passing mile. It was true what she'd said to Dan Ridley earlier, the serious crime rate was low. Resources were always under budget pressures, but Shona's main concern usually was not a backlog of cases stacking up, but how to prevent talented staff being lured away by busier and higher profile forces. The leviathan of Operation Fortress was a test of her leadership and, although she would have viewed it as a routine operation during her time in London, there were variables here in the experience and training levels of the staff that she'd have liked more time to address. She wondered if Baird had dropped the briefing on her at the last minute on purpose, just to keep her on her toes and in her place.

Rob had gone to the train station to collect some guests but left a chicken and tarragon stew in the oven for her. She fell on it with gratitude, having missed out on the office chips. Becca was in her room, wrapped in an over-sized jumper, once her father's. With headphones in and intent on her laptop, she grunted hello when her mother kissed the top of her head. Shona gave the screen a quick, parental glance and although the Spotify box showed The Clash's *London Calling* was playing, she was reassured to see an essay of some kind was also in progress.

She stood by the kitchen window looking out on the bay, massaging the tension in her neck. A quick walk, just down to the sailing club pier and back, would help her get some sleep before the three a.m. alarm call. Halfway along the seafront, she saw the light on in the lifeboat station and decided to update skipper Tommy on what they'd found at the Carmine warehouse.

The two-tone alarm of a call-out blared just as she reached the station door. A couple of cars were speeding along the road towards her, volunteers already alerted by pager. Inside, Tommy was in his kit and loading the first aid box into the boat. Callum the postman and Graham Finlayson, the landlord of the Anchor pub in the next village, burst through the door behind her.

'Got a man threatening to throw himself off Sark Bridge in Gretna. Coastguard want us to stand by,' Tommy said. 'It's at the limit of our range. To save fuel I'm only taking one crew. Shona, get suited up.' He turned to the other volunteers waiting by the door. 'Shona's a trained police negotiator and has experience of this sort of job from when she was based at Tower Lifeboat Station in London.' They nodded their agreement.

'Course,' said Shona. She reached for her immersion suit, suspended on the pegs behind her by its yellow wellies. Op Fortress was only hours away, but saving a life came first.

The sun had almost sunk into the western waves behind them as the *Margaret Wilson* set off on the long pull east up the Solway. Shona had fired off a quick text to Rob and Becca. Now she was out on the water all trace of tension and fatigue had gone.

'Sark Bridge,' Tommy shouted to her as they cruised at top speed up the middle channel. 'Funny how we were just talking about that. Did you have any luck with the lassie?'

'No. We recovered a haul of drugs next door, so not a wasted journey.' Mention of the drugs brought Baird and Operation Fortress back into her thoughts. She pushed them away, focusing on the job in hand. 'Any info on the potential jumper?'

'Cops are on scene. It'll be high water by the time we get there.'

An hour later, it was pitch dark. They followed the tide up the Solway and branched left into the River Sark. Shona's hands were numb beneath her gloves from gripping the anchor points and her knees sore from the battering of the waves through the few inches of foam that constituted the bottom of the inshore lifeboat. Tommy throttled back in the confused and choppy currents below Sark Bridge and Shona directed the powerful, handheld flashlight to a group of people up ahead.

Six feet below the parapet was a man, the light catching the wide whites of his eyes as he clung to the granite pier of the bridge. Blinded, he panicked, his legs flailing for purchase on the slanted stone. Shona dropped her arm down until the light shone instead on the churning water below. A red-haired constable and a member of the public, a thin, middle-aged man in a scuffed, brown leather jacket, were leaning over the bridge, calming the jumper down. On the road behind, a fire crew stood by. Other officers were keeping back a small number of cars and spectators.

Shona picked up the VHS radio handset, tuned it to Dumfries Police Area Control Room channel and identified herself. But before she could get an update there was a gasp from onlookers as the man slipped further towards the dark water. It was running at upwards of 6 knots with the turning tide.

Tommy gunned the engine and prepared to move in. Shona scrambled into position in the bow, ready with flotation devices and a grab pole. Suddenly the middle-aged man in the scuffed jacket shook off the police officer's restraining arm and clambered over the parapet. A moment later he reached down to the man, who after only a second's hesitation grabbed his wrist. The constable on the bridge leaned forward and took hold of the jumper's jacket collar. Together they hauled him up. Shona had a last glimpse of an anguished face, dark skinned and unshaven, caught in the beam of their search lamp, before he disappeared to safety over the red sandstone parapet.

'Another one for the mental health team,' commented Tommy, when they were stood down by the coastguard and eventually turned for home. 'It never ends, does it?'

Shona checked her watch. It would be after midnight when they got back. She had to be up at three. 'Aye, Tommy,' she said. 'Sometimes it feels that way.'

Chapter 9

At five the next morning, Shona and DC Kate Irving parked up in the Newington area of Annan, a market town fifteen miles from Dumfries and eight miles from the English border. The two specials waited by their van as the detectives double-checked the details on the warrant. One of the uniformed officers held a scarlet-painted door ram, in case the occupants were reluctant to open up.

Shona's eyes felt gritty and her arm muscles ached from last night's bumpy trip on the Solway Firth. The streets of 1960s grey, pebble-dashed terraces were quiet, but it wouldn't be long before the police presence was noted. 'I'd like a chance with the red key,' Kate said, giving the door ram its nickname. 'I've not used it since training.'

'Okay,' Shona agreed. She liked her officers to maintain their skills. Kate gathered her fine, fair hair, securing it with a hair band, slipped on the gloves and, weighing the device in her hands, adjusted her grip. 'Everyone ready?' Shona nodded to the uniformed officers. 'Let's go.' They rounded the corner and approached the house. The curtains were drawn but a light showed in an upstairs room.

Kate gave the battering ram an experimental swing, then paused to rip open the Velcro tabs on her stab vest, freeing up the movement of her willowy frame and toned shoulders.

Shona put out a hand to stop her. 'I had a colleague, DC Anya Carey, who did that. Know where she is now?'

Kate shook her head uncertainly. 'No, ma'am.'

'City of London Cemetery. There was a guy behind the door with a knife.' Shona remembered the metallic smell of arterial blood, the way it clung to the rims of her nails and grooves in the palms of her hands even when she scrubbed it.

'These vests aren't really designed for women,' grumbled Kate, readjusting the straps compressing her breasts beneath the thick Kevlar layer.

'It was a lot worse before Nike invented a decent sports bra,' replied Shona dryly. When she was satisfied Kate was ready, she tapped the special constable on the shoulder. 'Right, off you go.'

'Police. Open up.' He pounded on the door. 'Last chance. Open up, or your door's going in.' He put his ear against the white UPVC, listening for movement, then shook his head.

The door gave way on Kate's third swing. The specials were first through, shouting for occupants to come out with their hands in plain sight. From somewhere upstairs came the wail of a small child and a woman's raised voice. There was movement in the kitchen. The officers grabbed a skinny man in jeans and bare feet as he struggled with the locks on the back door. Kate identified him as the suspect, Billy 'Hammy' Hamilton, and cautioned him.

Shona took the stairs two at a time, pausing on the dirty pink carpet of the upstairs landing to draw her baton. 'Police. Show your hands,' she commanded, pushing open the three doors that confronted her. The two bedrooms were empty. In the bathroom she found a thin woman sitting on the edge of the cracked bath cradling her daughter. Both faces were streaked with tears.

'He told me he wasnae doing that stuff any more,' she sobbed, pulling a balled tissue from the pocket of a stained blue bathrobe.

Shona stowed the baton in her belt and called Kate. They identified themselves, then took the woman's name and details and helped the pair downstairs. Shona carried the sticky toddler, who eyed her with frank curiosity. The little girl touched Shona's pearl stud earring, then brought her hand up to her own ear. A tiny gold loop sat in the reddened flesh and Shona guessed she'd recently had them pierced. 'Pretty,' she said, and the child smiled.

As they entered the over-furnished living room, the woman let out a tirade of abuse, flying at the cringing, handcuffed Hammy. Kate hauled her off and she collapsed onto the sofa crying. The child looked uncertainly from her mother to Shona. 'Is there a neighbour we can call, Jax?' Shona said. 'We'll need to search the house and it might be better if you and Keana were somewhere quieter.'

'That's kind.' Jax sniffed, teasing a strand of mousy hair round her finger. 'But it's too early to get my neighbours out of bed. I'll stay. Just get that bastard out of my sight.' She took her daughter from Shona and glared at Hammy, who stood, head down, by the living room door.

Shona told the uniformed officers to take their suspect back to Loreburn Street for processing. Jax and her daughter sat together eyeing the police officers as they began to pull out drawers and cupboards. Kate searched a plastic toybox, placing it next to the little girl when she'd finished, but the child made no move to pick up her dolls.

They found a small bag of heroin taped beneath the kitchen counter and a thin roll of twenty-pound notes held by an elastic band in a cereal packet. 'What's this, Jax?' Shona said, walking back into the knocked-through living and dining room, holding the packages up in her gloved hand.

The woman shrugged and lit a cigarette. 'Don't know.' She nodded at the money. 'Hammy never gave me that for housekeeping, that's for sure. Bastard.'

Shona stood for a moment in the dining room, then turned to Kate. 'Does this room seem... odd to you? The dimensions? It's quite narrow compared to the front room, and dark. My kitchen wall's that colour. Taupe, isn't it?' She turned ninety degrees and pointed to the opposite wall. 'That wall's more like, limestone, wouldn't you say.'

'Housing association did it, before we moved in,' said Jax, getting up from the sofa.

'Yeah, not a great paint job,' said Kate, catching Shona's line of thought. 'I'll just pop outside for a minute.'

'Where's she off to?' asked Jax as Kate stepped out of the back door.

'Sit down please,' said Shona calmly. 'DC Irving just needs to check something.'

A minute later Kate was back. She leaned close to Shona and murmured, 'I've counted the windows, inside and out. They don't match.'

'It's a false wall.' Shona pointed over her shoulder. 'Get the ram, take it down.'

'Wait.' Jax jumped up from the sofa as Kate aimed the battering ram at the wall. 'What do youse think you're doing? My name's on the lease, I cannae pay for a new wall.'

'Sit down,' Shona ordered as the ram pierced the wall on Kate's first swing. Bags of powder, both dark and light, began to tumble from the hole.

Shona turned to see Jax rushing at her, a heavy glass ashtray in her raised hand. She stepped aside just in time to dodge the blow, catching the woman off balance and pinning her to the carpet. Kate dropped the ram and fished for her cuffs.

'You stuck-up bitch,' Jax spat in fury, her face pressed against the rug. 'My man will kill youse both, so he will.'

Shona was already on the radio, calling for a team to pick up a new suspect, then she helped Kate to prop the cuffed woman into a seated position on the floor, her back against the sofa where the child still sat staring blankly at her mother. 'You need to take a moment to calm yourself, Jax,' Shona said quietly. 'Tell me who these drugs belong to. Is it your partner Hammy? Were you coerced into keeping them by someone else?'

'Get tae fuck,' the woman spat.

Shona walked into the hall, where she could keep an eye on proceedings, and phoned DCI Baird with the news. It was a short call. Baird was jubilant, she could almost see him punching the air, drunk on the success of his operation, the credit for which would fall squarely in his lap. But through the open door to the living room all Shona could see was a sobbing woman in handcuffs on the floor and yet another child who would grow up without her family.

'Forensics are on their way,' she said to Kate when she'd come back in and sat down next to Keana. The child smelled musty and unwashed. Her cheeks, missing their baby curves, were hollow and grey. Shona couldn't help comparing the probable value of the drugs and the size and newness of the lounge's TV with the undernourished little girl. She'd grown up in a place just like this, knew there were choices to be made. She also knew women who went without so their kids were fed. Her own mother had chosen drugs and died young. Luckily for Shona, her grandmother had been around to pick up the pieces.

'That was quite a performance, Jax. Did you work it out in advance? You playing the innocent partner. Did you think it would distract us and we wouldn't do a thorough search?' Shona picked out the least mangled doll from the box and made it dance before the little girl. Keana's eyes showed a flicker of interest. 'Who do those drugs belong to?' She handed the girl the doll and was rewarded by Keana's attempts to copy Shona and make it dance too. The little girl smiled. Shona felt her heart contract.

'Don't you want to see your daughter grow up? Don't you want something better for her?' Shona leant forward to make eye contact, but Jax turned her head away.

Shona sighed and got back on the radio. 'Get the duty social worker down here. Female, two years old. Keana Cameron.' She listened to the dispatcher's query. 'Okay. She may already be on file but warn them, this time we're not looking at emergency care here, I think this will be a long-term fostering or adoption case.'

Jax looked up pleadingly at Shona, blinking away her tears. 'You think you know me? You know nothing. I talk to youse and she won't last five minutes. They'd kill us both, nae bother.'

'Jax, I can help you,' said Shona. 'But you need to tell me what you know.'

'You think you can help me, but you cannae.' Jax shook her hair back from her face and lifted her chin. She stared ahead. 'I've nothing to say to you, polis bitch.'

There were smiles all round when Shona and Kate finally made it back to the station. Dumfries's part in Operation Fortress had gone like clockwork, with all the suspects apprehended. Shona swallowed a large coffee and a couple of painkillers to keep at bay the headache that had taken root behind her eyes. She hated jobs with kids, most cops did. Even Kate, currently being patted on the back by Matthews, was more subdued than usual.

Matthews was teamed with a special, a young man with burnished red hair and pale freckled skin, colouring so distinctly Scottish you'd remember him. Copper Knob – the nickname would be irresistible to colleagues and felons alike. Bet he heard it a lot. An idea chased itself around Shona's mind for a moment, but she failed to catch it. There was a spark of recognition, then it came to her.

'You were at the bridge last night.'

Copper Knob looked uncertainly at Matthews. 'Yes, ma'am. It's Johnstone. I was at the warehouse too. If it's about my hours, I volunteered for this, I'm applying to join...'

She cut him off with a raised hand. 'How's the gentleman who was threatening to jump?'

He looked even more uncomfortable. 'I don't know. The paramedics were checking him. We went to disperse the crowd and he just vanished.'

'Were you wearing a BWV?' Shona asked. Body-worn video cameras were being introduced but issues with software meant they weren't universal.

'Yes, ma'am, I was.'

'Send me the footage.'

'Yes, ma'am.' His shoulders dropped. 'I'm very sorry, ma'am.'

'You're not in trouble, Johnstone,' she reassured him. 'I saw the way you pulled him to safety, that was quick thinking. Unfortunately, we often see people again. We'll circulate his picture, get mental health agencies involved.'

Shona returned to her office. Murdo tapped on her door and came in beaming. 'Great result.'

'Yes, it was, and largely due to your planning amendments.' She smiled. 'Well done, Murdo.'

'Ach, no,' he said with the hint of a blush. Her sergeant's lack of confidence in his own abilities was something Shona was determined to work on. 'Anyways, all safely gathered in, that's the main thing.' Murdo continued, 'The fiscal reckons as known faces they'll go before the Sheriff tomorrow and if we can link them to the drugs behind the wall they'll be remanded.'

One of the civilian data processors, a slight middle-aged woman with the air of a librarian, was hovering at the door.

'All right there, Amanda? Is it me you're after?' Murdo asked.

'Sorry, ma'am,' Amanda said nervously to Shona. 'it's just… the bracelet.' Both detectives looked at her blankly until she held up a printed out photograph of a young blonde woman who had one hand raised, brushing the hair back from her face. On her wrist was a silver bracelet stamped with the overlapping hearts of Luckenbooth design. 'You mentioned it the other day, Murdo.'

Murdo took the photograph. 'Where did you find this?'

'I've been going through the social media of the suspects picked up by Op Fortress this morning, like you asked, Murdo,' said Amanda shyly. 'Searching for links, pictures of them together, you know. This was on a Facebook page belonging to a James Buckland.'

'You wee belter, Amanda,' said Murdo, beaming at the woman, whose face was rosy with pleasure. He turned to his boss. 'Think that could be our girl?'

Shona pulled up the electronic file of the forensic report. She held the two pictures side by side. 'What do you think, Amanda?' asked Shona.

'Yes,' she said seriously. 'I believe it's the same bracelet. I couldn't say if it's the same woman wearing it.' She averted her eyes from the post-mortem photographs on the screen. 'The girl's not tagged or listed as a friend, so I couldn't trace her, but if you look at the detail of the bracelet, at the crown.' Amanda took the mouse from Shona and highlighted an area of the bracelet on screen, blowing it up. 'There's an identical flattened point and scratch on both pictures, where it's been damaged. I think it has to be the same bracelet.'

'I think you're right, Amanda,' Shona said. 'Murdo, we need to have a chat with this James Buckland.'

'Right, ma'am. Buckland wasn't a primary target; he was at a Dumfries address we raided and had drugs on his person. I'll see where we are on the clock with him.'

Shona checked her watch. 'If he was picked up at five a.m. we're still within the twelve hours. When the custody review is done, if there's any chance he'll be released, tell them I'll give my authority to hold him for another twelve hours, while we investigate this link to a suspicious death.'

'Okay, will do,' said Murdo, heading out the door.

'Amanda, can you get me all the pictures of this woman on Buckland's account, with dates?'

'Yes, ma'am, I'll do that now,' she said, following Murdo out.

Shona sat down heavily at her desk. She rested her chin on her hands and closed her eyes. Images from the last twenty-four hours played like a newsreel on the inside of her eyelids. The dead woman on the dissection table; Jax and her expression of defiant defeat when she knew she'd lose her daughter; flashes of the frightened face of the suicidal man on the bridge. Already the brittle lift from the coffee was speeding through her system. It would keep her going for an hour or so, but the double dip of sleep deprivation and caffeine ebb could affect her judgement and she needed to get this right. She needed some fresh air, but she could feel herself drifting towards sleep.

Her phone rang. Her head jerked upright, the muscles in her shoulders clenching in protest. She was about to decline the call when Dan Ridley's name flashed on the screen.

'I've been to see Nathan Jones's wife,' he said. 'Cops visited the house before, but only because *she* was battering him.' There was a pause. 'You still there, ma'am?'

'Yeah, sorry. Go on.' Shona massaged her neck.

'Do you think this might have been some form of revenge? That he killed the woman to get back against women in general?' Dan persisted.

'It's possible, I suppose, but we can't connect them, and Jones has come up clean here, no history of violence.' Shona saw Murdo at his desk put down his phone and give her the nod. The interview with Buckland was on. 'But listen,' Shona said to Dan, 'I've a possible lead on the jewellery. Come over tomorrow, I'll update you.'

'Great,' Dan replied. 'And I might have something for you too. I've been handed a bit of paperwork.' Shona thought it was more likely that a mountain of low grade files had been unceremoniously dumped on his desk courtesy of DCI Lambert. 'There's a mention of shop thefts involving baby milk,' he continued. 'I've asked the tech guys for any CCTV, I'll bring it over.'

'Good,' said Shona. If nothing else it would give Dan a legitimate reason to be in Dumfries if his boss got arsy about him pursuing the ID of the girl. 'Tomorrow it is.' She ended the call and stood up, tucking her blouse back into her waistband, shaking herself awake. She'd had two hours' rest in the last twenty-four, but she welcomed the pain, the tiredness. This was what hard graft felt like, and hard graft was how you got results.

Chapter 10

Jamie Buckland was in his early twenties but looked younger. Somewhere in his childhood all potential for growth and ripe maturity had been snuffed out. Scrawny and thin faced, Shona could see him becoming the kind of frail elderly man who shuffled between betting shop and boozer. That's if he made it to old age, which was by no means certain. She suspected he was a user and small-time dealer and there were a dozen beartraps waiting for someone in his line of work.

He sat opposite Shona and Murdo, the restless rhythm of his right leg a staccato beat on the vinyl floor of the interview room. Shown the blonde girl's photograph from his Facebook page, he denied he knew her. He did some casual bar work. She was just a girl he'd met there, or on a night out, he shrugged. No one he could put a name to. Murdo produced three other pictures taken at intervals over a few months showing Buckland with the girl. Caught out, he retreated into a no-comment interview. When Shona revealed this was a potential murder inquiry and he should have a chat with the increasingly nervy duty solicitor next to him, Buckland seemed to enter a state of suspended animation. The agitated tapping of his leg stopped. The muscles of his jaw clenched tight as if guarding against any outburst. Shona sent him back to his cell to think things over.

By the next morning, with Buckland remaining tight-lipped and no further evidence, Shona was forced to watch him go before the Sheriff on possession of a Class C drug, namely Valium. The amount was too small to charge him with dealing and his guilty plea provoked a ticking-off and he was released on bail to await pre-sentencing reports. Half the suspects Shona's team had picked up on Operation Fortress's trawl received the same treatment but the remainder, including Keana's parents Jax and Hammy, were remanded. It was a better than average result, but when Dan Ridley's hopeful face appeared at her office door, she felt an edge of disappointment that she had no good news for him.

Dan handed the CCTV from the Cumbrian baby milk theft over to Kate. Shona brought him up to speed on the bracelet photographs over coffee, drunk side by side as they leaned on her office window sill, taking in the view over Dumfries relief road to the umber-tinted trees beyond. He nodded, furrowing his brow and rubbing the stubble of his beard, as he jotted down Jamie Buckland's details and Carlisle address.

When she finished, he closed his notebook, his bright blue eyes alive with news he was bursting to tell. 'The DNA results came back. We have a hit.'

'You got a match? Why didn't you say instead of letting me rabbit on?' Shona turned her face up to him, hand on hip.

'Well, it's not a match as such,' he said, caution clouding his features. 'She's not on the database, but…'

Shona gave him a look that said, spit it out.

'But we've got a partial match to someone listed as living in your area.'

Shona held up her hand to stop him, opening her office door. Kate had headphones in, the new CCTV from the baby milk investigation playing on her screen. Ravi was out somewhere, following up on the witness statements. 'Murdo, a moment,' she called. When he came in, she nodded for Dan to continue.

'The girl in the Solway Firth. We've got a partial DNA match to Paddy Corr, fifty-six, address in Dumfries.' Dan flicked open his notebook again. 'String of previous. Convictions for aggravated assault, sexual assault and theft, also prostitution related offences including procuring, living off the avails...' Dan ran his finger down the list.

'Murdo?' Shona enquired.

'Aye, I know him. Lifted him a few times myself. We've got him on the Violent Offenders Database, though I don't recall hearing much about him lately. His younger brother, Tony, is in Barlinnie for culpable homicide. Glassed a fella in a bar and watched him bleed out. There's another brother, Gerry, doing a ten-stretch for robbery and possession of a firearm. There's also a posse of cousins who are known to us too. The lassie with the bairn you picked up yesterday, Jax Cameron, she's related. The whole extended family's been keeping us busy for years.'

'Yes. Name rings a bell. Let's pay him a visit,' said Shona, all trace of tiredness gone.

'Aye, why not,' said Murdo. 'But I warn you, you'll want to take a shower afterwards.'

—

Shona and Murdo spent a few minutes gathering up photographs of the woman from Jamie Buckland's Facebook account, the forensic shots of the bracelet and checking for the latest intel regarding Paddy Corr. Dan perched on the edge of Kate's desk, reading from his notebook as they went through the CCTV together. Shona noticed a definite thaw in her DC's attitude to the Cumbrian copper and hoped Dan's intel had brought a breakthrough in the baby milk case. Shona appeared in front of him, suit jacket on and handbag over her shoulder.

'Ready?' she said.

Dan looked surprised. 'You want me along on this?'

'Of course. I don't expect we'll get the warmest of welcomes, but we're doing this softly-softly. Follow Murdo's lead and keep your eyes open for anything that strikes you as odd. Okay?'

'Yes, ma'am.' Dan jumped to his feet. He gave a last nod to Kate, who glared after them before turning back to her screen and looking distinctly put out.

The Corrs' home was on a 1950s council estate of roughcast grey semis under grey tile roofs. Gap-toothed garden fences marked a permeable boundary between private and public. Nothing that happened here was out of sight of the neighbours, although most would claim, if asked by a police officer, not to have seen or heard a thing.

A short woman in her fifties with dyed blonde hair and heavy rose-gold jewellery opened the door, her face set like concrete, instantly recognising the trio on her doorstep as plain-clothes detectives.

Shona lifted her warrant card, looped on its Police Scotland lanyard around her neck. 'I'm Detective Inspector Shona Oliver, these are my colleagues DS O'Halloran and DC Ridley.'

The woman glanced at the card, then folded her arms and leaned against the door frame. 'Aye. What do youse want?'

'Mrs Corr, is it? We're here to see Paddy. Is he about?' Shona replied.

'Isn't he always?' She shrugged but made no move to step aside. They were about as welcome as Ebola in her household, and she wanted them to know it. Eventually she said, 'I suppose you'd better come in.'

Murdo touched her lightly on the arm and entered the hall. 'All right, Marie? How's the family?' She ignored him.

They followed her into an immaculate front room. Coy china shepherdesses sat on a teak shelving unit, a three-piece suite in polished leather was ranged back along the walls over a dark green carpet with a subtle fleck design. The room was dominated by a large flat-screen television showing the horse racing. A decaying man sat in a lounger, his swollen legs hoisted up to the near horizontal by the footrest. He breathed via a nasal cannula attached to an oxygen tank. When he saw Murdo he gave a gummy grin. 'Thought I smelled bacon.' His laugh subsided immediately into a fit of wheezing.

'All right there, Paddy. You were never one for the healthy lifestyle, but I can't say I'm happy to see you in this state.'

'Can't say I'm happy to see you at all,' breathed Paddy. 'What have I done this time?'

To Shona's surprise, Murdo shook the hand Paddy offered him and pulled up a stool next to the man's chair. He studied the television picture. 'The gee-gees, is it? You got a fix on the next race?'

Paddy shook his head. 'Strictly a spectator these days. In this as in everything else.' He swept his hand across his failing body, inviting sympathetic nods and noises from his audience. He got none.

'Well, you won't mind me turning this off then.' Murdo tapped the remote, placing it just out of Paddy's reach and provoking a scowl. 'This is my boss, DI Oliver, and a colleague from Cumbria. We need to ask you a few questions.'

'Can we sit down, Mrs Corr?' Shona asked.

'Suit yourself, hen,' the woman said, and turned on her heel. Dan chose a spot on the sofa, but Shona followed the woman out into an equally spotless kitchen. 'We'd like to talk to you too, Mrs Corr.'

'I've the dinner to make. That one's on special food.' She nodded through the wall to her husband as if she'd gained the advice of a vet rather than a doctor. 'Mair work for me, so it is.' She looked defiant, but Shona noted the edge of fear in her voice. Marie Corr crossed her arms and nervously chewed her lip.

'It will only take a moment,' Shona reassured her, ushering her back through to the lounge.

When they were all seated, Murdo took out a picture of a young blonde woman laughing into the camera and held it up. 'Do you recognise this girl?'

Shona saw the warning look pass from Paddy to his wife.

'No, don't think so,' Marie said uncertainly.

Paddy shook his head. 'What's this lassie supposed to have done?'

'She's not done anything,' said Murdo, ignoring the man and focusing on the woman, who seemed to be shrinking back into the armchair. 'Marie, we need to find her. We're increasingly concerned for her welfare.'

Marie reached forward and snatched the photograph of the smiling girl in the bar, peering at it, hungry for every detail. She turned in her seat, shielding herself and the picture from her husband's murderous looks. 'Have youse lot got her?'

'Got who, Marie?' said Shona inching forward. She took a second photograph from Murdo, the post-mortem shot of the bracelet removed from the victim and held it out to Marie. 'Who does this belong to?'

Marie stared at it for a moment. Then she took a deep breath. 'That's Isla's bracelet. My daughter, Isla.'

My daughter, not *our* daughter. Shona noted the demarcation. A line had been crossed, a subtle shift in the power dynamics of the Corrs' marriage. Marie was taking sole possession of their child, but Paddy Corr, even in his reduced state, wasn't giving way without a fight.

'Shut up, woman. We don't talk to the polis. Our family is our business.'

But Marie ignored him. 'This picture of Isla, where did youse get it?'

'From a Facebook page belonging to Jamie Buckland,' Shona said. 'Do you know him?'

'Isla doesnae do Facebook. But Buckie? Aye, they were pals from when they were wee.' Now the barriers had come down the words flooded out. Shona knew the moment was coming when she'd have to give Marie the bad news. No matter how many times she'd had to deliver the 'death knock' it never became easier.

'You're sure it's Isla?' Shona knew she was putting it off. Paddy Corr's eyes darted from face to face seeking an advantage but all attention had turned to his wife. Immobile and breathless, there was nothing he could do.

'I've got some pictures in the kitchen. C'mon and see.' Shona got up to follow Marie. Paddy turned to the now blank television screen, the rasping rhythm of his breaths the only sound in the room. Murdo had taken up a position in the bay window, one eye on the street outside. Dan's attention was fixed on the carpet. All were waiting for the storm to come.

Marie pulled a small pile of pictures from a drawer. Blonde pigtails and a school uniform. The long, white veil of first communion. Older now, holding a baby. An uneven row of teenage faces, cousins sharing out the Guess-Who game of family features; blonde hair, blue eyes, short stature, high hairline, sticky-out ears. Marie recited their names, her son Lewis, then Siobhan, Matty, Josh, Paul and on the end, recognisably herself, Isla Corr. The girl in Buckie's photograph, the girl with the bracelet. The girl on the slab.

'Marie, there's something I have to tell you,' Shona began.

'She's dead, isn't she?' Marie said quietly.

'I'm sorry, but the body of a young woman has been recovered. She was wearing the bracelet Murdo showed you. Her DNA was a match to Paddy. Do you have anything of Isla's, a toothbrush or comb? No? Okay, we'll do another DNA test with yourself, but I think you need to prepare for bad news. The young woman met her death through violence.'

'It's her. It's her for sure,' Marie moved the photographs around on the kitchen worktop like Tarot cards, as if a different combination could reveal a different fate for her daughter.

'Why do you say that?' Shona asked.

'She's gone off before, but always come back.' Marie tore off a sheet of kitchen paper and pressed it to her eyes. 'Ryan, you see. My grandson. He lives with me at the minute, but she's never left him for so long. I knew something wasnae right. She was just getting back on her feet. Her man's inside, he battered her and… she was just getting her head sorted.' She sobbed. 'Can I see her? Will I need to identify her? Paddy's no fit, he can hardly leave the house.'

'Marie,' Shona began, 'Isla's body was recovered from the Solway Firth. She'd been in the water some time. Like I said, we can confirm her identity through DNA. There's no need for you to come in.'

With the realisation that she'd never see her daughter again, dead or alive, Marie balled the tissue into her mouth and let out a stifled howl.

'It's okay, Marie. Take your time.' Shona put her arm around the woman. She could feel the tautness of her body, the physical effort required to stay upright, leaning on the kitchen counter. Together the two of them stood looking down at the relics of a young life, a life finished before it had barely begun.

Then, the jigsaw images of Isla Corr began to shift before Shona's eyes, forming themselves into a new alignment, opening a window of memory that illuminated everything in sharper focus.

'Isla's ex-boyfriend? Would that be Marcus Gregor?'

'That's the bastard, Gringo.' Marie nodded vigorously. 'Always said he was a bad yin. We fell out over it. He didnae kill her, did he? I thought he was in prison?' Anger was already battling the grief for pole position. Shona had seen it often, the swings and eddies that would roll on for months, even years, if answers weren't found. 'Do you know what he done to her?' Marie continued, 'He put her in hospital.'

'Yes,' Shona said quietly. 'I know.'

Almost two years had passed since Gringo had come at her with a broken bottle in that hospital room and she'd instinctively grabbed the special's baton. When she hit him, Gringo had gone down like a felled pine tree. She'd taken satisfaction from it, knowing all the while it could go badly for her if he made a complaint. But now the guilt flooded in. She remembered Isla propped up in a hospital bed, the small face swollen almost out of recognition. The eyes blackened, the lip split. Her name hadn't lodged in Shona's memory as it should have. Despite the girl's injuries, Shona should have recognised her in the Facebook photograph. For all she'd done, putting her career on the line, she'd failed. She'd set out to protect Isla, but now this vulnerable young woman was dead and nothing could change that.

She squeezed the woman's shoulder. 'Marie, I think you should sit down. I'm going to get a Family Liaison Officer to come over. They'll keep you up to date with what we're doing. When you're ready, I'll need you to tell my officer everything you can remember about the last time you spoke to Isla. But for now, is there anyone we can call? What about your son, Lewis?'

'No, he'll be at work. My sister, she lives close.' Marie sniffed, picking up the phone, but her hand shook so much that Shona took it from her and pressed the button marked Margaret. After explaining the situation, she took Marie back into the living room. When Margaret arrived a few minutes later, the women fell on each other, collapsing under their combined grief. Paddy sat sullen and silent, his mouth a hard line beneath the oxygen feed. After a moment he reached for the TV remote, scrabbling for it with his fingertips, and turned the horse racing back on. Murdo glared at him until he muted the sound. The three police officers left the family alone for their last private moment before the public business of an investigation began in earnest.

Outside, Shona started the Audi's engine. Dan sat squashed in the back. Murdo flicked through the collected pictures in the passenger seat. 'You mind her now, don't you, boss?' he said quietly. 'And Jamie Buckland, giving us the run-around. Saying he didnae know her. Maybe he was supplying her? Thought we'd get him for dealing instead of just possession.'

Shona bit her lip and made a show of checking her mirrors as she prepared to reverse out of the parking space. It bought her time to steady her voice. 'Murdo, check if Marcus Gregor is still inside. If he's not at Dumfries Prison, find out where he's been transferred to. I'm going to need a word with him, pronto.'

'I could do that, if you like,' Murdo said, also paying extra attention to the traffic-free avenue.

'No, I think it better if I see him myself. We've a conversation to finish.' She slammed the car into gear.

Dan had sat passively through the events inside, as instructed, observing the interplay of the Corrs' marriage, the firm but compassionate breaking of bad news by Shona and Murdo. Now he leaned forward from the back seat. 'Ma'am, if it's okay with you, I'd like to be present at that interview.' In the rear-view mirror Shona and Dan exchanged a glance. He was just as committed to finding answers as she was.

After a moment she said, 'Fine. Let's set that up for tomorrow morning.'

Chapter 11

Next morning, Shona called Murdo, Kate and Ravi into her office. Dan was already there, leaning back on a chair under the window, scrolling through his phone.

'So, is this our case now?' asked Kate bluntly, her eyes moving between Shona and Dan. Though she'd smiled and even flirted with Dan when he'd arrived, the question resurrected his uncertain status in the team. She was the senior detective constable here, and he shouldn't forget it.

'At present we're assisting an officer from a neighbouring force,' said Shona. 'But as head of CID in Dumfries I'm authorising the opening of a file to be shared with Cumbria in accordance with the guidelines laid down in the document "The Management of Cross-Border Crime in Dumfries and Galloway". Does that answer your question, DC Irving?'

'Yes, ma'am,' said Kate quietly. She crossed her long legs and shot Dan a malevolent look which he pointedly ignored.

'Okay, folks. Thanks to DC Ridley we have a positive ID on our girl in the water via a partial DNA match. Yesterday Murdo and I interviewed the family, who confirmed their daughter has been missing for over a month. Murdo, what have you found on the victim?'

'Isla Corr, twenty-one years old. Past convictions for possession of Class A drugs, a treatment order from the

Sheriff for her heroin addiction. We've had her in for public solicitation as well,' Murdo said. 'She dropped out of school and has been in trouble since her early teens. There's a son, Ryan, who's six years old, currently living with grandparents, Marie and Paddy Corr. I've had uniform check out Isla's last known address, the one she gave to the hospital when she was assaulted by her partner, but that was nearly two years ago and neighbours say she left a while back and they've no idea where she went.'

'Okay, lines of enquiry and persons of interest,' said Shona, squeezing across to the whiteboard propped up on the low filing cabinets at a right angle to her desk. She uncapped a marker pen. 'Former partner Marcus Gregor. Murdo?'

'He was out on licence when he assaulted her and went straight back to Dumfries jail.'

'Okay, he has an alibi, but we still need to interview him. Dan and I will be doing that later. Who else?'

Murdo cleared his throat. 'Her father, Paddy Corr. He has previous for violent offences including sexual assault on an eighteen-year-old girl. Pretty sure he brought his work home with him, but his wife Marie would never co-operate with police.' Murdo turned to Kate and Ravi. 'Paddy was hooked up to oxygen when we visited yesterday. Terminally ill, stage four emphysema Marie said, but if it wasn't for his health I'd have him in pole position.'

Shona nodded. 'Dan, what did you make of him?'

'He looked in a bad way, but he's a skilled manipulator. He could still have had a hand in her death.'

'Aye, that's true,' said Murdo.

'I'd want to check if he's really as ill as he makes out,' said Dan, tapping his teeth with his pen. 'From what I saw yesterday, there's something not right there. Marie would lie for him, no question. That might change though if she thought he had something to do with her daughter's death.'

'Good point,' Shona said. 'Okay, for now he stays on the list. Anyone else?'

'Nathan Jones?' said Dan. 'Is he still in the frame?'

'There's no indication he knew Isla,' Shona considered. 'Despite brandishing an axe handle at us he has no convictions for violence and he's a victim himself of domestic abuse. But, he's dysfunctional, aggressive and secretive, living alone close to the Solway Firth. I think he stays until we can rule him out completely.'

'What about Jamie Buckland?' Murdo said.

Shona nodded vigorously as she inked his name on the board. 'He lied to us about knowing Isla. We need to re-interview him. His gave his address as Carter Street in Carlisle so, Dan, re-interview him. And get Isla's photograph out to your uniform and PCSOs while you're at it.'

She stood back and looked at the spider diagram on the board, considering possible links and avenues. She turned to her two detective constables sitting side by side.

'Kate, I know you're full-on with the baby milk case, but check with the multi-agency hub if Isla Corr pops up anywhere in the months since she left hospital. We've an empty timeline, so let's fill it. And social media. Her mother said she didn't do Facebook but check the other platforms. Is that odd?' Shona paused, addressing the question to the room. 'A girl her age without a Facebook account?'

Ravi shrugged, picking a speck of fluff from his white, half-zipped hoodie. 'Social media is tribal, depends what your friends have. Snapchat, Instagram, WhatsApp groups. Facebook has an older demographic, but it's worth checking if she deleted her account and if she blocked anyone.' Beside him Kate was nodding and taking notes.

Shona replaced the pen lid. 'Ravi, I want you as FLO. Liaise with the family but also see if you can find out who Ryan's dad is and if there's still contact. Marie was evasive when I asked her. I don't want you to press them, that's not your role. But anything you pick up on, I want to hear it. As Dan said, there's something, probably many things, not right in that family. Oh, and we need a DNA swab from Marie, to confirm Isla's ID, and get any phone numbers Isla was using, see if we can get some cell site history.'

He nodded. 'Sure, boss.'

The Corrs' initial reaction to DC Ravi Sarwar would probably be hostile, and he'd certainly stand out in the all-white, working-class community of Dumfries. But his charm, tact and patience would pay dividends both for the investigation and for Isla's relations seeking closure.

'Anything else we should be looking at?' Shona said.

'Well. She was a prostitute and a drug user,' said Kate, doodling circles on her notepad.

'You talk like she deserved it. A young woman thrown in the sea like a piece of rubbish,' flashed Shona, causing Kate to colour. This was exactly the kind of comment, this lack of tact, that separated her two constables, and confirmed Shona's decision to appoint Ravi to family liaison. It was also the reason why Kate's career, talented though she was, could stall in an unguarded moment. A male officer might get away with it, just. But even in this era of diversity and apparent equality Shona knew the old adage held true. Women were held to higher standards and any who failed would be side-lined.

'I was just wondering why she didn't come up on the DNA database herself,' Kate said quietly.

'She was under eighteen at the time of the offence. The sample was discarded after three years,' Murdo said. 'She's not been in trouble since, or she learned not to get caught.'

'Lifestyle *is* a legitimate line of enquiry,' Shona conceded. 'But remember, Isla Corr has a son, a mother, siblings, friends who all want to know how and why she died. It's our job to answer these questions. There will be press interest, so let's watch our words as much as our actions. Isla's mother said she was clean, so we need the toxicology results before we jump to conclusions. Any sign of them, Dan?' Ridley shook his head. There was a moment of heavy silence before Shona wound up the meeting. 'Dan, with me. I want an update from the rest of you later today.' Chairs were pushed back, Kate and Ravi heading to the small kitchen area.

'Boss is taking this quite personally,' Kate said sullenly to Ravi as they stood by the kettle waiting for it to boil.

'I suppose if you recover the body yourself it's bound to affect you,' said Ravi, flicking through the tin of biscuit wrappers.

'Or maybe it's not that body she's interested in.'

'How do you mean?' Ravi frowned. Half a chocolate digestive, dusty and slightly soft, was his only option.

Kate tilted her head to where Shona and Dan were waiting for the lift. They saw Shona, six inches shorter and ten years his senior, smile upwards at something Dan said. Kate raised her eyebrows at Ravi and mouthed a single word. Cougar.

At Her Majesty's Prison Dumfries, the warning light flashed, and the reinforced glass door swung open. Inside, a second door buzzed and Shona and Dan entered the carpeted reception. At the desk they showed their warrant cards and deposited their bag and mobile phones in a lock box. There was a delay while they found a female prison officer to search Shona.

The repeated jingle and clang of locks and keys took them into an empty canteen area. Blocks of tables and benches, set out in rows, were bolted to the floor. A sneering man in prison uniform of jeans and blue T-shirt was already waiting, lounging back in the metal bench, one leg thrust out into the passage. A prison officer remained by the door.

'Thank you for agreeing to see me.' Shona took the seat opposite him. Dan sat down at the bench across the aisle, pulling his suit jacket straight, his expression parked firmly in neutral.

'Aye well, we're a bit short of the female form in here. It's nice to freshen the image. You'll be in my dreams tonight,' Gringo leered.

'I'm here about Isla,' said Shona, brushing aside the comment. 'When did you last see her?'

'She's not been to visit me thanks to you, bitch.' He glared at her.

Shona held eye contact and sat forward, leaning her elbows on the table. 'We've found her body. I'm sorry.'

Gringo stared at her for a moment then dipped his head, shaking it as if to loosen the grip of whatever emotion had seized him. He balled his fists. Dan shifted in his seat, ready to spring between Shona and Gringo.

He glanced up at the prison officer, who had also clocked Gringo's body language and was rocking on the balls of his feet, one hand on his radio to call for back-up. Shona didn't move.

But when Gringo finally lifted his head, she could see tears in his eyes. 'Was it the dope? Always thought it would get her.'

'Someone killed her. Threw her body in the Solway Firth,' Shona said bluntly. 'I recovered her myself. DC Ridley was there too.'

Dan reached into his pocket. 'I'm very sorry, Mr Gregor.' He slid a folded paper tissue across the table top. A sound somewhere between a grunt and a sob escaped Marcus Gregor's lips. He picked up the tissue and rubbed it across his face.

Given that he'd half-killed Isla himself, Shona thought he didn't deserve Dan's sympathy, but it wasn't her place to judge. The court had done that and passed their sentence. She needed him calm and willing to talk, and if Dan got him there that was fine by her.

'I've seen your file,' Shona said. 'Friends on the outside with previous form for violence.'

'Think I'd let anyone touch her?' Gringo swallowed hard. 'What's he doing here, you lot always swim in pairs. This an official interview? Do I need my solicitor?' he said, making a half-hearted attempt at defiance.

'Look, Marcus. I'm sorry we got off on the wrong foot.'

'You assaulted me with a baton.' It came out as a little boy whine.

'You decked a special constable and came at me with a bottle. I wasn't going to let you get at Isla, was I?' said Shona calmly.

'I wouldn't hurt her. I mean, I didn't mean to hurt her in the first place. I was high. But I was out on licence, if she went through with the complaint, I'd be back in jail. I only wanted to tell her...' He hung his head, radiating self-pity.

'You've a parole hearing coming up. If you've got anything to tell me, better do it now. Co-operating with the police will help your case.'

'I loved her. Ryan? What about Ryan? Is he okay? I hurt her, but I hurt myself too.' He shook his head, blinking back angry tears. 'I let her down and now she's dead. I wasn't there to protect her. The worst thing that could have happened to me already has, so you can threaten me all you like.'

'Okay, Marcus,' Shona said.

'You want to know who killed Isla? Ryan's dad,' Gringo spat. 'That bastard, Duncan Saltire. Wouldnae leave us alone. He was stalking her. I told him to back off and he had two of his thugs do me over. That's what we argued about the night... the night I hit her. I told her to keep away from him, but she said she needed money and he'd pay for her to keep quiet about how they used to score when they were together. Now fuck off and do your job.' He slumped in his seat and with a dejected flick of his hand, summoned the prison officer like a waiter and told him he was ready to go back to his cell.

—

'For someone who didn't want to hurt his girlfriend he made a damn good job of wrecking her life. But did he kill her? What did you make of him?' Shona asked Dan as they drove out of the prison car park.

'Weren't you worried?'

'What? That he'd see it as a chance to get even? I was banking on it.'

'How?'

'If he refused to see me, I'd need to interview him formally. He was banged up at the time of the offence, so a solicitor might raise objections. I was counting on his curiosity, his desire for revenge. He wasn't going to pass up the opportunity to try to humiliate or embarrass me. He gave it a go, he's just not very good at it.' Shona indicated and turned onto the main road. 'I needed to see his reaction to the news of Isla's death. Was there any hint of triumph? Did he know already?' Shona shook her head. 'He was devastated, that wasn't put on. I think his regret about hurting Isla and the guilt he carries was the one perceptive thought he ever had in his whole life. Pity it's too late for Isla.'

'What if he'd reacted badly?' Dan persisted. They stopped at the traffic lights.

'Well, I had you there to protect me.' She grinned, but instead of smiling back he looked crestfallen and embarrassed.

It had come out wrong. She'd meant it as light-hearted reassurance, something she could have said to Murdo or Ravi, and they'd have come back with a wry reply.

She felt a wrinkle of irritation. He'd obviously heard the story of how the last encounter with Gringo had ended. Did he really think she'd put them both at risk? That a detective inspector of her experience would needed rescuing? It was an insult both to her as an individual and a senior officer. Ridley had overstepped the mark. They travelled the short distance back to Cornwell Mount in silence.

Frowning, she pulled into a free bay in the car park. But her displeasure was tempered with the thought that he'd cared enough to be concerned. In a police officer of any level that was a reassuring quality. It was also something to be valued in a colleague, and a friend. She switched off the engine and unclipped her belt, turning to look at him.

'It wasn't that I didn't trust your judgement,' he said, as if reading her mind. 'I'm just trying to understand. You have some history with him. Murdo told me what happened when he attacked you at the hospital. That meant he was already hyped up. If he'd taken the news of Isla's death differently... he could have struck out at either of us, or a prison officer. He's a big bloke. Someone could have been badly hurt.'

'I'm aware of that, and took those points into consideration when I set out my interview strategy. I also spoke to the governor about Gringo's mental state before we arrived. They've been working with him and he's made good progress with anger management. Sometimes you have to hold your nerve, provoke an honest reaction, if you want to find a proper lead.'

Dan nodded. 'Okay, I get that. Duncan Saltire?'

'Oh, I know Mr Saltire, a wannabe local politician and small-time thug who the shit never sticks to. He pedals a particularly tasteless brand of right-wing ideology, the Sons of Scotia. That he's Ryan's father is very interesting, especially when you do the maths. Isla was twenty-one and Ryan is six years old.'

'She had his baby when she was fifteen.' Dan frowned. 'How come Saltire wasn't prosecuted?'

'Maybe she refused to name the father. We don't know for sure he *is* Ryan's dad,' Shona said. 'But Saltire has political ambitions. A grubby story about underage sex and drugs looks bad, even if you're a fascist. That's certainly a potential motive. Time Mr Saltire and I had a chat.'

'Want me to come with you?'

'No, I'll get Murdo to rattle his cage. You get back to Carlisle. Interview Jamie Buckland, check for sightings of Isla at his address. We need to fill in that timeline.' They got out the car and said their goodbyes. As Dan walked away, Shona called after him, 'By the way, you did well this morning. The hankie was a nice touch.'

He coloured slightly. 'My old sergeant taught me that.'

'Sounds like he knew what he was talking about.'

'She,' said Dan. 'And yes, she did. So do you, ma'am. Thank you for this morning. I learned a lot.'

Chapter 12

Shona stood by the bedroom window, putting in a pair of gold drop earrings Rob had bought her for their tenth anniversary. The early evening sun glittered on the Kirkness shore. A few dinghies and small yachts zig-zagged in the light breeze in front of the sailing club and she felt the familiar heart-tug of the water. The Scottish Trade Against Crime reception was taking place this evening at the Golden Eagle Hotel, a five-star establishment on Glasgow's Clydeside, owned by TV businessman Kenny Hanlon. It was a couple of hours' drive away from Kirkness. She knew where she'd rather be.

'Thought you'd given up the undercover work when you left Vice.' Rob came into the bedroom, struggling with the knot in his tie.

'Very funny. Do you think this is too much? Too tarty?' She spun this way and that before the mirror, suddenly unsure. She'd intended to buy something new, but Rob had discouraged her, pointing out she had a wardrobe full of clothes from London. The tight black vintage cocktail dress with its lace sleeves and beaded hem was his favourite. Maybe it was a little low-cut at the front, now she came to think of it. 'Should I change?'

'Don't you dare,' he said, his arm circling her waist. 'I'm so used to seeing you in trousers or waterproofs, I just forget how lovely you look in a dress.' He kissed her neck, nuzzling against her. 'God, you smell so good.'

'No, no, no.' She wriggled free. 'Mind on the job, Robert.'

'My mind's always on the job.' He made a grab for her, but she easily sidestepped him. He fell sprawling onto the bed, then grinned invitingly up at her and patted the duvet beside him.

She shook her head, laughing. 'Behave yourself. Your job is to get me through this STAC reception, stop me telling our host Kenny Hanlon what a total gobshite I think he is.' She secured the second earring.

Rob lay back, watching her, his hands behind his head. 'You never would. My Shona is never less than professional.' He smiled. 'But yes, *The Enterpriser.* Hanlon must be raking it in. BBC show, hotel group. Might put a business proposal to him myself. He's got fingers in lots of pies. Could tap him for the local tourism group, or my restaurant idea.'

'Well, if you're sharing a pie with Hanlon I suggest you use a very long spoon.'

Rob laughed. 'If you've already promoted him from gobshite to the devil himself I *will* need to watch you, lassie.' He wagged a finger at her. 'What's the problem? Got a nice fat CID file on him, have you?' He swung his legs out and sat on the edge of the bed.

Shona stepped into her heels and beckoned Rob towards her. 'No, should I have?' She unravelled his tie and started again. 'What have you heard?'

He shrugged. 'Nothing much. Has money to invest. He always turns the profit, others take the losses. Keeps on the right side of the law, just.'

'Regular businessman then. He's certainly keeping on the right side of the law with this STAC initiative. He's the Money Messiah as far as Division are concerned. A million for community crime initiatives. Mind you,' she said, patting his newly straightened tie, 'he's probably screwed double that out of his low-paid hotel workers over the years, so he can afford it.' She smoothed her dress and smiled at their reflections in the full-length mirror. They were a good match, a picture of respectable success.

Rob reached for his dark suit jacket and slipped it on. 'Maybe I should ask him the question everyone really wants to know?'

'Where he got his millions?'

'No. Is that his real hair? It's a very funny colour. Do you reckon it's his own?'

'No idea, but frankly, if that's the basis of your business pitch to Kenny Hanlon, I think it needs work.'

—

Shona scanned the room. A string quartet played in the background. On the dark red walls hung landscapes in oil and portraits of Glasgow's great and good, mostly white, mostly male, mostly dead.

'A top-up?' DCI Gavin Baird appeared at Shona's shoulder.

'No, I'm fine, sir,' Shona said. But Baird took her half-empty glass, flagged down a passing waiter and swapped it for a full one. 'Thank you, sir.' She had a two-hour drive home. This would put her over Scotland's strict, one-drink limit. Baird looked like he was already there.

'Call me Gavin. First name terms tonight. I'll go back to being detective chief inspector tomorrow. Cheers,

Shona.' He clinked his glass against hers, then watched her over the rim as he swallowed a mouthful of warm champagne.

'Cheers... Gavin.' Shona pressed the glass to her mouth, but didn't drink.

Across the room she saw Kenny Hanlon glad-handing through the crowd. In contrast to the sober dinner suits and uniforms around him, he was wearing a flamboyant saffron-coloured jacket in designer tweed, the fine check exactly matching the pale hazel-gold of his eyes. Hanlon paused to introduce two beaming businessmen to a third, thin-faced man with a smile like a knife gash. Hanlon's voice carried above the hubbub of the room. 'David, Andy, I'd like to introduce you to Evan Campbell, I know you will have lots to talk about.'

Hanlon must have felt Shona's gaze upon him. He strode over to join them. 'Detective Inspector Oliver, I just thought I'd take the opportunity to say hello. And your husband Rob? He's in banking, isn't he? Is he here with you tonight?'

Whoever had briefed him on the guest list had been thorough. Shona shook his hand. 'Mr Hanlon.' She kept her attention from straying to his hairline, and the peculiar upstanding brush of hair. 'Yes, Rob's here somewhere, but he's left banking. He's in hospitality and tourism now.'

'Smart move, man after my own heart.' He kept her hand tight in his grasp. 'Why haven't we met before?' He tilted his head to one side, a coquettish twinkle in his eye.

'I don't usually socialise in such elevated circles.' She smiled and retrieved her hand with a firm pull.

'Well, it's very nice to meet you. I believe you're the first female detective inspector I've met. So, what's next?' He looked at her expectantly, his hands clasped in front of him. Beyond the opening titles, Shona had never watched his show. Was this a catchphrase she should be smiling in recognition at? She had the sense that she was auditioning for something. Shona exchanged a quizzical glance with her boss.

'Come on now, Gavin,' said Hanlon. 'DI Oliver would be such an asset to our project, I hope you've brought her on board?'

'Of course,' Baird assured him.

'We might have a future chief constable here. Project like this is always good for the CV.' Hanlon beamed at them. 'No offence to you, Gavin.'

'None taken,' said Baird.

Shona smiled tightly. 'I'm very happy where I am but… thank you for the vote of confidence.'

'Inspector.' Hanlon gave her a little bow, running his eyes across Shona's figure, lingering on her neckline. He smiled. 'Excuse me.' Turning, he raised a hand and hailed a handsome, silver-haired man Shona recognised as a BBC Scotland news presenter. 'Alastair!' Hanlon set off like a vivid yellow speedboat through a sea of black suits.

'Why am I here, exactly?' Shona rotated the stem of her champagne glass between her fingers.

'Same reason I am,' said Baird, not looking at her. 'To celebrate the launch of the new crime prevention initiative and all the improvements it's going to bring, and to make sure we're all on the same page.'

Shona stared at him. Just what was he implying?

'I don't have to tell you the difference this will make to our budgets, and the community,' he added piously. 'And an initiative this size doesn't happen without a few hiccups, a few minor indiscretions. As local chief it falls to you to make sure some over-zealous officer doesn't balls things up.' He raised his eyebrows, seeking confirmation that she'd grasped the full implications of what he'd just said. The message was clear. I expect you to make this work, whatever it takes. You're either with me or against me. Time to choose a side.

'Ah, here's your husband.' Baird drained his glass as Rob arrived. 'Another drink?'

'No, thank you.' She put her hand over her glass. 'I'm driving.'

'No, no need for that. There's a room booked for you both here. Make a night of it.'

Rob's smile widened but Shona shook her head. She knew it wouldn't end with the free drinks. There would be a late meal, then somebody would mention the casino. No one was going to put temptation in her husband's way. Before she could answer, a tall, slim woman, polished to a hard shine, took Baird's arm. She wore a tight red dress made up of strips of fabric and her blonde hair was swept up into a complicated knot. On someone else the clearly expensive dress might have looked cheap, but this woman had the figure and authority to carry it off.

'This is my wife, Nicola,' Baird said with obvious pride. They shook hands, Shona aware how smooth and pale Nicola's hand felt in her own sun-browned, sea-roughened grip.

'What a wonderful evening, I'm so glad you could make it,' Nicola said, as if she was the hostess. 'The area where I'm a councillor will be greatly improved by this initiative.' Nicola was obviously in full, sound-bite mode. 'We aim to cut the re-offending rate, which is frankly atrocious, through a series of projects to educate these people to be better members of society. I think it's important for those of us who've been lucky in life to provide a moral lead. I just hope the people we're trying to help appreciate it.'

Rob smiled and nodded but Shona knew he hadn't been listening to a word Nicola said. Other people's problems bored him, and if he was thinking about Nicola at all it would be how she got in and out of the intricate wrappings of her dress and whether she was wearing any underwear.

It was the familiar prejudice, the deserving rich and the undeserving poor. 'Crime is a social issue, not a moral one,' Shona said flatly. 'The only difference between people in poverty and the rich is money. Cash in the bank doesn't give you a more refined morality, often the opposite is true.' And it doesn't give you carte blanche to be a condescending cow, she refrained from adding.

'Well,' said Nicola, momentarily lost for words, 'that's an interesting point of view.'

Shona could have sworn she saw Baird smirk at Nicola's discomfort, but he quickly suppressed it and, clapping his hands together, suggested they track down some canapes. He slipped his arm around Nicola's waist and guided her away.

To Rob's delight he spotted old friends from Glasgow University Business School and after much back-slapping and introductions to a group of red-faced, boisterous men who Shona thought looked like bankers, or a word close to that, he disappeared with them to the bar.

Detective Chief Superintendent Malcolm Munroe came up to her, stiff in his dress uniform. 'Shona, good to see you. Bit of a carry-on, this.' He sniffed over his ginger ale. 'Money better spent elsewhere,' he added, indicating a loud group at the free bar. Shona was mortified to see Rob among them.

'A high profile initiative with the business community to cut crime must be a good thing, sir.' She guided Munroe to a quieter spot away from the bar. 'I hear you're retiring soon.'

'Yes, I've done my bit. It would be good to go out on a high, leave a legacy.' He nodded. 'You did well with Op Fortress, I hear. I did the right thing putting you in charge in Dumfries,' he congratulated himself. 'Do you miss London at all?'

'Not at all,' Shona assured him.

'Keep in touch with your old boss, DSU Harry Delfont?'

'No,' said Shona evenly. Why was Munroe asking that? Delfont had given her a glowing reference only because he wanted her out. 'We never had that much in common.'

'So, liking it in Dumfries? Land of Robert Burns. A fine part of the world.' Munroe looked like he was winding up to deliver a sample of Scotland's national poet when there was an announcement over the PA and Kenny Hanlon bounded onto the stage to a roar of applause.

In the manner of a TV evangelist, Hanlon greeted a stream of celebrities, business leaders and senior police officers who pledged their commitment to the project. After a carefully choreographed ten minutes, the TV cameras were finished, and it was the turn of the photographers. Various combinations of people were corralled onto stage, officers lining up to have their picture taken with celebrities. Even Munroe was caught in a burst of flashlight like a rabbit in the headlights, a fixed grin on his face as he gripped Kenny Hanlon's hand. She should find Rob and escape before they came for her. Hanlon's jovial face beamed from the stage but as the cameras turned away and the lights dimmed his resting expression seemed to her to have a reptilian edge, the yellow eyes a predatory watchfulness.

When she finally located Rob at a corner table strewn with empty glasses he put up only a brief resistance. He shook hands with his old university friends with promises to keep in touch and followed her unsteadily towards the foyer. They were almost at the door when *The Enterpriser* himself stepped in front of them.

With the show over, Hanlon also appeared to have been sampling his own hospitality. Shona sidestepped his attempt to drape an arm around her shoulder. 'Oh, you're not going now?' He stuck out his bottom lip.

'So sorry.' She smiled regretfully. 'Our daughter's expecting us home and we have guests arriving tomorrow and… business is business.' She winked in a fair impression of *The Enterpriser*'s opening titles.

'Ha.' Hanlon laughed, obviously delighted with this homage to his brand. 'What a cherub you are. Oh, you must stay.' Shona managed to duck an attempt to take her face in his meaty hands.

Shona smiled through gritted teeth. She linked Rob's arm firmly. He had a look of bemused amiability on his face, having lost the thread of conversation a while back, but everyone seemed to be having fun. 'Cheers, big man,' he called boozily to Hanlon as Shona pulled him away.

They were heading towards the car park when Rob looked her up and down and said, 'Where's your jacket?' It was vintage Fendi and a present, too expensive to leave behind. Shona swore under her breath. 'Want me to go back for it?' he asked hopefully.

She raised her eyebrows at him and handed over the keys. 'Nice try. You sit in the car, I'll only be a minute.'

Shona retrieved her jacket. As she left the cloakroom she heard Hanlon's booming laugh and stepped back into a dim alcove hoping he'd pass. An angled mirror was set in the opposite wall. The reflection showed Hanlon and Nicola Baird. He was exploring the intricacies of her dress and she was doing nothing to stop him. After a moment they moved away.

Shona was heading back down the empty corridor when Baird appeared. 'That went well, didn't it?' he said, beaming.

'Yes, sir,' she said.

'Gavin,' he corrected her. 'You know, Shona, two good results on the drugs.' Baird bent closer to her, blocking her exit. 'What a great team we are when we work together.' His breath was hot against her ear. 'You and I are not so different, both clawed our way up, learned to make deals to get what you need. I can make it worth your while.' She could smell whisky on his breath. 'Rob looks pretty out of it,' he continued. Shona tried to take a step back, but he put out an arm to stop her. 'The room's booked. You could stay?' Baird was standing close, staring down at her with a hungry expression. The corridor was dim and stuffy, but the prickling of sweat on her back had nothing to do with the heat. She felt a wave of nausea, then anger. The drugs hauls had been down to her and her team. Baird had had nothing to do with it and now he thought he deserved, what? Her gratitude? Her fawning admiration? Her compliance? Her body?

She took a step to the side, but he followed, moving closer. She glared at him. 'Excuse me.' He leaned forward, pressing his body against hers, grabbing her wrists, pinning her to the wall. She felt a sick wave of panic. Turning away as he tried to kiss her, she spied Nicola coming along the corridor towards them, a deep frown on her face. 'I think your wife's looking for you,' she hissed at Baird as she prised herself free.

Why hadn't she seen this coming? She and Munroe were probably the only sober people in the room. Letting herself be cornered by Baird was pathetic. She hoped Nicola tore him to shreds. Her hands were shaking, tears of anger and shame pricking at her eyes. She should have engaged her copper's sixth sense, known what would happen. She was a fool. All she wanted to do was get back to Rob and go home.

As she reached the hotel entrance, Shona glanced back. Kenny Hanlon was talking to a frowning Baird. They looked at her keenly before Hanlon gave her a theatrical wave. As Shona turned and walked away, she had the distinct impression that both *The Enterpriser* and her boss were not nearly as drunk as they were making out.

Chapter 13

Despite the previous late night, and the fact it was Saturday, Shona arrived early for work the next morning in a well-cut dark grey suit and a lavender shirt. Murdo was already at his desk. She called him into her office and updated him on the prison visit with Gringo.

'Thanks for coming in. This should only take a couple of hours,' Shona said.

'No worries. My weekend on call anyway. What d'you have in mind?'

'We're going to have a chat with Isla's ex, Duncan Saltire. Do a background check on him first. Anything recent, firearms licence, the works. Don't want any nasty surprises.'

'You fancy him for the girl's killing?'

Shona nodded. 'Got to be in the frame. Saltire's a proto-politician who believes he's destined to lead. He has righteous anger and thinks he can get away with anything.'

'Thinks he's above the law.'

'Exactly. So, let's knock him down a peg or two.'

'I'll just finish typing up my notes,' Murdo said. 'I interviewed Isla's brother Lewis last night on my way home. He works in a fast-food restaurant, perfect cover for dealing. I wondered if he'd joined some arm of the family business, but he wants nothing to do with the Corrs. Threw some light on their appalling home life. Gave me a number for Isla's older sister, Eva. She's twenty-four and lives in Australia. I came in early to phone her. She got out quick, did a nursing degree then bolted for the other side of the world.' Murdo shook his head. 'Thought since she'd been away for so long she'd take the news okay, but she was in bits. Burdened with guilt, said she should have protected her little sister and wants to come back for the funeral. I told her it might be a wee while 'til Cumbria release the body, but we'd let her know.'

'Had she any recent contact with Isla?' Shona asked. She took a multi-vitamin pill and two Ibuprofen from her desk drawer, swallowing them down with bottled water.

Murdo shook his head. 'They didn't speak. Eva's first reaction was to ask if their father was responsible for Isla's death. Tells you all you need to know about that family.'

'Jesus,' Shona rubbed her forehead and took another swig of water. 'Did we confirm Paddy's state of health with the doctors?'

'Aye, he's out of the picture. Can barely walk. Marie's got a full time job caring for the bastard. I wonder she can stomach it.'

Shona crossed to the whiteboard and erased Paddy Corr's name with her finger, rewriting it at the bottom of the list. In its place she wrote Duncan Saltire. She replaced the cap on the marker and tapped the new name. 'Okay, Murdo. Let's see what this guy can tell us.'

–

Duncan Saltire's address was a property tucked in a quiet street not far from the centre of Annan. The house was a respectable double bay-fronted semi-detached built of red sandstone, which he'd inherited from his parents. Around that time, he'd changed his name from Duncan Ferguson to the more patriotic Saltire, the name for Scotland's national flag. The only sign of the house's noteworthy occupant was the heavy locks and the CCTV on the solid Victorian front door. The letterbox was sealed. Mail could be deposited in a locked metal container by the front gate. The background checks on his recent activities had come up clean, not even a parking ticket.

Murdo pressed the doorbell. Somewhere a tinkling sound from another era echoed. A shadow moved behind the peephole and Saltire himself opened the door. Short and lean, he was dressed in a white shirt with a light red willow pattern, cuffs rolled back to reveal muscular forearms. He wore jeans and his feet were bare. His fair skin was rosy from the shower and his cropped blond hair and moustache still wet.

'Yes?' he said, his face expressionless. Murdo and Shona held up their badges. She saw a flash of annoyance. 'Suppose you better come in.' He stalked off down the Milton tiled hallway, leaving the officers to follow. 'I've a meeting, you'd better be quick.' Murdo closed the door behind them.

They found him seated on a brown leather Chesterfield sofa in a tastefully decorated room that looked out over a neat back garden. The lawn ran down to a high brick wall topped with razor wire. Saltire was not looking at them but pulling on black socks. 'Our march permits are all in order. Or are the police wasting resources checking up on peaceful political campaigning while crimes committed by illegal immigrants go unsolved?' A pair of polished brogues lay on the carpet. 'What's this all about?' He didn't invite them to sit down.

'Isla Corr,' said Murdo.

Saltire said nothing, but Shona saw the missed beat, the fraction of a second when Saltire hesitated. Eventually, he said, 'What about Isla Corr?' He finished with the socks and lifted the shoes towards him.

'We've found her body,' Murdo continued, sitting down on the matching sofa opposite.

Saltire took a moment to answer. 'What does that have to do with me?'

'We understand you were previously in a relationship with Isla. We'd like to know when you last saw her.' Murdo took out his notebook.

Saltire shrugged. 'Wouldn't call it a relationship. I've not seen her for some time.'

'If you could be more precise, sir? This is a serious matter.'

Saltire gave a quizzical tilt of his head. He smiled. 'If this is official, maybe I need my solicitor?'

'If this was an official interview, you'd be down the station,' said Murdo flatly. 'We could do that if you wish. I'll radio for a squad car to take you in. Cancel your meeting. Call your solicitor if you like.' Murdo got up and buttoned his suit jacket in preparation to leave.

'Okay,' said Saltire, glancing at his watch, then motioning Murdo to sit down. 'I haven't seen Isla for a good few weeks,' he continued. Murdo raised his eyebrows, inviting him to be more precise. 'It was the Sunday of the Electric Forest Festival at Lanrig Castle, I'd just got back. She was waiting.'

'So,' Murdo flipped to the calendar pasted in the back of his notebook, 'Sunday, July 29th, that would be. What did she want?'

'She just dropped in to say hello.' Saltire slid one foot in his brogue and began tying the laces.

'What did you talk about? Did she seem distressed? Worried? Anyone threatening her?'

There it was again, the shrug. Confident the crisis had passed, Saltire pulled on the second shoe. 'Not that I know of.'

'Was Isla blackmailing you?' Shona had remained standing just out of Saltire's eyeline. 'Because you're the father of her child?' He turned and glared at her with such venom she knew she'd hit the mark.

. He concentrated on his laces. 'You'll need a court order to pursue that misguided idea.'

'Isla was fifteen and an addict. I believe the Sons of Scotia take a dim view of drugs.' Shona held up a campaign leaflet lifted from the hall table. On the front, a group of men marched behind the Scottish flag, a white diagonal cross on a blue background. Inside the leaflet was a declaration that they were taking back their country from a list of undesirables that included drug addicts, thieves and immigrants. Prospective supporters were urged to help at animal sanctuaries and hand out food and leaflets to white homeless people.

Saltire got up and walked slowly towards Shona. His posture became stiff as he sought to increase his meagre height. He leaned his face in close to hers and pulled up his unbuttoned shirt cuffs, showing her the inside of smooth pale arms, lightly covered in red-blond hairs.

'See any tracks? Think I don't believe what I say?'

'Do you believe it enough to kill for?' Shona challenged, her face impassive.

Saltire stared at her. 'To die for your beliefs is to become a martyr for your cause.'

'That's not what I asked you.' Shona kept eye contact. 'We have a witness who says you were harassing Isla.'

Saltire looked away first. 'I didn't kill Isla. I wanted her to join us.'

'But she refused? You wanted her back?'

'I was not having a relationship with Miss Corr.' Saltire returned to the sofa and sat down.

'But you argued the last time you saw her?' Shona took a seat next to Murdo.

'We had a lively discussion,' he continued. 'She needed something to believe in. She'd been clean before but lacked faith and direction. Our organisation would have looked after her, kept her off drugs, given her purpose in her life. A pure and united country is something to work for.' He was warming to his subject – Saltire as saviour.

'Did she ask you for money?' Shona said.

'I offered her a Tesco voucher for food but that was all.' He shook his head. 'You know we set up a food bank in Glasgow for white people, local people, and they shut us down. What sort of government wants its people to starve?'

What sort of human being denies another food based on the colour of their skin, Shona wanted to ask. Instead she said, 'Thank you for your time, Mr Saltire. We'll be in touch if we have any further questions. We'll see ourselves out.'

Saltire got up and held out the leaflet. 'Take this with you. Things are changing in Scotland. When the time comes, it might help you decide to do the right thing.'

They arrived back at the station and Murdo went upstairs to do further digging on Duncan Saltire, promising to call Shona at home if he found anything.

'Ma'am, your daughter is here,' the desk officer told her.

Shona checked her phone. No missed calls. Becca was studying at her friend Ellie's place for the day. What was she doing here at lunchtime? Perhaps she'd finished early, come into town and Rob wasn't answering his mobile for the obligatory lift home. Shona turned to go out into the public reception, but the desk officer stopped her. 'No ma'am, she's in here.' He indicated the cells and lowered his voice. 'The registration number you gave us. Uniform stopped the car for speeding, the lads were in it. Your daughter was with them. There was cannabis in the vehicle. I think you'd better have a word with the custody sergeant.' He pursed his lips, unhappy to be the bearer of bad news.

Two years before, at her previous school in London, Becca had been caught with a small amount of cannabis. At the time Shona had failed to identify any furtive behaviour linked to drug use, but no one can fool a mother like her own child. 'Thank you,' she said. Her knuckles showed white as she gripped the handle of the custody suite door. It buzzed open.

'Rebecca,' Shona barked, her face incandescent with anger. Becca, wearing ripped black jeans and a black hoodie, was perched on a metal bench opposite the custody counter. Her knees were drawn up to her chin, an attempt to make herself as small and unobtrusive as possible. Her dark eyes widened with apprehension when she saw her mother. The duty officer nodded to a room opposite and Shona hauled her daughter inside, slamming the door.

'I didn't know they had the stuff.' Becca was indignant. 'Why don't you trust me?' Her lip trembled and Shona could see she'd been crying.

'You know why,' Shona replied. 'You swore to me you'd never do this again.'

'I didn't!' Becca yelled. 'It was them. It was just a tiny wrap of resin.' She calmed herself down a moment, shrugging. 'The whatsit fiscal won't do anything cos they're seventeen and first timers. Don't sweat it, Mum.'

'Don't what?' Shona shouted, infuriated by her daughter's knowing air. 'I'm a police officer, Becca. Have you stopped to think how this affects me? My own daughter, dragged into the station.'

From Becca's expression, Shona could tell the thought hadn't even occurred to her. 'Sorry, Mum,' she mumbled.

Shona took a deep breath. She was livid, but a slanging match with her daughter wouldn't help. 'Do you want to get expelled, again? What will the school say? Why were you even in the car? These lads are two years older than you.'

'We were just in town and they pulled up. They said me and Ellie could go with them to McDonald's, get a burger. They're all right really. I was just trying to make friends. It was only a bit of weed. I wouldn't touch it. I've got more sense.' Becca folded her arms and slumped against the wall.

'You've let me down, Becca. I thought when we left London, we'd put this behind us. You know I lost my mother to drugs. I see every day what it does to people. Do you honestly think I'll let you throw your life away on the stuff?'

'I know, I know. You can trust me, Mum. But that's just it, kids everywhere do it. It's not just about partying.

Sometimes it's about helping to pass exams or relax after-wards, cope with anxiety.'

Shona thought about the Sweet Life group and the haul of prescription drugs she'd found at the warehouse. 'Have you been offered anything else? Pills?' She'd ask Ravi to check with the campus officers and his contacts at the hospital if there had been any more incidents.

Becca shook her head slowly. 'No. Oh God, you're not coming in to school to do a talk, are you?' Becca was so horrified Shona realised this might be the greatest punishment she could inflict.

'These pills are really dangerous, Becca. You've no idea what you're taking. Promise you'll tell me if you're offered, or even see, anything like that? It's important.'

'Okay, Mum. Chill out,' Becca agreed. 'One more thing.' She bit her lip. 'Dad doesn't have to know, does he? I mean, I haven't actually done anything wrong.'

'You kidding?' Shona almost laughed. 'It will be all round Kirkness by this evening.'

Becca looked so alarmed that Shona thought she might start crying again. 'Fess up, girl,' Shona advised. 'Right, let's go home. You need to tell him before he hears from someone else. And you can also tell him you're grounded for a month. School and home, that's it.' Shona held up her hand when it looked like Becca would protest. 'And if you argue, I'm having your new phone as well.'

Chapter 14

At Monday's case conference, Shona nodded to her team, 'Morning everyone,' then took a sip from her water bottle. It would be all round the station about Becca, but no one would dare say anything to her face. 'Murdo, let's get this briefing started.'

'Couple of weekend incidents…'

'Skip to the main event,' Shona interrupted. 'We'll take the other updates later.'

'Boss,' Murdo acknowledged. A few clicks on his laptop keyboard and a clip from a motorway surveillance camera, frozen in grainy black and orange, appeared on the screen behind him. 'Last night, the body of a young man was found on the hard shoulder of the A74(M) motorway. He appears to have fallen or been pushed from the back of a moving vehicle.'

Murdo picked up a small remote, the image on the screen sprang to life. A white van travelling north swerved and one of the back doors flew open. There was a sharp intake of collective breath as a man tumbled out, his head striking the tarmac, limbs tangled and lifeless as the momentum took him thirty metres along the carriageway, coming to rest beneath a large blue sign.

'Is that the Welcome to Scotland sign?' asked Ravi.

'Aye, it is,' Murdo replied.

Ravi frowned. 'What do we know about the victim?'

Murdo opened his notebook. 'The doctor who pronounced him dead said he'd received a cranial fracture resulting in traumatic brain injury, but he also had multiple facial injuries and broken bones consistent with the fall from the van. He estimated he was under thirty, lightly built and dark skinned. No ID.'

'Is the siting significant? Could be a racially or politically motivated attack?' Ravi said.

'Murdo.' Shona held out her hand for the remote. 'Let's keep an open mind at this point.' She ran the CCTV again, pausing at the moment when the victim left the moving vehicle. 'It does looks like there was someone else in the back.' A dark shape appeared as the door swung closed. 'He may have been pushed, fell out by accident or was trying to escape. Either way the driver didn't stop. The post-mortem will tell us more.' Her eyes met Ravi's. 'But yes, I'm not ruling out that he was dumped there on purpose.' A murmur ran around the table.

'Priorities,' Shona said, calling their attention back. She crossed to the map pinned on the wall. 'We need to find the van. It was stolen in the Newtown area of Carlisle last night. We tracked it leaving the motorway at the next junction, Gretna Green Services.' She tapped the map with her pen. 'The B7076 leads off from the services and into a network of smaller roads not covered by cameras. I've asked for uniform support to check businesses and farms along potential routes, Murdo will co-ordinate our efforts.' She looked around the table. 'Is Vincent still not back?'

'Op Fortress want Vinny Visuals a bit longer,' said Kate with a sigh. 'I gave him a call about the baby milk case, he reckons another week or so.'

'Okay, well image enhancement is our other priority. Kate, ask Vinny nicely which of his mates will do us a favour. Turn this around quick. I've got a date with Slasher Sue down the mortuary.' Shona began gathering her papers. 'Any questions?'

'The van was stolen in Carlisle,' said Murdo. 'Shall I give Dan Ridley a call? See if he can dig anything up for us down south?'

'Good idea, Murdo. We've access to the cross-border CCTV, but he has local knowledge. Right everyone, let's get cracking.'

As she picked up her notepad, Ravi came over and tapped her elbow. 'You asked for an update on that Sweet Life business?' he said quietly into her ear. 'A drop-off in the OD cases at the Royal Infirmary, and only a few confiscations of pills by the campus officers. I know it's Op Fortress's remit, but I'll keep my eye on it.'

'Thanks, Ravi.' Shona smiled. If Baird and Op Fortress did their job properly, Becca and her friends would be protected, and that was one less thing to worry about.

–

Pathologist Sue Kitchen was waiting for Shona when she arrived at Dumfries Royal Infirmary, having travelled down from Glasgow University where she taught forensic medicine. Tall and broad with tightly curled short blonde hair, her green eyes studied you from behind thick square glasses. Her nickname referred to the speed with which she conducted a post-mortem and also her ten-year tenure as Scottish National Fencing Champion (Epee). Having given up competition, she now judged at international level and remained a passionate advocate for the sport.

Shona greeted her warmly. 'I was hoping it would be you. I missed you the other night at the STAC launch.' They set off down the corridor to change into scrubs.

'Had a Royal College of Pathologists meeting in London, didn't get back until late, so I managed to dodge that particular trial. How was it?'

For a moment she wondered if she might confide in Sue. As a woman in forensic medicine she was a rarity. Surely she must have encountered similar treatment to that meted out by DCI Baird. But what had really happened? Her boss got drunk and tried to kiss her. Her suspicions that a leading television personality was a manipulative, whoring creep who made her feel generally uneasy were confirmed? Both figured low on the scale of gender-based crimes. Sue might give her a look that said, you're a big girl and you know what will happen if you complain, and Shona did know. So she rolled her eyes and said, 'Yes, a trial is just the word for it.'

In the pathology lab, Slasher Sue lived up to her reputation and quickly set out her preliminary findings for Shona. The victim was male, between twenty and thirty years old and had died from the skull fracture. His ethnic origin could be anywhere from the eastern Mediterranean to northern India, including Greece, Turkey, Lebanon and Syria. Dental analysis of his amalgam fillings might narrow it down but would take time. His injuries were conducive with a fall from a moving vehicle, possibly following a fight. Toxicology and DNA report would follow, radiography would be done now.

They waited in an upstairs corridor, Shona checking with Murdo for any updates while Sue got them coffee from the machine. Shona took the scorching plastic cup from Sue, holding it gingerly by the rim and setting it down on the floor next to her chair to cool.

'How's Becca?' Sue said with raised eyebrows. 'I heard you had a little trouble.'

'News travels.' Shona shook her head. 'I think she and her friend made a poor choice getting into that car and I'm not sure I believe her when she says she didn't know about the cannabis.' Shona remembered the small paper packet thrown by the boy to Becca outside the Royal Arms in Kirkness. Was that drugs? She'd been too concerned about her daughter's near miss with the car to ask. 'I think she just didn't take it seriously. Becca reckons the two lads will get a police warning, but she's in for a shock. Word is the fiscal wants to make an example of them. She might offer them a written warning if they'll admit to it. It's not a criminal conviction but it will still be a black mark against their names and they'll have to disclose it in some circumstances. I've grounded Becca for a month, but who knows if that will work. My daughter seems to attract trouble like a magnet.'

'Is she thinking about university yet? She should have a look at Glasgow. She's quite tall, isn't she?' Sue mused. 'Make a good fencer. Physical fitness, strategic thinking. Give her focus.'

Shona smiled at her friend's attempts to recruit her daughter. 'Did you ever have a brush with illegal substances?'

'Too busy with fencing and medical studies. What about you?'

'I never liked the smell of weed and couldn't afford coke. Plenty of glue sniffers around. I was too busy shoplifting lipstick from Woolworths to do drugs.' Shona grinned, her brown eyes alive with amusement. 'But seriously, I knew it was a trap. I've said before how I grew up with my gran cos drugs got my mother. Perhaps I don't talk to Becca about it as much as I should, but she knows how I feel. Drugs, violence, poverty. All that misery. I saw it every day. All I wanted was to get a career and get out of the place.'

'And now your career takes you to just the sort of places you wanted to leave.'

'Yeah, there's the irony.' Shona waved her hand around the pathology corridor. 'But I get to hang out with interesting people.'

'Yeah, *dead* interesting people.' Sue laughed. 'Come on, the radiography should be done.' She drained her coffee. 'Let's see what else our friend on the slab can tell us.'

In a borrowed office, Professor Kitchen scrolled through the MRI and X-ray images on the screen. They catalogued a sickening list of injuries to the skull, ribs, spine and limbs.

'The skull fracture killed him. The chest injuries, his rib fractures, were acquired pre-mortem.'

'He fought with his attacker?'

'That's a reasonable conclusion in combination with the soft tissue injuries to his body. The other breaks were post-mortem, most likely due to the fall. His heart had stopped beating so no bleeding into the bone. All except the hands.'

Shona peered at the side-by-side, crisp black and white images of skeletal hands on the screen. 'What do you mean? Injuries from the fight?'

'Possibly, but not this fight. In acute fractures there are sharp margins, without sclerosis. These breaks had begun to heal.' She pointed to the dark threads of fracture on the

X-ray. 'I'd say they occurred two to four weeks prior to death.'

'If we are talking about a trafficked individual,' Professor Kitchen continued, 'he could have sustained these injuries on his journey or in an unregulated workplace. I'd expect damage to the fingers if they were defence injuries.' She balled her fist, landing a soft punch on Shona's shoulder, then held her hands out as if warding off a blow. 'In both these scenarios it's the phalanges, the fingers, that receive maximum impact. Here,' she indicated the image on the screen, 'it's the metacarpals, the long bones in the hand.'

While Shona was considering this her phone rang and Dan Ridley's name flashed up on the screen. 'Sorry Sue, I need to take this.' She went back out into the corridor.

'We've recovered the van,' Ridley said. 'Burnt out near Carlisle. Not much chance of forensics.'

'Okay. So, we know they drove north, the victim fell or was pushed from the van, they immediately left the main route and doubled back on unmonitored roads. What does that say?' Shona replied.

'Local knowledge. After the incident they ran for home, burnt the van and called a mate locally to pick them up?'

'That's what I was thinking,' Shona confirmed.

'But was this a deliberate act, dumping the body on the border?'

'Or it was an accident. They set off from Carlisle with another aim in mind, maybe heading as far as Glasgow or Edinburgh. This ruined their plans and they were forced to turn back,' Shona said. 'Either way, we're looking for at least two people in the van and a third accomplice, who possibly didn't know what happened, and went to pick them up. Maybe a taxi driver. Murdo's just put out a public appeal and it should be on the lunchtime news. Let's hope someone comes forward.'

'What if dumping the body on the border was a deliberate act?' Dan persisted. 'I keep thinking of Isla and where we found her.'

The potential connection to Isla had occurred to Shona almost as soon as she'd heard the details of the case. None of her team, not even Ravi, had picked up on that, but Dan had.

'Have you got Isla's PM report there? Can you check something for me?' Shona asked. She heard him shuffling papers against the background hum of the CID office in Carlisle. 'Did Isla have broken bones to her hand?'

'Yes,' he confirmed. 'Her left hand was missing when she was recovered, but the right showed multiple fractures to the hamate bone and the metacarpals.'

'Did these injuries occur pre-mortem?' Shona asked.

'Doesn't say. Why?'

'I'm with the pathologist now. The victim has broken bones in his hands from a historic injury. Two to four weeks ago.'

'So, you do think there's a connection?'

'The time frame is interesting. However, once Isla's body was in the Solway it would be impossible to predict she'd end up right on the border,' Shona said. Not even lifeboat skipper Tommy McCall would be able to foresee that.

'But to most people the whole of the Solway Firth is the border,' said Dan. Shona conceded he had a point. 'What if the deaths are linked?' he continued. 'Bodies deposited in the border, broken bones to the hands, similar ages and both from groups targeted by right-wing vigilantes. I keep thinking about what Gringo said, how Duncan Saltire was threatening Isla. I've been doing some digging on him, he's a nasty piece of work, links with the English Defence League and alt-right groups in Europe. Disposal and display of the bodies on the border could be a political act.'

'I know all about Saltire,' said Shona. 'But presently we have two deaths that could equally both be road traffic accidents. That was mentioned as a possible cause of death for Isla. Someone panicked, got rid of her body. Our new victim could have been a drunken disagreement that ended in him leaving the vehicle by accident.'

'But you don't believe that?'

'What I believe doesn't matter,' said Shona testily. 'It's the facts that count. The Procurator Fiscal needs to be convinced by the evidence.'

'Okay, but this case has cross-border implications. Let's get the evidence. Let me have a crack at Duncan Saltire.'

'If anyone's talking to Saltire about this it's Dumfries Police. I'll consider your request to sit in on the interview, Detective Constable Ridley.' Shona ended the call. He had a point about the border, but she wasn't going to be pushed into any course of action before she'd considered all the options. And certainly not by a detective constable still wet behind the ears.

Shona said her goodbyes to Professor Kitchen and headed back to the office. When she arrived Murdo and Kate were eating a late lunch at their desks. The opening credits of an afternoon drama played silently on the TV.

'Anything from the public appeal?' Shona asked.

Kate finished her sandwich and lifted a sheet of print-out. 'I'll read you a few. "A waste of police resources on scum who got what they deserved". Or how about that old classic, "they should go back where they came from"?'

Murdo raised his eyebrows at Shona. 'Sound like anybody we know?'

'Is this the Scotland we know?' Kate said. 'Never used to be this bad.'

Murdo dusted crumbs from his fingers. 'That's because we were united in our distaste for the English. Border rivalry. Expected really. You tanned their hides at rugby, but not this.' He shook his head.

'If you asked Ravi that question, he'd say it's always been around, but I take your point,' Shona said. 'This rise of right-wing politics, it's a different sort of nationalism.'

'If it's murder, will we be handing this over to a Major Investigation Team too?' said Kate sourly.

'At present it's an unexplained violent death. Toxicology reports will take a few days. Since there's no match with DNA or fingerprints on our database let's use that time to identify the victim. I spoke to the Procurator Fiscal's office. They want more evidence before deciding if this is a racially motivated attack, so first thing tomorrow we're going to have another word with Mr Saltire.'

Chapter 15

The next morning, Dan Ridley tapped on Shona's office door. 'Thanks for giving me a chance.' He smiled. 'I won't let you down. What time is Saltire arriving?' He shrugged off his dark suit jacket and rolled up his white shirt sleeves.

'He's coming in at ten, with his solicitor,' she replied, concentrating on the morning roll call of action points on her screen. 'No one's reported our victim missing. Without any ID, we need to consider if he was here unofficially, but let's avoid the term illegal immigrant. Time of death is fixed by the motorway cameras for 11.56 p.m.'

'Okay. I've done the background,' Dan said, holding up a photograph. 'You'd think he was a student, or your local barista, rather than a tech-savvy neo-Nazi.'

She looked at Dan sternly. 'I hope you've prepared a watertight interview strategy. Saltire's no fool.' She took his sheet of notes, scanned it, and checked her watch. 'Okay, good. If we can get him on the back foot he might let something slip.' She took a swig of water from the bottle on her desk and tucked loose strands of dark hair behind her ears. Smoothing the purple silk blouse into her navy trousers, she motioned Dan to lead the way. 'Let's have a chat with our very own hipster fascist.'

Duncan Saltire, and a portly middle-aged man with bulldog jowls who introduced himself as Ross Balfour, solicitor, were waiting downstairs. When they were all settled in the interview room, Dan opened a slim folder and laid out a series of slogans taken from the Sons of Scotia website.

'The Islamisation of the West. The Great Replacement. What's this all about?' Dan asked.

'I'd have thought that was pretty obvious.' Saltire sat back and crossed his legs. 'Immigration policy is a legitimate topic for political discussion.'

'Is that what you've been discussing with far-right groups abroad?' Dan consulted his notes. 'Generation Identity in France and the New Reichsfolk in Germany?'

Saltire said nothing. He adjusted the cuffs of his Harris Tweed jacket then sat regarding Dan, a slight smile playing beneath the blond moustache.

'Neither of these are banned organisations,' Ross Balfour interjected. 'What exactly is it that my client can help you with, Detective Constable?' he added, pointedly consulting the time on his phone.

Dan cleared his throat and opened a second folder. 'The body of a man was found on the motorway late on Sunday night. He was beaten, tortured and dumped by the Welcome to Scotland sign. It's possible he was a non-UK national, here unofficially. Your client is quoted as saying, "The borders of Scotland shall be defended by all means necessary." Is this what he meant?' Dan laid the post-mortem photographs out on the table. 'Perhaps you recognise him? Is this the work of the Sons of Scotia?'

Saltire picked up one of the photographs, a close-up of the victim's smashed face. He studied it dispassionately before tossing it back on the pile. 'Nothing to do with me.'

Shona rested her elbows on the table and returned Saltire's cool gaze. Eventually she said, 'On Saturday, you handed me a Sons of Scotia leaflet setting out your aims.' She took the leaflet bearing the marching men beneath the Scottish flag from her notebook and laid it on the table among the photographs. 'When the time comes, do the right thing, you said. Was that because you knew this killing was being planned? Were you hinting that I should look the other way?'

'I'll tell you what happened.' Saltire leaned forward, stabbing the images on the table with his index finger. 'It's obvious. An illegal immigrant falls out with a criminal gang. Maybe he didn't pay them enough, so they dumped him, leaving the taxpayers to clear up the mess. This is nothing to do with my organisation. Why are the police wasting time and resources on this?'

'Do you mean this interview or this crime?' Shona snapped back. 'Are you saying that a falling-out of thieves is no crime, particularly if the thieves are foreigners? Just let them cancel each other out? You and I have very different ideas of the right thing. It's my job to uphold the law. Justice is blind, it doesn't discriminate by the colour of your skin.'

'I'm saying, my party are saying, this is exactly why we need to keep these people out,' Saltire replied. 'Now if there's nothing else...'

'There is something else,' Shona said. 'You claim not to know this man?' Saltire nodded. Shona continued, 'Ever see him in the company of Isla?'

Saltire stared at her. 'What has this to do with Isla?'

'Their deaths share certain features. Would you know if they were friends? Lovers perhaps? That would be a powerful motive to someone with your views, wouldn't it?

Quite a humiliation, your ex, former drug addict, *alleged* mother of your child,' she carefully emphasised. 'Taking up with an immigrant, illegal or otherwise. The media and your political opponents would love that.'

Saltire reddened, balling his fists.

'Where were you the night before last?' Shona continued. She'd seen Saltire had a temper at their first encounter. Getting him rattled was their agreed strategy. Dan turned a page in his notebook, a list of supplementary questions ready.

The solicitor began to intervene, but Saltire held up his hand to stop him. 'Let me make one thing clear, DI Oliver.' He smiled tightly, quickly recovering his composure. A useful skill for a politician, or a criminal. Shona watched the red tinge of ire fade from his pale skin. 'Times are changing. Scotland is changing,' he continued. 'The Sons of Scotia have enough public support to press our message through legitimate means, through social media campaigning and the mainstream political process. We don't need to go around killing people to get what we want.' In his confident smile she saw the sickening truth of his statement. 'As for Isla Corr, she made her own decisions. She was a former friend I tried to help. That help was rejected.'

'You haven't answered my question. Can you account for your movements around midnight the night before last?'

Slipping his phone from his pocket he gave her a pitying look. 'Oh Shona, don't you read the news?' Scrolling through, he held up a BBC Scotland website story detailing a speech Saltire had made at a business dinner in Glasgow that evening. The list of attendees included a former Lord Provost of Glasgow, a member of the Scottish Parliament and Shona's favourite celebrity businessman Kenny Hanlon. 'It started at eight p.m. and I was there until around one a.m. I stayed at Ross's flat.' He indicated his solicitor next to him, who nodded. 'We had a brunch appointment in the city next morning and I caught the train home afterwards.'

'How did we not know this?' Shona fumed as they left the interview. Dan followed her into the stairwell where she threw her notebook onto the window ledge and stood staring out at the traffic moving silently along the relief road. Below she saw Saltire patting his solicitor on the back as they got into their car.

'I'm sorry,' Dan stammered. 'I should have checked. If you want me off the case…'

Shona shook her head. 'No, don't be daft. It's just as much my fault as yours.' She sighed. 'You know, Duncan Saltire is, without doubt, a rancid bawbag of a man, but I hate to admit it, I don't think he's our killer.'

'A rancid bawbag…'

'It's a technical term we use in Scotland for…'

'It's okay, I get the picture. Very appropriate.' Dan grinned. 'But why do you think he's not involved?'

'Apart from the alibi?' She shook her head. 'He's just too… fastidious. He's all about control, and these deaths are messy, unpredictable. If these are vigilante killings by the Sons of Scotia, Isla is too close to Saltire, we were bound to make the connection. I can see the rationale for targeting an ethnic group. Asylum seekers, people who are already demonised by the right-wing media. But why kill a young mother, even if she was an addict? Big risk of a public backlash.'

'What about a breakaway group?' Dan asked.

'I've checked the intel on any current alt-right terror campaign in Scotland and there's nothing. I think if Saltire knew of anything, he'd be pointing us in that direction, hoping we'd take out his competition.'

'So, you don't think the deaths are connected?'

'Oh, I do think they're connected, I just can't put my finger on why,' she said, frustrated. 'Let's think about motive. No evidence that it's sexual. Neither victim was wealthy, so not robbery or ransom. So, if it's not sex, money, ethnic background, what is the connection? That's what we need to find.' She paused, turning the question over in her mind. 'How did you get on with Jamie Buckland?'

Dan let out a long breath. 'He admitted he knew Isla, that they'd been friends, but denied they had much contact now beyond the odd accidental meeting in a bar. My PCSOs have her photo and we've done the neighbours, but nobody wanted to speak to us. It's that kind of area.'

'We still don't know what she was doing with her time,' said Shona. 'Kate couldn't find any social media for her. Isla Corr was claiming benefits, but gave her old address and beyond fortnightly job seeker interviews she doesn't pop up anywhere.'

Dan was flipping through the pages of his notebook. 'Neither of our victims were reported missing. They're both from vulnerable groups, easy targets. Maybe that's the connection?'

'Go on.'

'We're looking for at least two people. What if they're a killing team? The dominant partner could be the individual in the back of the van, and the submissive partner the facilitator, the driver.'

'If you're thinking serial killers, you need at least three incidences to pursue that line,' she reminded him.

'What if there are more? Killings with body depositions on the border? There's a lot of rural areas...'

She held up her hand to stop him. 'Let's work with what we've got. We've already run it through HOLMES and other Home Office systems nationally, nothing's come up.'

'There's no link we can see between the victims, but what if the killers were mission-orientated, picking people they thought didn't deserve to live? Or hedonistic or control-driven, killing for pleasure or feelings of power? That fits for a duo.'

She shook her head. 'I've checked with Murdo. We don't get that many unexplained deaths here, so he'd know. I can't guarantee there are no unrecovered victims out in the hills, but what we need now is evidence.' Shona closed her notebook and leaned forward on the window sill, rubbing her face with her hands and shaking her head.

'What is it?' asked Ridley.

'I'm just thinking of Isla. Her father, Gringo, Saltire. Her killer or killers. How can a woman collect so many complete bastards in one life? You'd think the odds were against it. Poor wee girl.'

—

Murdo met Shona and Dan as they climbed the stairs back to the CID office. His face was set hard.

'Baird's been on the blower,' he said without preamble. 'That little shit Saltire has been mouthing off on social media about police harassment and general incompetence. Our local MP and MSP have both been complaining about the lack of arrests on the baby milk case and the media want to know if the motorway victim is a Nazi contract killing. It's not been the best of mornings.'

'Get the team together, Murdo,' Shona ordered, hurrying up the remaining steps. 'I'll have a word with Baird later.' She reached the door on the landing and turned to see Dan standing halfway up, unsure of his next move. 'Well, are you coming, or not?'

He took the stairs two at a time and followed Murdo in the CID office where Kate and Ravi were both sitting glumly at their desks.

Shona swept into her office. The Skype alert flashed on her laptop screen with DCI Gavin Baird's tag. She considered declining it, but if he'd already been onto Murdo he must have been looking for her. She checked her phone, which she'd switched to silent for the Saltire interview. A line of missed calls and texts showed up. Shit. She hurriedly shut the door, dragged her chair to the desk, smoothed her hair and blouse, and took a deep breath. She pressed the green phone icon and Baird's disgruntled face appeared.

'Shona,' he growled, 'what's been going on down there?'

'I'm sorry, I was in interview and couldn't take your calls, sir,' she said calmly. An image of when she'd last seen him, leaning over her in the hotel corridor, swam up in her mind. He couldn't have forgotten what happened. He didn't even have the decency to look shame-faced. She clenched her jaw.

'Mars Bar Munroe's been bending my ear. What's this about a Nazi killing gang patrolling the border picking off immigrants?'

It had Saltire's dabs all over it. He'd obviously been briefing the press as a result of this morning's interview. By showing his outrage Saltire was effectively protecting himself from criticism of his more extreme fascist views and positioning himself as a representative of all concerned citizens. She'd thought his connection to Isla would curb his tongue, but she'd been wrong.

'That's not our line, sir,' Shona replied. 'A suspicious death involving a man of Middle-Eastern appearance…'

'I know what it's about, what I want to know is what you're doing to wrap it up.'

'Sorry, sir?'

'I've seen the PM details. Fractured skull after falling from a moving vehicle. I've spoken to the fiscal, we agree that this is currently a road traffic accident until proven otherwise.'

'We think he was pushed from the van.'

'You *think*? Thinking isn't good enough,' Baird snapped.

'The driver didn't stop,' Shona countered. 'The van was recovered burnt out.'

'Then the driver is guilty of failing to stop at the scene of an accident. When you find him, or her, you can charge them with that offence. Understand?'

'Yes, sir, I understand completely.'

Baird cut the call. For a moment Shona stared at the empty screen. Then she slammed her hands repeatedly on the desk. This sleekit, sanctimonious bastard excuse for a DCI. All he cared about was his solve-rate, his budgets and his own career. When she was finished, she lifted her head, straightened her shoulders and went to do her job.

Chapter 16

DC Kate Irving pulled off her headphones and flopped back in her chair. In the far corner of the office Murdo was reviewing motorway CCTV footage with Dan Ridley. Ravi sat opposite her, beating out a rhythm with his pen on the desk. She caught his eye.

'What?' He smirked and resumed his tapping. But for once Ravi was not the target of her ire.

She leaned forward and hissed, 'What's he doing here again?' She jerked her head towards Dan.

Ravi dismissed her question with a shrug. 'Don't know what your problem is with him.'

'Suppose you fancy him too.' Kate pouted.

Ravi looked up at her, a mischievous grin spreading across his face. 'He is quite cute. What's the matter, girl-friend? Can't take the competition?' When Kate coloured, he knew he'd hit the mark and chuckled to himself. He was about to continue baiting her when the boss's door flew open.

'Murdo, Kate, Ravi. In here now.'

'Brace yourselves,' said Murdo under his breath. Dan slid into Murdo's now vacant seat and kept his head down.

Shona stood, palms flat on her desk. 'Updates?' She looked at each of them in turn, her gaze finally resting on Kate.

'I've collated the witness statements from the baby milk case,' Kate began. 'The CCTV from Cumbria is a match for two of our suspects but no reports of further thefts there. I'm still waiting for more image enhancement. Posters have gone out to the stores. Hannah and Ed are following up the calls. I pulled the mugshots of previous shoplifters. The witnesses couldn't give us a positive ID, but I've conducted three interviews and eliminated the individuals concerned.'

'So, as of now, we have nothing,' said Shona curtly. 'Ravi, can you do any better? Anything from Isla's family?' Kate, her face scarlet, dipped her head to her notebook and drew a line so heavy that the end of her pencil snapped.

'Do you want Dan in on this?' Ravi queried.

'I'll deal with DC Ridley in a minute. Get on with it,' Shona snapped.

'Okay,' said Ravi calmly. 'Isla's mother can't confirm Saltire as Ryan's father, but she isn't offering up any alternatives either. Isla was absent for six weeks before her estimated time of death. She contacted her mother only twice during that period to ask about Ryan. Said she was staying with a friend.'

'Any cell siting info on the phone?'

'Both calls made by Isla were from the Gretna area. Pay-as-you-go phone. Those masts cover a wide area. We've no associated address for Isla in the town.' Ravi closed his notebook.

'Okay. What are the family saying?'

'She was a nice kid, before the drugs. Smart. Good at maths. Her mother wanted her to be a bookkeeper. But the father, Paddy Corr,' Ravi shook his head, 'he's a deeply destabilising influence on the whole family. Still keeps Marie under the thumb. Drove a wedge between her and Isla. Dotes on the grandson, in a mini-me kind of way. Paddy hasn't got long. Probably a blessing.'

'Do you think Paddy had a hand in Isla's death?'

'I can't see any reason that he'd be involved. Isla was never there and she posed no threat to him.'

'So, no real progress.' Shona remained standing, glaring at her constables.

'I really don't think the family knew what she was up to, boss.' Ravi shifted in his seat, his customary bounce temporarily flattened. 'Marie's sister, Margaret, reckons Isla was an addict and her death is good riddance. She blames Isla for her own daughter Siobhan getting hooked and pissing off, leaving her kid behind. Marie's the only one upset about Isla, the rest of them couldn't care less.'

'Even more reason to get justice for her,' Shona exclaimed. 'One person, one agency after another, let this young woman down. I won't have her death swept under the carpet like she didn't matter.'

'It's okay, boss,' Murdo cut in. 'We want a result on this too.'

'Well, where is her social worker's input? Where's the timeline of her movements? Kate, I asked you to check with the multi-agency hub. Have you done it?'

DC Irving stopped doodling and sat bolt upright. 'I'll chase that up.'

'See that you do,' Shona ordered. 'All of you,' she pointed a finger at each of them in turn, 'want to keep the best cases from going to MITs? Then bring me something useful on Isla Corr, the baby milk thefts or the motorway victim by the end of the day, or Traffic will be gaining three new officers. Murdo, get Dan Ridley in here.'

They shuffled out, Murdo signalling to Dan that he was wanted. As Dan passed the subdued group Murdo whispered, 'Wee Shona's on the warpath. What do you English fellas use for protection? A cricket box is it?' He squeezed Dan's shoulder. 'Better get yourself one quick.'

Shona was rubbing her temples as Dan tapped the office door and came in. 'Anything I can do?' She was about to give him a suitably short and pithy reply but the sight of his hopeful, boyish expression and anxious blue eyes stopped her. She sighed and pointed to the chair in front of her desk.

'Isla's family think she was using again,' Shona said. 'Where are we with the toxicology report?'

'Still waiting.'

'Do us all a favour, get down to Carlisle pathology. Make a nuisance of yourself until they hand it over. We're losing momentum. If we don't get a break soon, we may never know what happened to Isla.'

'You think we should give up?'

She sighed again. Should she confide in him over and above her own team? He wasn't even her officer, but pursuing this case, following her lead, might land him in hot water with his own boss. 'Look, let's just say my boss and your boss are of a mind on this. They want these cases filed and forgotten. I know you're ambitious. You might want to think about your job prospects.'

'I don't need to think about that, boss,' Dan said firmly. 'Protect and serve, that's why I joined up.'

She smiled at his youthful naivety. But why shouldn't he mean it? She was just as resolved at his age and that hadn't changed. Fairness, integrity, diligence. These were the values that mattered, not just clear-up rates and paper targets.

'Off you go, let me know what you find. But Dan,' she stopped him at the door, her warm dark eyes full of concern, 'be careful.'

He nodded and was gone.

Shona returned to her desk. Craning her neck, she could see Murdo through the half glass panels of her office directing Kate, Ravi and two civilian assistants at the whiteboard, an action plan developing. On her screen, an email from Baird popped up requesting figures for a report. After his recent Skype performance, he could wait.

She scanned down through the heaving inbox. Among the internal memos, meeting reminders and inter-agency collaboration requests an email marked 'BWV' followed by Special Constable Johnstone's collar number and the date caught her eye. Attached were the body-worn video files covering the incident with the suicidal individual at the bridge. She'd told Johnstone she would arrange for the man's picture to be distributed, in case he made another attempt. It was a quick job, worth doing now. Besides, something about the incident, something half remembered, had been nagging at the back of her mind. Perhaps the video would show her what it was.

She clicked open the last file. There was the lifeboat arriving on scene, the searchlight illuminating the water, the terrified man clinging to the pier of the bridge. She could hear the Good Samaritan, the man in the scuffed leather jacket, reassuring him. Finally, he reached down and took hold of the jumper's wrist. Shona paused the video, taking it step by step until she was sure.

She went to the office door and called Murdo. 'Come and look at this.'

Next to the video, she pulled up the post-mortem pictures of the motorway victim's clothes. Murdo's eyes flicked between the moving image and the stills. 'Clothes look the same, but is it the same guy?'

Shona froze the video at the moment the man was pulled to safety. 'I think it is. Look at his hands. They looked odd at the time. I thought he was wearing finger-less gloves, but it's bandages.'

'The historic injury to the hands.' Murdo nodded. 'Was it another suicide attempt, him jumping from the van?' he said, doubtfully.

'I suppose we can't rule it out but, I agree, there are simpler ways to kill yourself.' Shona tapped the image on the screen with her finger. 'The jumper made off before he could be detained. We need to speak to our Good Samaritan.'

Murdo sat down in Shona's seat and played the video over a few times, peering at the screen. 'That's Tony Kirk-wood. I'm sure of it.'

Shona leaned in, resting her hand on Murdo's beefy shoulder, studying the man she'd seen through spray and darkness on the night of the rescue. His lean frame and deeply lined face said he might be a walker or climber. Shona put him in his fifties. 'Do I know him? Who is he?'

'Doubt you've met him. He's not a fan of the police, was in bother a few times when he was younger. Ex squaddie. He runs Hobo, the homeless charity off Irish Road.'

'Think he'll talk to us?'

'We can ask,' Murdo replied.

Shona took her hand from his shoulder with a final pat. 'Murdo, I swear there isn't anyone you don't know in Dumfries.'

Murdo frowned, considering the statement. 'Bound to be one or two,' he said, seriously.

'Well, I've yet to meet them. Come on, get your coat.'

—

Hobo had a boarded-over shopfront painted in a livid shade of green gloss. It was streaked with a fine drizzle, the rain adding to its general air of misery. The door was locked but Shona could see a light on inside, spilling weakly through murky glass panels. She rattled the handle and Tony Kirkwood's scowling face appeared behind the metal grill. He glanced at Murdo and his frown deepened. After a pause the door swung open. Shona and Murdo showed their badges as they crossed the threshold, but Kirkwood dismissed the IDs with a flick of his hand. 'What do youse want?'

A single bare lightbulb hung suspended from the ceiling. Battered sofas huddled in corners, the wooden floor covered by an overlapping network of mismatched rugs. The smell of fried food and damp lingered. Kirkwood regarded them, thumbs hooked in his jeans pockets, a posture of sullen defiance he had been perfecting since an early age.

'I was on the lifeboat called to Sark Bridge the other night. I saw you,' said Shona.

'What were you doing there?'

'Waiting for you to fall in.'

A flicker of amusement crept across the harsh expression. 'And you'd have hauled me out, would you?' he said sceptically.

'Well, it was before I'd met you,' Shona replied casually.

Kirkwood's lined face cracked into a grin. 'Ballsy wee thing, aren't you?' He turned to Murdo. 'Bet she keeps you on your toes.' Crossing to a sofa, he motioned them to sit down. 'I'll say nothing about my clients, so don't ask.' He took a cigarette from a packet on the low table in front of him and put it in his mouth, checking his pockets for a light, all the while fixing them with an uncompromising look.

Shona sat down next to him. 'The fella from the bridge. We think we've found his body.'

Kirkwood stared at her. 'Aw, fuck. Sami?' He threw the unlit cigarette back on the table and rubbed both hands across his shorn scalp. 'How do you know it's him?'

'The clothes, the bandaged hands. Did you not see the news? The body recovered from the motorway.'

'Didn't make the connection. So, was it suicide?'

'We're keeping an open mind,' Shona replied.

Kirkwood gave her a questioning look which she ignored.

'Was he a client?' she continued, nodding to Murdo, who opened his notebook and sat down opposite them. 'We'd like your help identifying him, so we can get in touch with his family.'

'You'll have a job. They're back in Syria, if they're still alive.' Kirkwood picked up the cigarette packet, offering it round. Shona and Murdo declined. He took one himself and lit it, shaking his head sadly.

'I'm sorry,' said Shona. 'This must be tough news to hear.' Kirkwood seemed genuinely upset. He'd saved the man's life, risking his own in the process, only to lose him again. Shona wondered how long you could work in a place like this before you became numb to the near daily doses of pain. 'How did you first meet Sami?'

Tony Kirkwood drew in a lungful of smoke and watched her with narrowed eyes, considering how far she could be trusted. She returned his stare with a steady gaze. Eventually he exhaled. 'His name's Sami Raseem. Found him on the street a couple of weeks back. Terrified. Injured here.' Kirkwood gestured to the backs of his own hands. 'Wouldn't go to hospital. It was an accident, he said, but it looked like someone had banjo'ed him. Black eye, the works. Patched him up. Fed him. Tried to get him to stay here, but he wouldn't. Said they'd come for him.'

'Who would come for him?' Shona asked.

'Too scared to tell me. My guess is the trafficking gang he was paying off. Said he couldn't do what they wanted any more. I don't know if that was because of his hands, he couldn't work, or...' Kirkwood shrugged, tapping the ash from his cigarette into a saucer on the table. 'One of the other guys called me when he saw him climb over Sark Bridge. Sami thought that was his only way out. The gang probably said they'd hand him over to the authorities if he didn't do what he was told, so he was just as frightened of the police as he was of the traffickers.' He smiled ironically at Shona. 'The gang had also threatened his family. I lost sight of him while the medics were checking him. They said the minute they turned their backs he legged it. Me and a couple of the guys had a look for him, but no luck.'

Shona sat forward. 'Do you know who this gang is?'

'If I knew who they were I'd be getting a few kicks in maeself.'

'I'd rather you left them to me.'

'Aye, mibbae,' Tony said, doubtfully, his eyes hardening as he expelled a line of smoke. Shona didn't doubt that he was capable of taking the law into his own hands.

So maybe Duncan Saltire had been right. Sami murdered by the gang who trafficked him. It wasn't a comforting thought. Shona wondered, if you put Kirkwood and Duncan Saltire in a room together, would they find common ground? Saltire's political rhetoric feeding Kirkwood's sense of righteous indignation. Perhaps they'd tear each other apart. The idea that they wouldn't was even more terrifying.

Kirkwood shook his head. 'Genuinely, I'd tell you if I knew. Traffickers. Modern slavers, they pick on people with learning difficulties, for fuck's sake. They find them easier to control.'

'Did Sami have learning difficulties?' Shona said.

'No, he was smart. English wisnae bad, spoke French and a bit of Greek too, all self-taught. I think I'd have persuaded him to turn the bastards in, given a wee bit of time. But he believed they could get to him anywhere. Looks like he was right.'

Shona thanked him. He promised to get in touch if he remembered anything else. 'And I'll give you a call, next time I fancy a swim.' He winked at her.

She and Murdo went back out into the steady drizzle. 'You were a hit with Tony-boy,' said Murdo, turning up his coat collar. 'Thought he'd show us the door.'

'It's my natural charm.'

'Nearly always fatal, so I've heard.'

'Less of your cheek, DS O'Halloran.'

'What?' he said, as she whacked him on the arm. 'I'm joking, so I am.' They walked to the end of the street where Shona's Audi was parked.

'Well, at least we have a name, poor fella,' said Murdo when they were seated inside. 'Isla Corr's death. Do you think it's linked?'

Shona pulled back the hood of her jacket. 'I don't know, Murdo.' She adjusted the rear-view mirror and tried to smooth the strands of dark hair, rapidly curling in the damp atmosphere. Then she sat back, staring through the windscreen, the drizzle turning the street outside to a wash of blurred lines. 'Two unexplained deaths. Whatever we have here, this isn't suicide or an accident, is it? This is murder, I feel it in my bones.'

Chapter 17

In Dumfries CID room, the two unidentified victims on the whiteboard now had names. Isla Corr and Sami Raseem. But how were they connected? For a long time, Shona stood before the photographs and scraps of information searching for links, but nothing fitted.

Murdo and Ravi had gone to tap their local contacts. Kate was putting in calls to the Police Scotland National Human Trafficking Unit and the Home Office and had even begged a favour from an old university pal, now with the Modern Slavery Helpline. She'd also demonstrated the value of her geography degree, talking Shona through the potential trafficking routes and points of entry. Shona called one of the specialist officers with the UK Border Agency operation at Stranraer Port to check if he had any leads. He promised to get back to them. Shona could only wait and pray all this effort would lead somewhere quickly. The time they could operate under Baird's radar was limited. Going over his head to Mars Bar Munroe wasn't an option. This close to retirement, her chief super wouldn't rock the boat with his favoured successor. Kate appeared at her side. It was late. She was off home, maybe Shona should go too.

Arriving back at High Pines she found a furious Rob sitting at the kitchen table, glaring at his phone. 'Didn't you get my texts?' he demanded.

'Yes, but I was already on my way. I wasn't going to stop to answer them.' She pulled open the fridge door, hoping for a meal to reheat, but found nothing. Rob often texted her with stuff that was sorted by the time she arrived home. God, she was sick of bread, but it would have to be another sandwich. 'What's the problem?' She took a packet of ham and dropped it onto the countertop.

'Becca's been excluded from school for a week.'

'You're kidding.' She turned to Rob, indignant. 'What do the school think that will achieve? She had nothing to do with the drugs. We've already grounded her. And when did excluding someone from an education improve anything?'

'It's not the drugs. She was fighting. Had some lass up against a wall, choking her apparently.'

'What?' Shona gapped at him. 'Jesus. At this rate I'll have to ASBO my own daughter. Where is she?'

'In her room.'

Shona tore up the stairs, hunger forgotten. She threw open the door to find Becca on the bed, her pale defiant face lit only by her phone screen.

'Right, I'll have that for a start.' Shona grabbed the phone from her. To her surprise, Becca didn't protest.

'You may as well, everyone's slagging me off anyway.' She glared at her mother.

'I'm not surprised if you go around assaulting people,' Shona replied.

'Oh, that's right, judge me,' Becca yelled back. 'They called Ellie and me names. Racist and homophobic abuse. They started kicking Ellie, taking her stuff.' She pointed a finger at her mother. 'You, you of all people shouldn't condemn me for defending someone and standing up for what's right.'

With stab of guilt Shona saw herself at the hospital, protecting Isla, beating Gringo to the ground. She winced at the unconscious bullseye her daughter had scored. 'I'm not judging you, but violence is never the answer.' She sat down on the edge of the bed. 'You were right to protect Ellie from these bullies, but look where your action's got you. Excluded and a black mark on your record. You should have reported this to the school, let them deal with it.'

Becca scoffed. 'Mum, you've no idea. They just ignore it, couldn't care less. Ellie came here with her family from Poland when she was three years old. She's white, so the school can't see the problem.' She leant forward, meeting her mother's gaze. 'This isn't like London. They haven't a single black or ethnic teacher. You just don't get it.'

'I do get it. I've had Ravi give the dedicated campus police officers a talk on just this issue. It's a first step and will help.'

Becca gave a weak smile. 'Yeah, Ravi's cool. If we had teachers like him, maybe things would change.'

'They will change, with more pupils like you.' Shona was surprised to feel tears of pride forming at the back of her eyes. She swallowed them down. 'Be patient, you'll get there.' Becca's motives might have been instinctive and sound but putting herself in the firing line was something she mustn't repeat. Shona knew the penalties of that approach. She hoped her daughter would learn this lesson and spare herself the inevitable consequences.

'About tomorrow? Am I still grounded?' Becca asked, tossing back her long dark hair in nervous gesture that Shona recognised from her younger self.

Tomorrow was Wednesday. Rob was off to the train station with B&B guests. Dental appointment? Other random family stuff? 'What about tomorrow?'

'Glasgow Uni open day. You were gonna take me?' Becca's eyes widened. 'Oh my God. You forgot!' Her accusation was tinged with glee at catching her mother out.

'I didn't,' Shona lied, quickly weighing up the pros and cons. She'd already cleared her schedule of meetings. Murdo could update her on leads. 'Okay, we will go to Glasgow. But Becca,' she took her daughter's hand and squeezed it, 'I want you to think seriously about what you've done. You need to understand your actions have consequences. You could jeopardise your future. No more smacking folk.'

'I won't, Mum. I promise.' Becca nodded seriously.

Shona returned to the kitchen and sat down heavily at the table. Rob gave her a questioning look. 'Sorted?'

'I think so. I'm taking her to Glasgow tomorrow for the uni open day, give you some peace. She needs focus and direction. Get her cleaning the B&B bathrooms when we get back. I want her to realise that will be her life if she doesn't stay out of trouble and get some qualifications.' Shona massaged her tired eyes with her fingers and shook her head. 'I understand why she did it, but...' She gave him a wry smile. 'God. It's like looking in a mirror sometimes.'

Rob raised an eyebrow. 'You can say that again.' He got up and kissed the top of her head, then placed the ham sandwich he'd made while she was upstairs on the table. 'Have some pity for me, darlin'. I get it in stereo.'

—

DCI Gavin Baird and Kenny Hanlon were finishing a bottle of chilled Louis Latour in the upstairs bar of a fashionable restaurant in Glasgow's Ashton Lane. They looked the part: a respectable Wednesday business lunch. Hanlon was soberly dressed in dark jeans and a sports jacket. If any fellow patrons recognised his celebrity status, they were cool enough to ignore him.

Baird was preparing to leave when Evan Campbell, one of Hanlon's trusted associates, pulled up a chair and joined them. At the STAC launch, Baird had watched Campbell tour the room like a heat-seeking missile, homing in on any information he could exploit. He had a reputation for clearing obstacles, making problems go away. His targets, initially uncertain, quickly recognised a top predator. These flaccid businessmen saw how they stood to benefit from a kill, if only they could avoid being devoured themselves.

Today Campbell was charming, groomed and fashionably dressed in a grey flannel three-piece suit. Smiling, he looked harmless, but in repose the skull-like face was chilling. It was like meeting death in Armani. Baird loathed him but, like the businessmen, he knew how much he could gain from this man.

Evan clutched Hanlon's offered hand in both his own, greeting him with the reverence of a Medici pope. Baird wouldn't have been surprised if Campbell had leaned forward and kissed his ring. Hanlon made a sad face. 'Gav is just leaving, what a shame. I'm sure he'd loved an update on the STAC issues we were discussing. Shall we order another bottle?'

The bar was filling up. Parents and teenagers from the Glasgow University open day had filed down the hill to the bars and cafes of the West End in search of refreshment. Baird shook his head and tapped his watch. 'Nicola has plans.'

Campbell nodded his understanding. 'Can't stop either, Mr Hanlon. Just popped over to say hello.' He tapped Baird's shoulder. 'Nice to see you too, Gavin. Here, I'll walk you out.'

Baird led the way. The stairs down to the street were narrow and dimly lit, with a sharp right-hand turn. They were halfway down when Campbell lunged forward, pushing Baird from behind. Baird tumbled down the remaining stairs, his face slamming against the tiled floor of the lobby. Stars bloomed before his eyes. The vignetting of his vision suggested a direct hit on the bridge of his nose.

'You going soft on us?' Campbell dragged him upright, growling in his ear. 'The Big Man willnae like it if you are. We've all got too much invested in the proper outcome to see it go tits up now. Solve the problem or I'll do it for you.'

He dusted Baird off as two teenage girls came down the stairs. 'Watch your step there, fella.' He gave the girls a charming smile, rolling his eyes at the pal who couldn't hold his drink. They giggled, squeezing past. Campbell pulled a still groggy Baird outside and propped him up in the shadow of the bar's awning.

Baird blinked, the lane swimming into view through involuntary tears. If he tried to arrest Campbell the man would claim Baird had tripped. Drink had been taken, conclusions would be drawn.

'Well, well. That's a coincidence,' Campbell said in a low voice. 'What a pretty pair they make, don't you think?' Baird screwed his eyes up, trying to follow Campbell's gaze. Then, just as he was seized by the arm, Baird glimpsed DI Shona Oliver, with a girl who could only be her daughter, coming towards him through the crowd. Campbell marched him quickly along the bustling lane in the opposite direction and out of sight.

–

Shona woke to the Sunday morning call of gulls across the Solway Firth. Thursday, Friday and Saturday had passed with frustratingly slow progress with both the baby milk case and the deaths of Isla and Sami Raseem. Tomorrow she'd have to make some hard decisions. To do that she needed to clear her head.

Rob had opened one of the full-length windows opposite their bed and the gauze curtains stirred in the faintest autumn breeze. Below, the polished silver of Kirkness estuary was marked by a single fishing boat drawing a plough-mark across its surface. Shona sat up and watched the boat's progress. Jimmy Hunter's *Orion*, out after some sea trout. She knew most of the local craft on sight now. She checked again that her RNLI pager was switched on. She was overcome by the urge to step off the land, let the sway of the sea dissolve away the tensions of her everyday life.

She dressed quickly and went downstairs to the kitchen. Rob and Becca were somewhere below on the guest level, holding a conversation that consisted of shouting to each other from different rooms above the sound of a vacuum. She left a note to say she'd be at the lifeboat station and slipped out the back door.

Coxswain Tommy McCall gave Shona the helm as they put the *Margaret Wilson* through her paces out on the firth. Then Shona coached a new recruit as he practised recovering 50 m of rope with a 15 kg weight attached in under

90 seconds, a test he needed to pass before his training could progress. The last of the season's holidaymakers lined up to cheer him on. The crowd broke into a spontaneous round of applause when, on the third attempt, Shona declared the recruit had done it. Tommy came out with the donations bucket and worked the crowd, who gave generously and felt they'd had their money's worth.

Shona spotted Becca in a small group gathered round Callum in the boat bay of the lifeboat station. He was giving a talk on the night bag, a satchel-sized extra loaded for shouts after dark, with extra flares. Becca was looking at the handsome village postman with a shy smile and rapt attention. If Becca ever showed any interest in joining the lifeboat, the RNLI wouldn't have her mother to thank for their latest recruit. When Becca spotted her approaching, her shoulders resumed their habitual slump and she scowled. 'Dad sent me to find you. Dinner's ready.'

Shona returned home with Becca, exhausted but renewed, to a family meal where Rob made them laugh with stories of his most eccentric university friends. He'd had a couple of trips to Glasgow since reconnecting with former fellow students at the STAC reception and had a potential investor for his restaurant idea. It was decided that their daughter would spend the remaining days of her exclusion from school helping Rob and both seemed happy with the prospect. Shona was just going to bed when Baird's name flashed up on her phone. What was so urgent that it couldn't wait until tomorrow morning? She felt a cloud pass across her sunny evening. She was tempted to decline it, but she'd only lie awake wondering what he wanted.

'Shona? Just a courtesy call, really. I'm about to make the final arrest on Op Fortress.'

Shona thought he sounded a little drunk. 'That's good news, sir.'

There was a pause. 'You know, if you crack the baby milk thefts, keep the local business community happy, you could be in line for my job. No one really cares about the deaths of a drug-addicted prostitute and an asylum seeker, it's giving the area a bad name. Tie the enquiries up now.' He paused again, breathing heavily down the phone. 'Trust me, Shona, it's best for everyone if you do.'

Chapter 18

On Monday morning, Shona pulled into the car park at Cornwall Mount HQ just before seven. She wanted an hour or so alone in the office before the team arrived, to gather her thoughts and plan a revised strategy. Dan Ridley's name lit up her phone screen.

'Morning Dan, how are you? Listen, I'm just having a wee think about our next move and I need to check some intel. Can I get back to you mid-morning?'

'I've got him,' Dan said, excitement bubbling in his voice. 'Your baby milk thief. I've got him.'

'What?' She grabbed her handbag. The driver's door flew open. 'Start from the beginning.' She clicked the electronic key fob over her shoulder as she hurried towards the building.

'I was in the office late last night,' Dan said. 'Patrol stopped a car for faulty brake lights. Driver tried to leg it.' Dan was getting into his stride now, relishing the news. 'They called me to talk to him. He was panicky and refused to give his name or address at first.'

'Yes, but how's he connected to our baby milk case?' Shona asked impatiently, scanning her pass and yanking open the security door.

'The car boot was full of the stuff.'

'You're kidding me.' She stopped on the stairs.

'Nope. Seventeen tins wrapped in black bags,' Dan said triumphantly. 'Plus, he's a possible for CCTV grabs of Suspect A. Right height and build.'

Shona punched the air. 'Dan, you've just made me a very happy woman.'

'That's nice to hear, ma'am.' Dan beamed.

'But listen, are you going to hold him for the motoring offences? I'd really like him up here.' Shona ran up the remaining stairs and into the empty CID office.

'That's why I'm calling you this early. Boss isn't in yet. No charging decision's been made. It's a bit complicated.'

'How?'

'There's some doubt over his identity. His English isn't great. We think his first language is Farsi. I'm waiting on a translator.'

'Where are you on the PACE clock?' Shona asked.

'We're fine. He was brought in just after ten last night, so we've got fifteen hours to charge or release. But there's something else. His driver's licence looks dodgy; it could be a fake. That means he's probably here illegally. We may have to hand him over to the Border Agency.'

Shona sat down at her desk and opened her notebook. 'Okay, what's his name?'

'He gave the name Imran Wazir and an address in Carlisle. I'm running ANPR checks on the car.'

Shona glanced at her watch. 'Dan, I can be with you in an hour. I'll find you a translator. Let's see how far we get before your guvnor arrives. Okay?'

'Yes, ma'am. I'll set up the interview.'

Shona was pulling the CCTV images from the white-board when she heard a noise behind her. DC Kate Irving hung up her coat. 'Morning, boss.'

'Kate, the very person.' Shona updated her constable on Dan's call.

Kate's pale grey eyes lit up with pleasure at the news. 'Want me to come with you to Carlisle?' she asked hopefully, her hand poised in mid-air in front of the coat stand.

'No, I need you here. Find me someone who speaks Farsi, I want a translator, quick as you can. We'll do it over the phone. I want him processed before the Home Office goons or immigration cart him off to a detention centre and I have to apply three weeks ago last Thursday, and in triplicate, to even talk to him.' Shona was brushing her hair back from her forehead and stuffing papers into her handbag.

'Maybe Ravi would know someone,' Kate said flatly. This was her case, she should be doing the interview with Dan.

'Why?' Shona challenged her. 'He's second generation Scottish Asian. His family came here from Uganda, his first language is Punjabi. Farsi is spoken mostly in Iran and Afghanistan. Did you say that because of the colour of his skin?'

Kate flushed. 'No,' she faltered. 'It's just…' She ground to a halt.

'You see, Kate,' said Shona, exasperated, 'it *is* a good idea. Ravi has contacts within the Pakistani community, here and in Glasgow, and that's relevant. He may know someone who speaks Farsi that we can access quickly. But when you field an idea, know *why* you are fielding it, and don't be fazed if it's questioned. Stick to your guns. Understand? Off you go, find Ravi.'

Murdo arrived just as Shona was running out the door, staring after her with a bemused look on his face. 'What's going on? Where's the fire?'

Kate returned to her desk and picked up her phone. 'Jesus. I swear serial killers take less pleasure in their victim's pain than she does,' she muttered.

Murdo raised an eyebrow at his DC. 'Okay, I'll get the kettle on. You can tell me in a minute.'

–

Shona pulled into a visitors' parking space at Carlisle Police Cumbria Division HQ shortly after eight a.m. Dan signed her in, taking her swiftly through to the custody suite.

'The duty solicitor is on standby, but Wazir's refused legal counsel,' Dan said. 'He's had something to eat and slept for a bit. I've arranged someone to sit with him. Custody sergeant is happy for you to interview him. Ready?'

Shona checked a text from Ravi. He had a friend, Shoku, an economics student who spoke Farsi and a bit of Arabic. Shona dialled the number provided. They would call in an accredited interpreter later. Was there a credible reason Wazir had this much baby milk in his car? If there was she'd be back at square one.

Shona explained to Shoku that everything she heard would be confidential. She could send a reasonable bill for her services. No charge, Shoku replied. Could Shona write her a reference for a translation company she was applying for? Shona smiled to herself. That was probably Ravi's suggestion, the kind of mutually beneficial deal that endeared him to both parties. It was exactly the sort of creative thinking that made him such a good officer. No dent in Shona's budget and a happy outcome for the student.

Imran Wazir sat in the interview room wrapped in a grey blanket. Even beneath the layers, Shona saw he was painfully thin. He shrank back when Shona and Dan entered, pressing himself against the wall, watching them with wide brown eyes. The vulnerable adult chaperone next to him, a pleasant-faced, middle-aged man in chinos and a pink shirt; the stark contrast in their relative lots in life wasn't lost on Shona.

Shona sat down and smiled. Dan switched on the recorder. She introduced herself, holding out her small hand out until Wazir shook it. Shona handed her phone to Wazir. He listened with trepidation to Shoku's voice, speaking quietly in response to her questions, then passed the phone back.

'I've explained why he's here,' Shoku relayed to Shona. 'I asked if he's given his real name. He says he has and that he's from Isfahan in Iran. He came here via Belgrade. He wants to know, will he go to prison here or be sent back to serve his sentence in Iran?'

'Tell him we're not the border police, we only want to ask some questions about the baby milk found in his car.' Shona smiled reassuringly and, setting her phone to loudspeaker, placed it on the table between them. 'So, is the milk for your family? How many babies are there? Seventeen tins is a lot of milk.' She watched Wazir as Shoku relayed the question. He didn't look at her, his eyes fixed on the phone.

'He just says it's for his family, that he bought them from a friend,' Shoku translated.

'What's his friend's name?'

'He doesn't remember.'

'Okay, how much did you pay? Did this friend give him a receipt?' Shona could see Wazir plucking at the edge of the blanket. 'Imran?'

At the sound of his name, Wazir looked up at her. In a flash, Shona was reminded of the night the lifeboat had been called to Sark Bridge. The expression of fear and hopelessness on Sami Raseem's face as he clung to the stone piers above the raging water. A man trapped. A man who saw no way out.

'He says he doesn't remember.' Shoku translated the murmured reply.

There was a knock on the door of the interview room. Wazir's eyes widened in alarm as a large, uniformed officer put his head in and asked to speak to Dan for a moment.

Shona touched Wazir lightly on the arm. 'It's okay.' She smiled. 'This is a good time to take a break. We'll get you something to drink.' Shona thanked Shoku. They'd call her back.

Outside in the corridor, Shona stretched, rolling her shoulders. A little further along Dan was talking to the constable, who shuffled through a series of photographs and pages of text. After a moment, Dan returned, his face triumphant. He held out a page for her to see.

'I asked for any ANPR hits on the car Wazir was driving over the last few months. He's been making regular trips up and down between Carlisle and Dumfries.'

Shona took the page from him scanning the familiar route she'd just travelled herself. 'That's good. It certainly puts him in the area on the day of the thefts.' She could see he was bursting to tell her something. 'What else?'

'I asked them to check his route into Carlisle. Did he trip any speed cameras?' Dan handed her a picture printout. 'He did. Two weeks ago.'

Shona studied the man hunched over the wheel. Without doubt it was Wazir's exhausted and fearful face caught in the camera's flash.

'Look there.' Dan was leaning over her shoulder, his finger pointing not to the driver but at the thin man with the high hairline in the passenger seat. He too had been caught clearly by the speed camera. Shona held the photograph closer, then looked up at Dan, her dark eyes wide. 'Is that our motorway victim? Is that Sami Raseem in the passenger seat a week before he was killed?'

'Worth asking our friend in there, isn't it?'

'Let's do that,' said Shona firmly. 'Let's see what's really worrying him, the faulty brake lights or that the police have just picked him up for murder.'

'Do you think Wazir pushed Sami from the van?'

'He hasn't accounted for the baby milk in his car. If we can prove it's been stolen, this is large-scale thievery. He's in the frame for Sami too, until we know otherwise. But Dan, one thing.' She drew him further down the corridor away from the custody desk. 'I want him back in Dumfries before this goes any further.'

'I'm not senior enough to authorise it.' He shook his head. 'Shit. It will have to be Lambert, my DCI.'

'Will he give me Wazir, do you think?'

'Not a chance,' said Dan, glumly. 'He'll either want the arrest himself or to hand Wazir straight over to immigration to avoid the paperwork.'

Shona pressed her finger to her lips, thinking for a moment. 'Okay. So, here's what we do.' She lowered her voice, glancing along the corridor to the custody desk. 'Right now, you're holding Wazir for a traffic offence. Get on the phone to the CPS, have him charged and bailed. I'll tell the custody sergeant he's wanted for questioning over a number of thefts in Dumfries. Soon as he's bailed, I'll re-arrest him. We won't wait for an escort team. I've been liaising with you on another cross-border case, you have business in Dumfries, and you're prepared to assist me in escorting the prisoner in the name of efficiency and good relations. Get this right and we'll be out of here before Lambert's blown the froth off his morning cappuccino. What do you say?' Shona could tell that the prospect of getting one over on his boss was almost more appealing than cracking the baby milk case and potentially the motorway death as well. Dan grinned. 'I'd say he was more of a tea with milk and two sugars man, but yes, you're on.'

Chapter 19

Shona drove and Dan sat in the back of the Audi with Wazir in handcuffs. She angled her rear-view mirror to keep watch on him. Wazir slumped in the seat, staring out of the window as the rolling green landscape of Cumbria gave way to the big sky of the Solway and they crossed the border from England into Scotland. Dan was checking regularly on their charge, offering him water and a thumbs-up sign. Shona decided they would head to Dumfries' Loreburn police station, where their arrival would cause less comment than at Cornwall Mount.

'I'll book him in,' she said to Dan as they took their prisoner from the car. 'All right, Mr Wazir, let's go.' She smiled politely. They took an arm each and guided the cuffed man through the door to the custody area. While they stood waiting for the sergeant to process their suspect, Shona leaned across to Dan and said quietly, 'I've updated Murdo. He's getting together everything they have on Sami Raseem. We'll get started once the official translator and a solicitor get here.'

'Sami is dead.'

Shona and Dan turned around, startled by the voice. Imran Wazir was looking at them sadly, his long body draped like rags over the coat hanger of his bones. 'Sami is dead. You can't ask me about Sami. They will kill me.'

'Mr Wazir, I know Sami is dead, we found his body,' Shona said, taking a step closer and gazing up at the anguished face. 'I need your help finding his killer, or killers. Do you understand what I'm asking?'

He nodded solemnly. 'I understand. I'm sorry I trick you. I thought you would just hand me over to the border police if I could not speak English. Just be another illegal to be sent away.'

'Mr Wazir,' Shona began, 'I understand you are afraid, but your residency status is not my concern. Crimes of theft and killing are my concern. You help me and I can help you. While you're in my custody, you have my word, no one will harm you.'

But Wazir just shook his head and stared at the ground. The custody sergeant, a burly man in his early fifties, was watching this exchange over half-moon glasses. He raised an eyebrow enquiringly at Shona.

'This is Imran Wazir. I've arrested him for theft.'

'Not often we get a DI in here, ma'am. Missing life on the streets?' the sergeant said, tapping on his keyboard, his eyes on the screen.

'I like to keep my hand in,' replied Shona, deadpan.

'Well, there's a Rangers and Celtic game coming up. Fancy signing up for some overtime? Eight hours in the rain, with beer cans full of piss thrown at you?'

'Aye, sounds grand, but I'll pass on that.' Shona turned back to her prisoner. 'Mr Wazir, we'll talk again in a minute. Think about what I've said. I can help you. The sergeant will ask you some questions. Would you like Shoku to translate for you?'

Wazir shook his head again. 'No. Thank you. I understand.'

Dan took Shona aside. 'What if he was the one who killed Sami?' he asked.

'If, at any point, it looks that way, I'll stop the interview and arrest him for murder. We'd better take his clothes for forensics. Let's just get him talking, part of him clearly wants to.'

Dan helped an officer bag Wazir's clothes. Shona called DC Kate Irving over from HQ. When she arrived, it quickly became evident that she was expecting to conduct the interview on the suspect. Her face fell at Shona's request to collect the clothing bags. Kate shot Dan a look of icy malevolence before stalking out of the custody suite and slamming the door. Shona felt a stab of guilt. It was Kate's case; she had worked hard. But only Shona and Dan knew about the traffic camera photograph. She had to find out what Wazir knew about Sami Raseem, and by questioning him herself, Shona was protecting Kate from future comeback from DCI Baird. She had her best interests at heart, but she doubted her DC would see it that way. Shona pulled open the door and called her back. 'Kate, a word.'

'What?' Kate looked surly and defiant.

'Don't dawdle with those forensics. I want you to draw up an interview strategy for Wazir. Keep it tight, just the baby milk thefts. You and Ravi will be handling this, I want you back here in an hour.'

'Oh, okay,' she said, brightening up. She was too pleased with the prospect to question Shona's reasoning or even Ravi's inclusion.

'I need a quick word with Wazir first. Go on, get moving.' Shona shooed her out of the building.

Wazir sat in the interview room wearing a grey sweat-shirt and jogging pants. He turned the plastic cup of tepid black tea in slow circles. 'You say you can help me. How?' He studied Shona and Dan sitting across the table from him with a calculating look.

'I will talk to the Procurator Fiscal's office. In Scotland they decide what charges you'll face, if any, based on the evidence the police put forward.' Shona held out her hands, palms up. 'But it's like balancing a scale.' She raised her left hand. 'We have evidence against you that will lead to criminal charges and potentially imprisonment.' Then she raised her right hand to the same level. 'You help us to bring others to justice. If you've been a victim of human trafficking, if you've been threatened or made to do things against your will, we will protect and help you. That is the law in Scotland.'

'You can judge a life that way?'

Shona folded her hands and rested her elbows. 'I'm not here to judge your life. I'm here to find out how Sami Raseem died, bring closure to his family and friends, wherever they are, and see that those who are responsible pay for their crime.' She took the speed camera photograph Dan had found from the file and placed it on the table. 'You and Sami.'

For a moment Wazir stared at the picture in silence, before picking it up. He could deny it was Raseem. Identification linking this image with the post-mortem photographs would require expert witness testimony to persuade the fiscal, a long, difficult and expensive process. Shona held her breath. But the man before her didn't deny it. Instead he pressed the picture to his chest and began to cry. He tipped back his head, his lips forming the words of a silent prayer as the tears ran back across his prominent cheekbones and into his cropped hair.

'What will happen to his body?' he said, rubbing at his tears.

'It will stay in the mortuary until his family are contacted. If they can't be found then the local council will arrange a funeral,' Shona said softly.

Wazir nodded. 'Samir Karam Raseem,' he said when he had composed himself. 'He came from Syria. Aleppo. He believed his family were still alive, in Damascus. Maybe they have fled now to Turkey.' He shrugged. 'I don't know. The men who brought him here said they knew where his family was and would kill them if he tried to escape or did not do what he was told. They said this to me also.'

'Thank you for identifying him,' said Shona quietly. 'We will try to trace his family and ensure he has a proper burial.' She set the cold tea aside and poured out a fresh cup of water, encouraging him to sip it. 'Imran, may I call you Imran?' She waited for the nod. 'A short time ago, Sami tried to end his own life. I was there at the bridge when he tried to jump into the river. He was helped by a man called Tony Kirkwood, who works at a charity in the town. Do you know him?'

Imran twitched his head in a way that said maybe he did, but he was undecided on whether to commit himself.

'Tony wanted Sami to go to the police, but Sami was afraid of the people that had trafficked him in to Scotland,' Shona continued. 'What sort of work was Sami doing to pay back the gang?'

At this, Imran's face creased in anguish and Shona thought he might cry again. After a moment, he bit his lip and said quietly, 'It is best you know what sort of people you chase. Sami was paying off his debt with children. That's why he tried to kill himself.'

Next to her, Shona felt Dan shift uncomfortably in his seat and rub his forehead as if trying to erase the mental images that had sprung up. She took a breath and pressed on. 'What do you mean, Imran? What did Sami do with the children?'

'I was working in a warehouse, moving boxes. But Sami, he deliver children like they were boxes. He did not know what happened to them. He thought people use them for bad things. That's what made him sick, here...' he touched his finger to his head, '...and here.' Imran pressed his hand to his heart. 'That is why we took the baby milk.'

'For the children?' said Shona, puzzled. The thought that this gang was trafficking babies for whatever purpose made her stomach tighten further.

But Imran shook his head. 'No. We take the milk to make money, to get away. Sami meet this girl and she tell him we could sell it online and make enough to escape. We could pay the traffickers, go and find our families.'

'So, what happened?' Dan asked.

Imran looked at him for a moment. 'You were kind to me when you did not need to be. Gave me water.' He made a thumbs-up sign, recalling their journey from Carlisle. 'So, I will tell you.' Imran leaned forward, resting his elbows on the table. His eyes became hard. 'The traffickers found out. They beat us and sell us to a new boss. He say, it's okay. Keep taking the baby milk. It's a good business, I look after you, give you new cars. Just pay me a little of what you earn. Sami handled the money. The girl, her name Ella, she help him. We hoped to take, maybe two thousand tins from all over Scotland and England. It was easy to walk in and out like a family. We would sell them with Ella's help on eBay. Make enough for everyone.'

'What went wrong?' Dan said.

'We sell them for less. Ella? I did not trust her. She a whore and took drugs. One day, she just vanish,' Imran said bitterly. 'The boss took what money was left and say we need to pay more. We are trapped like fish in a net that is smaller and smaller. We are squeezed so we owe him the breath in our mouths.' He shook his head.

Shona had watched Imran as he told his story. She saw the emotions flit across his face like cloud shadows across the surface of the sea. Hope, cunning, triumph. The grey bitterness of betrayal and defeat. As he spoke, an idea, caught on the breeze, floated before her eyes. Finally, it zig-zagged down, coming to rest like an autumn leaf landing on the water.

'This girl, Ella,' she said into the silence. 'What did she look like?'

Imran shrugged. 'Small, like you, but blonde. Always the short clothes.' Shona took out her phone and scrolled through. She turned the screen to Imran. He glanced quickly at it then turned away and nodded. 'That is her,' he said with a look of disgust. 'That is Ella. I hope you find her.'

'We have found her, Imran. Her name is Isla. Isla Corr. She's dead,' Shona said. 'She died about six weeks ago.'

'Yes, Ella, that is her name. She is dead? Then I am sorry for her family,' he said solemnly.

'I think whoever killed Sami killed Isla too,' Shona said.

'They will kill me now for sure,' he said, resigned.

'No,' said Shona. 'I meant what I said, we can protect you, but you must tell me all you know. Who was the boss who took the money?'

'I never knew his name. He just the boss.' Imran brushed his face with his hand. 'His face was thin. He had good clothes and a black car.'

'Did you meet anyone else? Any of Isla's friends?'

He nodded slowly. 'There was a man of business. He help her sell herself for drugs.'

'You mean her pimp? Do you know his name?'

'Jay, I think his name was Jay.'

Shona pulled up another photograph on her phone and showed it to Imran, who nodded. 'Yes, that is him.'

She tilted the phone to show Dan. On the screen was the arrest photograph of Jamie Buckland. 'Okay, Imran. Thank you. Let's take a break. Now, I want you to think very carefully about a solicitor.' She held up her hand when he began to protest. 'You have been very helpful, and I will do as I promised, but a legal representative can assist you in other ways. Please think about it.'

Shona and Dan watched a custody officer walk Wazir along the corridor to a cell.

'Do you think he's telling the truth?' Dan hugged his notepad to his chest, his eyes full of excitement.

'On Friday, Kate and I phoned around for trafficking intel in this area. There was none,' Shona said, chewing the end of her pen. 'Wazir said there's children involved. I need to flag this up with Division and the child protection agencies right away.'

'Perhaps there were no traffickers, and Wazir killed Sami and Isla to take the money for himself?'

'It's a possibility, but where's the money? He seems genuinely afraid of someone, more afraid than he is of us. He was almost relieved to get the story off his chest and get into that cell. If what he said is true, this is a gang that haven't been picked up by any agency yet. They must have a slick operation.'

'What are we going to do?'

'You're going back to Carlisle. Find Jamie Buckland. Wazir's identified him as Isla's pimp. I want that little bastard picked up and any of his associates. Ravi and Kate can get the baby milk case progressed. That will give us time.'

'Time for what?'

'Time to work on who killed Isla and Sami, and why.'

Chapter 20

Dan pulled up behind a squad car parked outside the flat-fronted, red brick terrace on Carlisle's Currock estate. As he got out, the two officers came to join him on the kerb.

'No sign of life,' said the larger of the two, hoisting up his utility belt and adjusting his stab vest. 'Should have tagged the bugger, least we'd know if he was in there,' he grumbled. 'Job for the Jocks this, aint it? Waste of bloody time.'

'Look,' said Dan patiently. 'Just go round the back. Check he doesn't scarper.'

The officer scowled at him but did as he was told, slouching down the street and disappearing into an alleyway.

Dan hammered on the door. The second officer peered through the dirty net curtain of the downstairs window but shook his head. Somewhere inside, a dog barked. Dan flipped open the letterbox. The hallway was filled with a stale, empty silence. 'Mr Buckland, it's the police. Open the door.' He checked with the cop at the rear of the property. Nothing.

Pulling out his mobile, he called the station. 'Has Jamie Buckland been in yet? He's on bail from the Dumfries Sheriff, reporting daily.' Dan listened to the tapping of a keyboard at the end of the line and the desk officer's reply. 'But that was three days ago. Is that the last time he was in? Why wasn't a no-show warrant issued? What do you mean, it's in progress?' Dan ended the call, shaking his head. 'Fuck.' He stared up the street.

The uniform officer had stood listening to the exchange. He rocked back on his heels, his thumbs hooked into armholes of his vest. 'That dog, sir.'

'What about it?'

'Your fella's a no-show? Might be lying dead in there. Can't leave the dog.' The officer gave Dan a knowing smile.

'Right, officer,' said Dan catching his meaning. He stepped back from the door. 'What are you waiting for? Kick the bugger in. But just remember,' he warned, 'you're catching the beast.'

They found the white Staffie pup in the kitchen, shut up in a soiled and stinking cupboard. It was delirious with joy to see them and ran trembling to the officer, who set down a saucepan of water which it lapped noisily. They searched the property but there was no sign of Buckland.

Dan called Shona. 'Bad news, boss. Buckie's legged it. Left his dog shut up. We can do the bastard for animal cruelty as well when we catch him.' The officer was rubbing the dog down with a wet towel, washing off the worst of the filth. It sat patiently, watching him with grateful eyes. The other constable came back into the kitchen with a metal tin. With his blue-gloved hand he pulled out a wad of cash and showed it to Dan. He dropped it back in the tin and held up four fingers.

'Shit,' Shona said. 'How long's Buckland been gone?'

'Last seen at the nick three days ago,' Dan sighed. 'Someone should have been round but they're still getting their arse in gear. Sorry,' he apologised, embarrassed by his force's lack of urgency. 'But listen, for someone who doesn't claim benefits and does casual bar work, there's a lot of nice stuff here.' He glanced around at the wide-screen TV, the expensive music system and high-end leather furniture. 'And we've just found about four grand in cash in a biscuit tin.'

'So, we're maybe talking alternative source of income, which fits with what Wazir said about him pimping girls,' Shona said. 'Okay, get an arrest warrant out. Put a trace on his phone. I'll make sure he's on our watch list too.'

'What if he knows we picked up Wazir?' Dan said. 'The money could be the proceeds from the baby milk thefts. Maybe he killed Isla and Sami and has taken off?'

'And left his cash behind? Wazir's got no love for the boy Jamie. He'd have handed him to us on a plate if he thought he'd killed Sami. But you're right, we can't rule it out,' Shona said. 'Do a house to house, ask the neighbours. I know you struck out last time, but we might get lucky. Listen, Vinny Visuals has just walked into the office, I've got to go. Stick with it. Update me later.' She ended the call.

—

'Vin, how's it going, pal? Dazzled by the city lights?' Murdo said, shaking his hand as the rest of the team said their hellos. 'Pleased to be back slumming it with us yokels?' he continued. 'Bet the beer prices in Glasgow were an eye-opener.' Vincent pulled at the sleeves of his plaid shirt, swept back his long, dark fringe and smiled shyly at his colleagues.

'Vincent, welcome back. Got a minute?' Shona indicated her office.

When he was seated, she said, 'We've been a bit stretched without you.'

Vinny nodded, crossing one long, denimed leg over the other, resting the ankle on his knee. 'Yes, ma'am. Kate said.' He eyed Shona nervously.

'Op Fortress must have been interesting work?' she said, smiling.

'Aye, great experience. Got all the best gear,' Vinny said with enthusiasm. 'Encrypted cloud storage, remote access. Top facial recognition software.'

Shona was sure Baird's team had secured the biggest bite of the budget cherry and, sooner or later, this would be reflected in her own slashed overtime resources. 'Sounds great.' She nodded, taking care to look impressed. 'You still got access to the CCTV footage?'

'Yes,' he said, shifting in his seat. 'Suppose so.'

'So, you could find me this guy?' Shona showed him a picture of Jamie Buckland.

'I might need permission from DCI Baird's team,' Vincent said uncertainly.

'Oh, don't worry,' Shona reassured him. 'I'll square it with DCI Baird. Buckland's not one of their targets. He's a potential witness on another case, but we picked him up on the drugs raids. Local address, Carter Street in Dumfries. Op Fortress were monitoring it.' She lowered her voice and turned her brown eyes up to him. 'I'll confide in you, Vincent. He's not been seen at his home address in Carlisle. There's concern for his safety. We need to trace any associates locally.'

'Fine, ma'am. If you think it would be okay,' said Vincent, reassured. 'I'll get onto it.'

'Can you do it now?' Shona turned her laptop towards him.

'Now?' Vincent said, a little surprised.

'Like I said, there's concern for his safety. Matter of urgency.' Shona fixed him with a firm look, pushing the laptop towards him.

Vincent shrugged, then shuffled forward in his seat. 'What's the address? Carter Street?' He began tapping into the CCTV cloud storage and an interface appeared, split into three areas. One showed the surveillance file images, the next detailed the watch team, and the third listed the suspects identified. The camera covered the entrance to a house and part of a street. Jamie's name was tagged to four separate clips, corresponding to visits he'd made to the target address, a dilapidated squat, the hangout of dealers and punters. Shona ran down the other names, all known to her and all currently on bail. She'd send uniform round for a chat just in case he showed up at any of their gaffs.

Vincent ran the videos, using the specialist software to jump to the sections that contained Buckland.

'That's odd.' He frowned at the screen. 'Some of this is missing.' He pointed to the time clock counter in the corner. It skipped forward in gaps ranging from a few seconds to nearly a minute.

'Who could have removed it?' Shona asked, peering over Vin's shoulder.

'No one,' he said. 'Well, maybe someone on the team. Thing is, there's a continual recording requirement, like a master tape. It's in case the defence say we've tampered with the evidence, made it look like something it isn't.'

'Yes, I know,' said Shona. 'Maybe there's a master somewhere else.'

'No, this is it. Something's gone wrong. If Op Fortress fails in court because of this...' He looked pale. 'We'll get the blame... I might not get another big job. Baird will side-line me, won't he?'

'Don't worry,' Shona soothed, patting him on the shoulder, 'no one will blame you. It will be one of the tech guys who've messed up.'

'But I am the tech guy,' said Vinny with a mixture of horror and indignation.

'Look.' Shona understood Vinny's distress, but she couldn't cope with a grown man crying in her office over an IT issue when she'd a couple of murders to crack on with. 'Can you give me a copy of the corrupted file?'

'It's not corrupted...'

'Just the file then. Give me a copy. I'll call Baird and we'll sort it out.'

A chink of light appeared in Vinny's darkness. 'Okay.' But then he frowned. 'I'm not sure your security clearance...'

'Vincent, listen to me.' Shona's patience was at an end. She drew herself up. 'I am a detective inspector and your line manager. I'm also the only one who can pull your cahoonies out of the fire if Baird does his nut over this. Get that file on my desktop now, then go back out there.' She pointed to the CID room, where a few heads had turned. 'And get on with the backlog of work your little jaunt to Glasgow has left us with. Understand?'

'Yes, ma'am,' said Vinny, hurriedly downloading the file and signing off.

'Murdo will give you the list,' Shona said, stepping back behind her desk and folding her arms. She stared after him as he scurried out of the room. Murdo caught her eye and winked. She shook her head in exasperation, pointing at Vinny's retreating back and the cases on the whiteboard, and mouthing 'get busy' at him. He replied with a good-natured salute.

Shona ran the file. There was Jamie Buckland arriving at his mate's house in Dumfries, then leaving twenty minutes later, sports bag in hand. In the intervening period, there were two short gaps totalling about ninety seconds. Without Vinny Visuals spotting the anomaly of the clock, Shona would never have noticed them. If it wasn't a software problem, a glitch or corrupted file, why would anyone remove such a short section? She played and replayed the file, searching the street for clues, but could find nothing. What would take about forty-five seconds? The file dated from a month ago, just before the raids. She watched a neighbour pull up, get out of his car and go into a house further up the road. She looked at the timer. He was in view for thirty-eight seconds. The gaps were enough time for someone to arrive at the house and then leave. The question was, who was that person, and why did Op Fortress want their identity kept secret? Only Jamie Buckland and DCI Gavin Baird could give her the answer. One was currently missing and the other was the one person she didn't want to ask.

Chapter 21

Shona was on her way home. Ravi and Kate had completed the interview with Wazir and the fiscal had approved the theft charge. He would go to court in the morning. Wazir had identified Isla and Sami as the two other people in the baby milk CCTV photographs. A lawyer had advised he apply for asylum and Shona had asked for protected custody as a potential witness, while her enquiries were ongoing. Finally, they had their baby milk thieves, but Wazir had remained tight-lipped about the traffickers and they were still no nearer to finding out who had killed Sami and Isla. She hoped for an update soon from Dan, saying he'd tracked down the elusive Buckland. Maybe the boy Jamie would bring them a step closer to the answer.

The low, late September sun shone directly in her eyes as she headed west along the A75. It caught every rise and undulation of the land, painting it with soft purple shadows and turning the wind-blown grass on the road-side to a fiery, flickering fringe. Shona thought of the estuary and the curlew's call on the mudbanks. She looked forward to the view from home.

The phone rang, showing Becca's name. She clicked the hands-free button on the steering wheel. 'I'm on my way back, darlin'. Be with you shortly.'

Becca's breath came ragged and uneven through the speaker. 'Mum… Mum.'

Shona felt the hairs rise on the back of her neck. 'What's wrong? Are you okay?'

'I was on my bike… I fell… a car hit me,' Becca said, the wind-noise almost overwhelming her weak voice.

'Where are you?' Shona sat forward straining to catch every detail.

'On the top road… near the farm.' Becca sobbed. 'I can't… get up.'

'Stay on the line, darlin'. I'm putting you on hold to call help. Don't hang up.' Shona flicked the controls and dialled 999. 'This is DI Oliver, Dumfries CID, I need an ambulance. RTA on the B712 by Mainsgill Farm. Casualty is a fifteen-year-old female cyclist. Attending. ETA,' Shona glanced at the clock on the dashboard, 'ETA, fifteen minutes.' She switched the call back to Becca. 'I'm coming, Becca, stay where you are. Keep talking to me. I'm coming.' Then she floored the accelerator and pulled out, overtaking a lorry and several cars, flashing her head-lights at an oncoming tractor before leaving the A75 and weaving through the tight lanes.

'Where are you?' Shona searched the road ahead, lined on each side with solid, drystone walls, but could see nothing. Then she gasped; the pink metal paintwork of Becca's mountain bike lay crumpled like a sweet wrapper against the moss-green of the verge. 'I see you, I see you.' Shona pulled the Audi to a halt, grabbed her phone and flew out of the car. 'Jesus.'

Becca was lying in a shallow ditch. She was dirty and wet, blood smeared across her face. She clutched her right arm, which flopped at an odd angle, the bone above her wrist protruding through the skin. Her bike helmet lay next to her showing a long split where it had struck the loose granite stones on a tumbled section of the wall.

'Becca.' Shona choked back a sob, tearing off her suit jacket and folding it under her head. 'The ambulance is coming. Where are you hurt?'

'My arm.' Becca tried to sit up. 'My head hurts.' Her skin was clammy and waxy white, the skin around her eyes and mouth blueish. Shona was afraid she was going into shock. She glanced at the shattered helmet and tried not to imagine what it signified. How bad was her head injury? Stay calm, deal with what you see.

'Don't move,' Shona warned her. She quickly assessed her daughter's condition, then ran back to the car for the first aid box and the thick tartan blanket she kept in the boot. She covered her, wrapping a triangular bandage loosely over Becca's wounded arm. Becca sobbed, biting her lip in pain, but she let her mother continue. 'Okay, okay, it's done,' Shona reassured her. 'Got to get you warm. Can you tell me what happened?'

'I was going up to the farm for eggs. A car hit me. Drove off.' Becca blinked slowly. She was shaking, letting go now that her mother was here. Cold, and dropping adrenaline levels were taking their toll.

'Did you know who it was? Did you recognise the car?' Shona was keeping her conscious and distracted from the pain. She dialled Rob's number. He was close by, at High Pines. Why hadn't Becca called him?

'No one comes up here, 'cept the farmer.' Becca's words were slurred.

'Your dad's not answering.'

'Out… with Uncle Sandy.'

Shona needed Rob, here, now. But there were other people she could rely on in an emergency. Her lifeboat family. Skipper Tommy McCall answered on the first ring. 'Becca's hurt, accident on Mainsgill Farm Road. Bring a spinal board.'

Tommy was there in minutes, his white Ford Transit van roaring up the tarmac track and pulling in behind Shona's car. 'For goodness' sake, Becca. What have you done to your mother now? She's enough to do catching robbers without you flinging yourself off bikes.' Tommy stroked Becca's hair back from her forehead, feeling the clammy skin and the rapid pulse beneath her chin. She gave him a weak smile in return. He confirmed Shona's diagnosis of concussion and compound tib-fib fracture. 'Pop this on for me, Becca, just to protect your neck.' He slipped the cervical collar over her head while Shona contacted the control room via Tommy's VHS radio.

'Ambulance is still thirty minutes away.'

'I'm not happy with her condition,' Tommy said quietly, his face grim. 'Let's get her onto the spinal board. We could call the helicopter, but it will be quicker to make our own way there. Agreed?' He waited for Shona to nod, then he turned back to Becca.

'Och, let's not wait for the slow-pokes,' he said, loudly. 'Becca fancies a ride in my van. Don't you, pet?' Becca looked back at him through half-closed eyes. 'Listen,' he said, half under his breath to Shona, 'I can't give her any gas and air, Entonox is contra-indicated for head injuries. Don't want her to slip under. Understand?'

Shona nodded, biting her lip. Then she squeezed her daughter's good hand. 'We're off to hospital, but we need to get you comfy for the ride,' she said brightly. 'I want you to take big breaths and be a brave girl for me.'

Becca cried out as they slid the orange plastic board beneath her. Shona could feel the panic rising in her own chest. Now Tommy was here, and Becca's rescue was not her sole responsibility, the anguish she felt as Becca's mother was pushing at her composure as a police officer. It threatened to burst through, as unstoppable as the Solway tide. She swallowed hard and forced herself to smile. Becca was whimpering, rivulets of tears forming paths through the blood and dirt on her face.

'Not long now,' Shona said, watching Tommy run to the van, turn it round then jump out again to fling open the rear doors ready to load Becca inside. She tried Rob's phone again meanwhile, cursing under her breath as it rang out before resorting to voicemail.

'Let's go.' Tommy lifted the bottom of the stretcher, Shona the head, murmuring a stream of reassurance to Becca. They slid her into the centre of the van, between the old fishing nets, wet-weather gear and boxes of spare parts. Shona jumped in beside her as Tommy closed the doors and ran round to the driver's side. As they set off, Shona updated the 999-control centre that they were on their way in with the casualty.

With the motion of the van and her body held rigid by the stretcher, Becca was drifting into sleep. 'Becca, Becca, open your eyes for me,' Shona said desperately. 'Dad will be at the hospital, so be ready to give him a big smile.' She lay down full length next to the stretcher, protecting her daughter's battered body with her own, bracing them both from sliding around as Tommy took the bends and inclines at speed. The steel floor of the van dug into her hips and ribs as she clung on, whispering old family stories into Becca's ear like charms to ward off the darkness that pressed on them both. How Becca had tripped as a toddler and knocked her front tooth out. How she'd once fallen in the lock on their only canal boating holiday and been hauled out by her mother grabbing the red ribbon of her pony tail. When those ran out Shona turned to snatches of favourite nursery rhymes, books that her daughter had loved as a child. She pressed her face close to Becca's. 'Not long now, darlin'. Stay awake. The car that hit you, what did it look like?'

'Big car... black.'

'Did you see who was driving? A man or a woman?'

Becca tried to shake her head. She grimaced in pain, the collar restricting her attempt.

'How long, Tommy?' Shona shouted desperately.

'Two minutes. How's she doing?'

Becca's eyes were rolling back in her head, showing white. 'Hurry, Tommy.' Shona was on her knees, checking her daughter's pulse and breathing. 'Becca? Becca? Come on, come on.' She rubbed her daughter's good hand, hauling her back as she teetered on the edge of unconsciousness.

Tommy pulled into a chequered ambulance bay outside DRI's Emergency Department and jumped from the cab. A man in a dark green paramedic uniform came towards him.

'Can't park there, pal.'

'Aye? Well if I didnae have to do your job for you, I wouldn't.' He glared at the man. 'I'm Tommy McCall, Kirkness lifeboat skipper. We've an RTA casualty. Head injury. Get a trolley. Now.'

They slid Becca onto the trolley when it arrived seconds later. 'Okay, you can leave her to us,' the doctor said, but Shona found she couldn't uncurl her fingers. Tommy gently removed her hand.

'Come here.' He pulled her into a fierce hug. 'Becca's going to be fine. If she's anything like her mother, she'll be telling the doctors what to do in a minute.'

Shona was shaking, a howl gathering in her chest. It pressed against her throat, choking her breath. A plea to a god she didn't believe in. Please don't take my girl. Please don't take my girl. Please don't take my girl. Over and over, it filled her consciousness. She was spiralling down into a darkness where Becca was the only thing that mattered. She could feel Tommy's lean body and smell his musky scent of salt and oil. She clung to his firmness to stop herself falling.

Gradually she stopped spinning, resurfacing amongst the light and noise of the hospital. No one was looking at her, she was just one drop in a sea of sorrows that washed through this place every day. She saw a woman, her battered face pale and drawn with fatigue. An old man who had fallen, his eyes roaming the ward for something solid and familiar to fix on. A crying child.

Slowly, her training and her anger began to kick in. Someone had done this to her beloved girl. She wiped the tears away with the heal of her hand. 'You know the best bit of my job, Tommy?' He shook his head, she continued. 'Whoever did this, the fucker who hit my child with a two-ton car and drove off? I get to see they pay for what they've done.'

'Aye.' He took her by the shoulders, looking her in the eye. 'You know what's even better? You don't have to do it on your own.'

'I know. I know. You're right.' She gripped his hand. He gave her a tissue and she blew her nose. 'Thank you.' Then she turned away and took out her phone.

'Murdo, I'm up at DRI.' She briefed him on what had happened.

'Dear God. Are you all right, boss? I'm on my way.'

'Listen, Murdo, it's okay. Tommy's with me. There's some things I need you to do.'

'Anything.'

'Get a team over there, it's a crime scene. Pick up the bike. Talk to Hector McCartney who owns Mainsgill Farm. That's a dead-end road, see if he's had any visitors today.'

'I will. Who would do such a thing? To drive away from an accident like that? Nobody local.'

'My thoughts exactly,' Shona replied. Thank God Becca had her new phone on her. Rob had complained bitterly about the expense, but her old one wasn't reliable. Shona shuddered. Becca could have lain by the side of that road for hours. 'Thing is, if the driver wasn't going to or from the farm, then someone must have followed her up there. Becca's had a bit of bother recently. It might not be an accident.'

'You mean the drugs thing with the lads? Bit of tit-for-tat revenge? Surely not?'

'Well, they may think Becca got off lightly cos her mother's a police officer. Plus, they might have meant to scare her, but it went wrong.' She cleared her throat. 'There's something else, Murdo. Becca got suspended from school last week for lamping a bully, who was excluded too. Her family might also have a grievance. And Murdo...' Shona said. 'You know I can't touch this. It will have to be another officer.'

'Hitting a young lassie on a bike? The traffic guys will be on this like a rat up a drainpipe, don't you worry. I'll get Ravi to work it from our side and talk to the fiscal,' Murdo replied. 'Anything else, boss?'

'Can you get my car back to my house? It's still at the scene, keys are in it. Rob is at home, but his phone is switched off,' she lied. 'If you see him, get him to call me.'

'Righto. Give Becca our love. Let me know if there's anything else. Anything. We're all thinking of you, boss.'

'Thanks, Murdo.' Shona ended the call.

'The doc will be out for a chat as soon they've assessed her.' Tommy handed her a large china mug of tea. 'Here, drink this first.'

Shona looked at the cup, then sipped the hot, sweet tea. 'This isn't out of a machine.'

'No, well, the eejit who made the fuss about parking had a change of heart. Brought these from the crew room.'

The doctor appeared an hour later and told them Becca had gone to theatre to have her broken arm set. Shona could see her afterwards. They'd be keeping her for a few days to monitor her concussion, but otherwise, he didn't think there was anything else to worry about. She'd been lucky and wearing a helmet had probably saved her life. Overcome with relief, Shona thanked him and felt suddenly exhausted. The orange plastic chair was heavy and hard beneath her aching muscles and she realised she must look a mess. Her work trousers and white blouse were stained with mud and blood beneath an old RNLI fleece of Tommy's.

'After you've seen Becca, you should go home. I'll take you,' Tommy said. Shona nodded, unable to put up further resistance. He sat down next to her and patted her hand. She felt her head droop against his shoulder and fell into a light doze.

Two hours later, they were still waiting when Murdo arrived with Rob. 'Found him in the pub, not fit to drive,' Murdo said sternly, his mouth a hard line of disapproval.

Shona looked at the swaying, pale-faced figure before her. 'Where were you, Rob? You're supposed to be looking after her.' It was all she could think of to say.

Chapter 22

As Shona sat in the hospital waiting for news, DCI Gavin Baird stalked into the CID room at Dumfries HQ. It was empty except for a slim young woman sitting at her desk with headphones on. She jumped when she saw him.

'Hello, sorry to scare you. DC Irving, isn't it?' He extended his hand and fixed her with his best smile. 'I've heard good reports about your work. Cracked this baby milk case, I heard.'

Kate blushed and took his hand. 'A team effort, really. Weren't expecting you, sir. The boss went home an hour ago.'

'Oh, that's fine, it's a social call. I'm looking for Murdo,' Baird reassured her. 'Was in the area, thought I'd better get my old mate that pint I keep promising him.'

'Have you called him?' Kate asked. 'He went out on a job this afternoon but I don't know where he is now.'

'I did call earlier, left a message.' Baird pushed out his bottom lip in a comic display of petulance. 'Can't believe I've come all this way to see my old mate and he stands me up.' He eyed her. 'Don't suppose you fancy a drink?'

'Er, well…Yes,' Kate stammered. 'I've just finished here. I'll get my coat.'

'Excellent,' he said brightly. 'We'll take my car. You know I haven't eaten, maybe we should get a quick bite. Know anywhere nice?'

It was a ten-minute drive to a small restaurant serving mid-priced Italian food that Kate told him she took her parents to when they visited. It was close to her flat and a safe choice for all appetites. Baird opened the restaurant door for her and asked the waiter for a quiet table for two. 'Don't want to scare the locals with shop talk, do we?' He winked at Kate.

They ordered, Baird insisting on a bottle of wine for Kate. He'd have one glass with his food, to toast her success with the baby milk case, but stick to mineral water after that since he was driving.

The waiter brought the drinks, Baird encouraged her to tell him about herself, how she came into policing. She recounted how her father was a dentist, but she hadn't wanted to follow in his footsteps and opted for geography at university as a subject that offered a broad choice of careers. She'd started as a special constable before she graduated and knew she'd found her perfect job.

'A scientific background, that's impressive,' Baird said, topping up her glass. 'We need a measured, analytical approach in modern policing. You know,' he looked at her shrewdly, measuring her through half-closed eyes as if judging her worth, 'it's no secret that I'm in line for promotion.'

'Really, sir? Congratulations,' Kate said.

He smiled, self-consciously modest. 'Oh, I'm not there yet. But it will come, and when it does, I want top calibre officers for my team.' He leaned across the table. 'Think you'd be interested?'

'Well,' she said with a show of studied consideration that failed to hide her desire to bite his hand off, 'I'd certainly think about it.'

'Seems I'll have to do my best to persuade you,' he smiled. Their main courses arrived. He signalled the waiter for another bottle. 'You see, I believe policing is about striking a balance. You'll never wipe out crime completely, but with a carrot and stick approach you can make crime regulate itself. It's always going to be there, but keeping it at its lowest possible integer is what we need.'

Kate smiled. 'Absolutely.'

'I need people who break the mould. People who are not afraid to voice their opinions.'

Kate nodded vigorously, swallowing a mouthful of pasta and picking up her wine glass, which Baird had quietly refilled.

'For instance, what would you change locally?' Baird said. 'How would you do things differently?'

Kate eyed him uncertainly. 'Well, I wouldn't want to appear disloyal... sir.'

'No, of course, Kate,' Baird soothed. 'No one would think that. Look, you're a talented officer who's just cracked a complicated case. You know what you're doing. I want to hear how you view the wider picture?' He looked at her earnestly. The waiter had brought a candle to their table. Tiny reflected flames danced in Baird's dark eyes. 'And call me Gavin. Tonight, we're just Gavin and Kate, two colleagues having a friendly chat.' He reached over and squeezed her hand. He could see she was tipsy now. He smiled his encouragement.

'Well, for instance, the baby... baby milk case,' she said, stumbling a little. 'We could have done with better tech support.'

Baird nodded sagely. 'Budget constraints. No magic money tree. What else?' He took a sip of mineral water, watching her from the corner of his eye. She was flushed and had drunk almost two bottles of wine.

'Wee Shona's a good DI.' She nodded her head emphatically.

'Absolutely,' Baird agreed, raising his glass of mineral water in a mock toast.

'And I'm gonna be a good DI.' She beckoned Baird closer. 'Maybe even better, because I'm smart.' She tapped the side of her head and attempted a wink. 'Scientific,' she said thickly. 'One day they'll all be calling me ma'am.'

'I'm sure they will,' he said earnestly, squeezing her hand again.

'You see, I'm all for lias...' it took her a few attempts to get the word out, 'liaising with other forces, but this woman in the water, she wasn't our case. Why are we wasting time on it?'

He nodded. 'Cumbria are dealing with that.'

Kate held up a finger in triumph. 'Ah, that's what you think. Dan Ridley, sure he's an okay officer, but why's he always here?' She shook her head. 'Waste of resources. Close cases. That's what we're paid to do. Guy who fell from the van? If it looks like a duck, and it quacks...' She blinked up at him having lost the thread of her thought. 'Accident. Misadventure,' she said finally. 'Waste of resources.'

'So, both those cases are still open?' Baird said lightly.

'Wide open.' Kate threw her arms out for emphasis, nearly smacking a fully laden waiter on his way to another table. 'Until the boss and her toy boy decide otherwise.' Kate leaned her chin on the heel of her hand. 'Poor procedure. You know... you know what the boss said? "Kate," she said, "restrict your questions to the baby milk case," like I'm the one who's gone off-piste.' She picked up her empty glass, then stared at the equally empty bottle. 'Is there any more wine?'

Baird made the waiter call her a taxi. Kate insisted she was fine; her flat was just round the corner. Why didn't he come up? They could talk more over coffee. She was a pretty woman, the type he liked, willowy and blonde. But Baird thought she was also the type to go running to Professional Standards if he fucked her. His old mate Murdo wasn't around but Irving had given him what he wanted. He made a show of waiting until the taxi came and saw her off. Then he came back, paid the bill, tipped the waiter handsomely so he'd remember him and set off back home to Glasgow. As he drove, the headlights of oncoming cars settled in the deep frown between his eyebrows. He'd told Shona Oliver to stop. She'd disobeyed him. It was time to do some digging. He'd call mates in London, get the gossip around her departure. Whatever happened now, she'd brought this on herself.

–

The next morning Dan arrived at Dumfries HQ just before eight o'clock. He knew he was early, but he wanted to get cracking. Murdo was at his desk in the CID room, several of the civilian support staff already busy at work. Shona motivated people to do their best; it was lucky he'd run into her that day at Silloth. His fortunes as a police officer were changing, he could feel it. Maybe he wouldn't apply to the Met. Instead, he'd come to Dumfries when the next vacancy arose. Murdo looked tired when he came over. 'Dan, pal. Good to see you.'

Dan held up a computer stick drive. 'Got this from a responsible citizen at the opposite end of the road from

Jamie Buckland's place,' he said excitedly. 'Bit posher there. They have front gardens, paved over. Bloke has a motor home parked on it. His missus says, "It's my husband's pride and joy, gets more attention than I do. He's got a camera trained on it day and night. He'll show you when he gets home from work." Had to wait for a bit, but I got it. CCTV of Buckland from a week ago. The boss will want to see this.' He paused, seeing Murdo's serious face. 'What's the matter?'

'Well, the boss might have other things on her plate this morning.' Murdo updated Dan on what had happened to Becca the night before.

'Shit, is Becca okay? Is Wee Shona okay?'

'We're both fine,' said a voice behind them. Shona swept into her office and stowed her bag under the desk. She looked pale and there were dark circles under her eyes that the subtle make-up she was wearing failed to disguise. Dan and Murdo came sheepishly to her door. 'Really, Becca's okay,' said Shona. 'Going to be off school for a while, which she's delighted about. Murdo,' she gave him a grateful smile, 'thank you for stepping up, last night.'

'No bother, boss. ID-ed a potential car belonging to one of the lads' mothers. Ravi's gone to lift it this morning.'

'Good.' She turned to Dan. 'What's this about Buckland?'

'CCTV from a neighbour. No sign of Buckland for the last three days, but there's footage from a week ago that's interesting,' said Dan, handing over the stick.

Murdo indicated he was leaving them to it while he got on with other work and chased up the whereabouts of DC Kate Irving, who hadn't showed up yet and wasn't answering the phone. 'Probably in the shower doing that hair stuff that women do.' He waved his hands uncertainly over his head.

'You mean washing her hair?' Shona said with amusement. 'Don't you wash your hair, Murdo?'

'Aye, I do.' He rubbed his shorn scalp. 'But I don't take all day about it.'

Shona grinned. 'Give her five minutes and call again. Kate's never usually late.' She slotted the stick into her laptop and motioned Dan to pull up a chair. 'Skip to the good part, will you?' She left him to set the CCTV going while she texted Becca at the hospital to say she'd be in this afternoon.

'This is it.' Dan turned the screen towards her. In the background, behind the white bulk of a camper van, an altercation was taking place between Jamie Buckland and a second man, who pinned him up against a car and punched him several times. Buckland fell to the ground, clutching his face as the man continued to kick him.

'When was this?' said Shona, pulling the laptop closer.

'Last week,' said Dan. 'There's more, the neighbour thinks she saw a girl matching Isla's description at the house back in the summer. Her husband only keeps the files for a month then deletes them, so I can't go any further back to check, unfortunately.'

'So, this is from a week ago, just before Jamie disappeared?' Shona reran the clip. The assailant stepped back from the car and straightened the jacket of his expensive suit, brushing down the sleeves.

'Wazir said Jamie was Isla's pimp. He must have had other girls. Could this be a dissatisfied punter?' Dan said.

'Maybe.' Shona squinted at the screen. 'You know, he looks familiar. Just let me ask our local walking Wikipedia.' She leaned back in her chair and bellowed,

'Murdo!' through the open office door. 'Let's test the geographical boundaries of his gift for faces.'

Murdo studied the footage then shook his head. 'Nope, don't know him. Vicious bugger, isn't he.' He ran the clip again. 'He must have form though, look at him. Practised. Professional. Delivers a beating and there's not a mark on himself. Suit's immaculate. Wouldn't look out of place in an expensive restaurant. Want me to chase him through the files, boss?'

But Shona was staring at the man. An expensive restaurant. Murdo was right, that was where he'd be at home. That's exactly where she'd seen him. Shaking hands, mingling with businessmen in a glitzy restaurant of Glasgow's top hotel. Having private chats. Private chats with DCI Gavin Baird against the background of celebrity businessman Kenny Hanlon and his glamorous STAC reception. 'No, it's okay Murdo,' Shona said with a creeping sense of unease. 'You can leave this with me for now.'

Chapter 23

Shona sent Dan and Murdo to check with uniform for any local sightings of Jamie Buckland in Dumfries while she paced the office. She was exhausted and the persistent pain was growing again behind her eyes. She ran through her options; they all came back to Baird. What he'd said was no more than any budget-conscious senior officer might say to his DI. But still there was something wrong. A picture comprised of jigsaw pieces forced together. When you looked closely, they didn't quite fit. All she had was a corrupted video file and the vague sense she was being threatened.

She passed her hand across her eyes. There was only one way to deal with this. She couldn't go around him, she'd have to tackle him head-on. Sami and Isla's deaths couldn't be the main focus of her enquiries, but Imran Wazir had linked them to Jamie Buckland and the baby milk case and that *was* high on Baird's list of priorities. She shut her office door, lowered the blinds and picked up her phone. His number rang once.

'Morning, Shona.' Baird's voice was hard, but the unexpected call put an uncertain edge to it, the cadence skipping up at the end as if a hidden question mark was lurking there.

'Morning, sir,' Shona said evenly. 'I've a quick technical query. Hope you don't mind me calling?'

'Fire away.' The claustrophobic silence in the background told her he was on his own. She knew she should probably step back, think it through. She was tired, she might miss something, but it was that very tiredness that drove her on. She was fed up with Baird blocking her, sick of people's passive lack of concern. A man and a woman were dead on her patch and she would not stop until she found out who had done this and why. It's a debt we owe to the dead, her sergeant used to say. It was a debt that must be paid before friends and family could move on and find whatever peace they could.

'I've been looking at some Op Fortress footage, a loose end connected with the baby milk case.' She reasoned this would divert his initial objection. 'Now, it may be a technical hitch, in which case I thought I better give you a heads up, but small sections of the surveillance on Carter Street are missing.' She let the question hang in the silence that followed.

'I know,' he said, eventually. 'It's to protect the identity of a witness.'

'Okay.' Shona knew Baird must have personally authorised it. 'The person who's been removed may also be a vital witness in the baby milk case. I need to interview the individual concerned,' she gambled.

This time, the pause was so long that Shona wondered if their connection had been cut. 'That individual is not your concern.' Baird's reply was a low growl.

'Why not, sir? It's procedurally appropriate—'

Baird cut her off. 'Are you not listening to me?' She could hear him breathing heavily and imagined his face puce with anger. 'Look,' he said eventually. 'We have someone on the inside. He's still in play. His codename is

Archer. That's all you need to know. He is no part of your inquiry. Understand? Op Fortress is not your concern.'

Whoever this individual, was, they potentially had contact with Jamie Buckland. Now that Buckie was a bail absconder it was a valid line of enquiry, but Baird hadn't even asked her why she wanted to speak to Archer. 'But, sir...'

'I know why you're really calling. I know you're pursuing the motorway death and that drowned addict you fished out of the sea.' Baird's voice dropped to a hiss. 'Now, what you get up to with Cumbrian constables in your own time is your own business, but do yourself a favour, send DC Ridley back over the border and wrap up these cases. Maybe you're missing the bright lights of London. Maybe you're out to make a name for yourself, I don't care. Take a telling, Oliver. This is your final warning. If you disobey my direct order, I will instigate disciplinary proceedings against you. Have I made myself clear?'

Shona picked up a paperclip, bending it back until the point pierced her finger. For a moment she was tempted to lash out at him. She was an experienced DI with fifteen years in the City Police behind her. She knew what she was doing. How good a detective was he? She remembered the scene in the STAC reception corridor. Nicola Baird and her paramour. Did he, for example, know his wife was playing away with Kenny Hanlon?

But to win your battles you needed to choose your ground, and Shona knew she couldn't win this particular skirmish. Baird would bring the full weight of the Division down on her and crush her. She wanted to ask him about the man who'd assaulted Jamie, the man she'd seen talking to Baird and Hanlon at the STAC reception. Did they know he was a businessman who hopped over the border to visit prostitutes in Carlisle? Maybe even purchase some recreational drugs? But she knew she was wasting her breath. A single drop of blood fell from her finger and stained the carpet. 'Yes, sir,' she said and hung up.

How did Baird know she was still pursuing both enquiries? No Divisional paperwork had been submitted so the cases were technically still open. But it was more than that. That crack about Cumbrian constables. Shona felt herself redden. There was no truth in it, but it was so personal that it could only have come from somebody in her office. There was always fun to be had at the boss's expense, and she wouldn't be the first copper to have an office affair, but this was someone whose loyalty was wavering, someone who had spied greener pastures. She rolled up the blinds and cast her eyes around the CID office until it came to rest on just the person to help her solve the mystery.

'Kate,' she called. 'Have you got a minute?'

DC Irving looked pale and sickly; strands of her blonde hair had squirmed loose from her pony tail.

'Listen, Kate.' Shona closed the office door but remained standing. She beckoned her closer, tilting her face up at the much taller constable. 'You're a mate of Vinny Visuals. What's he been saying?'

'Nothing, I think,' stammered Kate. 'Why?'

'Someone's been mouthing off to Baird about our case load and,' Shona paused, searching for a suitable term, 'operational matters beyond their pay grade.'

Kate turned an even paler shade. Shona considered how Vinny Visuals had probably gone straight to Baird, covering his arse when he first saw there was footage missing from the surveillance record. Well, if he wanted pastures new, that's what he would get. Next appraisal he'd be out.

'Kate, you really don't look well.' Shona wondered if she should offer her a chair. 'Is there anything you'd like to tell me?' Shona eyed her shrewdly and hoped she wasn't pregnant. Kate was a good officer and she'd rather not lose her, even temporarily.

'Er... no, ma'am.' Kate swallowed hard. 'Whatever's happened I'm sure it wasn't Vin.'

'Yes, I know, it's hard to believe someone could be that disloyal,' Shona continued. 'He'd still be flipping burgers and playing on his Xbox if I hadn't brought him in, the ungrateful scroat.' She pointed a finger at Kate. 'So listen. If he starts yapping again, come straight to me. Understand?' Kate nodded; she looked like she was about to throw up. 'Are you okay?' Shona asked.

'Yes, boss. Something I ate.'

She knew Kate wasn't a boozer, so she was probably telling the truth. Shona made a mental note to avoid anything from the office fridge until it had been properly cleaned out. It wasn't unknown for Murdo to sniff a pint of milk ten days past its date, and declare it fit for human consumption before sloshing it into everyone's tea. She sent Kate back to her desk with the proviso that she should go home if she didn't feel better soon.

Shona needed space to think. Should she do what she was told, tie up the cases and move on? She was in no doubt Baird meant what he said, but he wasn't the one who'd pulled Isla from the water or seen Sami's shattered body laid out on a mortuary table. Her debt to the dead remained. The memory of the mortuary filled her nose with the disinfectant smell of the hospital and then an image of Becca in Casualty, strapped to the trolley, flashed into her head. The thought of losing her, seeing her laid out on the same table as Sami or Isla, was a waking night-mare that made her tremble so much that her legs went from under her and she fell into the chair behind her desk. She felt a sudden overwhelming need to check on Becca, make sure the doctors were watching her carefully enough and that nothing could harm her. Taking a deep breath, she forced herself to get up. Her head pounded as she checked the wall clock. Doctors' rounds would be over.

She picked up her bag and coat. 'Murdo, I'm going out for a while,' she called, and held up her phone to indicate he could call her when he had something to report.

—

Becca was in good spirits, some of her customary surly defiance already in evidence at her mother's choice of reading matter. 'What's this?' She held a glossy page by the edges. '*Shout*. Really? Mum, I'm not a kid. And this?' She picked up a music magazine.

'It's got Fleetwood Mac on the cover. You like them. Don't you want to read about them?'

'I like one of their albums. Why would I want to read about anyone who's a hundred years old? Can't you bring my laptop in?'

'No, the doctors say you need to rest. What about some talking books?'

'For God's sake. You trying to finish me off?' Becca saw the stricken look in her mother's eyes. 'Sorry. Sorry, Mum. That was really stupid.' She lay back on the pillow, blinking tears away. The dressing above her eye and the bruising to her face made her look smaller and younger, like a kid who'd toppled off a swing. Shona took her unbandaged hand and squeezed it. Becca squeezed back.

'I'm okay. Really, I am.' She adjusted her head on the pillow to look at her mother. 'You know, you were amazing yesterday.' Becca's eyes were shining with admiration. 'Apart from the singing bit. What was that? Some nursery rhyme?' Becca started to laugh.

'What? "The Wheels on the Bus"? It's a proper song. You used to love that.' Shona couldn't help smiling back. 'It was all I could think of. I had to keep you awake.' Then the thick lump of terror that had been sitting in her stomach since yesterday welled up. Tears formed in the corners of Shona's eyes and she found she was crying and laughing with relief that her precious girl was still her precious girl in all her awkward, prickly, defiant self. Shona leaned over and pulled Becca into a fierce embrace, until her daughter again protested. 'Ouch! Mum, stop.'

'Ravi was in earlier,' Becca said, when her mother had given her a tissue and they'd both wiped their eyes. 'To take a statement. Is that what it's called? It's all a bit fuzzy, but I'm sure the car came from the direction of the main road, not the farm. I didn't recognise it as local. Don't think I was much help.'

'I'm sure you were,' Shona reassured her. 'Something more might come back to you, but don't try to force it. We can trace the car in other ways: CCTV, paint matches, tyre pattern analysis. You just need to concentrate on getting better.'

Becca nodded. 'Is Dad coming in later?'

'Yes, I'm sure he's on his way,' said Shona with brittle brightness. Rob was probably still over the limit to drive. He should take a cab, she wasn't going back to pick him up. No way. She knew it was stupid, but it was hard not to blame him for what had happened to Becca. Last night, Murdo had found Rob sitting in the corner of the Royal

Arms pissed out of his head. There was no sign of Rob's brother, Sandy. As soon as Tommy had left the lifeboat station in his van, news of a serious road accident on the farm road would have gone round the village like wildfire. Hadn't Rob thought to check who the victim was? That Becca was okay? Maybe that's why she blamed him, for being so wrapped up in himself. He didn't care that someone, anyone, was hurt. She just couldn't understand it.

'You need to rest now, darlin'.' She kissed Becca's forehead. 'I'm going back to the office for a bit. I'll be back in to see you this evening.'

Chapter 24

Dan met Shona as she came up the stairs to the CID office. 'No word on Buckie yet. I'm just on my way back to Loreburn Street for an update. Maybe uniform or the PCSOs... what do you call them here again?' He stopped on the half-landing.

'The special officers,' she said.

'Yeah, the specials...' Outside, rain was spitting on the stairwell window. 'Maybe they've heard something.' Dan zipped up his jacket.

'Wait, Dan,' Shona said, as he made to continue downstairs. 'Listen, I've had word from Division to drop both Isla and Sami's cases.'

'I know, you said before.' His frown deepened. 'I've already told you I'll be careful. I'm not giving up on this and I don't think you are either. If they sack us, we'll just have to get capes and become a cross-border crime-busting duo. Gotham City comes to Dumfries. What do you say?'

Shona shook her head, but Dan was grinning at her with such unfeigned enthusiasm that she found herself suppressing a smile. It was true, she had no intention of dropping the case. But if Dan could see through her then Baird would too, and with Vinny acting as a spy in the camp, that would come sooner rather than later. There wasn't much time.

'Okay, but you're gonna have to watch yourself. Understand?' Shona said. 'First sign of trouble you put your hands up and say you were acting under my orders.' She waited for him to nod before continuing. 'So, what have we overlooked? Wazir mentioned money.'

'We checked Isla's bank account,' Dan confirmed. 'Only a couple of quid in it and her card wasn't used after she disappeared. Still no sign of a purse, mobile phone or handbag.'

'We're going to need help to crack this.' Shona shook her head. 'We need Buckland.'

'He's a bail absconder. Every police force in England and Scotland is looking for him now. He won't get far.'

'Listen, Dan.' Shona put her hand on his arm. 'From now on we play this close to our chests.'

DC Kate Irving came through the glass door at the top of the stairs. Shona had the sense that she might have been watching them. She took her hand from Dan's arm. Kate's pale face was unreadable. 'Ma'am.'

'You looking for me, Kate?'

'Yes, uhm…' Kate came down to the half-landing. 'Isla Corr and Sami Raseem. I'd like to help.'

Shona peered at her curiously. 'You have plenty of work with the baby milk case. Fiscal's charged him but there will be a mountain of case preparation for the trial.' She couldn't fathom Kate's change of heart. Perhaps she *was* pregnant, and desperate to get as much investigation experience as she could before maternity leave. Whatever the reason, these murder cases would likely prove fatal to career prospects; Shona wouldn't put Kate at risk.

Kate chewed her lip for a moment and seemed to hesitate, but persisted. 'Really, boss. I want to help.

What you said is true. Closure for the family, it's really important.'

Dan was watching this exchange carefully. 'She's right, boss. DC Irving is a good officer and, speaking for Cumbria Police, I could do with the help.'

Kate shot him a look of gratitude. 'I was thinking, the social worker never came back to us. Perhaps I could chase that up? Just have a quick word with them?'

Shona looked at the two young officers and knew she was outnumbered. A trip to social work could be viewed as tying up a few loose ends. Isla Corr had been mentioned in connection with the baby milk case. It shouldn't put Kate in the line of fire. 'Fine. Get over to the multi-agency safeguarding hub. See if you can get anyone to talk to you, officers, civilian staff, case workers, anyone. Be respectful, social workers are overloaded at the best of times. See if you can get any background on Isla Corr. Anything we might have overlooked.' She turned to Dan. 'You clear on our next steps?' Buckland was his priority. He nodded and set off for the car park.

Shona and Kate headed back up the stairs. 'Wazir said that Sami and possibly Isla may have had dealings with child trafficking.' She saw Kate's shocked expression and pressed on. 'I've already informed Division, but I want you to double-check if anyone locally thinks that story is cred-ible.' Shona pushed open the door into the CID office. 'And I don't want any of that bollocks about scheduling it for a weekly meeting. Two people are dead, I want the individual or individuals concerned off the street before they can do any more harm. Verbal is fine for now. Get me the headlines, we can deal with the paperwork and the details later. Got it?'

Kate nodded and lifted her coat from the rack, swinging it round her shoulders and stuffing her notebook and phone into the pocket. Shona continued into her office and shut the door behind her. Murdo and Ravi were out somewhere, the civilian staff all busy at their desks. She sat for a moment, her head resting in her hands, then she pushed back her shoulders and surveyed her desk.

The screen grabs from the surveillance video that Dan had found were sitting on a folder in front of her. She picked up the pictures of Jamie Buckland and his unknown assailant scrapping in the street near Buckland's Carlisle home. The man with the sharp cheekbones and equally sharp suit stared back at her. Frozen now in black and white, stripped of motion and mannerisms, he looked less like the individual Shona had seen with Baird and Hanlon at the STAC reception. In fairness he could be any lean, shorn-headed, thirties guy with a taste for sharp tailoring. It was a popular look. But something in the video had struck a chord and Shona was convinced she'd seen this man at the STAC reception. She trusted her instincts. Holding the picture before her she picked up the phone.

Detective Superintendent Munroe answered after the first ring. 'Shona, I was just about to call you. Terrible, just terrible. How is your daughter?' His voice was full of concern.

Shona imagined this Glasgow bruiser had spent a large part of his career delivering bad news to families. It was his compassion as well as his toughness that had got him where he was.

'She's fine, sir. Doing well, thank you,' Shona said.

'I've just been talking to Baird, he's just heard about it too. He's suggested you take a bit of time off, compassionate leave. I must say, Shona, I'm with him on this.'

Shona felt a creeping cold travel up her spine. So, Baird was prepared to use her daughter's accident to get her out of the way. He'd probably bring in a temporary DI from his pals in Ayrshire, just to keep her in line. She forced herself to inject a note of calm in her voice. 'Oh no, it's really not that bad. She took a tumble off her bike, was sensible enough to be wearing a helmet. She'll be out of hospital shortly and Rob will be home to look after her.'

'And the driver…'

'Traffic are on it, sir. DC Sarwar is liaising. I trust them all to do a good job.'

'I'm sure they will. And what about you? I understand you were first on the scene.'

'I was, sir, but I had support from the lifeboat crew. So, you see, everything's okay.' Munroe couldn't force her to take leave, but he could make it very difficult to say no if he thought her mind wasn't on the job.

'Are you sure? It would give you a break, and girls like to have their mothers around when they're poorly.'

Shona bit her tongue. She was pretty sure a male DI wouldn't have to go through this grilling. Munroe had three grown-up daughters, so maybe he was talking from experience, but she was willing to bet he'd never taken time off for childcare. 'She will have her mother around, don't you worry. I'll be there every evening and I'll be sure to let you know if the situation changes, sir,' she soothed.

'Well, if you're sure.' Munroe sounded mollified. 'Keep in touch, and our best to Becca and Rob.'

'Sir,' Shona said before he could hang up, 'just one thing. I've been meaning to bolster our relations with the business community, part of the STAC initiative. Could your secretary send me the guest list from the launch in Glasgow? I'm thinking about setting up some cross-area networks. This baby milk case has thrown up a few ideas. Staff development, improved protocols.'

'Sure, I'll get Joan to send that through. I don't want to lose you, Shona, but remember what I said about the leave.' Munroe hung up.

Five minutes later, the guest list dropped into Shona's inbox. She printed out the three-hundred-plus names and began the slow job of eliminating them. Women first, then the males she already recognised. That still left over a hundred people she needed to identify and exclude. She couldn't risk giving it to someone else. She looked out into the office. Murdo was back at his desk. Shona decided she'd go home via the hospital, taking the list with her. Before she turned back to her desk, Ravi came into the office, shaking the rain from his parka and smoothing his hair. He said something to Murdo and they both headed for her office, tapping the door. 'Yes?' she said, not looking up from her emails. She should tidy her inbox before she left.

'I've just had a phone call from Marie Corr, boss,' Ravi said.

Shona frowned. 'What's the matter?'

'Paddy Corr died this morning.'

She nodded slowly, taking in the implications. 'Okay. Did he say anything about Isla?'

'Not a peep. If he knew anything, he took it with him,' Ravi replied. 'Marie asked if we had any news. I told her we hadn't.'

'How did she take it?'

'I think it's what she expected. She's got the wee boy to look after. Might be easier with Paddy gone.'

'I'll ask Marie to let us know about the funeral,' Murdo said.

'Are you planning on going?' Ravi said.

'Oh, aye.' Murdo nodded. 'It's worth making sure that bastard is definitely in the ground, no mistake.'

Chapter 25

The next morning Shona headed to the office late, stopping off at the hospital to get an update from the ward sister on the way. Becca was doing well, but still had spells of confusion and tiredness associated with the concussion. This was entirely normal. She'd need physio for her broken arm. They would keep her a few more days. Shona and Rob had orbited their daughter, taking turns to be at her bedside. They kept their distance from each other, pulled in opposing directions by the demands of Shona's work and Rob's B&B guests. When he'd suggested it wasn't fair to cancel them, Shona had quickly agreed. It would keep Rob busy and out of her way. Her disappointment and embarrassment at having her husband hauled from the pub by her sergeant still stung.

The CID office was buzzing and DC Kate Irving, looking smart and composed in a navy trouser suit and pale shirt, led a chorus of good mornings. She brought Shona a coffee in her Charles Rennie Mackintosh mug and said she had an update from the social services hub when Shona was ready.

'You can tell me now.' Shona took a sip of coffee and pointed to the seat opposite her. 'How did you get on?'

Kate crossed her long legs and opened her notebook. 'Well, there's nothing to indicate Wazir's claims about child trafficking are true. They haven't dealt with any out-of-area children, beyond placing a brother and sister from Glasgow with a local couple.'

'Okay, that's good to know, but it may be a new operation that isn't on anyone's radar yet. We need to keep it in mind, in case it becomes a potential line of enquiry. Situations like this, children at risk, it's important we all work together. It's why the multi-agency hub was set up in the first place.'

Kate nodded. 'How solid is this intelligence?'

Shona wrapped her hands around her cup. 'Uncorroborated,' she conceded. 'It may even be a fabrication by Wazir to misdirect us.'

'And we don't know anything about Sami Raseem's mental state other than it was fragile and he made at least one suicide attempt,' Kate added.

'True. God knows what he saw in Syria or while he was being trafficked himself.' Shona shivered, partly from thoughts of Sami's plight and partly from chilliness. She'd walked from the overheated hospital back to the car park without her coat and was paying the price. Even after nearly two years back in Scotland she'd still occasionally associate the late September sunshine with its counterpart in London and forget about the nippy wind and the ten-degree difference in temperature. She pulled the charcoal grey pashmina that hung over the back of her chair around her shoulders.

'What did Wazir think was happening to the children?' Kate turned over a new page in her notebook.

'He claims he didn't know, but it was something bad enough to tip Sami over the edge. As he told you, they were both in the grip of an organised gang Wazir's too scared to inform on. The baby milk scheme was a method of escape. I think we have to conclude that we're talking about sexually motivated crime, but where's the evidence?' Shona thought about her interview with Tony Kirkwood. She could ask if Sami had confided in him about a paedophile gang, but if he had then Kirkwood would surely have mentioned it when they spoke.

'Could the children be for unregistered adoption?' said Kate doubtfully. 'Or, since Sami came in on a lorry, is it possible the gang were bringing in lone children for families already here? Or on their way here?'

'Unlikely,' Shona said. 'Adoptions would have been travelling with at least one parent. If Sami was reuniting families, he wouldn't have been so troubled by his own part in it. What else?' she challenged Kate. 'What else are children and young people used for?'

'Well...' Kate dipped her head, concentrating on her notebook. 'County lines, drugs, but surely... DCI Baird would have picked up on this?'

She looked uncomfortable, perhaps expecting a reprimand for her lack of progress, but Shona appreciated that she'd volunteered to pursue an avenue that might lead to Sami and Isla's killers.

'Maybe they did, but preferred to go after the big fish?' Shona replied. Baird had shared only enough intelligence with her for her team to mop up the low grade dealers. The children and teenagers put on a cross-country train with a sports bag of cocaine were not the focus of his op.

Kate was nodding now. 'One of the outreach guys mentioned something. Town gangs renting rural Airbnb properties for a weekend. They bring in the local dealer network, kids mostly, to cut and package the drugs. They have an Xbox and send out for some pizzas, it looks like a family get together. When they're finished, everyone goes their separate ways. The place is always left clean, I mean forensically spotless, so the owners have no complaints, and no one is any the wiser.'

Shona shifted in her chair. Did Rob know what their guests were up to in their ensuite rooms with all those immaculate, white-tiled surfaces? She couldn't imagine the retired couples, their bread and butter, getting up to much mischief. Or the middle-class families arriving for the Kirkness Arts Festival next month, but surely that was the point. Make it look like normal activity and nobody batted an eye. 'What about Isla's social worker? Any luck with her?'

'There's been a fair turnover of staff, but I did speak to a woman called Sarah who'd been assigned to Isla and Ryan. They've had minimal contact, no causes for concern. With Marie Corr looking after Isla's kid, and no problems at school, the family have been low priority. Paddy Corr wasn't considered a threat, given his state of health and lack of recent convictions.'

'So, when did Sarah last see Isla and Ryan?'

'Months back. Isla never turned up for her last meeting, but that wasn't unusual. Another date was scheduled this month, but by then she was dead. Isla's movements have gone completely under the radar, for them as well as us.'

Shona sighed. She'd been hoping for more. Something, anything that filled out the picture of a girl whose whole life seemed to have been a spiral down to a violent death. Abuse, missing from home, addiction. Social services had done what they could, but no fairy godmother, no knight in shining armour was ever coming to save Isla. Shona wondered at what point Isla knew that. Seven or eight years old? Maybe even younger. The kids Sami was moving must have known that too. 'What about Sami Raseem?'

Kate shook her head. 'Nothing. Isn't on their files. Which is no surprise, I suppose.'

Shona drained her cup. 'Okay, thank you Kate.' She gave her constable an appreciative smile. 'Update me if you hear anything else from social services. Tell Murdo to come in. Let's see where we are on other jobs.'

Murdo took Kate's seat and ran through the case load, leaning on the far side of her desk while she nodded and jotted notes. Burglary, car theft, minor assault and a missing yacht.

'What's the name of the vessel?' Shona asked without looking up.

Murdo flipped back a page, '*The Solway Selkie*, a Westerly Conway 36.' He shrugged. 'Doesnae mean a thing to me. Is that a big boat or a wee boat?'

'Weekend cruiser. About ten metres long.'

'So quite wee then. Not my idea of a fun weekend. It was moored up at Kingholm Quay. Owner just returned from a fortnight away.'

Shona pursed her lips and shook her head. 'Worth about thirty grand. Probably stolen to order.'

'Can you hotwire a yacht?'

'Of course, same way you jump any diesel engine. Connect a battery across two wires on the solenoid. Bypass the starter button with one of your own. It's not difficult.' She pointed her pen at him in mock admonition. 'You see Murdo, if you'd grown up on a council estate, you'd have known that.'

'Oh right. Get many stray yachts in Glasgow, did you?'

'No,' she smirked. 'Actually, Tommy showed me. We had a fella who dropped his keys in the Solway rowing back to his boat from the pub. You let the coastguard know about the theft and I'll ask Tommy to keep his eyes open. Anything else?'

'Nope, that's the butcher's bill.' He closed his notebook. 'Where are we with Isla Corr and the fella from the motorway? Need anything following up?'

Shona didn't doubt Murdo's loyalty for a second, but he was an old mate and admirer of DCI Baird. It was best her sergeant stayed out of things.

She shook her head. 'Nothing outstanding. Any other issues? Cars? Overtime?'

'Not at the minute.' He got up to go, apparently unfazed by her reply. She thanked him.

Once she was alone, Shona slipped out the STAC guest list with its remaining candidates for Jamie Buckland's assailant. She started from the top, googling each individual name. Most had an internet presence. Councillors, businessmen, Chamber of Commerce officials. The profiles were mainly older and flabbier than her person of interest, but one or two looked possible. She pulled up their pictures. What she really wanted was video. The suspect's walk was distinctive; toes pointed slightly outward, the shoulder roll of a physically confident man. Vinny could probably ferret out something for her, but she couldn't risk it. By mid-afternoon, after exhaustive searching, she reluctantly admitted that she hadn't found a match.

She was stretching back in her chair, reaching up to the ceiling and rolling out tense shoulder muscles, when she spotted Dan Ridley coming into the office. He looked like he hadn't slept; his normally immaculate pale blue shirt was un-ironed under his grey suit. His bloodshot eyes met her gaze. She summoned him into her office with a jerk of her head.

'What is it?'

'Err, I could really do with some advice.'

She checked her watch; twenty minutes before a meeting with the local Police, Fire and Rescue Sub-Committee. 'Okay, close the door.' She pointed to the vacant seat by her desk.

'It's Lambert,' he said, sitting down.

He'd been reprimanded. She'd seen it coming. Her insistence on pursuing the Isla case had led a junior officer into bother. 'If he's telling you to step back from the Corr investigation you should do it.'

'It's not that. I've been working late, tackling the paper-work he's dumped on me, following up Isla in my own time.' Dan's hands were jittery. He put his car keys in his pocket before taking them out again. 'He's been mouthing off about you. There's something else. I overheard him on the phone to DCI Baird, Lambert saw me. When he'd finished, he came up to me. He had this big grin on his ugly mug. He said, don't hook up with Shona Oliver, she's not going to last.'

Shona felt a chill. She'd faced the challenges of the old-boy network her whole career. Even with Mars Bars Munroe's support it seemed she couldn't escape it. Munroe was retiring soon, Baird his likely successor. Had he already decided he couldn't work with her? Or was it what she feared, something that had followed her from London? Something that would wreck not just her career but her home life too?

Shona saw Dan watching her closely. 'Thanks for the warning,' she said with a confidence she didn't feel. 'If

Lambert is targeting you, you must talk to your federation rep.' She gave him a tight smile. 'And don't worry. It's the usual dick-swinging. I'm not going anywhere.'

Chapter 26

Shona sat through the hour-long session of the Police, Fire and Rescue Sub-Committee with Dan's words playing over and over in her head. She was determined not to let it get to her. Her results would speak for themselves.

As she left the meeting, she stopped one of the councillors, an upright man of military bearing, who she recognised as a STAC reception guest. She smiled, offering her hand and words of praise for his efforts on behalf of his community. When she asked about the suspect from the video, wondering if perhaps he was acquainted with the individual and knew his name, the councillor glanced at his watch, made a curt excuse and walked away. She stood processing this odd encounter when the answer came to her. The councillor in question had just received a drink-driving ban. It had been in all the newspapers. No matter what the topic, a police officer was the last person he wanted to chat to.

The CID office was quiet when she returned. Ravi was draped across a filing cabinet, his chin resting on folded arms as he chatted to Vinny Visuals. The surveillance expert dipped his head and got back to work when he saw Shona's fierce stare. Ravi pulled himself upright and came over to Shona's office. He tapped lightly on the door frame. 'Boss.'

'Hi, Rav, how's it going?'

'Aye, good. I can give you a progress report on Becca's accident if you want?'

'Go on.'

'The families of the lads caught in possession all seem to be in the clear.' He pursed his lips, pausing to see how she'd take the news.

Shona nodded. A local feud which had turned personal against an officer was often difficult to extinguish and had wider impacts on community policing. In pubs or shops, people would stop in mid-conversation, tyres would be slashed. She loved Kirkness, the community and the life-boat. It would break her heart to leave. 'Okay, can't say I'm not relieved about that. Any other leads?'

'Traffic have identified a suspect car, darkened windows, false plates. It popped up on the A75 then disappeared. There's a watch out on it but if the driver swaps the plates again...' He let the sentence trail off. 'What I can't understand is why a car like that would have been on a wee dead-end farm road?'

'Could have been passing thorough from England, heading for Stranraer. Stopped off looking for a pub, or a pee, and got lost.'

'But to avoid the cameras afterwards?'

'It's not hard. With a map or a Satnav and some common sense, you'd know we can't cover all the back-roads here. Could even have swapped the plates soon after. There's a Border Agency cop at Stranraer.' She wrote down a name, tore the sheet from the pad and handed it to Ravi. 'Worth asking if the suspect vehicle hopped on a ferry later that day,' Shona said evenly, trying not to get her hopes up. She would dearly love to see the driver nailed to the wall but knew she might never get the satisfaction. The cop in question hadn't got back to

Kate over the child trafficking inquiry – this might also serve as a reminder.

'Thanks, boss.' Ravi smiled and pocketed the name. 'How's Becca doing?'

'Good. Yeah, should be home soon.'

'That's brilliant.' Ravi's smile switched to full beam. 'She's a sparky girl.'

'Well, you were a hit at the hospital too.' Shona found her mood lifting, caught by Ravi's good spirits.

'Aye, mutual appreciation society there. She's a top lassie, you're dead lucky.'

Shona had a sudden vision of a few years in the future. Becca at Glasgow Uni, meeting up with Ravi and his mates, gay and straight, and going out on the town. She wondered if she should warn Hillhead police office. Glasgow wouldn't know what hit it. She laughed. 'Yes, suppose I am.' She picked up her coat. 'Although, some-times...'

'She'll be fine.' He touched her elbow and until that moment, Shona hadn't realised how much she needed to hear someone else say it. 'And,' he continued, 'we'll get the bastard, don't you worry.'

'Thanks, Ravi,' she said, and meant it.

'You heading up there now?' he asked. 'I'll come with you if that's okay? Social call. Thought Bec and I could crack open a few beers, celebrate her forthcoming release from custody.' He grinned at her.

'Get on with ye, she's fifteen and concussed.' Shona pushed him out the door. 'Which is what you'll be if you don't behave yourself, DC Sarwar.' She laughed. 'Come on then, Becca would love to see you.'

As they left the office, Vinny looked up from his keyboard, a goodnight on his lips. He hurriedly looked down again at the severity of the look Shona shot him.

Ravi chatted with Becca for fifteen minutes and Shona could hear the two of them laughing when she returned with coffee. She stayed another half hour and was pleased to learn that Becca was much improved and would be discharged tomorrow if the doctor okayed it.

As she drove back to Kirkness, she found herself humming along to Fleetwood Mac on the radio and planning her next free day with her daughter. Perhaps she could find someone from the Solway Yacht Club to take them out for a sail, if the weather held. Becca must be fed up with the stuffy hospital air.

The road dipped down into the village, the black mirror of the estuary reflecting the shore lights, doubled points of brightness in the dark. Shona pulled into the drive. The scent from the pine trees that gave the house its name filled the cooling evening air.

The lower floor of High Pines was dark and quiet. Normally the windows of the two ensuite rooms would be lit as people prepared to go out or relaxed after an early dinner. Shona came in through the back door and hung up her coat in the utility room. 'Where are the guests?' Rob was sitting at the kitchen table. It only took a moment for Shona to see how drunk he was.

'Gone. Checked out early,' he slurred.

'Because of this?' Shona said sharply, indicating the bottle and glass on the table. He shrugged.

Rob reached for the whisky, but Shona was quicker. She dumped the half-full bottle of Talisker Single Malt down the sink. 'Becca's coming home tomorrow. Do you want her to see you hungover, stinking of booze?'

He staggered upright and looked set to challenge her, but his resolve crumbled, and he sat back down again with a bump. Shona glared at him, her lips white with anger, until he fell forward onto the table, head in hands. 'You don't need to say it. It's my fault. Becca is my fault.' He sobbed. 'Jesus, she could have been killed.'

Shona took a deep breath, fighting to calm herself, and pulled out the chair opposite him. 'Look,' she said, 'you didn't hit Becca, an unknown driver did.' She reached across and took his hand. It was a natural urge, to blame yourself, to believe you could have saved a loved one from harm. Some people focused on an unlucky misstep, arriving late or a missed phone call, convinced this had precipitated the catastrophe. It was rarely true. Life and death were more random than most people were prepared to accept. She realised she'd fallen victim to this herself, blaming Rob for letting Becca ride up to the farm for eggs, a journey of a mile or so that she'd done multiple times. But he wasn't off the hook completely.

'I do hold you responsible for being out of contact. Why didn't you answer your phone? You must have seen all the missed calls from Becca and me, but you just sat in the Royal Arms drinking with Sandy.'

'I wasn't in the pub with Sandy,' he said quietly, wiping his eyes. 'I'd only been there a minute when Murdo came in.'

'Then where were you?' Becca had been in hospital for three days and this was the first he'd mentioned it. She sensed a shifting, a realignment. Was he having an affair? She searched for a likely candidate and realised she knew very little about the people he worked and social-ised with. Was there someone he'd mentioned? A name dropped frequently into conversation? She was a detective, this would not have got by her. But even as the thought formed, she knew it wasn't true. Anyone can be deceived if they're told a convincing enough lie.

Rob looked up at her, his tanned and handsome face a picture of misery. 'Shona, I couldn't help myself.'

Shona let go of his hand and folded her arms, hugging them tight against her ribs and looked down, avoiding his eyes. She felt the surge of anger returning and fought to control it. Now, the axe would fall, and she knew that even if he confessed and swore regret, this would be the end of their marriage. They'd survived many upsets; Shona's brush with depression after Becca was born, Rob being made redundant from the bank, the turmoil of Becca's expulsion from school in London, adjusting to this new life in Scotland. But all that was possible because they shared a fundamental trust in each other. An affair would shatter that.

He reached across for her hand, but she remained leaning back in her chair. 'Shona, I'm sorry.' He paused taking a deep breath. 'I was in the casino in Dumfries. I owe money. The car with the darkened windows? I think they were looking for me. What if they did this as a warning?'

Shona shook her head, trying to pin down the thoughts racing around her brain. Not an affair. 'What? No, the car wasn't local. It was passing through. False plates.' She stared at him. His expression wasn't one of guilt or remorse. It was fear. 'How much do you owe?'

'The debts have been building up for a while. But since that STAC night a couple of weeks back, seeing how successful my university pals were, I wanted that,' he said desperately. 'When I went back to see them, I tried to make back my losses and things just spiralled out of control. We went to the casino, Kenny Hanlon was there, he said he was interested in my restaurant idea.'

'All your redundancy money from Milton McConnell went into this place, we haven't got the cash to expand.'

'Don't call it that.' His voice was rising now. 'It wasn't redundancy.'

Shona looked at him, horrified. 'But…'

'I was sacked!' he shouted, getting up and staggering towards the sink. She thought he might be sick but instead he turned to her. 'The money was a pay-off to go quietly. Happy now? You've finally got it out of me.'

'You,' Shona stood up and pointed an accusing finger at him, 'you promised, you swore on our daughter's life you wouldn't gamble. Now this? What did you do, Rob?' She gripped the back of her chair and stood where she was. If she got any closer the urge to shake the truth out of him would be overwhelming.

Rob ran the tap and splashed water on his face. 'The bank was co-mingling legitimate transactions of a pharmaceuticals company with fake client accounts. Used it to buy gold. Smuggled it out of the country. Untraceable.'

'Money laundering?' For a moment she was almost speechless. Her Rob was smart, he had more sense. 'You knew about this and said nothing? Don't you understand? You could have helped fund the drugs trade, or terrorism.'

'They set me up. I signed off some of the transactions my team worked on before I realised what was going on. It was too late. I was in it up to my neck. I didn't know what to do.' He crossed back to the table and sat down, the cold water and the gravity of his situation having a rapidly sobering effect. 'I wanted to go to the police, but I kept it quiet for your sake. You and Becca.'

'My sake?' Shona scoffed. 'Don't make this about me.'

'But it *is* about you. You and Becca, that's all it's ever been about,' he said desperately. 'I'd lost my job, I didn't want to lose my family. Threats were made. You were with the City of London Police. Do you think they couldn't have falsified a bribe? Ended your career? We're talking millions here. Don't you think they had a few cops in their pocket? They'd have destroyed us both.'

Shona was shaking with anger. She felt utterly betrayed. She looked at Rob, unsure if she could even trust what he was saying.

She'd come from nothing; no money, no parents, no prospects, but she'd made something of herself. Rob had had everything; a private education, family money, good looks and natural charm, but he couldn't seem to stop himself from throwing it all away.

'The gambling? How much?' she said flatly.

'The cards are maxed out, savings account's empty.' Rob chewed his lip and watched her expression closely.

'The money for Becca's future?'

His face twisted. 'I'll pay it back. Just need to sort alternative funds.'

'How?' she shouted. 'How could you do this? Just when we were getting back on track.' Her hands flew to her hair and she stopped dead. 'The house? What about this house?'

'It's safe, it's okay,' he said, eager to placate her. 'Joint names, couldn't extend the mortgage without your signature.'

'Oh, so you tried, did you?' She advanced on him stabbing a finger in his chest. 'You'd have us homeless, on top of everything else. What do you owe? Fifty, sixty grand? More?'

'I'll work to pay it back,' he said. 'I'll get another job, I'll get help. I promise. Please, Shona.' He tried to hug her, but she pushed him away. 'Just let me try. I love you, Shona.'

'No!' she shouted, the tears pricking behind her eyes. 'You don't do this to people you love. You've destroyed everything and made me an accessory to your crime. I was a DI in the City Police, no one will believe I didn't know about this. Don't you realise? I have to report this fraud.'

'Don't, don't. I'm begging you, Shona. What's the point? They'll come after you.'

'Who?'

'I don't know. Whichever gang Milton McConnell are in league with.'

'Well, I've got news for you. My gang's bigger than their gang,' she said with a bravado she didn't feel. She wanted to scare him; it was the only way she could think of to make him realise the depth of shit he'd landed them both in.

'Look, just forget I told you. I'm drunk, don't know what I'm saying.' He tried a tentative smile. 'It's all my fault but I'll sort it, I promise. Just go to bed, you look exhausted. I'll sleep in a guest room. Here,' he filled a glass from the tap and held it out to her, 'get some rest.'

She felt the impulse to smash it from his hand, but he was right about one thing. She was exhausted. Becca's accident, the unresolved cases of Isla and Sami, the strain of keeping Baird at bay and now this. What had started as a trickle was now a deluge. It was like she was drowning, pushed further and further down by the weight of water.

She ignored the glass. 'I'm going upstairs. I need to think.' She looked him in the eye. 'Tomorrow, you call the doctor. You're an addict, Rob. You need help. You get an appointment and you tell him what you've done.' He nodded eagerly, feeling he was making progress with her, but when he reached out to kiss her goodnight, she turned away and slammed the door behind her.

Chapter 27

'Everything okay, boss? Becca all right?' Murdo's concerned face greeted her the next morning in the office.

'Yes, fine. Busy night,' Shona said distractedly. Her navy trousers and deep purple shirt were neat and pressed but her eyes were red-rimmed, and her dark bob was scraped back into a pony tail held in place by one of Becca's hairbands.

'You get called out on the lifeboat?' Murdo looked set to launch into a lecture about burning candles at both ends.

'No, no,' she said, irritated by the interruption. She picked up a pile of papers on her desk, then put them down again. There had been something she wanted to check about the Isla investigation but Murdo had distracted her and now she couldn't remember what it was. It had occurred to her, as she lay awake last night trying to grade her troubles into order of priority, but she'd omitted to write it down. 'No, just sorting out things at home.' She'd stood over Rob this morning, while he called his GP, but had said little else to him.

Murdo gave her a look which said that man of yours could do with sorting out for a start. Shona was aware that Rob's currency had slipped in the eyes of her deputy since he'd found him in the pub after Becca's accident. He'd said nothing, but a look from Murdo could say everything.

She stopped searching her desk fruitlessly for her lost thought. Murdo was watching her and frowning. 'Do you need me for something, Murdo?' The question sounded more exhausted than she'd meant it to.

He'd been leaning against the door frame but now stood upright and read from a Post-it note in his hand. 'Just a wee thing. A Nathan Jones called. Said it was urgent you got in touch.'

Shona felt the gears of her memory, heavy with fatigue, slip and judder.

'It's a Gretna number,' Murdo prompted.

It came to her. 'Nathan Jones, the yard next to the Carmine warehouse. Where the pills were found.'

'Okay, so, he wouldn't say what he wanted. Will only talk to you.'

'Murdo, I don't have time for this today.' She sat down, exasperated. 'I'm picking up Becca from the hospital in an hour.'

'That's grand.' Murdo smiled. He held the yellow Post-it note up. 'Want me to deal with this?'

'Yes. Please do.' She began opening and closing her desk drawers. 'Wait.' She stopped and looked at him. 'Could this be a change of heart from Jones? He must have seen the news about Op Fortress, how we rounded up the dealers. Maybe he feels safe enough to tell us something about the pills we found without fear of reprisals?'

'Aye, mibbae,' Murdo considered.

'Go and see what he has to say, and Murdo…' she hesitated. Right now, she felt like she was fighting a war on all fronts. She needed Murdo's help. 'Listen, technically we're not pursuing the Isla Corr case, but I still think it's possible that yard is where she went into the Solway. If Jones should happen to mention anything…'

'Aye, I know what you mean. It doesnae sit well with me that we never found out what happened to the lass.' Murdo nodded slowly.

'Take Ravi with you. As Family Liaison Officer he knows Isla Corr's background best.'

'Fine. Do you want me to pass anything onto Dan Ridley? Technically it's Cumbria's case.'

'Just bring it to me. We'll make that decision as and when.'

'Righto. What have you lost?' Murdo indicated her scattered papers and half opened drawer.

'I can't remember, but I'll know when I find it.' She smiled up at him. 'Thanks, Murdo. Update me at home if Jones says anything interesting.'

–

When Shona arrived at the hospital, Becca was sitting on the bed dressed in grey tracksuit bottoms and a yellow T-shirt. Her long dark hair was swept up in a pony tail and her right arm was in a splint and sling. To Shona's surprise Rob was next to her, holding her packed bag in his hand. Tommy McCall stood by the end of the bed, still in his blue overalls, feet planted apart and arms folded. 'Thought I'd pop in and say hello.' He was watching Rob with a canny eye. Shona wondered, with a stab of embarrassment, if he'd heard that Becca was due to be discharged and was making sure Rob turned up sober, and on time.

'Looks like you have a choice of rides home.' Shona hugged her daughter.

'I'll go with Dad if that's okay?' Becca said, getting up. 'He's got the nicest car.'

Rob looked relieved at this vote of approval. Shona said nothing. She had no wish to force a wedge between father and daughter, no matter what she felt about Rob herself. She knew he'd drive carefully.

'I'll try not to take that as an insult,' Tommy huffed.

'You can take me home next time,' said Becca magnanimously.

'Promise me there's not going to be a next time, lassie,' he said seriously.

'I promise, Tommy.' She shuffled forward and gave him a hug, 'Thanks for everything,'

He patted her shoulder. 'Off you go now, and stay out of trouble,' he said, ushering them all out of the ward. He winked at Shona and mouthed, see you later.

Shona followed Rob's car on the journey home. Ahead, she could see the outline of Becca turn and smile at her father from the passenger seat. She was unsure how much to say to Becca about her father's problems. First thing she needed to know was their financial situation. Could they clear Rob's gambling debts without losing the house? Who exactly did he owe the money to? She needed to know today where they stood.

After lunch Shona suggested that her daughter go up to her room and rest. When Becca protested Shona offered a bribe. If Becca did what she was told, Ellie could come over later and watch a movie. They could order in pizza. It did the trick. Shona helped her into bed and arranged a blanket over her. As she turned to go, she heard Becca say quietly, 'Thanks, Mum.'

When she came back down to the kitchen, Rob was staring morosely into the dregs of his coffee mug. Shona crossed to the table and lifted the plates to stack in the dishwasher. 'What time's your appointment with the GP?'

'Three o'clock,' he said glumly.

Shona checked the time on her phone; it was nearly two. 'Will you do me a favour before you go?'

'Sure.' He looked up with a flicker of interest. 'What?'

She lifted his MacBook from the dresser and handed it to him. 'Will you make a list of everything we owe, and who we owe it to? We need to know what we're dealing with.' She kept her voice level, her expression blank and deliberately used 'we' rather than 'you'. It signalled support and she needed him in a positive frame of mind, with no excuse to storm off in a tantrum and miss his appointment. 'Can you do that?'

'Okay.' His relief that he was getting off lightly was apparent. 'I'll just go into the office.' He took the laptop from her. A moment later she heard the door close on the small room next to the kitchen where Rob kept a desk and a filing cabinet of B&B paperwork.

Shona cleared the dishes and made herself another coffee. Then she sat down at the kitchen table and prepared to make a list of her own. Isla's file lay before her. It needed a full case review. Why was so little known about her movements in the last weeks of her life? Where hadn't they looked? Who else could they question? What unpromising leads should be reassessed? When exactly was Isla last seen, and who with? She took a fresh sheet of paper and opened the buff folder in search of answers.

Forty minutes later, Rob came back into the hallway and stood by the kitchen door. He'd changed into a jacket and tie. 'What?' he said when she looked up at him. 'I'm not going in there looking like an addict,' he challenged.

Shona bit her tongue. But you are an addict, a gambling addict. The sooner you face it, the sooner we can deal with this shit, the shit we're in up to our armpits, the

259

shit you've landed us in, she wanted to shout in his face. Instead she forced herself to smile. 'You look very smart. Good luck,' she said, and meant it.

He nodded, mollified. 'Thanks. Here's what you asked for.' He slid a sheet of paper, face down, onto the table like a schoolboy submitting below-par homework and stepped back quickly into the doorway.

Shona turned the corner up briefly, saw a row of numbers and dropped it again. Her heart pounded in her chest. Jesus. That much. 'Let's take this a step at a time,' was all she could manage to say.

Once he'd gone, she gathered up her cup. Her hand was still shaking as she switched the kettle on. She went out into the hall to listen for Becca. All was quiet. The office door was open, and Rob's dirty coffee cup sat on his desk. When she picked it up, the sharp, smoky smell of whisky stung her nose. Liquid courage. She pulled apart the desk and filing cabinet until she found the bottle, and marched back to the kitchen then emptied it, threw it in the recycling. Hiding from gambling in alcohol wasn't going to help. The doctor's surgery was a short drive away in Dalbeattie. She wondered how much he'd had to drink. If Rob lost his licence… stop, stop, she told herself. He's an adult, his mistakes are his own.

She took a glass of squash up to Becca, who was still fast asleep, then stood for a moment looking out from the panoramic window in the lounge. The days were already shortening. The trees on the far side of the estuary were a bright patchwork of orange, reds and gold. Their reflection lay like a fiery quilt upon the surface of the water. In a few weeks the winds would strip them bare. In a month or so, the trees would become a line of black tracery, stark against the vivid winter sunsets. Below, she could see the small boats rocking gently on their moorings, their noses all turned towards the incoming tide, like creatures scenting the wind. The thought that she might lose all this caused a pain in her chest so sharp that she gasped. She put a hand on her racing heart until the colour and sway and peace of the seashore infused her with calm again. She would fix this. This was her anchorage, she wasn't about to give it up without a fight.

Shona returned to the kitchen and by the time she heard Rob's car on the drive she had a list of action points in the Isla case neatly inked in her precise hand-writing on the cover sheet of the file. Rob came in looking calm and relieved. The doctor was referring him for CBT, Cognitive Behavioural Therapy, which was the best option for gambling. He'd given him some contacts he could talk to straight away. Rob had already called one who advised him to register online to self-exclude himself from all bookmakers and casino organisations, web-based and bricks-and-mortar. 'Can't even get into a bingo hall now,' Rob joked. It felt like a small step forward.

'We need to talk about the B&B business,' Shona said. 'Maybe we should close for a bit, till you feel better?'

'We can't, we need the money,' said Rob, flatly.

'Is the insurance paid? Can we even feed the guests?' Shona said. Detective Superintendent Munroe had offered her time off to be with Becca – should she take it and look after the guests? It took a millisecond to realise how impractical that was. They'd need to bring someone in to cook and they couldn't afford that. Her colleagues at Dumfries CID would likely have several cases of poisoning to investigate if she took charge in the kitchen.

'Thing is, Shona, it's not up to us,' Rob said quietly.

'What do you mean?' Shona had the creeping sense that a wave was looming that she couldn't see.

'The interest rates on what's owed are crippling. If those loans aren't cleared quick, I'll be declared insolvent.'

'But you're a banker, what do we do? Can you ask Sandy for a short-term loan?'

Rob shifted uncomfortably. 'Already had one. Times are tight for him too. Anyway, I don't see Caroline agreeing to any more.' He came towards her and took her by the shoulders. 'But don't worry, Shona. I'm so grateful for your support. I'll fix it, don't worry.' He was so earnest that she could see he really believed it himself. She shook herself free.

'One thing you need to understand, Rob,' she said, 'is you need to complete your treatment and face up to your financial responsibilities, then we'll talk about whether this marriage is working for both of us.'

Shona's phone rang and she saw Murdo's name. Rob was staring at her as if he couldn't comprehend what she'd said.

'I have to take this.' Shona went into the utility room and closed the door.

Murdo's voice was low and serious. 'Really sorry about this, boss, but you need to get over here.'

Shona listened with a frown to the brief details. 'Okay, I'm on my way.' She picked up her jacket and car keys and went back into the kitchen. Rob was still standing where she'd left him. 'I have to go. Can you keep an eye on Becca?' For a moment he said nothing, then he nodded. She went out and started the car. As she backed out of the drive she caught a glimpse of Rob standing at the kitchen window watching her go.

Ravi was waiting by the kerb, barrier tape already strung across the gateway to the old Carmine industrial unit. 'Murdo's inside,' he said, lifting the tape for her to duck underneath. Behind the chain-link fence that separated the two lots, Nathan Jones stood with his hands in his pockets and his habitual hang-dog expression on his face. Once he'd seen Shona arrive, he turned and shuffled back to his caravan and closed the door.

'Is the body in the warehouse?' Shona asked.

Ravi nodded. 'Jones heard a car pull up around four a.m., two nights ago. Dark blue or black BMW, no plate.'

'Why not just report it? What made him so keen to talk to me?'

'Guilty conscience, I think. He now admits he saw a girl matching Isla's description.'

'Why did he wait to report this car?'

'He was waiting to see if it came back. Apparently, he watched Isla through binoculars while she had sex in the car with an unknown male. Jones was worried he'd be labelled a peeping tom and be implicated in her death. I think he's more concerned for his own skin now. Cars turning up again at night, him on his own.'

'I'll give him something to worry about. If we'd known any of this earlier...' She bit her lip. 'Get a statement off him. Give him a good shake, see what drops out.'

'Think he's involved?'

'I doubt it, but he withheld evidence, so feel free to put the fear of God into him.'

The light was fading. A keen breeze blew off the Solway as she crunched across the scuffed tarmac and broken glass. She caught the smell of salt mixed with diesel and decay and fished a pair of blue latex gloves from her pocket. Murdo was standing just inside the roller door, shoulders hunched against the cold and damp.

'Confident on the ID?' Shona said.

Murdo pursed his lips and nodded. He pointed to the far corner of the unit and handed her the torch. She tucked it beneath her arm as she pulled on the gloves. The body was on the ground behind a low wall of crushed cardboard boxes. In the pool of torch-light he lay on his side, hands tucked between his knees, like a sleeping child overcome by tiredness mid-game and resting for a moment in a makeshift den. She nodded to Murdo, her voice caught by the pathetic sight. She swallowed. 'Yes, it's Jamie Buckland.'

Murdo walked out to Ravi and instructed him to chase up forensics. Now, the wheels of justice, whatever that might be for Buckland, would be set in motion. Shona turned back to the body and ran the torch around the scene. There was very little blood and nothing obvious to indicate how he'd died. She leaned closer, taking care not to disturb anything. He was facing towards her and she could see he'd been dead for some time. She looked for stab or gunshot wounds but could find none. Murdo came to stand beside her.

Shona shone the torch on Buckland's hands. 'Is that a ligature? Are his hands bound?'

Murdo leaned in close to her. He narrowed his eyes and nodded. 'Could be.'

Shona shifted the angle of the torch and looked again. 'No, they're not bound. It's just one hand, his right hand. It's not tied. It's bandaged.'

She lowered the torch and they both stepped back. Outside Ravi was peering at them through the twilight, the glow from his phone lighting up one side of his face. He lifted his hand and signalled 'two' with his fingers. It would be two hours before forensics would get here. Shona prepared to keep company with Jamie Buckland's body until they did. After a moment she took out her phone and dialled Dan Ridley's number. Tonight, she'd give him the news that they'd found his missing bail absconder. Tomorrow, Dan would be making the drive north, not to interview him, but to attend his post-mortem.

Chapter 28

Dan was waiting by the entrance to Dumfries Royal Infirmary when Shona arrived just after nine a.m. She felt as if she'd hardly left the place in the last few days, that somehow it had acquired a gravity that was pulling her into a closer and closer orbit. She nodded hello to Dan and they went upstairs.

'You won't have met Slasher Sue before,' Shona said, and then explained the origin of the pathologist's nickname.

Dan's face fell. 'I told my boss I'd be here all morning.' He was clearly in no rush to get back.

'Thirty minutes, tops. You'll still have time for a full Scottish breakfast in the cafe afterwards, if you feel like it.' Shona smiled.

Dan put his hand on his stomach and made a face.

'Not a fainter, are you?' The tall figure of Professor Sue Kitchen came out of a side door and looked him up and down like a lab specimen. 'If you feel funny, kindly stand by the wall or sit down. Haven't got time to whip out the smelling salts.'

Once they were dressed in green scrubs, they followed Professor Kitchen into the autopsy theatre.

Buckland's corpse lay fully dressed in a grey hooded sweatshirt, jeans and trainers. Professor Kitchen adjusted the round examination light, clicked on a digital recorder and quickly assessed her subject.

'Well-nourished, adult male, approximately five foot, five inches and in his early twenties. Rigor has passed, and there are early signs of decomposition suggesting death occurred two to three days ago. There are a number of injuries to the body including the right hand, which is bandaged, the face, and the right side of the head.' She glanced up momentarily. 'Now this will be of interest to you, Shona.'

Professor Kitchen pushed her glasses up the bridge of her nose with one gloved knuckle then pointed to a purple discolouration along Buckland's cheek.

Shona held her mask over her nose and mouth and leaned forward. 'Is that bruising?'

'There's some lividity, the pooling of blood in the lowest parts of the body after the heart stops beating. However, this is secondary lividity, which means he was moved between approximately two and six hours after death. I'll need to see the rest of him to tell you more. Right, kit off and let's open him up.' Professor Kitchen waved them back as her assistant began cutting and bagging up the victim's clothes.

Shona turned to Dan. 'You better get Carlisle to check Buckland didn't go back to his home address. If the body was moved, that could be our primary crime scene.' Dan pulled out his phone and took the opportunity to leave the room just as Professor Kitchen dug the scalpel into the skin below the subject's breastbone.

Slasher Sue lived up to her name, and within twenty minutes Buckland's internal organs had been removed and placed in containers for analysis. 'You're in luck.' She directed Shona to a metal dish containing Buckland's stomach contents. 'Meal of noodles and vegetables. See these bright flecks?' She teased out three small blue objects with the point of her scalpel and scrapped them into a clear plastic tube. 'Partially digested pills.'

'An overdose?' Shona said studying the sample.

'Hard to say. Toxicology will tell us more.'

When Dan returned Shona updated him on the partially digested pills already taken for testing.

Shona, Dan and Professor Kitchen stood looking down at the body. This close, a sour-sweet scent lingered beneath the masking disinfectant, and the marbled skin had a hard, smooth look.

'So, what are you thinking, Sue?' Shona said.

The pathologist tipped her head to one side, considering. 'He was on his back when he died, then someone moved him into this foetal position.' She curled her hands in front of her and turned to one side, demonstrating.

'So, someone else was present at or near the time of death. Could he have been transported in the back of a car?' Shona asked. 'Curled up in the boot then left the same way at the final locus.'

'That theory would not contradict my findings,' Sue replied.

'The pills,' Dan said uncertainly. 'Could it have been an overdose? Suicide?'

'Someone moved the body after death,' Shona reminded him.

'His dealer panicked and dumped the body?' Dan suggested.

'Key questions would be, is he self-medicating for depression or chronic pain?' Professor Kitchen cut in. 'He's well nourished, if small. His teeth are okay, looks like he's visited his dentist regularly. He's physically well cared for. That's not what I'd expect to find in a current user.'

Professor Kitchen shifted up a gear. 'Two things.' She lifted Buckland's head and pointed to a wound in the short blond hair above his ear. 'This blow to the head would be sufficient to render him unconscious.' She moved swiftly in long strides around the table and lifted his arm. 'Old track marks here too, but this one is fresh.' She pointed to a small mark almost hidden among the freckled skin. 'He was beaten prior to death. It's possible he self-administered drugs for the pain, but it's also possible he was injected while unconscious.'

'And the bandaged right hand?' Shona asked. She exchanged a look with Sue that showed they were both thinking the same thing. Was self-administration even possible with this hand injury? Shona pictured Jamie Buckland after their interview, at the custody desk signing for his possessions. 'I'm pretty sure he was right-handed.'

'It might explain the clumsy injection. We'll do X-rays and we've fast-tracked the toxicology and bloods,' said Professor Kitchen, pulling off her gloves. 'It shouldn't be long.'

Shona and Dan had paced the corridor, exhausted their small talk and finished a cup of indifferent machine coffee when they were called back in. Professor Kitchen pulled up the results on the computer screen.

'Your man died of heroin overdose. The pills are benzodiazepines and a small amount of alcohol is also present.'

'Could the benzos be Quinox? It's mostly available in the Far East.'

Professor Kitchen spent a few moments tapping on the keyboard. 'The recovered sample and Quinox are both

269

2-keto compounds, so it's possible. I can't tell you if the heroin was self-administered. It's a clumsy job but he could have done it himself. Now, Shona.' She replaced the lines of numbers and figures with X-ray images of Buckland's bandaged right hand.

Shona leaned closer. 'Is it the same as Sami Raseem?'

'Partially healed fractures to the metacarpals.' A second image appeared on the screen, side by side with the first. 'And, yes, the injuries are almost identical to your road victim, who also showed small traces of benzodiazepines in his blood.' The pathologist swivelled in her seat to look keenly at Shona.

Shona turned to Dan. 'You said Isla Corr had broken bones in her hand?' Dan nodded and Shona continued, 'Did you ever see the toxicology report?' It was the detail that had been nagging at her, the question at the top of her newly written list pinned to the front of Isla's case file.

Dan looked apologetic. 'I tried. I did what you said, went over there, but I just got the run-around. I had a case in court the next day, paperwork to finish, so...'

Professor Kitchen pushed her chair back from the desk and looked at Dan over her glasses with the kind of withering pity her students would immediately recognise. 'Leave this with me,' she said curtly, and left the room.

Shona perched on the edge of the desk and bit her thumb. Dan was still smarting from the exchange and sat down at the desk opposite, picking silently at the elastic band around his notebook.

'I've seen something like this before, a long time ago,' said Shona eventually, indicating the black and white pictures on the screen. 'London gangs used to punish thieves by breaking their hands. The victim was given a time limit to repay four or five times the value of what was stolen, or they'd get a return visit. A visit that usually proved fatal.'

Before Dan could respond, Professor Kitchen came back through the door. 'I called Carlisle. No drugs found in her system except small traces of 2-keto benzodiazepines, so potentially your Quinox. There were similar injuries to the metacarpals, but these were sustained peri-mortem, with no time to heal.'

'Wazir confirmed Buckland, Isla Corr and Sami Raseem knew each other. Now it looks like their deaths have a physical connection. Thanks, Sue, I'm really grateful for your help.' Shona got up and motioned to Dan. 'We'll let you get finished now.' They all shook hands.

At the end of the pathology corridor Shona stopped by a row of plastic chairs. 'What if they'd all been caught skimming from the same boss and had been trying to pay off the debt?' she began. 'What if they couldn't source enough baby milk? Wazir said they didn't get what they thought they could for it. Wazir doesn't have the same injuries – could he have been the one doling out these beatings? Doesn't strike me as the enforcer type,' Shona said. 'But could he be the boss behind this?'

'He's smart,' Dan agreed.

'Maybe, but he doesn't fit for Buckland's death. He's inside.' Shona began chewing her thumb nail again. 'Dan, get onto his solicitor. Wazir's in protective custody in Glasgow, see if we can set up a meeting. We need another chat with him. You're right. I'm not convinced he's told us everything he knows about Sami's death. I'll give Murdo a call, update him on the PM.'

Dan got out his phone and walked to the other end of the corridor but a few minutes later he returned grim faced.

'No joy?' Shona asked.

'It's worse than that. Wazir was found this morning hanged in his room,' Dan replied. 'The doctor's been in. They're saying suicide, no question. Tore up his shirt to make a ligature. No one thought him at risk, so there were no extra checks.'

'They can get to you anywhere,' Shona murmured. 'That's what Wazir said Sami told him.'

'You think someone got to him?'

'I think the fiscal should consider the possibility. He was in protective custody for a reason,' Shona said firmly, then sighed. 'Jamie Buckland, our best lead, is dead. Now Wazir's gone too.' She shook her head. Witnesses were disappearing, avenues of enquiry closing off. Shona searched back for any potential living source and landed on Tony Kirkwood, the ex-soldier who ran the homeless support centre and who knew Sami. He was a second-hand witness at best and there was no guarantee Kirkwood would talk to her again. 'I'll just be a minute.' She pulled out her phone, took up Dan's spot at the end of the corridor and dialled his number.

'Well, well, if it isn't the little mermaid.' Kirkwood's sleekit tones, set against a background of a muffled radio and the clatter of plates, sounded uncomfortably intimate.

'Mr Kirkwood,' Shona ignored the comment, 'I've a couple of questions about Sami I think you could help me with.'

There was a pause. 'Hang on a minute till I close the door.' The background noise died away. 'Okay, what is it?' His voice dropped and acquired a harder and more cautious edge.

'Couple of things, and I'd ask you not to repeat these matters to anyone.'

'Fire away.'

'Did you ever have contact with a friend of Sami's, Imran Wazir?'

'Nope, don't think so.'

'Okay. Was Sami caught up in the trafficking of children?'

'Paedophile stuff? You kidding me? Think I'd have given him houseroom if he was?'

'Okay, so one other thing. Drugs. Was Sami involved selling pills?'

This time the pause was longer. 'I don't tolerate dealers here. Nae sympathy for them. Parasites.'

'Tony, I've got three young people dead. There's a drugs link and both knew Sami. For Sami's sake, and all those who come after him who deserve a second chance, tell me what you know. Help me shut these networks down.'

He sighed. 'Yeah, Sami did mention something about selling pills. Said he'd got scared and stopped. I told him he'd done the right thing. He'd wind up in jail if he was caught. No chance of asylum or anything. Jail and deportation.'

'How did he react?'

'Seemed to hit home, promised he was done with that game.'

'Did he tell you anything about the operation, who he was involved with?'

'Not my job to ask, is it? Had enough to do keeping him here till I could patch him up,' he said indignantly.

'Yes, I know, Tony. Thank you,' Shona soothed. 'You've been very helpful.'

'Aye well, don't bandy that about. I've got my reputation to think of.'

Shona smiled. 'Of course. We are on the same side, you know.'

'Not always obvious though, is it?' he said, and hung up.

Shona walked back to where Dan was scrolling through his messages.

'Kirkwood just confirmed Sami was selling pills. Now we have three deaths with the same MO. Still think this is a serial killer?' Shona quizzed Dan.

He nodded slowly. 'In a sense. I think we're looking for the same perpetrator or perpetrators in all three cases. This isn't political. Or some ritual notion about the border, although I still think people like Duncan Saltire need locking up.' Dan shook his head. 'This is about revenge, or a turf war. That's the more likely motive.'

'Revenge for what, though? If it's a turf war over drugs, then Op Fortress would have had more intelligence on Jamie. He was bycatch. Surveillance identified him but he wasn't scheduled for arrest. We only rounded him up because he was at his mate's house. He literally had a couple of Valium pills in his hand when we nicked him.' Shona looked at him, her eyebrows lifting as an idea occurred to her. 'Do you think he did that deliberately?'

'How do you mean?' Dan frowned. 'You think he stuck his hand up for a Class C offence, knowing he'd walk, and we wouldn't look too closely at him? Yeah, I'd buy that. If he's gone under the radar, he's either been exceptionally clever or very, very lucky.'

Shona nodded slowly. 'Oh, I think he was much cleverer than we gave him credit for. And I think Isla, Sami, Buckland and Wazir are connected by more than baby milk. Dumping Buckland's body at the Carmine warehouse can't have been an accident. It was a warning to others. I think the pills, this Quinox, is the key. I think there's a connection to the Sweet Life group here somewhere. I should have seen it sooner.'

'How could you?' Dan said. 'Everything was passed to Op Fortress.'

'I know,' Shona conceded. 'But if I had seen a link, then maybe some of them would still be alive.'

Chapter 29

Shona and Dan spent the next hour preparing the conference room at Cornwall Mount CID office. It was early afternoon, but the overheated, south-east-facing room was close and dim, for the autumn sun had already left it far behind. Shona shrugged off her navy suit jacket and sent Dan to get a jug of water and two glasses.

When they were ready, the dozen officers and staff trooped in and gathered round the rectangular table stacked with files. Some sat on chairs, some perched on side tables, notebooks clasped to their chests. They shot furtive glances at the three photographs on the whiteboard and speculated quietly with their neighbours on the reason for their summons.

'Afternoon everyone.' Shona got up and all conversation died away. She tucked a strand of dark hair behind her ear and turned to the board. 'Isla Corr, Sami Raseem, Jamie Buckland.' She stabbed the board under the headshots with her marker pen, emphasising each name. 'Three deaths we now have reason to believe connect our baby milk case to the Sweet Life drugs group.' There were murmurs and exchanged glances around the table. 'All knew each other. All display injuries to their hands sustained weeks before, or at, their deaths. These are possibly punishment beatings,' she continued. 'All have traces of the prescription drug Quinox in their systems.'

'Our key witness Imran Wazir was found dead this morning.' Shona stilled the bubbling chatter with a glance. 'A doctor has ruled it suicide, but since he was supposed to be in protective custody in Glasgow, I've asked the fiscal to consider any anomalies in the case and ask for a second PM if necessary.' Shona had spoken to Professor Kitchen, who had promised to make herself available for it and would be formidable if crossed. Shona was assembling a strong team around her. They would solve these cases.

'Could Wazir have been involved in Isla or Sami's death? Did he think we're closing in on him?' Murdo said. 'It's a motive for suicide?'

'Can't rule it out,' Shona admitted, 'but while Wazir was in custody, Buckland was beaten, potentially forcibly injected with heroin, and his body dumped at the Carmine warehouse. Given what we previously found in the warehouse, a drugs turf war is a primary line of enquiry. Could this be a message to anyone thinking of reviving the business? Let's find out.' She looked directly at all the faces around the room; everyone understood her seriousness. 'I'll be seeing DCI Baird later to discuss proceeding these deaths under a single investigation, and any possible links with Op Fortress.'

She could have called Baird by phone or Skype but it was better to do it face to face. She wasn't leaving his office without getting what she wanted. The evidence of three connected murders was compelling. There was no way Baird was shunting this off to the sidings. Someone was loose on her patch, killing and getting away with it. Her relationship with Baird had got off to a bad start, mainly due to his stupid and unreconstructed behaviour, but she didn't believe he was a bad officer. In person he might listen to her and they could start to mend bridges.

'Okay. Where do you want us to start, boss?' Ravi ventured, and there were nods of enthusiasm around the table.

'Lines of enquiry.' Shona took out a screen grab and fixed it to the whiteboard. 'This man who assaulted Buckland is a priority.' Shona had failed to find him among the STAC guests – her memory for faces was good but not infallible. 'Vinny...'

The visual analyst jumped at the sound of his name. Shona didn't care if he reported her actions back to Baird, she'd get there first. Vinny was still on his way out, but until then she'd make him sing for his supper. 'Vinny, I want you to look at the footage Dan got from the neighbour. Clean it up. Also, I want you to review the baby milk store footage. Can you track them further from the scene? Railway station, bus station. Who were they meeting?'

Vinny nodded and looked down, busy typing notes into his tablet.

'Ravi, go back and talk to Isla's family. Emphasise she was clean, no heroin, but check with them and her GP if she was on anything for anxiety or sleep problems. That could account for the benzos in her system. We need to rule that out.'

'Kate, I want you to liaise with Dan over Jamie Buckland.' Shona thought she spotted a flash of enthusiasm cross her detective constable's expression, but it was quickly mastered. 'Buckland grew up with Isla.' Shona turned back to Ravi, but he signalled he'd already noted that and would pursue it with the family. 'Buckland had no previous,' she continued, 'but check around Carlisle, Dumfries, Annan and Gretna. Was he known to us? Any associates known to us? Also, any social worker contact as a kid?'

Kate exchanged a smile with Dan, who shifted round the table to sit next to her, opening his notebook and showing her addresses and other details to copy.

'Questions. I want to know where the Sweet Life group were getting the drugs. Who was supplying them? Talk to local users, see if they give us any clues.' Shona ticked them off her fingers. 'I want three fresh timelines, one for each of our victims. I want to know where they intersect.' She paced the room. 'Isla and Buckland were childhood friends, but how did they meet Sami? Why did they use the Carmine warehouse?'

'Nathan Jones has given us a new statement,' Murdo broke in. 'But I think we should talk to him again. Show him pictures of the three victims, see if he can give us more.'

'Yes, good,' Shona said. 'And Murdo, I spoke to Tony Kirkwood. He admitted Sami talked about selling pills. Get a statement, see if there's more. Suggest he comes to us, but if he gets stroppy, tell him we'll be round to his place mob handed and I'll be asking the fire service about certifications for that building.'

Murdo smiled and raised his eyebrows. 'That'll shake him up.'

'Good,' said Shona, firmly. 'Shaking up's what we do now. Everyone clear?' She waited for the nods and 'yes ma'am' responses. 'Okay, off you go.'

She said goodbye to Dan in the car park, with final advice on how to handle DCI Lambert. But as she got into the Audi, she saw a stream of texts from Rob alternately begging forgiveness and claiming he'd sort it all out and a little voice in her head piped up. 'Who are you to hand out advice? You're a fraud,' it said. 'A gambling addict husband, a wayward daughter and a business on the brink of bankruptcy? What about all the secrets you're keeping, enough to end your career and your marriage?' She dismissed it. That would come, but not now. Isla had been dead for seven weeks. With the passage of time opportunities had been lost. She needed to hurry. The chance to speak for the dead was slipping away.

Two hours later she pulled into the car park at Divisional HQ, a squat 1980s brick and concrete structure, in the centre of Kilmarnock. Shona showed her ID at the desk and was directed up to Baird's office on the top floor. As she left the lift, she felt her heels sink into the thick carpet and caught the scent of beeswax polish, two features noticeably absent from her own workplace. Baird stepped out from a glass-panelled side office.

'Shona.' He ushered her in, grasping her hand and expressing sympathy for her daughter's injuries. His jacket hung neatly on a coat hanger on a rack behind him, the buttons done up. Placed prominently on his desk was a silver-framed family photograph and the glass shard of his Scottish Policing Excellence award. As Baird returned to his chair, he gave the trophy a discreet half-turn, better to show it off. Shona suppressed a smirk.

Baird pointed her to a seat opposite and offered her coffee, which she refused. He rested his forearms on his desk, his white shirt cuffs rolled back, exposing thick dark hair. 'I appreciate you coming all the way here, but there was really no need. I'm happy to approve your compassionate leave, we could have done this with a phone call,' he said. 'Not that it isn't good to see you.' He smiled with an effort at sincerity.

'Oh, it's not about the leave, sir, though thank you for the offer.' Shona shifted in her seat. 'It's about a case, or rather a number of cases which appear to be linked. I'd like your approval to group them under a single investigation.'

A cloud passed across Baird's features, but he quickly regained his composure. 'Go on.'

Shona laid out the evidence connecting the baby milk thieves and the gang behind the Sweet Life drugs operation. She detailed the common factors in the murders of Isla, Sami and Jamie Buckland, citing a drugs turf war or gang violence as potential motives. She told him of Wazir's death and his allegations of threats against Sami, his link with Isla and Buckland.

Baird's frown became steadily darker until he held up his hand. 'Stop. You have two road accidents, an OD'd junkie and a suicide. At most you've got mates panicking and dumping the bodies. I appreciate you recovered the woman from the water, and therefore believe you have some sort of personal stake in this, but none of it adds up to murder.'

Shona started to reply but Baird cut her off. 'We know who was behind the Sweet Life group, an organised crime syndicate from Edinburgh which was dismantled by Operation Fortress. You really believe a bunch of shoplifters could run a drugs operation?' he scoffed. 'I gave you a direct order to drop this, remember?' He levelled an accusing finger at her.

'Yes, sir, but that was before Jamie Buckland's body was found at the Carmine warehouse.'

'A dead junkie in a warehouse. Seriously?'

'But he knew Isla and Sami...'

'Listen, Oliver, you're not in civilisation down there. It's the wild west, everyone knows everyone and half of them are related.'

'There's forensic evidence...'

Baird got up from his chair and loomed across the desk at her. 'I've got cases going to court from Op Fortress. Your meddling endangers potential convictions.' His voice was climbing. 'You start throwing up doubts about the Sweet Life group and the defence will jump on it. We've got Archer, an important informant, still in play out there. You could put his life in danger.'

'Sir, I need access to Op Fortress intelligence. I'm prepared to go to Munroe with this.'

Baird stopped dead and stared at her. 'You think he'll back you over me?' he challenged. For a moment Shona hesitated. Munroe was due to retire, he wouldn't want the success of Op Fortress jeopardised, but the bottom line was four people were dead. No one could provide a satisfactory explanation why they'd died. She wasn't suggesting the deaths were linked to some failure of Op Fortress, but she could see how Baird might feel it reflected badly on him. It was something he'd missed, and that would injure his pride. He was prepared to put his reputation before justice for the victims and their families.

Shona sat back in her chair and crossed her legs. She wasn't going anywhere. 'Why don't we ask Detective Superintendent Munroe for his opinion and find out?'

Baird paced the room then came to stand before her, hands on his hips, shaking his head. 'I really didn't want to go down this route, but I've heard things about your time with the City Police. Things that make me doubt your fitness for this job.'

Shona stared at him, shocked into silence. What did he mean? Did he somehow know about Rob's dismissal from the bank? His fraudulent dealings? She'd only just learned this herself. Or had he heard how her old DCI had given her a choice; transfer out of the City of London force or face a drunk-driving charge that would see her sacked. Baird lifted the phone on his desk. 'Sergeant, can you come up here for a minute.'

'I don't know what you've heard, but whatever it is, it has no bearing on these cases,' said Shona carefully.

A moment later the custody sergeant appeared. Baird motioned her to stand up.

'DI Oliver, I think you're under a lot of strain at the moment. I've offered you compassionate leave, which you've rejected. I've previously warned you about your failure to follow orders and maintain procedure. You've given me no choice. I believe you are currently unfit to serve. As of,' he looked at his watch, 'as of five o'clock today, I'm suspending you from duty. Please hand your warrant card and police phone to Sergeant Simpson. He'll escort you from the building.'

Chapter 30

Shona sat in her car and stared blankly ahead. Around her the street lights were coming on, orange outposts against the monochrome of evening. The teatime traffic was in full flow, leaving neon trails of brightness in the wet streets.

She'd left Divisional HQ with no clear idea of what to do next and pulled into the public car park across the road. Moments before, as she was being escorted out, the sergeant asked apologetically if she had arrived in a police vehicle. She'd need to hand over the keys. Though in a daze, she had enough self-possession to reply that when pool cars were introduced to cut costs that she'd opted to keep her own car and take reduced monthly expenses for it. She'd rather have a car she could trust to get her to jobs than be left on the roadside thumbing a lift. The sergeant had smiled and agreed that budget cuts were a shocking state of affairs, then he'd stopped. He gave her a guilty look and Shona realised she was no longer a colleague to share a grumble with. She was already an outsider.

She should tell Murdo what had happened. Shona reached for her phone, then remembered Baird had taken it. She felt like part of her had been lopped off.

'Shit, shit, shit.' She banged the flat of her hands on the steering wheel, then leaned forward and rested her forehead against it. Tears of rage and frustration were pricking her eyes. Nearby, two elderly women in bucket hats and raincoats were loading their car with shopping bags. They looked curiously at her. One came across and tapped the window, making Shona start.

'You okay, hen?' she mouthed through the glass.

Shona wound down the window, the fine drizzle misting her hot face. 'Yes, sorry. I... err... lost my phone.'

'Jeezo, I do that all the time.' The woman pulled a high-end smartphone from her pocket. 'Ma grandson sorts mine. Here, d'you want to borrow it? Report yours stolen?'

'No, it's fine. Thank you.'

'Sure? Cos, I tell you something, that shower there willnae help you.' She nodded to the police station Shona had just left. 'Ma grandson got his car taken. Three days it took the polis to turn up. Never found it.'

The other woman had finished loading the shopping and came over to join her friend. 'Aye. Shocking, so it is,' she agreed. 'It's a pure disgrace. Better off doing it yourself.' She took her friend's arm. 'C'mon you, let the lassie get home to her man.' She winked at Shona, 'This one would talk a glass eye to sleep if you let her. You sure you're all right?'

Shona smiled gratefully. 'Yes, I'm fine thank you.'

'Better off doing it yourself, hen.' The woman nodded sagely as her friend pulled her away. 'Cheerio, then.'

Shona watched the woman's multiple attempts to re-pocket the phone in her raincoat before she gave up and hauled open the passenger door of her friend's car. They both waved as they drove away.

Shona's first thought was to query her suspension, hit back at Baird with an allegation of sexual harassment at the STAC reception, but it would look like a petty attempt at revenge. She'd appeal of course, get hold of her Police

Federation rep and fight every inch of the way, but even if she won, and that wasn't certain, it would be too late. By the time she was reinstated, any chances of solving the deaths of Isla, Sami and Buckland would be long gone. The woman was right. Better off doing it yourself, hen.

Shona grabbed her wallet from her bag and flung her waterproof jacket around her shoulders. On the opposite side of the car park, shoppers in silhouette passed across the lit windows of a small retail estate. Between a McDonald's and a carpet shop was a Carphone Warehouse. She picked a mid-range pay-as-you-go and handed over her card. A moment later, the salesman handed it back. 'Sorry, your card's been declined. Do you want to try another?' All her cards were for joint accounts she shared with Rob. She remembered the row of figures on the spreadsheet he'd shown her, the unmet payments on Rob's car. They must all be maxed out.

Her salary was all they had to live on. Did her suspension mean the money wouldn't arrive this month? She didn't know. The bank certainly wouldn't unfreeze their accounts if they knew her job was in jeopardy.

'Wait a minute.' She sorted through her wallet. 'How much is a sim card?' There was that old phone of Becca's in a drawer at home. That would have to do. She handed over ten pounds in notes and coins. That would get her a couple of hours of calls and plenty of texts. 'Lost my phone, not worth getting another. My insurer will sort it out soon.' She felt compelled to explain to the dubious salesman.

When she got back to the car, she checked the petrol gauge and was relieved to find the tank half full. She'd need to ration her journeys until she was sure she could top up. In two hours, she'd be back in Kirkness. Home, food, sleep. The weariness, the injustice, the self-pity was creeping up on her, but she pushed them back. She took a swig of water from the bottle on the passenger seat and started the car. In two hours, she'd be back. Now she needed to think. In two hours, she'd have figured out what to do.

–

'I've been trying to call you,' Rob said impatiently as she came through the back door just after eight p.m. 'Becca won't leave the house. She should have a walk, some fresh air. I think the accident's still on her mind. You need to talk to her, convince her the driver's not coming back.' He was repacking the freezer, on his knees in jeans and an old checked shirt. A family-sized homemade lasagne lay on the countertop. Next to it was a colander containing the last of the salad leaves Rob grew in the garden. At least they wouldn't starve. Not yet, anyway. 'Becca's already eaten, do you want me to put this on now? It's going to be at least an hour. The guests for the Rood Fair in Dumfries will be here next week, if you're not hungry I'll save it for them. Murdo called looking for you, by the way.' He stopped at the sight of her pale face and red-rimmed eyes. 'What?'

Shona stood looking down at him, clenching and unclenching her fists. 'Who knows what happened at Milton McConnell? Who did you tell?' she said. All the way home in the car she'd thought about this, more and more convinced this was what Baird meant about her unfitness to serve and rumours from London: her association with Rob and the bank fraud. All it took was whispers.

'No one, I swear,' Rob said, shocked. 'It's hardly something I'd boast about, is it?'

'I've been suspended,' she spat.

'How can that be my fault?' he challenged, getting up and kicking the freezer door shut. 'Look, I know I messed up, but I'm getting help.'

'You know what that means?' Shona yelled. 'Thanks to you we're finished. No money, no jobs, no business. Think, Rob, think hard. Who knows about this?'

'Look, Shona, I'm the victim here. They screwed me over at the bank.' He stabbed a finger at her. 'If someone's out to get you, don't blame me.' Rob stalked out of the kitchen and left Shona staring open-mouthed after him.

'Thanks for the support!' she yelled. 'Rob!' She went through the kitchen after him, but he'd already sprinted upstairs. High above she heard their bedroom door slam.

Becca's pale face looked down over the bannisters. 'Everything okay, Mum?'

'Yes, yes, darling. Sorry I'm so late.' Shona's smile was brittle and unconvincing. 'How are you doing? Did you get out today?'

'Didn't feel like it.'

'Right, well I've got some time off coming. Maybe we could take a boat out? It's not too cold yet, is it?'

'Dunno.' Becca slouched back from the bannisters and Shona heard her bedroom door close.

'Becca? I'll be up in a minute. Where's your old phone?' Shona called after her, but there was no reply.

Shona's hands trembled as she pulled out the drawers in the kitchen searching for Becca's discarded handset. It lay under a under a pile of tea towels and red bills. She wasn't even going to look at those. Bundling up the envelopes, she went into Rob's office next door and dumped them on the overcrowded desk beneath the window. Plugging the phone into the wall, she inserted the SIM card bought in Kilmarnock. 'C'mon, c'mon.' The sluggish battery blinked slowly back at her.

Shona's RNLI fleece hung on the back of the utility room door. She searched the inside pocket for the business card Dan had given her the first time they'd met at Silloth Lifeboat Station. It was there, folded in half. She blew off the fluff and returned to where the phone was slowly coming back to life. One bar showed on the battery, that would be enough if she kept it plugged in.

Becca's music drifted down from above. There was no sign of Rob. She closed the office door over and punched Dan's mobile number into the phone.

'Hello?' he answered cautiously after the fifth ring, not recognising the number.

'Dan, it's me.'

'Boss, at last,' Dan sounded relieved. 'Are you okay? Murdo told me he'd had a call about a temporary guvnor. What happened?'

Shona filled him in, omitting Baird's inference about her past. There was a long silence from Dan. 'I think you've been treated appallingly,' he said eventually.

'Dan, listen to me. You've got to let this go now.'

'Not a chance,' he said flatly.

'I mean it. Your DCI isn't interested, you said so yourself. Murdo won't be able to help you,' she warned. 'Let it go, Dan, you did what you could.'

'You're not letting it go, are you?' It was half statement, half question.

'I'll go and see Isla's mother tomorrow. Tell her I'm sorry we couldn't find out how her daughter died. I owe her that much at least.'

'Want me to come with you?' Dan said. She was touched by the generosity of his offer, but what Dan needed to do now was keep his head down. She had misjudged Baird. If he spoke to Dan's boss, the bull-headed DCI Lambert, then this conscientious young officer could be caught in the fallout of her suspension.

'Thanks, Dan. It's better if I do this alone. Take care of yourself.'

'You too, boss.' Dan hesitated. 'If you need me, you know, to talk or anything, just call.'

'Okay, Dan. Thanks, I will.' She ended the call and stared for a moment at the handset. She would miss his company. She left the phone to charge. She'd call Murdo shortly, when she'd worked out what to say to him. From the office window the estuary was calm, the sky clear, and the temperature dropping. Later, a mist would come up and, in the morning, there would be a silver sheen of frost on the cars and pathways. She pinned a note of her new mobile number to the kitchen noticeboard for Rob and Becca, then took her fleece from the peg and closed the back door behind her. She would enjoy this beautiful place while she still could. They might not be here much longer.

Now the shock of her suspension was sinking in she felt an overwhelming sense of guilt that Murdo and her colleagues would suffer for her mistakes. It would be her sergeant who faced the questions tomorrow morning, standing up in the Dumfries CID and explaining to the frowning faces of her former team that they'd be carrying on without her. There would be a disruptive enquiry. Later, a disciplinary board might ask Murdo why he hadn't questioned his DI's maverick behaviour. She worried he'd stand up for her, talk of the values they shared; loyalty to the community, defending of the defenceless, the pursuit of justice for all. Murdo and his wife were churchgoers, steadfast in their beliefs. He would hold to his and pay the price with his own career. Dumfries shouldn't lose a copper as good as Murdo.

She walked down to the water's edge. The lifeboat station was dark. She hesitated by the door. Tommy must have gone home. She cupped her face against the shopfront glass. She could see the lifeboat asleep in its metal cradle. She thought of the original Margaret Wilson, the Solway Martyr, a woman tied to a stake and slowly drowned by the incoming tide for holding fast to her beliefs. As the water had reached her chin, the executioner and local church minister had given her the opportunity to recant and be saved. She'd refused. Shona hoped, in the face of this unstoppable tide of disaster that seemed to be racing towards her, her courage and resolution would be as strong. Pulling up her collar, she set off along the seafront path.

How did this all happen? What sign had she missed? Her marriage to Rob might not survive this, the burden of deceit and lies pulling it apart. There was a part of her that still loved him; they'd come so far together. Her anger at learning what he'd done was still fresh, but he was right about one thing, no one at Milton McConnell would want fraud rumours to get out. So, who told Baird? Maybe this wasn't about Rob at all. More likely Baird was in contact with her old boss DSU Harry Delfont. Delfont was unscrupulous and corrupt enough to turn the knife. Either way, if it all came out, she was finished.

She stopped by the Wee Pier. The tide had not yet turned, slack water lay quietly against the lichen-covered granite, invitingly calm. She could just walk in. Walk until it covered her head. Walk until it took her away somewhere peaceful and still. But as soon as she thought this, she saw Becca. Her life would be blighted by the grief Shona knew took root in those left behind. Tommy and her RNLI colleagues hauling Shona's lifeless body from the water. Professor Kitchen conducting the autopsy before Murdo's bleak and uncomprehending stare. She saw all this in a fraction of a second and knew there was nothing to be done but face what was coming. She had failed Isla, Sami and Jamie Buckland. Their deaths would be listed as unfortunate but not unexpected. A junkie, a whore, an illegal immigrant; people would say they'd got what they deserved. A least she could tell Isla's family she didn't agree, and tomorrow she would do just that.

Chapter 31

On Saturday morning Shona drove to the Corr house in Dumfries. She didn't have Marie's number to call in advance and knocking brought no reply. Shona peered through the front window to a room unchanged in its neatness, but with Paddy Corr's reclining chair no longer in front of the TV. In its place was a child-sized beanbag and a plastic toybox. A neighbour said Marie had taken the kids to Southerness beach where she had a caravan. Shona used her precious petrol on a trip that took her halfway back to where she'd started out an hour earlier.

There were few visitors despite the dry weather and the September Weekend holiday. She left her car in the village car park and headed towards the dense white block of Southerness lighthouse. The tide was low, the sky grey. Mudbanks and small islands floated in the pewter vista as if suspended between sea and sky. The lighthouse, the second oldest in Scotland, was a familiar landmark she'd seen often on journeys up the firth with the lifeboat.

Shona, in her off-duty uniform of jeans, trainers, and RNLI fleece, stood for a moment above the beach. She swept back her hair, which blew about her face in a dark mass of waves and curls, and scanned the sparse dogwalkers, fishermen and day trippers for a clue.

She spotted Marie about a hundred metres away looking out at the Solway Firth. As Shona set off towards the lone figure, she felt a renewed stab of guilt that she was bringing no fresh news and no real answers.

Two boys in bright anoraks and wellies played nearby. Shona recognised one of them as Isla's six-year-old son Ryan and her courage nearly failed her. Did he miss his mother? Or had he become accustomed through her long absences to life with his grandmother? She supposed he had. Shona had been the same age when her mother went. She couldn't recall missing her. That came later. Her wedding, Becca's birth, Christmases and birthdays, a subtle gap in the family photos she was sure no one else noticed.

Ryan wheeled and swooped like a gull, intent on some game only he could see. The other boy, a little younger, moved with a listless boredom, hood up against the breeze, shoulders hunched, his hands in his pockets. He dragged loose circles with the toe of his boot on the muddy sand. A ball lay untouched nearby. Marie might not welcome a conversation in front of either children, but the space and distraction of beach and rock pools was better than a stuffy front room for what Shona had to say.

Suddenly, Ryan ran to his grandmother, pulling at her sleeve, pointing out to sea. A row of bobbing heads just offshore looked back with interest. The grey seals, like bathers in swimming caps, studied the figures on shore before slipping back beneath the choppy water.

Shona understood how the stories of selkies, half-human, half-seal folk who lured young people away into the sea, had taken hold around the Scottish coast. A tale to comfort the loved ones of drowned souls. Did Marie come here to search the faces of these sea creatures in the hope she would catch a glimpse of Isla? Isla reborn, Isla free.

Marie turned and looked back at Shona's approaching figure, shading her eyes from the wind to study her. Recognition followed by a flicker of hope. Then her jaw set firm in a frown. The police never brought good news to her door.

'Hello, Marie.' Shona smiled at the woman, who seemed to have grown younger since their last meeting. She wore a brightly patterned waterproof jacket and wellies, and her hair was subtly coloured with blonde streaks.

'Youse got nothing better to do than hang about outside in this weather?' Marie said with a habitual stab at aggression, but Shona could see her heart wasn't in it.

'Day off,' Shona replied.

'All right for some.'

'My condolences for Paddy,' said Shona.

Marie shrugged. 'Good riddance.' She glanced at Shona. 'You don't look shocked.'

'I understand he wasn't an easy man to live with,' Shona said carefully.

'Led us all a dog's life, that's for sure. Better off without him.'

Ryan studied Shona for a moment with serious blue eyes she recognised from Isla's picture, then headed back to his game. The smaller child leaned against Marie.

'Who's this young man?' Shona said.

'Liam. One of the family. I look after him.'

'Hi Liam.' Shona crouched down and smiled at the child, but he looked past her, unwilling to meet her eyes.

'Got problems. Doesnae talk,' Marie said. Liam turned away and followed Ryan to where the older boy was dropping stones into a rock pool.

Shona nodded. 'Must be hard for you.' They watched him go then Shona cleared her throat. 'I'm sorry we couldn't do more for Isla,' she said. Marie looked surprised at this admission. 'I think you need to prepare yourself,' Shona continued, 'for the possibility that we may not be able to determine how she met her death.'

'You mean, you don't know who killed her?'

'No, I'm sorry,' replied Shona. Out over the water, a flock of seabirds were a percussion of dark dots against the sky. 'I have a daughter myself. She's nearly fifteen. I don't know what I'd do if I lost her. She's been in trouble a few times over the years, gave me a few sleepless nights, but still…'

'Aye, they do that right enough.' Marie gave a short laugh. 'Lads and lassies, both.'

'I'm thankful I've just got the one then.' Shona smiled. 'What was Isla like, as a wee girl?'

'Smart,' Marie said with pride. 'If she'd stuck in at school mibbae she'd have had a chance. She could have worked in an office, good with numbers. I don't know where I went wrong.' She sighed. 'That's a lie, I do know. I was terrified of Paddy, but I couldnae leave. He told me plenty of times how he'd kill me and the kids. I was doped up to my eyeballs on Valium from the doctor. The tables turned when he got sick. I got off the pills, but by then it was too late. I should have done more for her.'

Shona could think of no reply. They stood and watched Ryan, now jumping in a shallow stand of water, the muddy spay leaving dimples around the edges of the pool.

'I saw on the news that Jamie Buckland's dead.' Marie said. 'Nice lad that, Isla was fond of him.'

'Do you know if he has any relatives? Who's his next of kin?'

Marie shook her head. 'His ma was in and out of the jail and his father drank. They're both dead. Brother and sister were jakies, OD'd years back. Suppose he was always gonnae go the same way.'

'It always comes as a shock though, doesn't it? Someone so young.' Shona paused. 'My daughter recently had a serious accident. It brought home to me how fragile life is, how one action can sweep away someone you love. I know an explanation of what happened is no substitute for your daughter's life, but I hoped I could at least give you that. I'm sorry I failed to do that.'

'So, you'll not be investigating it any more.'

'Another officer will take over the case and I believe, together with the fiscal, they'll conclude that Isla died as the result of a road accident, that the driver panicked and disposed of the body unlawfully. Anyone caught in relation to her death will face that charge. But Isla will be released now, so you can have the funeral.' She tried to end on a positive note, but how could telling a mother she would soon be free to bury her daughter ever sound anything less than tragic.

'How come you're not in charge?'

Shona sighed. 'I didn't see eye-to-eye with my boss. He thought I shouldn't have been investigating Isla's death in such detail.' She paused and took a breath. 'You know, I brought her body ashore with the lifeboat.'

Marie's eyes went to the RNLI logo on Shona's jacket then back to her face. 'No. I didnae know that.' Shona sensed she was under scrutiny, Marie's shrewd expression softening.

'Maybe that's what made me want to find out what happened,' Shona said quietly. 'Maybe I let it affect my judgement. I'm sorry. I feel that I've let you both down.'

Marie turned away and Shona saw her take out a paper hankie. 'This wind goes for your eyes,' she said hastily, wiping away tears. After a moment she said, 'You shouldnae blame yourself.' Her eyes were on the far horizon of the Solway. Then she put out her hand and gripped Shona's arm just above the wrist, and the two women stood watching the waves and the boys playing by the water.

'Listen,' said Marie eventually. 'Mibbae you should have a cup of tea at my place. There's something I'd like to show you.'

–

DCI Gavin Baird was in his office early after a sleepless night. Nicola had complained about his tossing and turning, she had an important day ahead, a meeting with a local party executive that might back her for a Scottish Parliament seat at the next election. She needed her sleep. For a moment he almost told her, told her where her ambition and social climbing had led them. But he was the one doing the climbing, Nicola was already up there.

Finally, around four a.m., he'd gone downstairs, padding into the kitchen in sleep shorts and T-shirt to make some warm milk. He'd had one of the tech boys unlock Shona's phone. Now he slipped it from the evidence bag, turning it over and over in his hand while he sipped his drink. He'd checked the call log, then opened the picture files. There was the woman Shona had fished from the Solway, before and after. Headshots of the illegal immigrant found on the motorway, and Wazir, the guy they'd nailed for the baby milk thefts. In the middle was a low-quality still from a CCTV camera showing two men in a street of Victorian terraced houses. Baird had scrolled past it but flicked back, scrutinising the monochrome blurs. Then he searched the original video files. He'd sat forward on the edge of the sofa, the milk going cold in his cup.

Fuck. She had almost all the pieces. He'd been right to suspend her. He'd made a call, but it went straight to voicemail. He'd tried over and over with the same result, then spent the rest of the night on the sofa wrapped in one of Nicola's fancy blankets, Shona's phone in his hand, waiting for the dawn.

Now, Baird paced his office. DCI Oliver's phone lay on his desk like an accusation. Things should never have gone this far. Three murders, that's what she was talking about. He glanced at the chair where she'd sat the evening before, looking at him. Her expression was plain: he was a plod, a dull copper who couldn't join the dots. She was wrong, he had joined the dots. But he saw an entirely different picture.

He remembered the look she'd given him when he'd taken her warrant card. She wasn't going to let this go. There would be scrutiny. He'd stop her in the end, everyone has weaknesses and he'd found Shona's. Was that enough? Things might come out along the way, things neither he nor, God forbid, Nicola would want made public. But he got results, that was the bottom line. That's what kept him moving upwards. He could fix this.

Baird ignored his police-issue mobile on the desk, went to his jacket and pulled out his personal phone, his 'secret shagging phone' as Nicola called it. As if he'd time for an affair. Her little joke. His obsession, his love for Nicola was both his strength and his greatest weakness. Did she have secrets from him? He didn't doubt it.

He called a dozen more times, all straight to voicemail. What would he say when they finally picked up? He had an alien sensation lodged in the pit of his stomach. It took him a while to identify, it was so long since he'd felt it. Fear, plain and simple. If he wasn't careful everything he'd achieved would come tumbling down, pulled apart by some wee woman sat in some arse-end town in the borders. Damage limitation was called for. He dialled. This time there was an answer.

'Listen, I've sorted that problem in the south,' Baird said to the gruff greeting at the other end of the line, 'but you need to keep things calm for a bit.'

'Too late for that, Gavie-boy.'

'What do you mean?'

'Had your go at fixing it. It's my neck on the line. You want a job done properly, do it yourself, it's what the Big Man says.'

'You got us into this mess. Now you listen to me…' Baird was used to respect. The top brass, inspectors, sergeants, tough coppers with years of experience, hung on his words.

'Or what?' the voice challenged, and Baird knew where the fear he felt came from. It came from the feeling of powerlessness. You can't reason with a mad dog. There's only one way you teach it respect. Be quicker, scarier and have a bigger bite. Baird knew the day had arrived when he'd have to shrug off his fine suits and go back to the sticky end. He'd been too soft, he looked weak. Well, that was soon fixed. He wasn't afraid to get his hands dirty. He remembered his father, a peaceable man, back in their pit village, slugging it out with another miner who'd goaded him once too often. The blood mixed with sweat and coal dust, streaks of red and black across the sun-starved flesh of his muscled arms. Eventually his father had lost patience with the mouthy upstart and felled him with a single punch, the man hitting the ground like a dislodged pit timber.

'My turn now, Gavie-boy,' the voice said, hauling him back to the present.

'Listen to me, you sick bastard,' Baird growled, but no one was listening. He heard the click and empty buzz of silence on the line. He threw down the phone, hauling his jacket from the back of his chair. He fumbled his car keys, ran down to the car park and sped from the station, heading for south.

Chapter 32

Shona expected a photo album. Tea and tears. She felt an obligation to stay, it would be a kindness. But the truth was she had nowhere else to go. Another DI would already be sitting at her desk in the CID office. If she went home, the guests would be out and she'd have to face Rob. Becca would still be in bed. Shona wasn't looking forward to breaking the news of her suspension or Rob's insurmountable debts to her daughter, but it needed to be soon. It was time Becca understood what was going on and prepared herself for the changes to come. But Shona could put that off for an hour to sit with Marie. If nothing else, Marie reminded her that no matter how bad things were, Shona was still the luckier of the two.

The boys raced ahead across the beach; Marie had promised them chips. Liam seemed content to let Ryan lead him, stopping by items of interest along the way, a coloured rock or a feather, which he pocketed. At one point Ryan picked up a discarded toy car, the dull metal showing beneath the chipped red paint, and handed it to the younger boy, folding Liam's fingers tight around it. Liam looked at it blankly but didn't let go.

Marie's large static caravan sat at the far end of a row. Most of its companions were already locked up for the winter, their windows shuttered against the coming storms. At the door, the boys kicked off their wellies.

Ryan placed both sets carefully upright next to Marie's rubber clogs. There were more wellies and a pair of trainers too big to fit either boy. A Nike hoodie lay next to them. He led his cousin up the metal steps and pulled open the door. Inside, Shona could hear his excited chatter, a second voice replying. Marie must have other family staying. Shona's heart sank. They'd react badly to the news that the investigation into Isla's death was over, bombard her with questions she couldn't answer. Marie might join in, or leap to her defence. Either way, a family row would ensue. She turned to the woman at her elbow. 'Marie, listen, maybe I should go. I don't want to make this any harder for you than it is.'

Marie put a hand out to stop Shona. 'I want you here.' She bit her lip. 'Just remember one thing. I did all this for her,' she said simply, before motioning Shona to go inside.

'What do you mean?' Shona frowned. But Marie was still ushering her forward, so she kicked off her shoes and climbed the steps.

Shona's eyes took a moment to adjust to the dim light inside the caravan. To her left, the boys were already on the banquette seat that ran around the bay end of the caravan facing out to Solway Firth. On the table, a magazine and a coffee mug lay abandoned by a small, dark haired girl, late teens or early twenties, indistinct against the grey autumn light. She wore a black fluffy jumper and jeans, her legs curled up under her. The girl smiled at the treasures Ryan spilled from his pocket. Shona looked around. Through open doors she saw three small bedrooms, two with double beds and one containing bunks and cartoon duvets, but there was no other family in sight.

The dark-haired girl glanced up at the new visitor. The smile faded. 'What's this?' she said to Marie.

'Hello, I'm Shona Oliver.' Shona smiled, coming forward.

'I know who you are,' the girl said.

Shona stopped in her tracks. A pair of blue eyes stared defiantly back at her. Shona looked from Ryan to the young woman and back. There was no mistaking the resemblance. Shona blinked. The face was small and pointed. Shona took a step closer and saw that blonde roots pushed up into the short dark hair. Could this be the young woman sitting in a hospital bed, battered by her boyfriend? The pale body tangled with ghost gear lying on the sandbank in the middle of the Solway Firth? It couldn't be. Shona felt her heart leap in her chest. She took another step closer. 'Isla? Is that you?'

The young woman shifted in her seat, pulling Ryan closer. The boy put his arm protectively around the woman's shoulders. 'Aye,' she said eventually. 'Aye, it's me.'

Behind her, out of the window, was a glint of brightness, the sun coming from behind a cloud out over the firth. This was the woman in the water, but out here on the coast, by some miracle, the sea had given her back.

'So, who?' Shona asked. 'How?'

'Think you better sit down,' said Marie. 'I'll away and take the boys over to the cafe for chips. I'll let Isla tell you.'

Once they were alone, Isla pulled a packet of cigarettes from their hiding place in an overhead locker. If she was conscious that Shona was staring at her she didn't show it.

'D'you mind if we go outside, my mother doesnae like me smoking in the van.' She wrapped a chunky white scarf around her, opened the door and slipped her feet into the Nike trainers on the mat. They stopped in a sheltered spot between the caravan and a low hedge of yellow gorse bent double by the wind.

'You okay here? You warm enough?' Shona asked, conscious that she was slipping into lifeboat mode, caring for a casualty, as if Isla had only just been plucked from the water. Isla's pale face looked as fragile as bone china and she barely came up past Shona's shoulder. One strong puff of wind might blow her away.

Isla shrugged. 'I'm fine.' She put a cigarette between bare lips and with a practised stance lit it first time. From the packet she also drew a folded photograph, holding it delicately between third finger and thumb, and positioning it for Shona to see. It was the line-up of Isla and her cousins that Shona had seen in the kitchen when she'd first told Marie the news of her daughter's death.

'That's me.' Isla pointed to the blonde teenage girl with the centre parting on the far right, then worked her way along. 'Paul, Josh, Matty,' she skipped a face, 'and on the end's my wee brother, Lewis.' She came back along the line, her child-like finger with its chipped polish and bitten nail resting tenderly on the only other girl in the photograph. A slight girl with blonde hair and Isla's blue eyes. 'That's my cousin, Siobhan.' She faltered. 'It's... it's her body you found.'

'Marie's sister, your Aunt Margaret? It's her daughter?'

'Aye, that's right.' Isla blew out a trail of smoke. 'Though Maggie the Misery never wanted much to do with Shiv, even before she was a jakie. Shiv's sister, Neve, was the favourite. Neve got hit by a car coming home fae school and Margaret told Shiv the wrong girl had died. What a bitch. Then Shiv had Liam, and, well, he spends all his time with us.' Isla shrugged. 'My Auntie Margaret has religion. Thinks she's above us all. And Shiv's dad, my

Uncle Joe, gave his daughter a bit too much attention, if you ken what I mean. We had a lot in common, me and Shiv.' Isla's expression darkened.

More in common than you know, thought Shona, remembering the file she'd just reviewed. Identification of the body was via partial DNA match to Paddy Corr. So, Siobhan must be Paddy's daughter, Isla's half-sister, rather than her cousin. There was no record in the file of the DNA sample Shona had asked Ravi to collect from Marie. It was the second question she'd written on the review list pinned to the front after 'Toxicology report?' Now those questions had both been answered. Was Quinox present in all three victims? Yes. Confirmed ID through maternal DNA link to Marie Corr? No.

Did Paddy have an affair with Margaret, his wife's sister? Or, knowing Paddy's record and reputation, was Siobhan the result of rape? That was a question Shona couldn't answer, but it might be one explanation for Margaret's estrangement from Siobhan.

'So, you both had bracelets with the twin heart design?' Shona asked, focusing on the details of the case.

Isla shook her head. 'It was mine, I lent it to her. She'd come down from Glasgow for a few weeks. I was living sometimes in Gretna, sometimes in Carlisle at Buckie's place. We had a wee project on the go,' said Isla evasively.

'The Sweet Life?' Shona hazarded.

'Aye.'

'So, what happened to Siobhan? When did you last see her?'

'She went out one night and never came back. I thought she'd just skipped back to Glasgow, but then I found out Buckie was fixing her up with punters. I'd told him not to, but she needed the cash.' Isla turned away, narrowing her eyes as she looked out over the water. A man was chasing his dog on the beach, the shouts drifting across the scrubby foreshore as he tried to persuade it back.

'Do you think someone mistook her for you?' Shona asked. It would be an easy mistake to make, she thought ruefully.

'I didn't at the time, but now with Sami and Buckie gone...'

'Siobhan, Sami and Jamie Buckland all had injuries to their hands sustained before they were killed. In Sami and Jamie's case, days or weeks. Does that mean anything to you?'

Isla took a long pull on her cigarette and nodded. 'Buckie suggested we sold prescription pills through Facebook. He had a supplier; it was a side-business for Buckie but Sami and I just wanted enough cash to get out. Start over somewhere new. Shiv didn't know any of this. I couldn't trust her to keep her mouth shut. When I had enough money, I would've told her. Then we could've both got out.'

'How did you and Sami meet?' Shona was aware she was straying from the main narrative, but she was hungry for detail. Isla might refuse to repeat her story to anyone else. She couldn't arrest her, she couldn't stop Isla and Marie running off to hide elsewhere. Shona needed to harvest every detail, sketch the web of connections as quickly as she could.

Isla threw away the stub of her cigarette and pulled her scarf closer. 'Sami was doing some courier work for a contact of Buckie's. We just hit it off. He was dead clever, but he'd had some bad times back home in Syria, done his head in. The traffickers had sold his debt on to this crazy gang of dealers. He'd had enough.'

'Did Sami ever tell you about trafficking children?'

Isla shifted uncomfortably. 'He'd get upset and say stuff, but I think it was in his head. He'd get mixed up with things that had happened in Syria, you know, like flashbacks, but it was like he was actually re-living them. Kids being taken and killed. People getting blown up. He wasn't sleeping. Buckie gave him some pills to help him but it just made things worse. Suicidal, like.' She stared at the ground, pushing the extinguished cigarette butt with the toe of her trainer.

'How did they injure their hands?' Shona pulled Isla's attention away from thoughts of dead children and back to her earlier line of questioning.

'Buckie's main drugs suppliers found out we were selling pills on the side. They weren't happy,' she said with ironic understatement. 'We were all too scared to go back to the Carmine warehouse and get the rest of the gear. Thought they might be waiting for us. We'd undercut them, stolen their market. Why would you pay ten pounds for heroin if you can get pills for two or three pounds a time through the post, in the comfort of your own home? No risk. Buckie said he'd bring them in on the business, like a merger. He had big ideas, I helped him draw up a business plan. That looked like it might work, but then some new faces took over at the top, a new crew who didn't want the competition. Plus, someone, probably Sami or that creepy pal of his, Wazir, was syphoning off cash. Sami was so desperate to pay off the people who brought him here. Desperate and scared.'

'So, the baby milk?'

'Thought we could use it to generate some quick cash and get out. But Buckie's supplier heard about this too and wanted a cut. We couldn't shift the stuff quick enough.'

'And the injuries to their hands?'

'There was one guy. Buckie used to call him El Chapo, or the Big E, like he was a celebrity. Dressed smart. Face like a skull. Said he'd take a hammer to anyone with their hand in the till. I think he killed Siobhan because he thought she was me.'

Shona's heart was beating fast. So, she'd been right, punishment beatings. Siobhan's injuries were close to the time of death; perhaps they were a bid to extract information. But Siobhan wasn't Isla, there was nothing she could tell her captors. Shona thought of the man in the video that Dan had found. The man punching Jamie Buckland in the street outside his home. Expensive suit, face like a skull. 'What's his name?'

Isla gave a short and bitter laugh. 'You're wasting your time. You willnae get this guy. He's got protection. He used to say he was like the devil himself. He could get rid of folk and no one could touch him. I believed him.'

'Isla, four people are dead.' Shona saw her do the maths. Good with numbers, her mother had said. Shona supplied the missing figure. 'Wazir apparently committed suicide in custody yesterday morning.'

'And you think someone got to him, don't you? Fuck. I told you, this guy's protected.' Isla shook her head. 'Used to boast he had cops in his pocket, judges, the lot. You know what? I should just stay dead. Don't tell anyone it wasn't me in the water. I don't want to stop being Shiv and go back to being Isla.'

'Is that what you really want?' Shona folded her arms, letting the question hang in the air.

'Being Isla wasn't really working for me. Safer being Shiv.'

'We can protect you. Give you a new life. Ryan will have questions as he grows up. He knows you're Isla. Will you tell him you're not his mother? Will you make him keep that secret?'

Isla bit her lip and leaned back, her shoulders resting against the side of the caravan. 'No really fair to the wee man, is it?' She let out a long breath. 'When me and Shiv were kids, we delivered drugs around the estate on our bikes. Got me away from my dad, he was never into that scene. Thieving, gambling and girls was his thing. Running with a gang got me some protection.' She took out another cigarette, offered the packet to Shona, who declined. 'One time me and Siobhan were delivering to a squat and this big crackhead, nasty looking fucker, didnae want to pay. He just laughed at us, pulled out a knife and took what we had. Locked us in a flat overnight, we were shit scared he'd come back. We were about fourteen. I was so angry I nearly went for the guy, knife or no knife. Shiv pulled me back. That's when I knew that what I needed more than drugs was respect.'

Isla paused and clicked her lighter. 'So, I picked up with the scariest, most violent bastards I could find. That's how I met Ryan's dad, Fergie. Duncan Ferguson as he was, before he cleaned himself up and changed his name to Duncan Saltire. Back then, he ran with this skinhead gang who controlled the drugs market in Dumfries. I used to bag the stuff, count the cash, balance the books.' She saw Shona's expression. 'Aye, funny isn't it, him being so anti now.' She laughed, taking a pull on her cigarette. 'You know he's never paid me a penny towards Ryan? I asked him again a few months back, but he wasnae having it. What a dick. He used to batter me of course, but even wi' that it was better than being at home, or out there on my own.'

'You're not on your own now, Isla,' Shona said quietly.

'You really think you can get this guy?' Isla looked coolly at Shona, assessing her, and Shona had a glimpse of the streetwise intelligence, the head for figures that had kept this tiny, fragile creature alive against the odds.

'I can nail him, with your help. I owe it to Siobhan.' She paused. 'You owe it to Siobhan and yourself. He's never going to stop unless we stop him.' She watched as the young woman made the calculation, a look of resignation signalling she'd balanced the odds.

'Aye, maybe you're right.' Isla stubbed out her cigarette. 'Okay. His name's Evan Campbell. He's from Glasgow but he's got a flat in Carlisle too. Jamie took me there once.'

'Do you know the address?' Shona pulled out her phone and pressed Dan Ridley's number.

Isla shrugged. 'No idea.'

Shona quickly updated Dan. When she gave him the news that Isla was alive and had information on their suspect he was shocked into silence. Then she could hear him beaming with enthusiasm, the keen, urgent edge back in his voice. With a witness and a suspect, they could build a case. Show Shona was right, get her reinstated. Shona reminded him they'd have to catch Evan Campbell first.

'Can you describe Evan Campbell's flat? Did you go by car?' Shona asked Isla.

'Aye, underground car park. Lift to the penthouse suite, all very flash.'

'Did you hear that, Dan? Ring any bells?'

'Could be any number of places,' Dan replied glumly. 'What else, Isla? Anything?'

Isla screwed up her face with the effort of remembering. 'There was this chimney, this big brick chimney. Like it was an old factory or something, but really tall.'

'Shenton Mill,' said Dan triumphantly. 'It all flats now. I'll get over there with back-up.'

Shona gave Isla the thumbs up and moved away, lowering her voice. 'That's great, but listen, Dan, I want you to keep the fact Isla is alive between you and me for the moment. Officially, Campbell is wanted in connection with the death of your bail absconder, Jamie Buckland. That's all anyone needs to know. Do you understand what I'm saying?'

'Okay,' Dan said slowly. 'You think there's a leak? You think Isla could be in danger?'

'I think whoever killed Siobhan thought she was Isla. Let's not take any chances.' She paused. 'Dan, what happens after a big drug raid?'

'A new team takes over in a couple of months and we're back to square one,' he sighed.

'Isla's just told me the new crew had people in place before the raids.'

'How could they do that?'

'Maybe they knew we were coming,' Shona said. There was silence as Dan digested this possibility. 'Just be careful,' Shona continued. 'We're on our own now.'

'Okay, boss.' He ended the call.

Between the leaden boxes of the caravans, Shona could see two bright dots. The boys in their colourful anoraks were orbiting Marie, refuelled by chips and coke, running wide circles around her. Shona returned to Isla.

Isla took a mint from the cigarette packet. 'If she asks, I'll say you gave me the fags,' she said, a twinkle in her eye before turning sombre. 'You know, I never really thanked you for what you did in the hospital. That night you stopped Gringo hammering me. I guess I knew then I could trust you.'

'Will you go back to him, when he gets out?' Shona asked. She'd seen it time and again.

Isla shook her head. 'No. I need to stay clean, help my ma with the boys. She wants me to go to college, but, you know.' She shrugged. 'No one off my estate goes to college.'

'No one off my estate became a police officer either,' said Shona. Curiosity flashed in Isla's eyes so Shona continued. 'I'll tell you a secret. I came from a place like you. My mother OD'd when I was a kid, never knew my dad. But I was lucky. I got an education and my gran taught me you can do anything you put your mind to. You were right to get angry, it's still about respect. So, Isla Corr, just you remember, you've been given a second chance. Get out there and teach the world to respect you.'

'Aye.' Isla grinned, linking her arm through Shona's as they watched Marie and the boys walk towards them. 'Who can stand against two angry wee women when they put their minds to something?'

'Naebody I can think of,' Shona replied, solemnly.

Chapter 33

Marie boiled the kettle and doled out tea to Shona while they waited for news from Dan Ridley in Carlisle. Isla found a charger for Shona's phone then got out a pack of cards and showed the boys how to play patience.

'About a week after you told me she was dead, she turned up at the house,' said Marie quietly. 'It was dark and raining. I heard this noise in the garden, opened the back door. There she was. Nearly gave me a heart attack. She was all wet. I thought I was seeing things, that she was a ghost, come back from the sea.' Marie shivered. 'I wanted to say something to that nice lad of yours, Ravi. Should have told my sister Margaret I suppose, but she didnae care about Siobhan. Seemed better to just keep quiet until you got the guy. Isla's been here ever since. I'm sorry.'

Shona touched her arm. 'It's okay.' She thought of Becca and how far she'd go to protect her. 'In your shoes I might have done the same thing.'

Liam was coaxed into offering Shona a biscuit from a packet of chocolate digestives he gripped tightly. Shona took one and thanked the little boy who walked slowly back to his cousin, giving no sign that he'd heard her.

When she'd drunk her tea, Shona distracted Liam and Ryan by building a Lego garage for the battered toy car they'd found at the beach, giving mother and daughter some space. Marie took her daughter into one of the bedrooms and half closed the door. Shona could hear her rising voice and worried tones as she questioned Isla on what was happening. Then Marie came out and gave Shona a look that said, you better be right about this.

As the day wore on and the skies grew darker, Shona could feel the elation from finding Isla alive and a lead on the murders begin to ebb, with no news from Dan forthcoming. The atmosphere inside the caravan was close and tense. Condensation pooled on the windows as five warm breaths raised the temperature of the confined space. Marie made sandwiches. No one wanted more tea. Ryan was restless and pleaded to go back to the beach with Isla, but with the full threat against her family now laid bare, Marie didn't want anyone leaving the caravan. Even with Isla's blonde hair dyed black, and few neighbours, her mother was taking no chances.

Marie finally shooed the boys into her bedroom and a few seconds later Shona heard the jaunty sounds of a kid's cartoon start up on the TV.

Shona took the opportunity to step outside for a moment, holding her phone up to check the signal. The strong four bars said she hadn't missed any calls. In ordinary circumstances she would be badgering Dan, demanding an update and issuing fresh orders. The wind cut through her fleece and she shivered as she stared south across the Solway Firth, across the border, as if the pressure of her gaze alone could bring some news. The claustrophobia of the caravan and her own powerlessness pressed on her, raw and heavy. She wanted nothing more than to dive into her car and head for Carlisle, but she wasn't even sure she had enough petrol to get there.

'C'mon, what are you doing?' she muttered at the phone. They should have heard something by now. She checked the time. It was just after six p.m. In less than an hour it would be dark. They must have risk-assessed the building. Campbell might be armed. Perhaps they'd decided to go in early tomorrow, catch Campbell in bed. After ten minutes of cold, damp air she could see the women's anxious faces through the van window and she went back inside. 'No news yet, sorry.'

'Fuck, I need a fag,' Isla muttered, and her mother frowned at her.

Shona sat back down. Her phone pinged. Marie and Isla both jumped in their seats. Shona had only put a few close contacts in the directory. Becca's name lit the screen. 'It's okay,' Shona smiled and reassured them. 'It's just my daughter.' She opened the text message. *At lifeboat station. Pick me up.*

Shona tutted. She thought she'd at least succeeded in bringing Becca up to use please and thank you when she wanted something, but the thought was quickly overtaken with relief. At least Becca was getting out. Rob's worries about the effect of the accident were an overreaction. Tommy had probably coaxed Becca into some small life-boat task, counting donations or polishing brass, pointing out she still had one good arm and may as well make herself useful by using it. On this holiday weekend there would have been some visitors to keep her busy. This might be Shona's chance to have a word with Becca away from Rob. *Ok, back in a bit.* Shona hit send. The reply was immediate, *Come now.*

Before Shona could remind Becca of her manners, Dan's name appeared on the screen as an incoming call.

'I'll just pop outside and take this.' Shona got up from the table. Marie's hand reached across and took her daughter's.

'No sign of Campbell at the flat,' Dan said. 'We're got a watch on it and doing ANPR checks on a vehicle registered to him, a dark grey Land Rover Discovery.'

Shona's heart sank. 'Okay. Listen, you've got the CCTV footage. Campbell's wanted in connection with the death of your bail absconder, Jamie Buckland. Get it out to the media and put a cross-border alert out on him.'

'Already done, boss,' Dan replied. 'Don't worry, I'm on this,' he reassured her. 'You should really talk to Murdo though, he's beside himself.'

'Why? What's happened?' Shona felt guilty she hadn't called her deputy, but any association with her left him open to disciplinary proceedings.

'A temporary DI, some guy from Ayr station, is pulling the place apart. He's suspended all investigations into the deaths and is reviewing cases from the last six months.' Dan hesitated. 'He's also told all staff not to contact with you. Murdo's attempting damage limitation but I don't think it's going too well.'

It was as Shona had thought. 'Then while I'm suspended, it's best I don't phone him.'

'He's really worried about you. He's been calling your house on the sly. Rob said you we're out, but he didn't know where.'

'Will you tell Murdo I'm fine, Dan? But don't mention Isla,' Shona said, biting her lip. 'Concentrate on finding Evan Campbell, he's the key to this.'

'Okay, boss. You still with Isla?'

'Yes.'

'Do you want anyone with you? I mean, if she's a target?'

'No, we're safe enough here. Only you and I know she's alive. Make sure it stays that way until Campbell's in custody. Keep me posted.' Shona stepped back inside and delivered the news that there was no news. Marie had opened the kitchen window and was furiously washing a set of already clean mugs.

'How can youse no find this guy?' Marie's frustration boiled over. 'You've got cameras all over the place. You cannae move without getting nipped for drink driving, but murder folk and suddenly you're invisible?'

Isla was sitting curled up on the banquette. Her gaze met Shona's. A small, perverse smile of triumph. I told you so, the girl seemed to say. The devil himself. You won't find him.

'Look, it's still early. Officers are at his flat and tracking his vehicle. If he's out there, they'll get him. We just need be patient. It will be on the local news. Web, radio, TV, the works.' Shona saw Isla's look turn to alarm. 'Don't worry, Campbell's wanted for Jamie's murder. No one knows you're alive. No one knows you're here.'

'But we cannae stay here for ever,' Marie said. Isla sat biting her nails. 'Maybe we should go to Spain, there's family out there. Isla's got Siobhan's passport. We could get the kids away,' Marie said desperately.

'No,' Shona said firmly. It was what she'd been afraid of. If Isla and Marie fled, she'd have no witness and no way of protecting them. The gang would find Isla, even in Spain. Marie and the boys would be collateral damage. 'You need to stay here. You need to trust me.'

'Aye, but how can we? You're not even with the police, are you?' Marie's mouth was a firm line. She pointed to the open window above the sink. 'I heard what you said. You're not on a day off, are you? You're suspended.'

'Is that true?' Isla looked up at her.

Shona sat down heavily on the end of the banquette. 'Yes, it is,' she said quietly.

'How come?' The young woman's eyes were hardening.

Shona propped her forehead on her hand for a moment, the cold fingers a relief against the dull throb in her head. She looked sideways at Isla, who was still studying Shona with her sharp assessing look.

'I was told to stop investigating your... Siobhan's... death. But I didn't,' Shona said simply. 'Cumbria Police are chasing Campbell. DC Ridley will get him.'

'You trust this guy?'

Shona thought of Dan. The earnest schoolboy in his raincoat waiting on Silloth shore for the lifeboat to bring in the casualty. His sometimes fanciful notions of serial killers and political plots. Others might have doubts, but underneath it all Shona saw an officer as committed and determined as she was. More than once she'd offered Dan the chance to walk away. He'd refused every time. 'Yes, I trust him.'

Isla looked up at her mother. 'And I trust her, so we're staying.'

Marie folded her arms and leaned against the sink, her expression set firm. She shot daggers at Shona. Her whole posture said, we'll see about that.

Shona's phone pinged. There was a stream of missed texts from Becca. *Hurry up. Where are you? Come now.* Shona checked the time. The grey day was sinking into a greater gloom. The sun had dipped down unseen behind the flat clouds. Shona considered the frosty stand-off between Isla and Marie and decided Isla was the more determined of the two. Nothing more could be accomplished here. The women wouldn't be going anywhere tonight. She could safely leave them to smooth things over for a few hours. *Coming*, she replied to Becca.

'Look, I'm going to leave you for a bit. I'll be back later.' Shona calculated her fuel situation. Tommy had spare jerry cans of petrol for the lifeboat. Would he lend her some? She'd have to explain the situation, her suspension and lack of cash, but she could rely on Tommy McCall to keep it quiet.

'What? You're leaving us?' said Marie, who a moment ago had wanted Shona gone.

Shona put her hand on Marie's arm. 'I just need to see my daughter. Someone hit her with a car a few days ago. She's all right but… you know?'

'It's fine, Mum,' Isla said getting up. 'We'll be fine,' She put her arm around Marie and nodded to Shona. 'Off you go.'

Shona put her head into the bedroom to say goodbye to the boys. Ryan lay back propped up on pillows, eyes fixed on the TV, while Liam dozed next to him. Shona felt a moment of uncertainty about leaving them without an officer to protect them, but if Isla was right about Evan Campbell's connections then it wasn't safe to involve social services or even her own colleagues. Murdo. She really wished she could call Murdo, but it was too much of a risk. She would only be a couple of hours at most.

Shona walked quickly between the shuttered caravans back to the car park. She kept a sharp watch for any suspicious vehicles, especially a dark 4x4 Land Rover Discovery, but her own car sat alone in the deserted car park like a shiny black rock left behind by the tide. She jumped in, pulling away with a spray of gravel, and headed inland along the poker straight road. Past a scattering of low, white-washed houses with black slate roofs, their windows bright in the gloaming, along a long single-track stretch between flat fields and up to the junction with the main coast road. On the way she called Becca to say she was coming, but to her annoyance her daughter's phone went straight to voicemail. The slick tarmac of the A-road began to climb through stands of saplings already bare for winter, their pale trunks whitening like bones in the headlights. To her left, Shona glimpsed the bright silver of Southwick Water snaking its way across the marchlands to the Solway. With each mile, and no news from Dan, her hopes of Campbell's arrest were evaporating; she saw how far away she was from being reinstated. She tried Becca's phone again. She wanted her daughter to be ready when she arrived but, as usual, whatever she was doing was of a higher priority than answering her mother's calls.

Twenty-five minutes after she'd left the caravan park, Shona came in on the back road to Kirkness, dropping down between two big Victorian villas which had travelled from private homes to nursing homes and back again, only to be carved into holiday flats.

It was almost dark, the estuary was quiet and calm, a streak of indigo between inky shores. The main street lay empty. At the far end, the bare bulb above the shop door of the lifeboat station was unlit, but Shona saw the glow of the crew room lamp upstairs. Tommy's van was parked across the road between tourist 4x4s. She slotted the Audi next to them.

The roller door of the boat hall and the shop entrance were both locked so Shona made for the side door that led straight into the crew changing area. Inside, all was dark. Tommy and Becca were obviously too busy gassing in the cosy crew room to come down and attend to the lights. She felt for the switch, but nothing happened. The building was 140 years old and, despite rewiring, intermittent faults with the electrics were becoming a regular feature again. Her eyes were slowly adjusting. She saw the glimmer of white helmets high above the hanging forms of dry suits, their yellow wellies, monochrome in the gloom. Shona huffed, her hands stretched out in front of her. She took a step towards the door at the far end that led direct to the boat bay and the stairs to the mezzanine level, but her foot caught. She tumbled forward onto the bags someone had left on the floor. She swore under her breath. As she put out her hands to right herself, her fingers touched not plastic or canvas but skin and hair. She flinched, scrambling back, fumbling for her phone. The ghostly glow showed a horror scene; a slumped body, a red-smeared floor.

Tommy lay on his side. Shona gasped and leaned quickly forward, feeling for a pulse. It was slow but strong beneath his chin. She searched for the source of the blood. A deep gash above his eye running into shadowy streaks down his blue overalls, but she couldn't find any other wounds.

'Tommy? Tommy, can you hear me? What happened?' Shona shook him. He didn't look like he'd fallen. Where was Becca? Had she gone home? Tommy only groaned, blood and saliva bubbling from his nose and mouth. Shona wiped his face with the sleeve of her jacket, then bundled the garment under his head to keep his airways clear. 'Tommy?' She shook him again as she dialled 999.

'This is Detective Inspector Shona Oliver.' She fought to keep her voice steady. Becca? Where was Becca? 'I need an ambulance. Kirkness RNLI station. A fifty-year-old man with head injuries, possible victim of an assault.' They never kept cash at the shop but he could have disturbed thieves. Her phone went silent, the battery exhausted, but the ambulance was on its way. She prayed Becca had gone home, but then a noise came from upstairs, a muffled scrape and thump of something dragging across the floor. Becca? Shona jumped to her feet and felt her way to the door that led from the changing room to the boat hall. Light and voices spilled from the crew room above. Becca. She could hear Becca.

At the top of the stairs she stood blinking in the sudden brightness, then gasped. A nightmare tableau greeted her. Across the room, beside the crew table, Becca was slumped in a chair, her eyes closed. Six feet away, hands outstretched in a gesture of propitiation, was DCI Gavin Baird. Between them, a gun levelled at Becca's head, his sharp suit creased and bloody, stood the man with the skull-like face. The man DC Dan Ridley was hunting fifty miles away in Carlisle. The man Isla said had killed Siobhan. Evan Campbell.

Chapter 34

For a second Shona stood frozen. A single upturned chair seemed too little for the latent violence, the brimming brutality of the scene. Shona recognised Campbell immediately as the man from the STAC reception. She'd been right all along. Blocks were shifting into place. Campbell, Baird, Kenny Hanlon, they were in this together.

Campbell pulled Becca to her feet, his arm around her neck. Her phone lay on the table by Campbell's elbow. There were smudges of blood on her jeans and yellow T-shirt. Her sling had been used to tie her good hand to the splint on her broken arm. A muffled '*mum*' escaped the gag across her mouth. It took every ounce of Shona's training not to rush forward and tear her daughter from his hands. Stop, she told herself. Stay calm. She didn't doubt for one minute that Campbell might kill them all.

'Okay, okay Evan.' She raised her arms in a placatory gesture. 'What do you want?'

'Late to the party, Shona, but what I've got to say willnae take long.' He grinned at her, the angular lines of his face became even more skull-like. He motioned her to drop her phone on the table. 'Smart bitch like you can probably work it out for yourself. Although my last wee warning went unheeded.' He gripped Becca's broken arm with his free hand. Becca flinched, the pain showing on her face. She stifled a sob and shot Campbell a defiant look. The dark 4x4. It was Campbell in the iron-grey Land Rover Discovery who'd hit her daughter. Shona wanted to rip his throat out. A savage panic was forcing its way out of her chest. She pushed down the urge to scream at him. Let my daughter go. I'm the one you want.

Instead she said, 'It's okay, Becca,' and tried to smile reassuringly, but her expression felt white hard. She kept her eyes not on Becca or the gun, but on Campbell's leering face. Whatever he meant to do, she would see it there first. 'I'm here now. Tell me what you want, Evan. Put the gun down and let her go,' she said with false calm. In the corner of her vision, Baird was tense and poised to intervene, but on whose side?

Baird took a step towards Campbell who turned and levelled the gun at him. 'Now, now Gavie-boy, no interrupting.'

'Let the girl go, Campbell,' Baird persisted. 'I told you, it's sorted. My guy's in Shona's seat now, the cases are wrapped up. Back to business as usual.'

'Aye, so you keep saying, but the bitch doesn't take a telling.' Campbell switched his glare back to Shona. It was like an icy blast, straight from hell.

'Okay, okay. Put the gun down, Evan,' Shona said. 'There's nothing I can do to you. I'm out of the force, I'm no threat to you. Let my daughter go.'

'Not good enough. I say we kill them both now, keep it tidy.'

'She's right,' Baird broke in. 'You got away with the others cos nobody cared about a couple of junkies and an illegal immigrant. Kill a police officer and her daughter, and they'll never stop hunting you. I'll not be able to save you.'

A flicker of doubt crossed Campbell's face. Baird pressed his advantage. 'Know why she won't talk? Because I've had a chat with Harry Delfont, her old boss. He says hello, by the way, Shona. Lots of dirt on this lassie, Evan. Juicy stuff.' He raised his eyebrows chummily at the gunman. 'And that dodgy banker husband. All those gambling debts Kenny helped him run up? The big man was right, should have just offered her a cut. No need for all these dramatics.'

Shona felt a wave of hot nausea. So, Kenny Hanlon had targeted her family. He'd preyed on Rob's weakness, sent Campbell to run Becca down, all to get at her. And Delfont, she thought she'd escaped him. It would all come out now, everything she'd tried to hide. It took a fraction of a second for Shona to realise she didn't care. Becca was the only thing that mattered. Shona's world narrowed to her daughter, Campbell and the gun. The ambulance, the squad car despatched with them, Dan Ridley, Murdo, even Rob were all too far away. She dragged her eyes from Campbell and swept the room for a weapon. A heavy wooden oar, engraved in gold with the names of past Kirkness rowing champions, was propped in the corner by the door. Pictures flooded through her mind; Siobhan's lifeless body, Jamie Buckland curled like a sleeping child. You couldn't reason with Campbell. He would always take what he wanted unless someone stopped him. Unless she stopped him.

'Put the gun away, let the lassie go,' Baird hissed, red-eyed. 'It's fixed. You walk. Get back to business. Keep the big man happy. We all get what we want.'

Campbell grinned. 'Aye, maybe you're right. Not worth the bother.' He let the gun fall to his side but kept hold of Becca.

Baird's shoulders relaxed. 'Let's get out of here.'

'Seems a shame, I was looking forward to topping that bitch.' Campbell licked his lips and leered at Shona.

'You're a sick fuck, Campbell. Get out of here.'

'What, no got the balls for it? Seems to me it's your lack of balls that landed us here. Hanlon always said you were weak.'

Shona saw the flash of anger twist on Baird's face. He was a DCI, used to respect. He stepped up to Campbell. 'You're the weak link, Campbell. You should be on a leash.'

'Is that a fact?' Campbell threw Becca aside and brought the gun swiftly against Baird's chest. The two men stood toe-to-toe, neither willing to give way. Baird's bulk blocked Campbell's view. Quickly, Shona pulled Becca's towards her and with clumsy fingers pulled down the gag and undid the sling binding her hands together. The stairway down from the mezzanine floor was only a few feet away. Shona put her mouth close to Becca's ear. 'Get out. Run.' She turned her body to shield her daughter's escape. But Becca hesitated, unwilling to let go of her mother. 'Go, go. I'm right behind you,' Shona urged, eyeing the two men.

'You're an animal, Campbell.' Baird was spitting, the tamped-down anger bubbling up. Campbell's scorn, the humiliating shove down the restaurant stairs. 'You're gonna bring us all down. Think the Big Man's going to like hearing about this?' he threatened. 'Thugs like you are ten-a-penny. Just a cog. Probably got someone lined up already to take your place.'

'Maybe he shouldn't hear it then.' Campbell's savage face was inches from Baird's.

Baird barked a laugh. 'I'm a detective chief inspector. You need my protection. Shoot me and you're dead too. Hanlon will drop you like the turd you are.'

'You…' as Campbell's left hand went to Baird's throat, the detective made a grab for the gun. The two men lurched sideways, locked in a vicious embrace. Shona pushed Becca stumbling down the darkened stairway and took a step after her. Then she stopped.

Baird had prevented Campbell shooting them both. He was mixed up with the Hanlon, with the supply of drugs, but his hatred of Campbell showed it wasn't too late for him. With his help she could bring down Campbell and Hanlon, end this nightmare of killings. Whatever he'd done, it was her job to protect a fellow officer and ensure the safety of the public. She turned back just as the flash of light and the roar of the gun's explosion filled the room. Both men were thrown backward. Shona saw Baird fall, the stench of cordite caught in her throat.

Baird stayed down, blood blooming across the detective's white shirt, but his opponent scrambled to his feet and aimed the killing shot. Shona grabbed the oar and swung it at Campbell, catching him a glancing blow. The bullet missed Baird and sent up a plume of plaster as it struck the wall. Shona jabbed again at Campbell's outstretched arm, but he sidestepped her and the weight of the oar sent her crashing to the floor. Baird lay next to her, his breath fast and shallow. Campbell levelled the pistol at her. Time slowed as Shona's mind raced to a thousand different places. No matter where she looked the dark circle of the gun barrel swallowed her. There was no way out. Campbell's death-head stare would be the last thing she saw. 'Should have done you first, bitch.' She heard the bang, the flash wiping out all vision. The room tilted and tumbled in an arc of noise, a red stench filling her nose and ears.

Campbell let out a howl as he was flung backward. Shona scrambled to her knees. Smoke arced through the room. Becca was at the top of the stairs, the launch tube of a red parachute flare still gripped clumsily in her hands. The rocket, having struck Campbell a glancing blow, ricocheted off the walls and cupboards. Shona heard it chime loudly against the metal roller door of the boat hall then clatter onto the concrete floor. Shona blinked sweat and smoke from her eyes. Campbell's prone form lay by the mezzanine rail, writhing in the thickened air.

Below, in the boat hall, the delayed ignition of the flare exploded into life. The thousand degree burn of bright red magnesium crackled and popped. It sent up a glow of leaping, bloody shadows over the walls and rafters. Suddenly, a solid mass twisted through the smoke and darkness. Campbell was on his feet, one arm hanging strangely from the impact of the flare. But he raised the other, the gun levelled at Becca.

Shona grabbed the heavy wooden oar, the smoke swirling as the blade cut through the fiery air. 'Get away from my daughter, you bastard!' she roared, swinging at Campbell with all her strength. Before he could alter his aim, the oar caught him square in the chest, propelling him back against the mezzanine rail. He scrabbled desperately for purchase, but the slippery forms of the immersion suits hanging like chrysalises over the barrier offered none, and with a scream he tumbled backward out of sight. Shona heard the crack as he hit the metal outboard of the *Margaret Wilson*. She rushed forward and looked cautiously down. The scarlet flare lit the boat bay like a scene from hell and the devil himself, Evan Campbell, lay motionless in the lifeboat.

Becca ran to her mother, cradling her injured arm against her chest. 'I got it from the night bag. Callum said... Callum said it must never be pointed at people and property, but I had to stop him. I had to...' Shona pulled her daughter into a fierce hug. 'It's okay, it's okay. You saved my life. You saved all our lives, that's what you did.' She pressed Becca's face against her own, taking deep breaths of her daughter's scent.

If time had slowed before, now it sped up. Baird lay on the crew room floor gasping, his eyes wide and fixed on the ceiling as blood bubbled from the corner of his mouth. The urgent tick of a life draining away. Shona pulled a towel from a kitbag in the corner and pressed it to the chest wound. Becca slid to the floor. She took a quick sideways glance at Baird. 'He tried to save me, but the guy wouldn't listen.'

Shona leaned over Baird. His eyelids were drooping, his face a deathly white. Blood was seeping through Shona's fingers. 'Gavin, can you hear me?'

'Hanlon... got to stop them,' he gasped.

'How, Gavin? How do I stop them?' Shona leant forward; his whispering breath fluttered like birds' wings against her cheek.

'I... Not money... clean.' Baird's fingers were searching for something to cling on to and she took his hand squeezing it tightly. 'Never meant... to harm you...'

'I know, I know, Gavin,' Shona said desperately. 'How do I stop them?'

'Hard...' He breathed, his eyes rolling back. Shona felt the blood soaking her jeans, seeping up from the carpet as struggled to hold onto Baird.

'I know it will be. Help me stop them.'

'Shared...'

'What? What did you share? Gavin, open your eyes for me,' she called desperately. 'The ambulance is coming.' But as the faltering red glow of the exhausted flare was replaced by sweeping blue lights, Baird's slackened muscles and glassy stare told her it was too late.

She heard a commotion in the boat hall. Voices yelling, 'Police, show yourselves.'

'Up here,' she shouted. Constable Guy Matthews appeared at the top of the stairs, followed by the bright red hair of Special Lewis Johnstone, torches waving like searchlights through the lingering smoke. Their jaws dropped at the scene of horror before them. 'Get the paramedics,' Shona yelled. Her last ditch attempts to revive Baird were failing, blood seeping from the gunshot wound with every chest compression. 'Matthews, that's the shooter.' She pointed a bloody finger over the rail at the boat bay. 'Secure the weapon, it's down there some-where.'

Suddenly, Murdo was at her elbow, pulling her away. Outside, Becca ran to Tommy, who was sitting on the pavement, a dressing held to his head. Kirkness resid-ents were gathering, drawn by the sirens descending on their village. Shona searched in vain for Rob among the shocked crowd lit by the flickering blue beams of the emergency vehicles.

'Boss?' Murdo's face had a thousand questions. 'You okay?' He gripped her shoulders.

'Yes, yes.' She nodded. 'I guess you'll need state-ments...' She was suddenly overwhelmed with exhaus-tion.

'Never mind that now. I'm taking you and Becca to hospital.' Murdo kept one arm round Shona as he led her to where Becca sat, a blanket over her shoulders. Shona leaned gratefully against his solid bulk, her limbs suddenly heavy with tiredness. 'It was Evan Campbell. You need to secure the scene, get forensics down here...'

'Aye well, never you mind that. Campbell's dead, broken neck. He's not going anywhere. Ravi and Kate are on their way. I think you should get checked.' He motioned to a bruise on Shona's face which she had no idea how she sustained. 'Is Baird really...'

'Yes, Campbell shot him. Dan...' Shona felt her pockets. Her phone was out of charge and lying somewhere in the crew room with Baird's lifeless body. 'Tell Dan what's happened.'

'Shona, Shona.'

The voice sounded fuzzy, far away over the tinnitus roar, a residue of the gunshots. Rob had burst through the police cordon and seconds later enveloped Shona and Becca in a tight embrace. She could feel the wet smear of tears across his cheeks. His breath came in huge gulps and he was shaking with shock. Murdo motioned away the constable who'd run after Rob and was trying to restrain him.

'Right, no arguments,' said Murdo. 'Have you had a drink today, Rob?' He turned to Shona's husband, once more the severe officer in charge.

Rob looked chastened by Murdo's tone. 'No, I haven't.' Shona thought of the whisky she'd emptied down the sink and their lack of cash, and decided he was telling the truth.

'Right well, I've a job for you. Take your wife and daughter to hospital. Get them checked over. Think you can do that for me?'

'Yes, yes, of course,' Rob said, pulling Shona and Becca close. 'I can look after my family.' He sounded as if he was convincing himself as much as Murdo, but when Shona looked at the firm set of his jaw and the determination in his eyes, she knew he meant it.

Chapter 35

Nearly two weeks later, on a bleak Thursday afternoon, Shona buttoned up the front of her black wool coat and straightened her shoulders. The mournful drone of bagpipes filled the damp October air. The guard of honour came to attention as a single piper led the funeral procession towards the crematorium. DCI Gavin Baird's coffin was carried on the shoulders of uniformed officers and draped with a white banner showing the Police Scotland shield. Detective Superintendent Malcom Munroe, in full dress uniform and medals, walked behind the piper. Baird's widow Nicola and their children were in the following car.

Shona had given a brief statement about Gavin Baird's death. Now she heard echoes of her own words in the police chaplain's address. A brave officer. Cut down in the line of duty. Gave his life to protect others.

Murdo was waiting for her in the car after the tea and ham sandwiches at a local hotel. 'Let's give her an hour to get back to the house,' Shona said, and Murdo nodded in agreement.

They pulled up to Baird's detached villa in Newton Mearns just as the light was going. The orange glow from the picture windows spilled out onto the gravel drive. In the living room, Nicola was still wearing her fitted black dress but had shrugged off the matching coat. Her phone was pressed to her ear. She laughed at something the caller said as she unpinned her tightly wound chignon of blonde hair and shook it free.

'I shouldn't be long,' Shona said to Murdo.

Nicola was composed when she opened the door, but her expression turned to ice when she saw Shona. 'Come to give your condolences?' she spat. 'Gavin died saving you and your daughter.'

She was right. Shona felt the stirring of compassion for the woman's loss, but it soon faded. She'd held Gavin Baird's hand while he died, but Nicola had not asked her for a single detail of her husband's passing. Did he suffer? Did he ask for me? Shona had been ready with a softer, sanitised version of the truth, but it wasn't needed.

'I'm sorry for your loss, but I'm not responsible for your husband's death,' Shona said levelly. Nicola tried to slam the door, but Shona stepped forward, her raised arm blocking the doorway. 'Can I come in for a minute? There's some files of Gavin's I need to retrieve.'

Shona saw a flash of fear, then calculation in the woman's eyes and she wondered how much Gavin had confided in Nicola and how far she herself was involved with Kenny Hanlon. Shona remembered the scene she'd witnessed at the STAC reception. Nicola Baird and Kenny Hanlon. Was it a drunken grope in the hallway of a posh hotel after too much champagne, or something more? An affair? An alliance? Shona guessed a bit of both, but she didn't have energy to go softly-softly with Nicola.

'Two options,' Shona said. 'I can come back with a warrant and this will be all over the media. Or you let him rest the gallant officer he was, and you stay the grieving widow.' Shona had done her research. Nicola had political ambitions. At the polls she could turn her sacrifice into votes. 'I'm not after you or Gavin. Think of your kids.'

For a moment Nicola held the door firm, the gym-toned bicep taut beneath the year-round tan. She gave Shona a look of pure hatred, then allowed the door to swing open. Shona stepped into the hallway, the Edwardian quarry tiles clicking below her heels. Nicola, in her stocking soles, loomed over her. 'What do you want?'

'Ten minutes in Gavin's study.' She calculated Nicola might agree to a short, timed visit just to get rid of her. 'I'm not after Gavin, remember,' she repeated.

'Why? What are you looking for?' Her eyes narrowed. 'Gavin's laptop isn't here. He never kept anything at home. The guy who shot him is dead, so isn't that the end of it?'

'There's a few details to clear up. Ten minutes.'

'Okay.' Nicola shrugged eventually. She waved Shona through a polished teak door behind the main staircase. 'Then I never want to see you again.'

As Shona went into the study, Nicola remained in the hall, her arms folded, watching her. Shona closed the door firmly and scanned the room. Old leather-topped desk, dark wood bookcases built into the alcoves beside the fireplace. From Shona's brief glance of the rest of the house, modern and sleek, this room owed its décor to previous owners. Perhaps Nicola was right, Baird didn't bring his work home. It didn't look like anyone had spent much time in here.

The box files on the shelf contained household receipts, a guarantee for the ride-on mower. The ten minutes were ticking away fast. What if Nicola phoned Hanlon? Shona needed conclusive proof of his involvement in the drugs operation. Murdo would warn her if anyone approached the house, but she wouldn't get

336

a second bite at this. Hanlon was wealthy, powerful and connected. She was, technically, a suspended police officer with a gambler husband and a daughter recently hauled in for drug possession. The lawyers, the media, her own force, would crucify her.

Frantically she scanned the room. What had Baird said? It would be hard. He'd said the word 'shared'. She saw again his bloody fingers grasping her own, the incredulity in his eyes that death was coming for him. Hard. Shared. She looked in vain for a hard drive. How would he share the information she needed? Not cloud storage, that wasn't secure, Baird would know that.

She flipped open cardboard storage boxes. Holiday brochures, books. In the corner, a plastic crate. Shona spotted the framed picture of Nicola and the children that had sat on his desk at Kilmarnock HQ. Kneeling on the carpet she emptied the jumble of personal items, stacking them one by one onto the desktop. An almost empty diary, Scottish police mug, pens, the glass tower of the Policing Excellence award, an A4 pad with jotted notes from a budgeting meeting. There was nothing.

Outside in the hall she could hear Nicola's urgent voice. She was on her mobile to someone. Baird had recruited his own team. Some of those officers might be in this up to their necks. They could arrive any moment to see her off the premises. Harassing the widow of a hero. Even her own colleagues would shun her.

She checked her phone. Nothing from Murdo. The final seconds were tickling down until Nicola threw her out. Hard. Shared. Still kneeling, as if praying for a miracle, she looked up desperately at the personal items from Baird's office now on the desk. Nicola opened the door and the light from the hallway reflected off the glass tower of Baird's award.

In a flash she saw it. She was back at Tower RNLI station on her final visit last year, standing on the pontoon on the Thames' north bank, looking south at the night sky ablaze with all the life and brightness London possessed. She'd laughed as the skipper had said he loved coming to work because his office had the best view in London. On the eastern horizon the City pulsed with light. On the south bank, new skyscrapers were springing up, painting the surface of the river and the black sky behind the OXO tower with colour; the new Southbank Tower, One Blackfriars and between them the slim pinnacle of the Shard. Baird's mouth formed the shapes. Not hard. Not shared. Shard.

Shona snatched the glass tower of the Scottish Policing Excellence award from the desk. Nicola stared at her in astonishment. Shona turned away, her fingers found the hollow dip below the red felt cover of its base. She ripped it back and extracted a slim metal shape. A memory stick. She slipped it into her pocket.

'What are you doing with his award?' Nicola said between gritted teeth. Shona held it out and the woman grabbed it from her, cradling it against the dark front of her widow's outfit. 'He was going places, you know? Could have been chief constable one day.' She stood looking down her nose at Shona as if she was a particularly disappointing domestic servant.

Shona brushed past her. In the hall she stopped and turned. For a moment she was tempted to tell her what her husband really was but found she couldn't. 'Every day I will be thankful to DCI Baird for the life of my daughter.' The woman stared back uncomprehendingly at her. To serve and protect. Baird had understood what it meant, even if Nicola couldn't. 'I'll see myself out. Thank you.'

Murdo had the engine running, the heater on full. 'Did you get it?' She held up the memory stick. 'Bastard,' Murdo muttered. Shona felt they wouldn't be seeing that leather jacket again. He put the car into gear, and they drove away.

They stopped in the car park of the first fast food restaurant they could find. Shona sat in the passenger seat, her laptop before her. She held her breath as she wondered whether she would need a password, but whether due to Baird's arrogance or an oversight the memory stick was readily accessible. She quickly went through the files. Murdo returned with coffee and donuts.

'It's all there. Recorded phone calls, finance documents. Baird's put together a good case.' Shona took the coffee beaker, holding the hot cardboard gingerly between finger and thumb, and placed it on the dashboard.

'How ironic,' Murdo said, taking a savage bite from his donut. Shona watched Murdo chew gloomily. 'I looked up to that guy. Thought he was sound.' He shook his head.

Shona sighed and closed the laptop. 'This wasn't about money. I think Baird genuinely set out to cut drugs crime. Maybe Kenny Hanlon persuaded him drugs was a business like any other. You can't eradicate it, but you could run it cleanly. Hanlon might say he was just a service provider. Between them they could cut the violence, clear out the competition. Start fresh. They could keep the crime figures to a minimum. They'd both get what they want. The Enterpriser. He's very convincing. Once Baird took the first step, he was hooked, there was no getting out.' She took a sip of coffee. 'Or maybe he thought he'd never beat them playing clean, that he'd give them a go at their own game. It just didn't work out as he planned.'

'Aye, I suppose,' Murdo conceded.

'But neither Baird nor Hanlon could control Evan Campbell. He killed Siobhan, Sami and Jamie Buckland because they'd set up a little enterprise of their own.'

'Will we be able to link Hanlon to the killings? Conspiracy to murder?' Murdo asked.

'We'll have a damn good go,' Shona said. 'We've no forensics. No witnesses, except Isla. There's the risk a good defence lawyer will take her apart in court. Former addict, prostitute. The jury might not believe a word she says, but she's bright and she might just sway them. She's determined to testify, get justice for Siobhan and the others, if she can.'

Murdo nodded. 'Good girl. At least Campbell won't be troubling us again. Maybe that's some justice.'

Shona took another sip of coffee and swallowed hard. She'd already decided to get Becca into trauma counselling. Her daughter was having nightmares and was horrified by the part she'd played in Campbell's death, even though she'd saved her mother's life. The Procurator Fiscal had decided there was no case to answer but Shona didn't want recent events, decisions made in a fraction of a second, to cast a long shadow over her daughter's life. She knew how that could happen.

'Anyway, let's give Mars Bar Munroe the good news.' Shona drained her cup and picked up her phone.

Murdo chuckled. 'It looked like it was killing him today at the funeral. Keeping a lid on this.' He wiped the powdered sugar from his fingers and began clearing away the cups.

'Well?' Detective Superintendent Malcolm Munroe answered after the first ring.

'It's as we thought,' Shona said simply.

'Okay, bring Hanlon in,' he said testily. Shona knew he was thinking of his retirement, his legacy. He wanted Baird buried a hero and Hanlon nailed with minimal fallout and no talk of police corruption.

'So, I'm no longer suspended?' Shona asked.

'I never saw any paperwork, Oliver. As far as I'm concerned it never happened. Swing by HQ and collect your warrant card. Seems you left it on my desk.' He ended the call.

–

When Shona and Murdo arrived at the TV studios, the bright block of glass and steel which sat on Glasgow's dockside, crowds were streaming from its main entrance. Filming for *The Enterpriser* had just ended, the receptionist told them when Murdo showed his warrant card. The studio was on the second floor. Security would buzz them through.

Kenny Hanlon, in his bright blue checked tweed suit and cockatoo quiff of stiff blond hair, was still on the set and evidently still on a high from his show. He bounced on the balls of his feet like he was about to take off, calling farewells and waving to the dregs of the audience as technicians packed up around him. The neon sign, Your Business is My Business, glowed a deep red behind him.

Shona and Murdo stood for a few moments, assessing the layout, exits and potential risks to the general public should Hanlon attempt to flee. The floor manager, who'd frowned at them until Murdo flashed his badge, was looking at his watch. Hanlon showed no sign of winding down.

'Mr Hanlon.' Shona stepped onto the brightly lit stage. Hanlon turned, shielding his eyes. He saw Shona and without missing a beat came towards her.

'Shona, I was so sorry to hear about your trouble. How is your daughter?' He took in her dark suit, black coat and low heels and nodded soberly. 'A sad loss of your fellow officer, I'm sorry I couldn't be at the funeral.' He spread his hands wide; it looked for one awful moment as if he might try to hug her. Shona knew the consequences for him would be brutal. Instead, he spun around, rotating through his kingdom. 'Filming commitments. My fans. I have a responsibility to them all, you know.'

'Aye, that's you, pal. Scotland's answer to Gandhi,' muttered Murdo.

Shona snapped a handcuff on Hanlon's outstretched arm. Shocked, he jerked his head round to look at her, but his momentum kept him turning. Shona grabbed his other arm and spun it into the waiting metal link, which clicked shut around his wrist. He came to rest with both arms pinned behind his back.

Heads began to turn among the backstage crew, who paused mid-task and gaped at Hanlon held securely between a small, dark haired woman and her companion with the rugby player's scowl.

'What are you doing? This is ridiculous,' he blustered as Shona read him his rights. Supplying Class A drugs. Conspiracy to murder. 'This is a prank. Is this for Comic Relief? The director never told me. Douglas, Douglas, you cheeky swine,' he said into his lapel mic. 'Just so we're clear, what's going on?'

Shona reached across and pulled the mic from his chest. She turned him round to face the neon sign. Your Business is My Business. In the blood-red glow she put her mouth close to his ear. 'This is no joke, Mr Hanlon. My daughter is fine, and Rob will be too, but a police officer and four other people are dead. You've made *your* business *my* business. Just so we're clear, I'm going to nail your bollocks to the floor.'

Chapter 36

In Dumfries CID office, Ravi returned to his chair and sat down with a bump. DC Kate Irving glanced at his shocked face from her desk opposite. She swallowed a bite of her Kit Kat.

'Well? You're still in one piece.' She grinned. Over his shoulder she could see the boss in her office, mid-call with the desk phone tucked into her shoulder and papers strewn around her.

Ravi shook his head. 'I can't believe I forgot to DNA Marie Corr.'

'Will you get an official reprimand?' Kate's expression turned serious. Ravi shook his head. 'Well then,' she continued, 'you got off lightly.'

'I've just been beasted by Wee Shona. You call that getting off lightly?' he said, indignantly. 'You wait till it's your turn.'

'Already been there,' Kate replied. 'Suck it up and move on, that's what the boss says and it's my advice too. Here.' She held out a finger of her Kit Kat. 'Get your blood sugar up, it's good for shock.' Ravi took the biscuit from her.

'I know,' Ravi sighed. 'But a mistake like that? If we'd known it wasn't Isla…'

'It wouldn't have made any difference, Rav,' she replied, then paused. 'Look, it's my fault Baird knew we were still investigating. He came to the office one evening and I just let it slip.' She decided to gloss over the full extent of their conversation, the drunken dinner and sexual near miss. 'The boss thinks it was Vinny, I'm going to have to tell her. I can't help feeling if...'

'Don't,' Ravi said. 'Vin's the blue-eyed boy for trawling up CCTV of Evan Campbell and Kenny Hanlon, all is forgiven as far as the boss is concerned. Learn from it and move on, that's *my* advice.' Ravi looked past her at a new arrival. 'Well, well. If it's not our pal from the south.' Ravi got up and shook DC Dan Ridley's hand. 'Nice to see you.'

'Hi Kate.' Dan gave her his shy smile. 'Let me know if there's anything you need to tie up the baby milk file. I'd be happy to help. Is the boss free?' He pointed towards Shona, now replacing box files on top of the filing cabinets in her office.

'Looks like it. Go and ask.' Kate smiled back. 'Oh, and thanks for the offer, I'll let you know.'

'Looks like you've made a wee conquest there,' Ravi said slyly to Kate as Dan tapped on the glass of Shona's office and was waved in.

'Jealous? What's the matter, girlfriend? Can't stand the competition?' Kate shot back, arching an eyebrow.

Ravi laughed. 'Aye well, I'll let you have this one, but I still think he's too nice for a crabby tight-arse like you.'

Kate balled the silver paper from her snack and threw it at him, earning a frown from Murdo in the corner. 'Hoy, youse two. Back to work.'

Shona pulled her navy coat over her dark suit. 'To what do we owe the pleasure?' She smiled at Dan. 'You flavour of the month in Carlisle? You should be – all that evidence from Campbell's flat. Linking the murderer of a police officer to a major drugs dealer. It was you knocking on doors in Jamie Buckland's street that set us in the right direction. Well done,' she said.

'But I wasn't quick enough to stop him getting to you and Becca, was I?'

'Nothing you could do. Campbell came straight from Glasgow.' Shona dismissed his guilt. 'The fact you're beating yourself up for it shows what a good cop you are. What are you here for anyway?'

'Nothing, I just… tie up some ends.' Dan shrugged.

'I'm off to Kilmarnock. Walk me out.' Shona grabbed her handbag.

In the car park she stopped by the Audi. 'Everything all right with DCI Lambert, Dan?'

'Yeah, he's busy claiming all the credit he can. He hasn't said a word to me but that's a bonus as far as I'm concerned.'

'Good,' said Shona firmly as she unlocked the car.

'Boss,' said Dan. 'I don't suppose there's any vacancies coming up here?'

Shona leaned on the half-open car door. 'You want to work in Scotland?'

'I want to work with you, boss,'

Shona smiled. 'We'll that's very flattering to hear.'

'I mean it,' said Dan with resolve. 'I've learned more working with you than I have in the past five years in Carlisle. And we get on okay, don't we?'

'Yeah, we do.' Shona had to admit she liked Dan a great deal. He had the makings of an excellent officer. Maybe an even better friend. He was clever and thoughtful, and she'd had no hesitation on calling on him when the chips were down.

'Okay, here's the deal. Stick in at Cumbria, build your skills. You're good, and one day you'll be very good. If there's any cross–border stuff, I'll make sure we give you a call. Okay?'

'Yeah?'

'Yeah.' Shona couldn't help smiling at his enthusiasm. 'I have to go. See you soon.'

–

Detective Superintendent Malcolm 'Mars Bar' Munroe beamed at her when she arrived at his corner office with its view over Kilmarnock. A cafetière of freshly brewed coffee sat on the low table in front of Munroe's desk. Shona shot a surreptitious glance at the plate placed next to it. There were none of the eponymous chocolate bars, only biscuits. 'Knew I did the right thing appointing you,' he congratulated himself as he took her coat and bid her sit down. 'Procurator Fiscal is beside himself with glee over that dossier of Baird's you found. Looks like Hanlon will put up his hands, plead he was on a social mission to reform the drugs trade, or the like. Mind you, he'll probably do his time, write a book and be on every chat show as soon as he gets out.'

'What about the murders?' Shona asked, accepting coffee from Munroe.

'The lawyers will distance him from Evan Campbell, even with the CCTV and documents. Can you imagine how Hanlon will work a jury?'

Shona could imagine it. The contrite martyr led astray. His charity work, his role in the Scottish Trade Against Crime project, which she was convinced was little more than a cover for his criminal activities. The jury would probably give him a round of applause. 'What will happen about DCI Baird, sir?'

'DCI Baird was compiling the dossier as part of Operation Fortress. He had his suspicions about Mr Hanlon but, due to *The Enterpriser*'s high profile, the information was kept between Baird and me. Unfortunately, DCI Baird fell in the line of duty before he could complete the case. That's the line we're sticking to, Shona, understand? I expect scrupulous honesty in my officers, but Baird has paid with his life. I'm no friend to a dishonest cop but there's nothing to be gained from making Baird the scapegoat in this.'

'Do you know how far this goes? Hanlon's connected and Campbell boasted he had judges and cops in his pocket.'

'Let me tell you about Campbell. He was Hanlon's man, but Baird brought him in originally as an informer, codenamed Archer. He was with an Edinburgh county lines set-up, a disaffected grunt with notions of grandeur. There's no institutional corruption, just straightforward greed and stupidity. It gets people into bother more often than you'd think. Baird played this close to his chest. His officers are loyal to him, but I saw nothing in the file to suggest they knew about Hanlon. Did you?'

'No sir.'

'Good, let's keep it that way. There will be scrutiny, internal and from the media. Let's stick to the facts.'

'The children Sami Raseem said were being trafficked?'

'It's more likely they were mules, county lines kids, but I've asked the child protection team in Edinburgh to go through what we have, just in case.'

Shona nodded.

'One more thing.' Munroe continued placing his cup and saucer carefully on the glass-topped table. 'I'd like you to take Baird's job.'

Shona stared at him. 'Me?'

'You've got the experience. All that time in the City of London force, you're a bit wasted down in Dumfries. I'll back you, it'll go before an interview panel, but you'll get it. I want you here running the big cases. You can pick your team.' Munroe sat back and folded his arms, confident that the deal was done. 'You'd need to move closer to Kilmarnock. It would be less hands-on, but that happens to everyone eventually.'

Shona thought of her young officers, Kate and Ravi. They'd be thrilled and rise to the challenges. She could bring Dan in full-time and show Murdo that promotion hadn't passed him by. She could give good, solid Murdo a role that played to his strengths and kept everyone's feet on the ground. She saw it all. This could work. But then the dark mass that had hovered by her shoulder ever since her husband's drunken confession stepped forward.

'Sir,' Shona began; her hand shook as she replaced her cup in its saucer, the china chiming like a passing bell. Her whole world was about to come crashing down, all she'd worked for – career, reputation, financial security. It was over. 'Sir, I don't think I'm the right person for the job.' She told him of Rob's gambling and the Milton McConnell bank fraud. How Hanlon knew of this and might use it at the trial.

Munroe's face clouded. 'I see. Thank you for telling me.' He paused and shook his head. Shona knew her chief inspector prospects had gone for good. 'This is bad, Shona. Your husband,' he continued, 'will need to report this to the City of London police right away. I said I expect scrupulous honesty in my officers and you've just proved yours. Providing no blame attaches to you, and I don't expect it will, I'm still offering you the job.'

She could just nod, walk out a DCI with a pay rise, God knows they needed it. It would mean choosing between her work, her family life and the lifeboat. A move closer to Glasgow. Becca might like that. A fresh start, another one. But the shadow by her shoulder hadn't gone. It lingered. How many times did she have to start over before it ended up being the same? The gambling, the running, the lies.

'Sir, there's something else.' Shona swallowed hard. No more running away. This was her chance to face up to the past and take the consequences. She might leave this office without a job, but the prospect of finally laying down the guilt she had carried for two years rushed over her like a wave. 'I left the City because DSU Delfont gave me no choice.'

Munroe shifted uncomfortably in his chair, but Shona could see he was listening intently. She hurried on; there was no going back now. 'I was caught drunk at the wheel of a car, although I think, in retrospect, my drink was spiked. He told me I could leave or be charged.'

Munroe folded his hands and bowed his head for a moment. 'Shona,' he said gently. 'Are you aware that DSU Delfont was arrested recently on charges of corruption and sexual misconduct? Two female officers alleged he drugged them and filmed himself sexually assaulting them.'

The darkness rushed to fill her vision. Shona dug her fingernails into the palm of her hand. She remembered waking up, her car pulled over on the hard shoulder of the Docklands expressway, a traffic officer tapping on her window. She'd been at a leaving party and had one drink, wanting to get home early, but had woken up with no idea how she got there. At the station she'd gone to the bathroom and found her underwear was on back to front. Delfont had bought the drinks. Did he assault and film her while she was drugged? It was what she'd always feared. She let out a shuddering sob. She'd had no physical injuries, but that didn't mean it hadn't happened.

Munroe leaned forward and put his hand over hers. 'Delfont will go to jail, lass. You've nothing to fear from him and nothing to repent for yourself.' Shona nodded, the biblical language recalling Munroe's status as a teetotal church elder. But she did repent. She'd made a bad decision. Two women had been brave enough to come forward. The fear was ebbing, anger was flooding into its place. Well, now there would be three women standing up to the bastard. She would have to talk to Rob and Becca first, but it was time to set everything straight, everything she could. Munroe was handing her a tissue.

She took it and rubbed her nose. 'I'm all right, sir.'

'That man, a police officer. He's a disgrace.' Munroe was grim. 'If he'd laid a finger on one of my girls, I'd have strung him up myself. I understand why people take the law into their own hands, I really do.'

'You said corruption charges. Why corruption?' Shona had worked for Delfont for two years. She knew the rumours and had flagged a couple of case anomalies which she was convinced led to Delfont targeting her.

'It's alleged he was helping drugs gangs launder money through City companies. It involved buying gold, I don't know more than that.'

Buying gold. Untraceable. That's what Rob said. It was Delfont. Had he set them both up? If Rob revealed the money laundering fraud, Delfont could use Shona's alleged drunk driving to keep him quiet. If Shona threatened Delfont, he'd make sure Rob went to jail. She must talk to Rob.

'Listen, Shona.' Munroe was getting to his feet. 'I've got to go, but you've had a shock. Sit here till you feel better, my secretary's just down the way if you need anything.'

'Thank you, sir, I'm fine.' Shona gave him a weak smile. 'I'd just like to get back home.'

'Of course, of course.' He patted her shoulders. 'Listen, you did a brave thing telling me this. I believe you're a fine officer and I'd still like you to consider the job.'

'Thank you, sir. I'll think about it,' Shona said, but she already knew what she wanted to do.

–

Shona took Rob's hand. 'I made a really bad decision once.' She saw the look of apprehension in his eyes. 'It was when Becca was expelled and you left the bank.' She felt him try to pull his hand away. 'No, wait. Listen to what I have to say. I buried my head in the sand, for years I pretended it didn't happen.' She told him about Delfont, how he'd pressured her into leaving and what might have happened in the car. For a moment Rob said nothing, he just stared at her, open-mouthed, then his face crumpled and he pulled her close and started to cry. 'I'll kill him, I'll kill that bastard for what he did to you.'

'Listen though, there's more. He's been arrested for corruption. Money laundering via gold purchases.' Shona saw the spark of recognition in Rob's eyes. 'You know what this means?' She continued, 'He targeted both of us. That's why Milton McConnell set you up, they wanted you to go quietly. It also means we both have to face up to what happened, tell the investigators what we know and take the consequences. But I think we can survive that if we support each other. If you want to, that is.'

'You kidding? Shona, there's only ever been you. You're like no one I've ever met. I don't know if I can beat this gambling thing, but I'm gonnae give the therapy everything I've got, because the one thing I do know is my life is infinitely better with you in it. I love you.' He kissed her. 'So you're no getting rid of me just yet. You're the one sure thing in my life and I never, never want to be without you.'

'We're going to have to look at the financial situation,' she warned.

'I know,' he said seriously. 'I think there's a way to continue the B&B, but it will mean re-mortgaging.'

'Well, let's not make any other decisions right now. I need a cup of tea.' She smiled at him. 'I do love you too. Come on, get the kettle on.' She pulled him from the office and into the kitchen.

Becca had her back to them, washing up with one hand. Outside, the sun had vanished behind the hills across the estuary and the day was dimming down. 'By the way, I've decided I want to be home schooled. I've worked out a timetable.' She didn't turn round, but Shona knew she was watching their reaction in the reflection of the kitchen window.

'Okay, but won't you get lonely?' Shona said neutrally, exchanging a glance with Rob, who didn't seem too worried by the idea.

'I've decided to do archaeology at Glasgow University.' Becca slid a plate onto the draining board.

Rob leaned past Shona to grab a tea towel. 'Archae-ology?' he said under his breath. 'Where the hell did that come from?'

'Don't look at me,' Shona muttered.

'I can apply without A-levels or Highers if I have voluntary and practical experience,' Becca continued. 'But I'll need maths and English. Since we've got Bees Wing Community Teaching Co-operative nearby, I thought Dad could teach maths there and they'd let me sit my exams with them. Maybe he could get some paid tutoring, I know we need the money.'

'Great, I'll have a home-grown crop of embezzlers and insider traders on my patch to deal with,' Shona muttered to Rob.

'I'm genuinely hurt by that remark,' he said, handing her the second tea towel, but he didn't look it. Perhaps the thought of losing everything – home, family, her – had given him everything he needed to change. She knew she was outnumbered and out-gunned. 'I'm not saying no,' she said eventually. 'We'll need to talk it over a bit more.' Behind her, Rob and Becca bumped fists and smiled.

–

Shona walked down to the lifeboat station. She'd call Munroe in the morning and thank him for his offer. There'd been enough change, enough running. She was staying here, for now. The main road along the seafront had been closed off and Kirkness Arts Festival was in full swing. The smell of haggis burgers and cooked fish drifted on the wind, making her stomach rumble. A man in a kilt wheeled a trolley of gin along the pavement in front of her, the bottles clinking like an advancing army.

Tommy McCall stood on the concrete apron outside the station and brandished his RNLI donations bucket. The dressing had come off and a neat line of stitches along his brow and a shiny black eye gave him a pirate air. 'That piece in the papers and on the news has done us the world of good,' he said to Shona, easing the almost full bucket to the ground. Callum the postman was showing a group of giggling girls over the *Margaret Wilson*. The crew room was out of action, but with donations pouring in it would soon be fixed.

Next door, Tommy's boatyard had been given over to a group of artists busy hanging exuberant oils of seaside scenes and displaying sculptures fashioned from driftwood. A crowd out front was cheering a young man juggling lit-up neon clubs. It would soon be dark. Later, Shona planned to watch the yacht club fireworks with Rob and Becca.

Shona saw Tommy's expression change. He reached into his pocket for the vibrating pager. 'Shout,' he called to Shona, pulling out his phone and hitting the entry marked *Coastguard Red Line*. 'Family with children caught by the tide on Rock Island.' He relayed the distress call that had come in to the coastguard minutes earlier. 'Shona, I'm giving you authority to launch. This is yours and Callum's, if you want it?' He gave her a calculating look.

'I'm fine and I want it.' Shona ran past him. 'Callum,' she called. 'You and me.' The postman gave her a thumbs up and quickly loaded the first aid bag into the *Margaret Wilson*. Tommy started the tractor and prepared to back her out.

Other crew were arriving and cleared the visitors from the path to the slipway. Shona took the helm as they launched lifeboat D-855 to enthusiastic applause from the crowd, who assumed this was all part of the festival show. Four minutes later they spotted the family; parents, two children and a small dog, shivering and cut off on the tidal island by the rising water. White foam arced above the rocks as the short, sharp sea advanced towards the stranded visitors.

'Callum!' Shona shouted over the noise of the engine. 'Here, take the helm. Nudge us in.' They swapped places. Shona leaned over the bow. The parents' faces were white ovals of fear. She reached out her hand and smiled. 'Hi, I'm Shona. I'm here to help.'

Acknowledgements

To my agent Anne Williams, who possesses the magical ability to turn dreams into reality. Thank you, and all at KHLA, for your expertise, persistence and encouragement.

To my editor Louise Cullen and the dedicated and passionate team at Canelo, especially Siân Heap and Deborah Blake, my sincere thanks for making it all happen.

I'm enormously grateful to Steve Austin, Lifeboat Deputy Launch Authority at RNLI Cleethorpes, for the technical advice and wisdom. Thank you also to former DCI Stuart Gibbon for an early insight into police methodology and best practice. Shona and I were listening, any errors are mine.

To Charles Simpson, thank you for being my first intrepid reader and for your wise comments and enthusiasm.

To my friend Fiona MacDonnell, who was there just at the right time and provided such excellent research suggestions.

Crime writers are a supportive bunch and my special thanks go to authors Meghan Taylor, Stephen Booth, Henry Sutton, Tom Benn, Nathan Ashman & Julia Crouch for pointing me in the right direction and pushing me on, and my fellow UEA Crime Fiction students for their excellence and strength.

A huge thank you to my family; my parents John and Netta McEwan, brother Eric, and Cath and Hugh Oliver, who loaned more than a name to Shona. And finally, Leo, Chloe and Mickey, I couldn't have done it without you.

CANELOCRIME

Do you love crime fiction and are always on the lookout for brilliant authors?

Canelo Crime is home to some of the most exciting novels around. Thousands of readers are already enjoying our compulsive stories. Are you ready to find your new favourite writer?

Find out more and sign up to our newsletter at
canelocrime.com